Lilly's Story

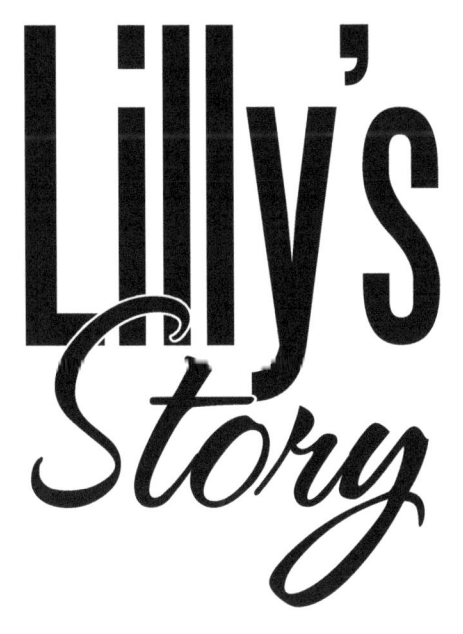

Making the Tour

RL Monsheimer

authorHOUSE

AuthorHouse™
1663 Liberty Drive
Bloomington, IN 47403
www.authorhouse.com
Phone: 833-262-8899

© 2024 RL Monsheimer. All rights reserved.

No part of this book may be reproduced, stored in a retrieval system, or transmitted by any means without the written permission of the author.

Published by AuthorHouse 01/22/2024

ISBN: 979-8-8230-2032-9 (sc)
ISBN: 979-8-8230-2031-2 (hc)
ISBN: 979-8-8230-2030-5 (e)

Library of Congress Control Number: 2024900070

Print information available on the last page.

Any people depicted in stock imagery provided by Getty Images are models, and such images are being used for illustrative purposes only.
Certain stock imagery © Getty Images.

This book is printed on acid-free paper.

Because of the dynamic nature of the Internet, any web addresses or links contained in this book may have changed since publication and may no longer be valid. The views expressed in this work are solely those of the author and do not necessarily reflect the views of the publisher, and the publisher hereby disclaims any responsibility for them.

Contents

Chapter 1	Who I am	1
Chapter 2	Flushing Meadows, Final Day of Qualifications, (Friday)	5
Chapter 3	The Beginning Story	15
Chapter 4	US Open Weekend:	25
Chapter 5	The Tennis Beginning	39
Chapter 6	Round 1 US Open	47
Chapter 7	From the Beginning to High School	62
Chapter 8	The Second Round	78
Chapter 9	The High School Experience	96
Chapter 10	The US Open Mixed Day and Third Round Women's Singles	112
Chapter 11	The Recruiting Year	128
Chapter 12	Mixed Doubles Second Round	142
Chapter 13	The First College Years	149
Chapter 14	The Fourth Round	170
Chapter 15	Senior Year at Longwood	185
Chapter 16	Mixed Doubles Quarters US Open	202
Chapter 17	Beginnings and Endings	221
Chapter 18	Asian Swing	241
Chapter 19	One More Tournament	261
Chapter 20	Home and Then Australia	270

Chapter 21 The Journeyman..284
Chapter 22 Wimbledon..298
Chapter 23 Time for Mrs. Wilson...327
Chapter 24 US Open Again 340

Chapter 1

Who I am

Who I am: My name is Lillian Jarman and tonight is a very nervous night. I am staying here at the local Motel 6 near Flushing Meadows, NY. I had to extend my room for the second time this week. I am now a professional tennis player waiting on the third round of the US Open qualifying, having upset the 3rd seed in the last round and an up-and-coming NCAA player in the first round. The match yesterday went 3 sets having to come from behind in the third set from 1-2 and then reeling off 5 straight games to win the match and get me in to this position.

I am now 5'10" tall, with mostly European features, light brown to blonde hair and weigh according to the program 140 pounds. I have green eyes like my grandfather. My facial features look mostly Asian as my grandmother is Korean and I guess like Tiger Woods, I am a combination of features. I am now 28 years old and will be 29 during the tournament, and as a first-time player here, I must be the oldest first-time player in the qualies as they are called.

My parents are trying to come up to the match tomorrow, they are trying to drive up from Radford, VA where my father is a history professor, and my mother works as the manager of a local bank. Ken Jr and Barbara Jarman have lived in Southwest Virginia most of their lives. They have not watched me play tennis since college. It seems so long ago I played for a small division 1 school in Virginia, Longwood University. Longwood was the only one that offered me a scholarship to play tennis and even then, it was only a half scholarship. My younger brother James was a swimmer and unlike me received a full scholarship to the University of Kentucky, after he won the 200 IM, and the 500 freestyles in the state meet and was at that time top 50 in the United States in the 200 IM. He is now finishing law school, at George Mason University and was in DC clerking for a local lobbying firm all summer. I was really hoping he could see me play what could be my only chance to play at a tour level event.

My grandparents met while my grandfather, Ken, was serving in the Army during the end of the Korean war. My grandmother Dea was working as a waitress at the military PX where she learned to speak English. Apparently, the romance blossomed and while it took a lot of effort for them to get married and for Dea to come to the states, they settled into Blacksburg, VA. Both worked at Virginia Tech, until they retired. My grandfather passed away five years ago, having had prostate cancer that took him from 220 pounds to 145 when he passed away. Dea is very frail now as she approaches her 80th birthday. She called me to wish me luck on my matches this week. Hard to believe this little woman who probably never weighed more than 95 pounds had three boys to raise and still worked at Virginia Tech cafeteria and attending various baseball games on the weekends. My family says my resolve to play professional tennis comes from her.

I received 2 texts from my uncles Karl and Kevin, and of course my dad is Ken Jr. Obviously, someone liked the K's for names. They texted me good luck and proud of me for getting this far.

I bet my teammates and neighbors from Virginia will be surprised that I will be connected to South Korea and not the Unites States. When I won a level 125 tournament in doubles, I received a call from the South Korean company, Hyundai Motors and they offered me a 100K sponsorship, but I had to play under South Korea flag and not the United States. Because my grandmother was Korean, they said I was eligible and with that money, I finally had enough seed money to try to play more tournaments. So, as I said earlier, with my nice southern accent I will be representing South Korea.

I have been told that the Tennis Channel will be airing my match against the number 13 seed opponent for a chance to play the main event of the US Open. My opponent is Bulgarian, Anna Georgiev, has played in numerous grand slams and is playing the qualies only due to recovering from a knee injury and losing her rankings. At one point she was up to 40th in the world, so obviously as a wild card entry the odds makers are betting on her.

2 years ago, I started to date a former soccer player at University of VA, who just finished his graduate MBA a year ago. Larry Wilson grew up in Fairfax, VA, and was a top athlete and student. Larry works for a Wall Street company and since he is only in his second year, he has had very little time to watch me play this year. He was able to see me play the first-round match as it was not played until 5 PM, and he was able to leave directly from work via the subway. He missed my second-round match as it was scheduled at 11:00 AM, and Wall Street is main action at that time. Since my match is third on tomorrow, I am hoping he can catch the match. It could be an interesting stand if he starts yelling for me, my parents have never met him, and when they realize that he is my boyfriend. I can't imagine what dad will say to this guy.

So, this is where I am and what I am about to do. I had to make sure that I ate right this week, the US Open people had a great spread so all I had to do is buy breakfast. I found a little bagel place, (Elijah's Bagels) around the corner who had the ability to get me a healthy breakfast of oatmeal, fruit, and a health drink. They told me I had to eat with them tomorrow as they are my good luck breakfast. If somehow, I win, I am going to say how nice they are on my post court interview. I know at least 1 waitress is coming to root me on.

If I can somehow get some sleep tonight, I want to be ready for the biggest match of my life. Not only would a win be worth over $100,000, I would get enough points to get in to the top 200 of the worlds in singles I am currently 125 in doubles but as of, yet nobody is calling me to play doubles with them. I would never have to play qualies for the 125's again. If it was not for the last tournament with a wild card attached to the qualies I would not be here today. 2 rounds of qualies then a week full of matches with higher ranked players and the next thing I knew was after my 6-7, 7-5, and 6-4, win in the finals I had a wild card invitation to the US Open. Losing doubles at the quarters was disappointing but I had just met my partner a week ago. She has a partner lined up for this US Open, so I am on my own to find someone else.

Good night. Tomorrow is the key. I don't even have a real agent, so if I qualify, how do I get the calls for endorsements that all the others have. Wow so far ahead of myself, time to chill out and get some sleep.

Chapter 2

Flushing Meadows, Final Day of Qualifications, (Friday)

Larry is in the stands and said he would write this portion of the story.

Larry here, Lilly is the lower rated player than Anna, so they will introduce Anna, and state her career accomplishments which include a couple of championships at 250 level tournaments, plus a quarterfinalist at both Wimbledon and the Australian open.

Lilly is being interviewed before the match by Brad Gilbert, basic questions. Asked how it feels to finally be here at the possibility of qualifying.

Lilly was good at answering with her southern draw, basically saying, I always knew I could be at this level it just was very hard to do without sponsors, and without the US Tennis Association support.

"Brad then asked her how it was that she is here representing South Korea?"

Lilly was so good at this question, said "she was honoring her grandmother, and that South Korean Kia Motors had given her enough money to enter Futures and 125's this year to get the points required to make it here."

Brad just finished the interview by saying "good luck Lilly". Then he said to the ESPN audience, "this is what qualifications are for to allow those without the pedigree or sponsors a chance at making the main draw".

ESPN Discussion:

"Brad Gilbert - Anna is an experienced player and being here will not make her nervous, so expect an easy journey here, predicted about an hour or less to win the 2 sets."

"Pam Shriver disagreed, I am predicting that Lilly is so hungry, she is playing so well, look for her to qualify this afternoon. What a great story, without a major sponsor, she was outside the top 600 in singles this year, and now is playing for a chance to make the biggest tournament of the year. Just shows you what can happen if someone helps you out and sponsors you."

"Patrick McEnroe was the tiebreaking predictor, and he agreed with Brad and said that Lilly has a great year to get to this point, but she has never played a player with this pedigree, and she will be likely overmatched."

Introductions:

The players today are Anna Georgiev, career highlights include top 40 and reached the quarterfinals of two majors. Anna has won four tour level championships in singles and 2 in doubles. Anna is playing on a protected ranking today and is the number 13 seed for seed for this tournament.

Now introducing her opponent, who represents South Korea, and recently won the tournament in Bethany Beach, Delaware receiving a wildcard into the tournament. Lilly Jarman is from Virginia and played collegiately at Longwood University. This is her first appearance at the US Open.

No applause for Lilly, except for her parents and me. I told Lilly this morning I was going to be at the match no matter what work had me do.

The First Set:

The coin flip then warm-ups went off on time, as the match before ended early with a player retirement. Lilly called heads and the coin was a head. Lilly chose to serve, as she has a very hard serve and can often get up to 110 plus.

Lilly starts off the match with a service winner, that Anna could not return. Shortly after she holds off Anna for a 1-0 advantage.

Anna's serve is well placed and after 2 aces she also holds for a 1 all.

The remainder of the set goes that way, strong service games and no potential break points for the opponent. At 5-6, Anna was serving and up 40-30, and Lilly hit a backhand down the line to make it deuce. We were hoping she could break but alas an ace and a service winner later the match was tied up at 6 all forcing a tiebreaker.

For those not familiar with tennis set, at 6-6, a 7-point tiebreaker decides the set. The winner must get 7 and be ahead by at least 2 points, thus 7-5 or better. If tied at 6 each they keep going until someone gets 2 points ahead.

During the tiebreak, each server was holding easily, but at 5-4, Anna served a soft second serve that Lilly hit down the line for a winner, putting Lilly up 6-4. After Anna held her second service point, Lilly was up 6-5. Lilly then steps up to serve and with a strong 100 mile an hour serve up the middle, Anna can only put her racquet on the ball, and it does not clear the net. Lilly wins the set 7-6 after the tiebreak.

Second Set:

Anna appears to be recommitted to the match in the second set holds early and the for the first time, breaks Lilly to go up 2-0. After another strong service game Anna, is up 3-0.

Anna looked like she had this gear that Lilly was not going to be able to match. But after an 8-minute 3 deuce game, Lilly finally got on the board and down, 3-1.

It took Anna less than 3 minutes to take a 4-1 lead and it was looking bad for Lilly. Lilly looked like she was pressing and at 30-40, double faulted so she was behind 5-1.

Anna served out the set with her 8th Ace of the day and completed the set 6-1.

Third Set:

Now with the match tied at 1 set all, Lilly initiated the set, and just like the first set won easily the first game of the set. Anna matched with an easy hold only giving up a point when she double faulted at 15-love.

The rest of the set went quickly and soon it was 5 all with Lilly serving with a chance to go up 6-5. At 40-30, Lilly hits a wide serve which Anna simply barely gets over the net, Lilly hit the ball into the opposite corner for a clean winner.

Anna is serving to force a match tiebreak and immediately goes up 30-0 and we fear for a match tiebreak. Anna shows her rust and double faults to let Lilly back in and with the opening Lilly fires another backhand down the line, and the game is 30-all. Now with a new intensity, Lilly returns another strong serve, and wins the point when Anna hits the ball into the net with her shot. For the first time Lilly has the chance to win the match.

At that point Tennis Channel coverage again goes live with the match Anna showed her veteran ways and hit a strong serve wide Lilly was able to get the ball back to the baseline but Anna hit behind Lilly for a winner.

Deuce now, and Anna hit a serve down the T and Lilly must have guessed it well and hit an inside out backhand cross court out of the reach of Anna to give Lilly a second match point with a break point. Anna hit the net with her first serve and set-up a match point with her second serve to Lilly. Lilly caught the wide second serve and hit a backhand screamer down the line out of Anna's reach. With that shot Lilly qualified for the main draw of the US Open.

Lilly screams with the results, falls to the ground, and covers her eyes. We can hear her sobbing intently and we could see the tears streaming down her face when she got up to give Anna a handshake at the net.

ESPN Broadcast booth:

Patrick McEnroe says" well Pam I guess we tip our hat to you. Lilly Jarman was much more the aggressor in this match. Who would have thought that this American who could not get enough money to continue her play, now plays for her grandmother's home country, and now South Korea will have a flag in the main draw."

On court Interview:

Brad Gilbert says to still shaking Lilly, "so Lilly we can see how much this win means to you. I want to ask you what you thought after the first match point was lost and Anna was then serving at deuce".
Lilly responded, "I thought 2 more points to play, and you will achieve the dream for the year. No seriously, all I could think of what my coach kept telling me in practice, it is one point at a time, and remember what your weapon is and figure out how to use it."
Brad, "I see your parents are here for the match what do you have to say to your family and boyfriend."
Lilly responded, "Can you please take me shopping I only brought enough clothes to get through 2 days of qualification. I think I need some clean new clothes for the first round."
"Brad starts laughing, and with the additional 100K you have just earned what does that mean for you later this year."
Lilly starts crying again, "I guess it means that I can enter the challenger tournaments on a routine basis now. Oh, thanks to Elijah's bagels who have fed me all week, they made me feel welcome and they fed me a healthy meal and a friendly conversation every day."
Brad then concludes the interview, "Lilly Jarman welcome to the main draw of the US Open."
Lilly just starts crying again and barely can say "thank you," she won't like the look tonight as her mascara started to run all over:

ESPN Broadcast booth:

"Pam Shriver says to Patrick, now you can see what qualifying means to those tennis players, that are on the fringe. Those tears are not because she simply won the match it is what the match will mean to her. With the points and the money, Lilly will find new opportunities that she never has had access to before. This will be the story of the first round, those players looking to just get the first-round money and those that have a real chance of winning the tournament."

Lilly packed up her tennis bag and we met her outside the court. Her mascara that she had taken so much time to make sure she looked good on the television today was running down her face. It may be sweat proof, but it was not crying proof.

She jumped in our arms and said to us, "we need to go to Macy's, I need some clothes if I am going to stay another couple of days for the first round."

I spoke up and said what happens if you make the next week?

"Lilly responds you may have to help me do laundry or go shopping again."

I don't have an agent or a clothing sponsor at this point. I am going to look like a country bumpkin at the first round with old clothes no logo's and the shoes that I purchased on my own.

Lilly's parents simply stated to her, "we are country bumpkins from rural Virginia and now we are in the biggest city in the USA."

A man approached us as we were walking with Lilly to the players locker room and said to her can I talk to you for a few minutes. He introduced himself as Jacques Dumas, and he said he was from clothing company Lacoste. "Lilly, we would like to sponsor you for the tournament to wear the famous Lacoste alligator. Your story is something we feel we need to be a part of whether you make it through one round or numerous rounds. We will pay you five thousand dollars to wear our clothes through this tournament and through the end of the year. We will need you to come to our offices this afternoon, so we can find some clothes that you can wear and feel comfortable with. I am afraid that the custom clothes that our lead players have were fitted several weeks ago, you will have to probably use whatever they did not choose to wear for the tournament. We will also fit you for the clothes you wear here so you will have an adequate supply for the tournaments the rest of the year."

Lilly said to Jacques, "I thank you for the offer and I will wear the Lacoste brand for the rest of the year. Can you tell me where we need to go to look at the leftover clothes. This is so appropriate that the girl that nobody thought could make it here wears the clothes others did not want to."

With a handshake, Lilly now had a clothing sponsor for the first time in her 7-year professional career.

After Lilly had showered and changed to her jeans and Walmart polo shirt, she was about to meet with us again and a woman came to us and asked if we knew Lilly Jarman. Lilly came from behind us and said, "I think I know her what you need?"

"My name is Allison James and I represent Mizuno shoes and they were trying to get some professionals to represent them as we are trying to get our Pickleball and Tennis shoes more exposure."

Lilly to Allison, "I have been wearing Asics shoes for the last year, they feel comfortable, and I was able to get 6 pairs at the outlets in Rehoboth, Delaware.

"Alison responded you will love these shoes. Lilly, I think we can help you out here. We have these new lines that we are about to launch, and we are willing to pay you $7500, plus all the shoes you need for the season. I have a pair in your size 8.5's for you to look at and decide if you like them and want to endorse them."

Lilly took the shoes from Allison and put them on. She looked up at Allison and said, "these are fantastic, but I think they are a little large for me."

Allison then presented the custom insoles that the company also sold and told Lilly put them inside the shoes.

"Lilly exclaimed these are the best shoes I have ever had, but won't they hurt my feet I have not had time to break them in."

Allison laughed, "we have shoes stretching equipment and we can make it just like you would have worn them and broken them in. As an extra incentive let us know the name of your favorite charity and we will send the organization enough shoes for all the participants."

With a handshake Lilly now had a new shoe company and collected $12,500 for traveling expenses for the rest of the year. "I would love it if you could provide shoes to the kids in Radford that would like to play tennis but can't afford it. I will have the information from the head pro at my home tennis club in Radford, VA, and can provide you with the details of our outreach to the community and the kids that would love new shoes."

As we were walking out of the player parking area, a call came on Lilly's cell phone, the number said spam, so Lilly ignored it and turned it off. A minute later a man came running out of the facility and said to Lilly can I talk to you for a minute.

Lilly says, "I am busy I must go look at clothes this afternoon and get some new shoes."

"That is exactly what I want to talk to you about Lilly, I have been an agent for several players, and I think you could use an agent to represent you for the rest of the year. My name is John Littleman, and I represent second tier athletes all over the world and think we can help each other out this year. I noticed you play with a Babolat racquet, but you don't have a deal with them. If you work with me, I can guarantee you will get a deal with them that will go way beyond simply getting free racquets and strings, I am thinking about at least another $10,000, for the rest of the year, and possible another $25,000, if you can crack the top 100." "Lilly, you received a little over ten thousand today and I think with your story the 2 companies came out cheap. I think we could have pushed for at least double, every year a Cinderella story comes out of here and you could be it. An American playing for South Korea because she could not get any US sponsors, is just the tip of the story. Here's my card if you want me to represent you let me know. I think we can get you wild card entries into the Asian tournaments in South Korea and Japan, they will be clamoring for your story and the publicity of getting that miracle player that qualified on a wild card entry into the qualification tournament and took out her three opponents to make the main draw. The press will eat you up as you play in the Asian tournaments of the blond girl with the southern accent that plays for South Korea.

Lilly just said "thanks let me think about it, so you want to represent me get 5 to 10% of my winnings. So funny because this year you might have only received about $2500 for efforts."

John said to Lilly "Lilly, I think you have the potential to earn over a quarter of million dollars in prize money this year and another $100,000, in endorsement deals by the end of the year. The deals you agreed to today only are for the rest of the year and you should be asking for custom sizing of clothes and shoes for every tournament after this. Just think about it, because I know you don't have representation and you really need it, your boyfriend may be good with stocks, but this is a different game and I know how to play this game."

Lilly told him "she would call some time Saturday afternoon if she chose to have him represent her, but again in her mind nobody else has been calling."

When John had left, Lilly said to me, "where were all these people for the last 7 years. Let's get out of here and get the leftover clothes that Lacoste has promised. We must figure out if they have the clothes here or elsewhere. Who would have thought that all of this was happening after I started learning to play tennis at the Radford college tennis courts. This is so funny; a couple of wins and it is like everyone wants to be my friend."

Before we do anything, I need to make a call this afternoon. I need to call the club at Radford and let them know I won't be back for the September start of classes. I guess they will need to replace me.

Lilly calls the Radford University tennis club and finally gets in touch with the head Pro, Jake Willis. "Hey Jake, it looks like I will be busy this week not sure you should plan to have me on the roster to coach the Fall Junior tennis."

Jake just starts laughing, "the whole junior tennis camp was watching you this afternoon Lilly. I am sure that we can wait until later this Fall for you to come back to teach here. I will let you know though the club has sent Paul, (Paul Nelson) up to New York this afternoon. He will be staying near you and he has agreed to act as your coach for training and arrange practice hit for you for as long as you need it. Consider this a gift from the club, I know you and Paul have been working on a barter system for his services, because you did not have enough money for a full-time coach. The club is paying for Paul, and if he is wearing Radford Tennis, he is yours for free for the rest of the US Open. You should call him to coordinate your practice times, he will be your hitting partner this week unless you find another partner." Good luck and do the club proud, so happy for you and the whole club was standing and cheering when you made the main draw. The college girls were in tears as their part-time assistant coach made the main draw."

Lilly said "Thanks Jake, I can't thank you enough for your support over the last few years. Paul will be a great training partner for the time being and maybe we can get him some Lacoste gear, I just got sponsored by them this afternoon and on my way to get fitted for the clothes shortly."

I then commented to Lilly, "I know it has been a struggle to get here but truthfully you have never talked about how you started tennis and I think we need you to be able to tell the story, of how the country bumpkin without much fanfare learned tennis, made it to college and then the story of life in the low levels of tennis."

Lilly stated to Larry, "Larry let's write the story of Lilly so others can read about it. I feel uncomfortable and have been told that ESPN wants to interview people I know, and I think you and I need to write it down, so the real story comes out from my point of view. The tears, the crazy events, the working at night so I could play during the day. Nobody ever wanted me as a player and now it appears everyone wants a part of me. Maybe it is time to write the real story, the ugliness, the prejudice of my Korean looks, it should all come out. The tears of not being recruited by anyone, finishing near the top of the NCAAs from a school that nobody had ever heard of and even then, nobody would sponsor me for events, I had to work to just make the entry fees and hope I covered them with prize money. The long years without a sponsor and having to turn it around by myself with a part-time job and coaching is now over. I have received over 110,000 for the win today and that will fund me for the next year."

Chapter 3

The Beginning Story

So, this is the beginning of the journey, I am going to talk about my parents and how they met.

My parents both went to college in Virginia near I-81, my father Ken Jr, was a business major at James Madison University. Dad is about 6 feet tall with his hazel eyes and very dark brown hair, and he was very athletic. Or at least that is what my grandparents said. My dad was on the James Madison Football team, although from what I heard he played sparingly until his senior year. His senior year he was a blocker on special teams and the extra safety when needed for 3rd downs. He played enough his junior and senior years to get a varsity letter. James Madison was a very good team and won the National title at least one year while he was on the team, he has a ring somewhere. James Madison probably has 20,000 students on both sides of I-81 and dominates the tiny town of Harrisonburg.

From what I understand my father Ken was good at many sports and was a good student also. He was popular apparently with the girls in Blacksburg, but never dated any more than a few times the same girl. I knew my dad played basketball as a small forward and baseball as an outfielder, but his love always was football. From what I understand from my grandmother, the girls knew he was going to college and was going to make something of himself, and the local girls did everything to make it known they wanted their hooks on him. One such girl was Maggie Crenshaw, who was very Barbie like and had her hands on dad at the senior prom. She decided that Ken was the perfect guy to get her out of Blacksburg and have a life with a very successful guy. Ken was definitely a little naïve when it came to the girls, his mom had made sure that he did not date and concentrated on school and athletics with little time else. When February of his senior year was ending Maggie found a way to get close to him at basketball games and at the last game of the year asked why he had not asked her out on a date. Ken is not blind, he said to her I thought an attractive girl like you would have all the guys you wanted. Apparently, Maggie was able to convince him to date her and as I said she was an extremely attractive girl. I know for a fact from others in Blacksburg, that she was sexually aggressive with Ken, and that she convinced Ken to get a room at the local hotel one night, and that they did not leave until noon the next day. I believe that was dad's first-time making love to a woman, I doubt it was Maggie's first time with a guy. They did date through senior prom, and I think they reunited on prom night at a cabin the guys from football had rented nearby. It was Dea, who said to her son, I know you like this girl, and she is very attractive, but she is not the one for you, she is not a strong enough woman for you, she just looks at you as a ticket out of here and you need a real woman that is smart and a partner. I understand that the first week of June, Ken told Maggie that they should just be friends because he was about to go to college, and she had one more year of high school. Maggie did not take this very well and spray painted my grandparents' garage and stated loser in red paint. Ken went to James Madison with no ties to the Blacksburg community and with a little nervousness apparently never dated much during his freshman year of college other than a couple of double dates with the football players asked him to cover the other girl.

My mother was from Farmville, VA and while she could have gone to a lot of schools, decided to attend Bridgewater College, which is about 10 miles due west of James Madison. Bridgewater is a very small university, mostly women even today and she had majored in liberal arts with a teaching certificate. While at the university, she pledged and was an active Greek member of Phi Sigma Sigma, a large sorority. My mother is a typical small-town girl, was in a lot of clubs has dirty blond hair, about 5"2" tall, and maybe 110 pounds when she was in college. I heard she was at one time a track sprinter, but she never pursued track and field in college, and I don't think she ever was good enough to place in high school despite the stories she has told me. I do know that my mom is very smart and is an extensive reader even today.

Both of my parents are typical of western Virginia, grew up in Episcopalian churches, went to services every Sunday, and I don't think either was allowed to date much in high school. I did hear my dad may have had a secret girlfriend in high school, but nobody ever talks about it.

My mom Barbara Miller was the middle child of three children. Her older brother Thomas, became an electrician, never went to college, and I don't think he ever has been more than an hour away from Southwest Virginia his entire adult life. He is married and has 4 children. My other uncle is mom's younger brother, chose a different path, he lives in Orlando with his partner James, and together Albert and James adopted a daughter a few years ago. Obviously, he is not welcome at a lot of the Farmville gatherings, and I only met him twice in my entire life, the last time at a tennis tournament he came to visit. My grandparents Susan and Joseph Miller are the nice couple owning some land that they rent to farmers in the area, Susan teaches Sunday School, but likes to be called Suzi, I have no idea where that came from. Joseph owned a garage and managed a team of 4 mechanics that work for his shop. I understand he was very good with his hands when he was younger and the many upgrades in the house were from his personal projects. I think he was supposedly athletic but chose to be a mechanic instead of pursuing a minor league baseball contract. I guess I come from 2 athletic families of men, and I guess I am the female extension of both of my families' athletic jeans.

To understand my mother, you had to recognize that she was not interested in sports, much or a book worm, and preferred nature walks by herself that being with girls in gossip groups. She always knew she wanted to escape Farmville, and she graduated with a very high-grade point average from high school, just short of being the top student at her high school. A lot of schools came looking for her and I know she was accepted into the University of Virginia but did not want to go to a school that large and with scholarship money available she found her way to Bridgewater. She was on the school newspaper and the guys in Farmville never really pushed to date her she was a little too mature for them. She never played the southern bell game and was ready to go to college having never gone to a prom or any real dates, so you could say she went to college pretty naïve and a little immature, but she is smart, and college was her way to a new life. That is why it was so amazing that she fell in love with my father and that seemed to change her personality. She was very confident with him, no longer shy or alone.

As I stated earlier, my dad had 2 brothers both with K names, and both received teaching degrees at Virginia Tech and neither ever taught a single day. Karl is the oldest brother, and he is an engineer for the State of VA and works from Glen Allen, VA near Richmond. Kevin is the younger brother, and he sells life insurance in the Roanoke area and is very successful. Kevin did not get married until he was in his mid-forties, and at the age of 50, his first child was born, I bet that was funny when he went to the PTA meetings, but his wife is only about 10 years older than me now so there is like 20 years of age separating them.

How is it a jock at James Madison and an academic shy girl got together when they went to different universities, and nobody thought they had anything in common. The stories I heard were that my parents met at a sorority formal. My dad had a fellow football player that was dating a sister of the sorority, and my poor dad was asked to come as a blind date to the sorority formal event. Yes, my mom was too shy to ask a guy out, but her friend Judy Canoe asked her boyfriend Jason Bello, to find a nice guy for her to have a date. I don't know what had to be done but my dad agreed to both a blind date and a formal dinner as the first time he ever met what would become my mom.

The story you are about to be told is mostly from Judy, as my mom and her have stayed friendly most of their lives.

Ken was wearing a dark grey suit when he was driving from James Madison to Bridgewater. Apparently was having second thoughts about having a blind date and having to spend all night at the formal and no drinking etc. Jason just kept telling him Hey, it's only 1 night, you can leave by 11, and then we can go back to James Madison. We won't miss practice and you won't have to see that girl they are setting you up with again. It's not like you have been dating much as James Madison anyway, I can't remember the last time you went on a date. Yeah, let's get this over with Jason, you will owe me.

My dad and his friend Jason got to Bridgewater college, they had to ask for Judy and Barbara to come down from their rooms to the front desk. According to Judy, the two of them locked eyes and both were tongue tied when trying to talk to the other. The friends were worried this was not going to be an easy night, they thought they were quiet because they took a dislike to each other. My dad apparently provided Barbara with a corsage, and she put it on her arm herself. The ten miles back to the Hampton Inn near Harrisonburg, the two opened-up and became very chatty as the two just kept asking each other lots of questions and they apparently just started talking and the shy Barbara eased into the lead of conversing with her blind date.

While Jason and Judy never got married to each other, my parents apparently were lock stepped in love from the first night. I was told that they danced together most of the night including the slow dances and the good night kiss at Bridgewater lasted several minutes. This was the end of Dad's junior year and mom's sophomore year, so they were lucky that they were only an hour apart during the summer. The weekend after Barbara watched Ken at the James Madison spring game, and they went out again that night. I have been told that nothing went on that night other than a lot of kissing, but that is probably the clean story that Judy told me as opposed to the facts. Over the summer the relationship began to blossom, and the distance from Blacksburg to Farmville was a good distance but somehow, they dated every week during summer break.

With late July, came football practice and Ken was back at James Madison, so dating for the next 4 weeks was not possible. I knew that James Madison was having a good year and Ken was doing well, and when they decided to have a homecoming event, Barbara was there.

Judy has told me that they were holding hands and listening to the music but that nobody thought they were all that serious. She later said we realized we were oh so wrong. As soon as James Madison was eliminated from the NCAAs in the semi-finals, Ken kept coming over to Bridgewater at least a couple of times per week. While men were not allowed in the dorms past the front room, the two were known to be there at least one evening and then on most Sundays. Judy said that Ken and Barbara went to the local church together on most Sundays during Ken's senior year. They would then go out on a date Sunday after church and were becoming well known in the church community as the cute couple. That cute couple supposedly took the relationship to a higher physical level during the spring formal at the Hampton Inn during the Spring. I was told that Judy got a call from Barbara that they were still at the Hampton Inn and would be back around noon after brunch. Judy told me they were surprised that the couple had gotten a room, again nobody knew that they were dating twice a week and were really falling for each other. Ken graduated after his four years at James Madison, but did not want to be far away Barbara, so he enrolled in a Master of History program while Barbara was doing her senior year. At graduation, Ken introduced his girlfriend of the past year to his parents for the first time. Apparently, the family took a liking to the little blond girl that had fallen in love with their son and approved of the couple. Dea was so happy to meet Barbara for the first time, later she told me that she wondered when Ken was going to bring her home, she knew he was going to Farmville to meet a girl but upon seeing Barbara for the first time realized that she was going to be her daughter-in-law at some point. Barbara decided to move in with Ken and commute from Harrisonburg to Bridgewater four days a week for her classes. This continued until the spring formal of Barbara's senior year.

As Judy related to me. Ken had told her earlier in the week that he intended to ask Barbara to marry him. The plan was for the announcement time Ken would be asked by Judy to present the academic award for the sorority to Barbara. Barbara did have the highest GPA, so she was not expecting the change in plans. Well instead of presenting the award, Ken waited for Barbara to come up to the podium, Ken then got down on his left knee and grabbed Barbara's hand. In front of all her sorority sisters, Ken then proposed to Barbara with the microphone in his hand. Apparently, my mother said yes, and she leaped into my father's arms, and proceeded to knock the ring out of Ken's hand and they had to find it as it rolled on to the floor. The ring was found and was placed on her finger to the applause of all that were at the formal. Then Judy came by, gave her a hug, and presented her with her award of the academic member of the sorority.

One week later, Ken drove down to Farmville, VA, and formally asked Barbara's parents' formal permission to marry her daughter and that same weekend Ken came home to Blacksburg and introduced Barbara as his fiancé. A lot of driving but the couple enjoyed their time together. Both families approved of the marriage and with crying and wine the approvals were done. Ken had beer with my grandfather, still does not like to drink wine.

Nine months later the first day of spring, (March 21) Ken and Barbara were married. Judy was the maid of honor and the other K brothers walked as best men. Barbara filled out the party with one friend from her Farmville church, Christina Smith who she knew since she was 5 years old, and another sorority sister Wendy Torrance, who had been her big sister in the sorority. The reception while enjoyable at the church was a dry reception except for the flasks that seemed to appear throughout full of moonshine and other spirits not on the formal menu. I was told that they had nearly 100 people attend in the church, and that the local community turned out and wished the couple their best by honking horns as the couple drove by.

After they honeymooned near Disney, in Florida, they returned to James Madison, where Barbara started working in a bank, and Ken taught and took classes at James Madison. They lived in graduate school housing and while they did not have much money, they continued to do Sunday dates after church every week. Friday nights were movie nights as Ken finished grading papers and exams, so he could be free to be with his young wife on the weekends. On Saturdays, they would often find a place to bike and picnic.

Ken and Barbara lived there for three years and at the end Ken received his PHD in History, and shortly after received a job offer from Radford University, a small university in the southwest portion of Virginia. Radford is a distance from his hometown of Blacksburg, and just like his hometown the university dominates the local community.

The week after Ken received his PHD, Barbara nestled up to him and said "while we are moving, we will need to make sure we have at least 2 bedrooms. She announced that she was pregnant with their first child. Laughing, I guess one of those remote bike spots must have been the trick".

My father hugged her and said, "I guess we really need to be a little less enthusiastic in finding places to play on our bike rides."

I was born in the spring of my father's first year as a college professor. 2 years later my younger brother James was born.

When my brother was very young, we moved from a 2-bedroom apartment to a small three-bedroom house not far from campus, which is good because dad walked to school, and mom started working again at a local bank as the assistant branch manager. I understand that both sets of grandparents donated $5000, towards having enough money to buy the house. My parents only needed 1 car for a long time and that is all we had for the first five years of my life.

This is the story of how my parents met, nothing fancy but now you know how I ended up in Radford, VA when my grandparents were at Virginia Tech in Blacksburg and the others were in Farmville. My father loved Radford University and he never moved once he received tenure really did not have much of a reason to. He later published 2 books for his studies of the history of western Virginia and how the area lacked slavery, and some thought they would have been a part of West Virginia, but for some reason the local's felt alignment with Richmond and the Confederacy. The second book focused on the post-civil war conditions of SW Virginia and the coal mining that was the primary industry for years.

Now comes the part of the beginning that was not so friendly. As I stated my grandmother was Korean, and while none of the K boys took after her except for Ken's very dark hair, I have her facial features so when I was born and thereafter in the town of Radford, I really was not accepted as I had the Korean facial features, and very blond hair much like my mother. So, growing up we would hear things like poor Barbara must not have been able to have children and she adopted this child. Others would whisper that my mother must have had an affair with an Asian, that is why I had blond hair and Korean facial features. While my parents tried to ignore this underlying discrimination, very few of the kids in the neighborhood would play with me or have play dates with me. My mother tried to make me believe that people were just jealous that I was reading as a 4-year-old and many of the other little girls were just learning to read in kindergarten while I was reading books like second graders.

I will relate a story that my mother told me regarding my first year at pre-school when I was age 3. I was already pretty smart and learning the alphabet, ahead of many of my peers. A mother came up to my mom and said it is so nice of you to adopt a Eurasian child.

My mother said, "what made you think she is adopted",

The other mother said "well look she has blond hair, looks like she has a tan, and her facial look is Asian.:"

My mother simply said, "well that would make sense her grandmother is from Korea and of course Lilly has some Asian features, you do realize that her father has very dark hair just like his mother."

The other mother simply said "oh, well it must have been nice for your family that your son looks totally European." Then she ushered her daughter away from me and this was just the beginning of what I experienced in Southwest Virginia. Whenever there was an opportunity to be with other little girls my own age, I noticed that I was never invited to birthday parties and had no play dates. I learned to rely only on my family and myself and that no matter what I did I was never going to be accepted in this community. So yes, I spent very little time with other little girls in the area, the parents did not want the snowflakes to be exposed to a multi-cultural child. Well, that and I was as smart as the best of them and more athletic than any of them. My mom said they were just jealous that I could read at an early age, and they could not. Now we all knew the truth, they simply were never going to accept me not for me, but simply because I did have some looks from my grandmother.

It did not help that my younger brother was very much facially a European, and with fair skin, light brown hair, and blue eyes we just did not look like we were from the same family. That just did not help my case for being accepted by the community of Radford, VA, who was very much a white European Christian community. My friends in the Asian community complain about discrimination at least they are only from one world, I was from two worlds and accepted by neither. I would say that was from the community and not from either set of my grandparents, they just loved me for being Lilly, the first grandchild. Since I was not wanted or desired to play with others, I was not really interested in being on teams with others, my parents found another way for me to get my exercise. So that is how my parents chose for me to try individual sports. I did not have to deal with being withdrawn from others in my community.

I do know that when someone what was my age teased my then 3-year-old brother about me being adopted, he beat the heck out of him. My mother wanted to punish him for getting into a fight and had to relent when dad said he was defending his sister, give the kid a break. Later I was told that dad went to James and said while I don't like you fighting thanks for taking up for your sister. Even then James was my height, and I was 2 years older. James is very attractive from what I hear, the girls are always trying to be more than his friend, but he is really focused, and these debutantes will not alter his goals.

This is the story of my first five years and how my parents met, wed, and settled in Radford Virginia. You can see what drove me to be my own character as the other little girls were never my friends. I have to say all the time with the family, we spent Thanksgivings in Farmville, and the Christmas holidays at Blacksburg, because with the kids out of school, and with my grandparents' ties to Virginia Tech, we were able to get a reduced rate at a local hotel, often in was a Comfort Inn. With the family it was fun times, outside I developed a bit of a shell and to be independent.

Chapter 4

US Open Weekend:

With the qualifications over, I went back on the grounds to the Lacoste storage area. I was looking for the right look for a 5'10" girl that was athletic build.

With the match ended at 2 PM Eastern, and by the time we got out of the locker room and dressed it was 4 PM, before we could get to the Lacoste area. So many of the outfits were taken and reserved, but I was able to get a yellow knit top, with a white stripe across the middle, they recommended a traditional tennis skirt, that was orange in color, but they had another traditional red, so I chose that one. I then thought about it and that would have looked like a traffic light, so they were able to find a blue skirt that nobody had chosen, so that is what we agreed upon. A dark blue tennis skirt with the pink top with a white strip across it.

While I was there, they asked would I like to have the South Korea flag on my wrist bands. "I said sure, but I don't see any."

They said they were having the small flags printed and would be sown and complete for my first match Monday or Tuesday. The last thing they provided was 10 pairs of tennis socks.

Jacques then came by and provided a check for me for what was promised and then he asked me "would I like to get a better hotel room for my coach and myself." With that they found us both rooms at the local Hilton Garden near the airport for as long as we needed.

I called up Paul and let him know where were staying he typed the address in to the Waze AP. I told him "We have 2 windbreakers for him to wear along with his Radford Tennis clothing."

For the tournament they provided 5 sets of clothes that we had chosen, yes, I was able to get the pink top and a blue skirt that nobody else I guess wanted, plus the socks and then provided 10 windbreakers with the alligator logo. The windbreakers were of various sizes light green with a dark green alligator on it. After committing two to Paul, we still had enough for myself, Larry, and my parents to wear if the weather required. Then they sent us all sort of fun things, bags, water bottles you name it we had it with the alligator logo on it. I had already checked out of my Motel 6, my clothes were in my 8-year-old malibu, so next was to check in at the Hilton Garden and check in to the room.

When Larry and I went to the Hilton Garden Inn, we saw a sign that said welcome to Lilly Jarman and coach. When I introduced myself, the front person told me I had a basket of fruit that was sent to me courtesy of Elijah's Bagels. A note simply said, thanks for the mention, good luck, we will have someone at all your matches and will give your party a breakfast they want. Then a box of shirts was available saying Elijah's Bagels. I guess that was for my family and friends. I started laughing and showed the card to Larry.

The manager said "your coach has already checked in; we are so happy to have you here. Anything we can do to help you let us know, you are our only tennis player here, most are at the full-service Hilton closer to the facility. We don't have a full-service restaurant, but you call our staff, and we can get you anything you need."

I showed them the Elijah's Bagels note, and told them, I will need someone to make a run for breakfast from them every day. I gave them what I was eating with them and said I want this breakfast, if possible, every morning until I am eliminated.

After I checked in and Larry and I got everything in the room, I was amazed, they have given me a converted conference room, with a sofa bed, separate kitchen facility, and a large conference table. A note on the table said put your dirty clothes in this bag and we will launder them every day. "Management"

Larry helped finish getting all my clothes equipment and new stuff to where I wanted to have it so we could use the conference table for our meetings with my friend and coach Paul. I then called Paul and asked him what is up. We scheduled a meeting for 5 PM which was in 30 minutes, meanwhile I went to the refrigerator and noticed it was stocked with Gatorade, diet sodas and bottled waters. I pulled a water out and threw Larry a Gatorade.

With a ring of the doorbell, I opened the door and gave Paul a hug. I gave him the credential badge he will need for the tournament and a big hug thanking him for how we got here.

Paul had already made calls for us and stated" You will have practice time on Saturday for an hour at the practice courts at 11:00, we get half the court, you are sharing with a Russian male player, Dimitri Romanov, who is top 60 but not seeded. We have the court for an hour, and I am suggesting that we just do a general workout, no serving, and then stationary bike and light lifting. We should be done by 1 PM, and then we can start reviewing video files with your opponent in the first round. The draws will be out fully by 7 PM, and the Monday matches will also be posted by that time. Once we know who, when and where you are playing for the first round, we will plan more specific strategy. The one thing that is great, because you have played mostly in small tournaments, nobody has tape on you, so they are at a disadvantage on getting to know your tendencies. If we don't get a top seed, we just may be able to find a way to win a round, and then we can see what's next. For now, let's look at when your new shoes will be available, we need them by practice Saturday, so can you place a call to Allison James to make sure she has the shoes ready for practice or have her team deliver them to the hotel this evening. We will bring your regular shoes if the new shoes don't work for you. I know they promised $7500, but if they hurt your feet or don't help, then you just don't take the money. I do want to understand who is this other guy that wants to represent you, we still don't have a deal for your racquets, and who knows who else wants to place a logo on your clothes for the tournament. Let's take this opportunity to get you enough money so you will not have to coach and bartend at night. By the way, I don't know if you know it but just winning the qualifications has moved you up on live ratings. This means that you will not have to do any qualifications for ITF's this year. Enjoy yourself for the next hour plus, and we will get together and look at your opponent and start our strategy sessions. Also call that potential agent so we know that we need to work on your current Babolat or if they will be your new supplier and brand-new sticks."

Paul left for his room, and Larry left for his apartment in the city. My parents were going to come by, and we were going to go out for dinner. Meanwhile I need to call my prospective agent and let them know that I need support.

Good evening, John, "this is Lilly, we met this afternoon when you talked about representing me. I would like to have you do that, so we need to get some paperwork together. Also, can you call Babolat, I use them, and have purchased them at a discount, but need new ones for the tournament if I can, I only have three of them with me and I have been told for this tournament I should have 6."

John said to Lilly, "I already made some calls on your behalf and Babolat is one of them. I have a 25K, offer if you are ready to go with them, and I can have 6 new sticks delivered to you this evening. I already know how you like them strung, so you need them delivered to the Hilton Garden Inn, near the airport, I will let Babolat know, and you will have them delivered by 10 tonight. I have made some other calls on your behalf thinking that you would want to work together. I have a series of 5 people that want to place their logos on your equipment, Motorola, NTT Telephone, T-Mobile, Makers Mark, and Kroger Supermarkets each are paying us $5000 each so I will bring the paperwork over later tonight for you to sign and I will have someone pick it up early Saturday morning at the front desk so let's get this arrangement started. That is 50K, in our first days of the relationship, and who knows what will happen if you can manage to win a round."

My head began spinning, even after my agent's fees, I had nearly 60K in endorsement money, all the seed money I will need for the rest of the year.

John yelled at me, "oh do you have a passport because you are getting one of the four wildcard entries in to the Korean Open. I believe that you get at least $5K, for getting in the main draw, and we have a slot open for you in the qualifications at the Japan open."

I responded "I have a passport because I have played in Mexico, Canada and in Jamaica and they needed a passport. I just finished the call saying thanks for everything, I can't believe this is happening."

John just said, "get used to it, this is your new reality, no more trying to pay for things, you are now in the big league."

7:15 Conference room at the Hilton Garden Inn.

Larry had to miss the group get together to see the draw and the Monday schedule. When we looked at the US Open draw, we saw that I was in with two qualifiers, a top 75 from Brazil, (Maria Schindler), and the 12 seed Susie LaPointe, from France, who has made it to the quarters of the French open. My quad was slots 45 through 48, part of the top portion of the draw. My opponent for the first round was the NCAA champion from University of California at Los Angeles, also known as UCLA. Marianne Jackson recently won the NCAA as the 6 seed and is like 19 years old. I know that she was an African American player from Los Angeles area. Out match is third on Monday on the most outer court, number 4, which is right by the road and seats less than 1000 people. This makes a lot of sense I'm an unknow, and my opponent has very little matches at the ITF or professional level. Third match out will mean we have a women's match they will end by 1 PM, and a men's match that should be done right around 3:00 and expect to play at around 3:15 PM. This odd time for a start means having lunch at about 1:30 and a few minutes practice hit at the courts around 2:30. 3:15 PM, Also means we will be playing with a temperature in the upper 80's humid, and with no shadows in the beginning of this match and then shadows if we have to go three sets.

Paul says well, "this is about as good as we can have a rookie that got a direct entry in to the tournament. She has only played a few ITF's and has never gone beyond the second round this summer. The seed in our group is mostly a clay court player so who knows what can happen."

While everyone was here, I got a text from Mike Finley, a British men's top 50 player who has won professional event but is a top 25 player in doubles. The text stated, I have been asked if you would like to play mixed doubles in the tournament, the US Open has stated they will give us one of two wild cards if I want to play.

"Ok, everyone what do you think, I have been invited to play mixed doubles, that will start on Friday, it means staying here probably through the weekend, but just for showing up we each get $5000."

Paul says, "so you stay to the weekend and make a few thousand dollars. We get to use the practice courts through the week, so why not."

I texted Mike back that I would be honored to play mixed doubles, and to let me know what is required on my part to be registered for this event. Text came back, you just did it, I have all the paperwork for the event ready to go.

Larry called-in and I put him on speaker, good draw for you Lilly, "I will make sure I can be there somehow Monday afternoon."

Given the money I had just received, I asked the front desk for where they would recommend for an Italian dinner. They made a recommendation of a small family-owned place. Paul reminded me no alcohol for this evening. The restaurant Magna Restaurant, very nice place not far from the tennis facility. We got an Uber to get us there and we had a great meal a lot of pasta, iced tea for most of us except Paul who was able to get some chianti. While we were there somebody came over to our table and asked, did I see you playing at the US Open today. I simply said yes and thanked them for watching.

My dinner of ziti and meatballs came, and we ate until the restaurant staff looked at us impatiently, I looked up and it was quarter to ten and the restaurant closed at 10 PM. We left after spending $150, with tip. The Uber was there at ten and we were back at the hotel by 10:15. I hugged my parents and they drove off and said they were going home but would be watching on ESPN for the match Monday.

I hugged them and said, "I want you back if I get to play next weekend."

My dad said, no problem, but we may need to have you find us a hotel. I hugged them both and said is this real or am I just dreaming.

Dad, with tears in his eyes "this is not a dream just a beginning. And with that my parents were going back to Virginia, and Paul called it a night also."

Saturday:

With a knock on the door at 08:15, breakfast was delivered, eggs, oatmeal, and a bowl of fruit from Elijah's. They also packed 2 more things, a plain bagel with butter and jelly, and a note in the bag. "Thanks for the publicity yesterday good luck on Monday"

I went on my laptop and went to see what e-mails I had to respond to and when I went on to my Gmail account, I saw well over 100 e-mails congratulating me on making the main draw. So many of these were from Radford area, and a few were funny as these were the same people that shunned me as a child. Now that I have a few minutes of fame they want to become my friend, I don't have time for them, and I am not going to allow myself to be bitter about my lack of debutant friends growing up.

Only 2 e-mails were important, my new shoes will be delivered to the front desk at 9:15, and a second one from the Korean Open granting me a "Wild Card" entry to the tournament. The tournament is a 250, and just one win is worth 20 points, minimum prize money $5200, US. That is enough money to cover my airfare and costs in Korea. I guess John has already been working on my behalf, where were all these people the last 8 years.

As soon as I finished breakfast, I received a call from the front desk, numerous boxes of shoes had been delivered. I asked how many boxes, and they said you have 8 boxes for you and 2 came for your coach. They were up in my room ten minutes later delivered on a luggage cart by the staff. There were 4 colors with 2 of each per color in my size with inserts and ready to go. All I could think is that this is a fairy tale, new clothes, new shoes, customized wrist bands. I started to cry, this is unbelievable, a week ago I only had old clothes, racquets, and it all could be over Monday night.

I called Paul to make sure we were still scheduled to hit at 11:00, and he responded "yes, and John stated you need to wear your new sponsors clothes for the practice hit today in case people are watching we want to make sure that we don't violate our just signed agreements. We have a potential new sponsor if you get to the third round, Chevrolet heard that you are driving a Malibu with almost 200,000 miles on it, and they have a brand-new vehicle waiting for you and a logo patch to put on your sleeve.

"I just said but won't Ruppert get mad if I don't use him to drive everywhere.

Paul responded" I think Ruppert will be retired to your parent's home in Radford, let's just drive Ruppert to the US Open grounds and get our practice in."

I gave the name to the car several years ago, and Ruppert has been great hardly a single repair and the car has 175K in miles on it. The red car is hard to miss with the 5'10" blond driving it. I really don't want to retire Ruppert; he really is the symbol of my struggle to get to the main draw.

Showing our credentials, we go to where they allow the players and coaches to park cars for matches and practices. I look at the cars in the lot, all new things like Mercedes, Audi, Lexus, and Bentleys, and then there was Ruppert. I hid Ruppert in the back section near the employee section of the lot. We walked over to the practice court assigned to us and noticed a ton of Wilson tennis balls at the side of the court, looked like they had never been played with. Paul said let's do it like we are in Radford remember this court is the same size as the courts in Radford, just has a different view. I know he was joking and yelled yes just like Radford.

John came by as we were finishing our 1 hour of practice with the contracts to sign. "Sorry I did not send them over last night, let's sit over here and sign the numerous contracts and deals for you."

I must have signed like 7 contracts.

"John then asked how did you like your first tournament invite in South Korea?

I laughed "my grandmother will appreciate it, but I don't think she is healthy enough to go home. I may have some distant relatives that I have never met that she may want me to visit, remember she has not been back since she fell in love with my grandfather. With the contracts all signed, my money was official I would have enough to play the rest of the year.

John asked me "are you good to play the mixed doubles later this week and said so you had something to do with it."

I responded yes, "the tournament was open to finding a way for you to be in more than one event, and they had already given all the wild cards for women's doubles so playing mixed doubles was going to be worth a little more money and the only thing they had open."

Finally, John stated "there is a challenger that many of the people that lose the first week play in to get some points, I am going to see about getting you a wild card so you can get some points this is a top-level ITF event if you need it. I will be in the stands on Monday watching your match, I won't be there for the entire match I have 3 other players playing on Monday. Live rankings have you as number 175 in singles we really need to get you top 100 by the end of the Asian tour, so you get a direct entry in to Australia."

I responded "John, that is so funny, I only got into this tournament by winning a wild card into the qualifications and now you are talking about a main draw directly."

"Lilly, you just win some matches and let me manage the rest, we will get you in to the top 100. The next talk we will have to talk to you about your coaching relationship, I know you are getting some help from the local club but that only works for this tournament, so we will have to talk about what is next after this tournament."

"I just shook my head, wow I never thought of it, I have been basically working with Paul for the last few years on a barter system. I think he needs to be a part of the coaching no matter what."

John reminded me that Paul has a job at Radford but could be a good base coach when you are back in Virginia on holiday. The other alternative is that you choose him, and he can travel with you for the rest of the year. It could be a great relationship for both of you. That is something you don't need to think about now, but once you get to the top 100, you may need a full-time coach.

After a 30-minute workout, mostly bicycle and then stretching we were done with the tennis portion of the day. It was time to get lunch at the players area and then a little time to nap and then have dinner with Paul and Larry this evening in Manhattan. Larry wants to take me to one of his local places he likes.

While eating lunch, I got a call from one of the directors of the Tennis Channel, to do a brief interview they want to do a quick background story with Lindsay Davenport.

Interview with Lindsay, "Good afternoon, Lilly, I was asked to do a little background on you to be used this week for the matches. Can you please tell me a little about you, and where you grew up, where you went to school, and then a little about you personally, (dating)."

"Thanks, I am a little nervous about the interview but let's go at it. Lindsay, I am from Radford, VA, which is in the southwest corner of the state. I played high school tennis for Radford High School, and then was a last-minute recruit for Longwood University between Richmond and the middle of nowhere. My grandparents on my mother's side were here and they knew the coach. I was not rated very highly by others in the state as we did not do all the bigger tournaments, but I made the state finals as an unseeded player. Nobody has a lot of money left except Longwood, so that is how I ended up there. I am currently in a relationship with Larry that you see over my shoulder, we have been dating for over a year, and he works on Wall Street."

Lindsay asked, "so how is it you are playing for South Korea, you have naturally blond hair, and a deep southern Virginia accent."

"I am bi-racial, and my looks come from Korea and Europe. This is a funny story. My grandmother Dea is from South Korea, so I was eligible based on her heritage. I was playing an ITF last year and won the doubles when I was approached by a representative of Hyundai/Kia motors, and they said that they would like to sponsor me, but I had to play under the South Korean flag. They offered to sponsor me for

$100,000 for expenses, so that sealed the deal given that I had to play a light schedule previously due to the costs."

Lindsay asked, "Who is your coach I see with you."

"Paul is an assistant coach at Radford University, and we have worked together for the last few years. We have an odd coaching arrangement; I pay in private lessons for some of his better students, Radford University pays me a small fee as a training assistant coach and instead of paying directly he arranges for me to practice with the college team. The local Radford club is paying for him for the rest of the US Open, so right now I get his services for free."

Finally, Lindsay asked "I want to ask what the prize money means for you for the rest of the year?"

"The money I earn will make it that I can play all the ITF's this year, have money to pay a coach, and possibly qualify for WTA main tournaments. I have already been given a wild card entry to the Korean Open. So, it is a big deal."

Lindsay just said, "thank you and good luck."

The interview took no more than 15 minutes, I'm sure a puff piece for later.

Now it is late about 2 PM, time to go back to the hotel take a long shower and then get ready to leave by 5 PM. I checked in on my parents they were just entering the VA border on I-81. They were doing ok, going to stop at James Madison and then lunch at Harrisonburg. They expected to get home at about 8 PM. Called Larry and we were to meet up at our hotel about 5:30 and then take the subway back to Manhattan.

Paul and I got through traffic and back at our hotel at 2:30, I took my shower and then sat down, the next thing I knew it was 5 PM, and I had to rush to find clean clothes presentable for tonight. I had a nice polo top and skirt, about as fancy as I get. Paul said no high heels until after the tournament is over, so flats keeping me about 3 inches shorter than Larry.

We went to a nice Irish restaurant, that I forgot the name of, and I had bangers and potatoes. Paul told me to get a salad to balance out the dinner and told me to be careful about dessert. So much for the cheesecake, just some ice cream and a couple of cookies. Of course, the men had heavy shepherd's pie, 2 beers each while I got to drink iced tea. Then they had the cheesecake I wanted to have, really such a mixed blessing. What a bummer.

By 9 PM, we were done, and Larry and I spent time together until 11 PM, and then he reminded me it was chill time. Nothing more than some hand holding and kisses while watching "Saturday Night Live" I think it was rerun, but the company made it better. With a hug, it was time to call it a night. Paul called me and said look at the tape I sent you, see what your opponent does well. Looks like we can get her in the forehand corner and crash the net. I finished watching the tape and then crashed on the sofa-bed and with my water from the fridge, I crashed. It took less than 10 minutes to fall asleep.

"Sunday Morning" 1 day before US Open Main Draw.

Just like Saturday, I heard a knock on the door and the breakfast from my Elijah's was waiting for me. A note in the bag said, enjoy your practice we want to see you win Monday. A smile came to my face, they were so nice all week, and I felt like for once in my life I had someone that accepted me for just being me, and not having to worry about being different. While eating my breakfast, I went on to the laptop and looked at my e-mails. A lot of junk that I got rid of. Welcomes from my new sponsors, created a new folder for sponsor activity and requests. Then the schedule from Paul, same times as Saturday. I have been asked to walk through the crowd near Ashe Stadium, bring my bag with me so they will know I am a tennis player, and sign those huge tennis balls if requested. This will take up to 30 minutes after practice and before lunch. I so much wanted to skip this as nobody knows me, but the word mandatory appeared and was directly from John, so I am sure that this is in my best interest even if I have no idea. The last thing it said was make sure you are wearing the clothes and shoes from the sponsor. "Smile" if anyone asks for you to sign.

We took an Uber to the stadium this morning. I had all my new clothes shoes, and waiting for me was a box of white wristbands with the South Korea flag on them. I looked at the player list that they showed by country on the outside of the practice court. I noticed South Korea, with 2 players, one man and then me. It struck me, I was going to be in the main draw and tears started to come to my face.

I guess Paul saw me and said "did they spell your name right."

"Yes, they spelled my name right, the thing is my name is on the list. I'm way too old for this to be my first time through. When people see my age at 29, they are going to say why is she still playing tennis."

Paul says, "because they all had big-time donors, don't overthink this and let's play it a point at a time. Let's kick the door down Lilly Jarman. I would give you a hug, but Larry may not be too happy about it."

Practice finished and then the walk through the crowd, I had two requests for me to sign those large green tennis balls. Another person asked me if I knew a player and said just like you, I am a fan but nope I don't know them. I yelled but you can watch me play on the outer courts Monday afternoon. She yelled back, what's your name. Reality check, I am the country bumpkin trying to break into the big time. So many years, so many rejections and now I can play where a million tennis players have dreamed of. My name is Lilly Jarman, I am playing for South Korea, and then threw her a wristband. The lady yelled sure you are, tall blond lady.

I wonder how those little debutantes in Radford who never would be my friends, let me be a part of their world, see me now. Time to have lunch and get away from here before I start crying again. How am I going to play, if just being here puts me in tears. I got to get it together otherwise I will be the blip the person who lost 6-0 6-0 in her one and only time in New York.

We wandered off to the players food area in Ashe stadium and had lunch that was provided just before they closed the place down. The food left was mostly salads and desserts, but we did manage to get a good sandwich from them before they closed it out. I guess we meandered too long after practice so we got what we could. Turkey and bacon on rye bread still was not bad, a small salad, and then some Jello with fruit for dessert. Of course, some type of Gatorade was what I had to drink to rehydrate. I had some time to wander the ground before our uber was coming, and so went down the main areas between the courts to see where I would be playing on Monday. At least my court was way outside, only about 1000 fans. Probably a lot less but maybe some that follow college tennis would like to see the NCAA champion. I saw the cameras but know that they won't be live except maybe the clinching point.

Wow, time to chill in New York and it was 4 PM, and time for the uber to take us back near the airport. Dinner was going to be nearby at the closest Olive Garden, I need the pasta and it is affordable. Larry will be coming by, afterwards while I am watching my opponent tapes, he will be watching me. That will make it a fun evening even if it is brief, he must be gone by 10:30, I need my sleep. Only the biggest tennis match I will ever play, Lilly Jarman is going to play the main draw of the US Open.

I was thinking about the day I learned how to play tennis and the first matches. I guess we should write down the beginning of the Lilly tennis world.

Chapter 5

The Tennis Beginning

Before ESPN calls everyone and we get a different story about my tennis beginnings I wanted write down the story as I see it. I was five years old when my mother took me to a summer camp at Radford High School. We the participants did different sports at the summer camp, and then on the third day they introduced us to the sport of tennis. With adult racquets and counselors that simply tossed the ball to us and had us try to get the ball on the other side, this was my introduction to the sport, that now I am playing at the pinnacle. While most of my other camp mates, (not friends), were trying to hit the ball, I found it was easy to get the ball over when they fed it to me. By the end of the first week in camp, the counselor, (Lisa) took me to where the 7- and 8-year-olds were playing and told the instructor, Lilly here seems to be pretty good at getting the ball over the net in our feeds wondering if she might be able to join the kids here and try to hit the ball with a partner on the other side. I would love to say I was an instant hit but truthfully, I had an adult racquet and could barely move it but was able to get the ball over at least once just not always in the court. When I told my mother what was happening, my dad and I went to the local Walmart and got my first tennis racquet, a junior version from Wilson, because that is the only one, they had in stock. Dad also bought a mesh bag full of tennis balls, so he could feed me these practice balls.

We went to church on Sunday just like we did every Sunday, but afterwards my dad convinced my mom to let me go play at the Radford tennis courts with him feeding me the practice balls and trying to get the ball over the net. My baby racquet made my ability to swing the ball so much easier and by the end of the hour I was getting every ball over the net and most of the time, I was able to hit it on the side of the net my dad said to hit it to. The local pro came over, His name was Jake Willis, and he asked how long I had been learning to play tennis. My dad laughed, she just learned it this week, she appears to be able to get the ball over when I feed it to her. Jake, if nothing else is a good hustler, and said let me feed her some real balls from my basket and see what happens if I hit them to her instead of just feeding them to her. I was just hacking at the balls and then he stopped me, came over to my side of the court, and showed me what is called a topspin forehand. He had me shadow what I just had been showed, moved my hands around to do what we now call a western grip and fed me a couple of balls and the next thing I know I am hitting these balls with lots of spin and could keep it in the court. He went to the other side and said now let's see if you can play a point. Instead of serving it, he simply started the point and to my surprise, I was able to get the ball over the net and play a point for at least three times over with this little racquet, and the topspin forehand. Jake gave his card to my dad and said, she is capable of being a pretty good player, if you want lessons, let me know and I can set them up with our junior professionals have young people clinics with three to six kids learning the sport. I think your daughter here could be a pretty good player, she is smart and learns the things I just taught her easily, plus she listens without arguing.

My dad took the card and said to Jake, "we don't have a lot of money, but maybe after summer we can do 1 day a week. I will call you in August and find out if you have anything for the Fall."

Jake responded, " I don't think we have any indoor courts so not sure how long we can play outside. Jake said sounds like a plan, and then nice to meet you, Lilly Jarman."

When camp started again the next week, I could not wait to play tennis with the older group. On Monday afternoon, Lisa walked me over to the older tennis group and said I will pick her up to finish the day with the other 5-year-olds. An hour later, after dominating all the next older group, I was asked would I rather play with the ten-year-olds or go to the regular camp, I chose to go with the tennis, and from after that I chose to go to play tennis rather than do other activities. In other words, the sport and me were now going to be best friends. I thought I was pretty good but when you are five and trying to hit with ten-year-olds, obviously I had my leveling that afternoon, and after that I never played with anyone my age, I could dominate them and just used this as another wedge not to play with Lilly.

For the last 4 weeks of the summer camp, I would do the general camp stuff with the others my age and then the afternoon would come, and I would leave and the rest of the day I would play tennis for two hours once with each group. My father watched me the last day of camp and said to me, Lilly do you like tennis and do you want to take lessons this fall? After I said yes with a lot of energy, my dad called Jake to see what was going to be available for a beginning tennis player.

Jake had lessons starting in September, with groups starting from very beginner to competitive player practices. Jake said "let's try Lilly in the intermediate group, she showed me enough that she could be quickly up to what the others in that group can do. Lilly would practice from 5 PM to 6 PM, three afternoons per week through the end of November, we end our fall programs at that point and don't pick-up again until the Spring."

With money being tight at home, my dad asked "how much this tennis was going to cost for the three months?

"Jake said we can do it for as little as $400, and he told my dad pay each month because we you don't a lot of savings and as a professor, I know you are not highly paid."

Apparently, they were more interested in me getting started than getting cash up front, so we were able to work out a plan for my first serious tennis lessons.

Radford University – tennis courts

Radford University is a division 1 program so while they have 12 courts, the juniors only get 2 to 4 courts to play. Jake had his program, after assisting the women's team until 4 PM. From 4 PM to 5 PM, were the real beginners, mostly the kids my age. They were there to just learn how to get the ball over do a topspin etc. At 5 PM, we had 4 courts, the intermediate and completive players both had 2 courts three days a week, and the other 2 days a week, it was only the competitive junior players.

I remember the first day of practice was the first Monday after Labor Day. I had turned 6 over the summer and getting ready to enter first grade. One of my classmates Joanna Kearns, started pointing at me and laughed, look who showed up an hour late.

"I yelled back, Joanna, I am right on time I'm here for the intermediate group."

"Apparently, she asked why I was allowed to practice with the 7- to 10-year-olds and she was in the beginning group."

The young coach told her that Lilly has mastered all of what we are teaching you, so she is playing up with the next group. I know for sure that the other girls in my first-grade class were informed that the weird girl was being allowed to play with the older kids and like always she was just showing off. You see I was reading at a second-grade level already, and the other kids were always commenting that my head was too full of it. Of the 12 girls in my class only one or two ever spoke to me, I was not part of the click and really, I had very little in common with them. My parents pushed us academically to do our best, we read early learned basic addition before we ever entered elementary school.

Getting back to the first day of tennis lessons at the Radford courts, I was the only one that was under eight, so I looked so funny in my pigtails, pink tennis outfit, and my little racquet. The older kids already knew the basics about serving, I had to watch them and then the assistant coach showed me the way to do the ball toss and then what I had to do to get the ball over. I will admit I was not very good at it; I think I got like 2 of these serves into the proper box that day. Two days later I was able to get almost half of them in and by Friday, I was able to get three-quarters of them in. The older kids were surprised that when we were just hitting at the base line with each other I was able to keep the ball in the court as much as they could even if my racquet was much smaller than theirs. You want to know how I improved my serve so fast, on Tuesday and Thursday, my parents took me to a local park with a couple of tennis courts and with my bag of balls my mom took my brother to play and for me to try to learn how to serve for over an hour each day. By the end of Thursday, I could basically toss the ball up and find a way to get the ball over, nor pretty, but at least I could get it to them. My dad would come by after doing his papers each afternoon, and helped retrieve the balls so I could concentrate on the lesson.

The following weeks were great, three days a week I would play with the older players at the practice, and by the first of November we started to play points and learn how to keep score. Tennis scoring is so strange, must be a purpose I have never looked up to find out why. So, with the practices ending, a suggestion was made that I play my first tennis tournament. Jake said we must get Lilly a USTA number, but there will be a "Little Mo" Tournament in Blacksburg the week before Christmas, and I think Lilly should play there so she gets a feel of what competition will be like, she has some potential to be a pretty good competitive player. She will be playing with other 8 and under, so she will be probably the youngest. No matter what happens this is just for her to learn what it's like.

My parents apparently gave in to my whining and on the 21st of December, I played a tournament for the very first time. I got my Christmas present early; my dad gave me a brand-new junior racquet that was 2 inches longer than the one I had been playing with but was the same size as most of the other players. Since we had 24 players for this tournament, I had to play a Friday night match to qualify for the top 16 match the next day. Did I forget to mention that we left Radford early Friday afternoon, and we were going to stay the weekend with my grandparents. I got the best of the weekend my first tournament and get to see my grandparents. My opponent for the Friday match was a girl named Mary Smith, not kidding, she was about 5 inches taller than me and was completely decked out in matching designer outfit. I was lucky to be in my little sweatpants and t-shirt, yes, she was from

Fairfax, VA and looked like the wealthy area of Virgnia. She was kind of conceded you could tell right away the way she talked and a little overconfident, I guess. Well after about 90 minutes, I had upset her 6-3, and 6-4. Maybe this was something I should have known was coming the wealthy spoiled kid, and country bumpkin from Radford. When we got back to my grandparents' house, they gave me a big hug and said, wow athletic just like your dad, Ken showed himself early-on also. On the 22nd of December, I found out what a seeded player meant, I had to play the number 2 seed, who was almost 9-years old. Tania Sing told me this was like her twentieth tournament and had placed at the recent National "Little Mo" Tournament in Florida. The 6-year-old was somewhat in awe, and I ended up losing the first set 6-1, and she outlasted me 7-5 in the second set to win the match. The match barely took an hour. Since I got to play 2 matches, my first tournament was over, but I learned that competing with these girls was going to be hard they are a lot older and bigger than me. I would find as I grew it got a lot less difficult but, in this area, I always played older girls than me.

We went back to my grandparents' house and Dea, gave me a big hug. She put this in perspective you competed with girls 2 years older than you and competed well. You are playing with a new racquet, and you will get better, and they have played many more matches than you and you were still competitive. No crying or being upset, this is just the start of the journey.

Dea's words while they had some comfort, I think that weekend the drive to be competitive was born in me. The problem was that while those in the DC area had a lot of indoor courts to play, Radford did not have any courts, so that was going to be a problem. Nobody wanted to play tennis when it is thirty degrees outside, so we had to get creative. My dad called several places in the area, and someone mentioned a Country Club in the Roanoke area that had a couple of indoor tennis courts and had a small junior program for members and community members could learn. A tryout was arranged at Hunting Hills Country Club for the first week of January, but first, Christmas in Farmville. We spent the Christmas day at Farmville with my mom's parents. We went to Midnight mass and went to sleep. In the morning we got to open presents and I received a doll from my uncle in Florida, ok, but not a big doll person. My grandparents held out my present from them, it was 2 complete tennis outfits from Nike, one my current size and one the next size above for later in the year. The skirt, which had a pocket in it for placing tennis balls, was dark blue, the tops were both pink. I was not sure that the two went together, but my grandmother said you will be an athlete and you are a girl, so the pink and the blue will be your strength. I saw a second box, which contained a pair of Nike shoes and 6 pairs of socks and that was from my other uncle who was with his wife's family in the morning but would join us in the afternoon. I gave a big hug to both of my grandparents and showed all of this to my mom and dad. My dad said I think we can have you wear this next week in the tryout. For the next twelve years it became my trademark combination, Navy blue skirts and pink tops. I know not the girly colors or combinations that others had, but this was how I saw it would be, blue was the fierce competitor and pink was the girl inside it kept me balanced.

One week later, my dad and I were on our way to Roanoke and Hunting Hills Country Club. The place was beautiful, and while I was used to college campuses looking nice this country club was twice as nice. They had 8 courts outside, 4 looked like they were green dirt, my dad said those are called clay courts, and 4 hard courts like I was used to seeing. We then went in to the 2 nice indoor courts, and met the head pro Joseph Mikulska, who said to us welcome to the Country Club, you ready to play.

"Please call me Coach Joe, that is what I liked to be called."

"I introduced myself as Lillian Jarman, and that I liked to be called Lilly."

"Well Lilly, let's find our way to the court and start doing some warm-ups."

After Coach Joe went through warm-ups with me, he said let's go to the baseline and hit some rally balls. After about ten minutes, he said that's enough. He called my dad over and inquired about my previous lessons?

Dad stated, "The answer she has had one private lesson, she has been playing with group lessons for the last 3 months, but not a lot of personal coaching.'

"Joe said, she has the desire but runs around her backhand to hit a forehand, what's that about."

"Jokingly my dad said, nobody had taught her one, so she runs around to get a forehand."

Coach Joe then proceeded to asked to have Lilly with our young juniors, "we have a starting program on Sunday afternoons, and I would recommend that we get her with a junior pro once or twice a month initially to learn basic strokes and strategy."

My dad had a worried look on his face, "I am a professor at Radford, I'm not sure we can afford a membership here much less private lesson."

That was alleviated when coach Joe explained that we would not have to become members for the winter seasons, and that using a junior pro he could reduce the cost to $35.00, an hour because his rates were double that. With a handshake, my winter tennis began and with the Radford tennis the rest of the year, the beginning or my tennis was cemented.

During the Spring, the 6-year-old would play with the older junior players three days a week, and in the winter every Sunday afternoon, and twice a month would stay for a private lesson with a junior pro. I will tell you that there were rotating junior pros, so my backhand was a work in process, some days I played a 2-hand and other days a nice slice single hand backhand. I would not know until later that this gave me an advantage, my opponents would not know which one it was going to be.

So that is the beginning of the Lilly tennis chapter. But would like to tell you that playing tennis made me closer to the girls in the area, but it did just the opposite, even at first grade I heard things like "Lilly, thinks she is a boy", or the other "Lilly only seems to play with boys, I guess she thinks she is one". The little cheerleaders chose things like gymnastics and dressed up in pretty dresses, went to the pool. They went to pageants, and had sleepovers, and I was not invited, the Eurasian girl was not accepted anyway based on my looks, I was as smart as any of them, and played a sport they only wished they could play. The way of dresses and gossip were never going to be my world, but getting used to being the youngest player I felt like everyone treated me like the baby sister.

Chapter 6

Round 1 US Open

I had a hard time sleeping last night, finally fell asleep sometime after midnight. I can't believe I am getting to play the US Open, 7 years trying to prove myself and finally I get this opportunity. I only hope that I get to see more than one round. The first thing I did was check voice messages from the hotel. Just times from Paul for the match and our practice time is 10:45 to 11:30, this morning. I decided that the warm-ups would be a blue skirt, plus I would wear the white polo shirt from Elijah's bagels. The match is third on way out court 4, almost no fans at the court but the better players are at Armstrong, or Ashe stadium, or even the round one they call the bull ring. The first match will be played at 11:00 AM, and we are scheduled at a minimum of 3PM, the hottest part of the day. With the temperatures expected to be in the upper 80's and humid, I feel right at home with the summer weather at Radford. Marianne plays on the West Coast, so wait until she sees what this humidity feels like, I bet she is already moaning about the weather here. I just love it, grew up in it, so I will make it a part of my game to make her sweat right off. The other voice mails were from Radford Tennis and some others wishing me good luck today. I did notice none of the girls I went to school were any of these messages.

Larry just sent me a text on my phone, saying he is getting permission to leave at 3 PM, so with the Uber he is taking and the security he should get there at 3:45, he said hope your match is not over by then. He should at least see me play 1 set of tennis in the tournament.

Day of the match:

At 8:00 AM, a knock on the door, and breakfast was served from Elijah's, they were great for me. A note was attached, Lilly kick butt today. I popped in some sugar-free Gatorade, orange flavored, and started hydrating. I really would rather have coffee this morning but know that was not going to help much. By 8:30 breakfast was over, and Paul called Uber would be here at 10:00, so be down at the front desk by 09:55. I love his instructions.

I made a call to my parents and mom answered. I never call my mom Barbara, which was her given name, because she is and will always be my mom. She was my defender and protector, when the little girls tried to tease me and when I punched one out when she tried to bully me, she was standing up for me. She was excited to hear from me this morning. "I asked could she put dad on the phone?"

Mom said "she would love to, but he was at the Richmond Airport currently. Last night we got a call from a Jacques, said he would love to have one of us attend the match today. We got a ticket for a flight from Richmond, through BWI, and then to JFK airport and since the University does not start until Thursday, your dad grabbed at the thought and will be with you this afternoon. His flight gets in at about 1:PM, and Lacoste has a limo and credentials waiting for him at the airport. I was offered the same but said I will be too nervous to watch in person. I just got the ESPN+ application and I have been told that all matches will be available and will watch your match that way. I am so proud of you, and this is not lady like, but go out and kick some ass today. You deserve this time and no matter what happens this afternoon, know we are so proud of you."

She started to stutter, and I started to cry. Mom said "let's end this call before I start crying"

"I told her it was too late I already was crying."

I had time to shower select clothes get my bag ready and thought about preparing a water bottle with Gatorade in it for practice and then remembered it was all provided to us. Before the shower I texted Larry know I would look up at him and wave when he sits in my player box and then reminded him, he has no player credentials we have arranged for his ticket though and his line is short because he gets it like other sponsor pick-ups.

After the shower and getting dressed I packed for the day, I just looked into the mirror and started to cry again, I really need to get it together, my young opponent will not have these issues. It took a couple of minutes and then it was time to go downstairs and meet with Paul. All the new equipment shoes and racquets were ready, the new sweatbands were packed for the occasion. I felt like Cinderella, I was in beautiful clothes and equipment, and I was just an imposter in this world. I wonder if Marianne will have any of these thoughts.

Paul met me in the lobby at 9:55 exactly, I was a minute or 2 early but he is always prompt and on-time.

We were waiting for our Uber and Paul said "we need to try something different with this experienced college player. The only tape she will have on you is as a baseliner in the last round of the qualifications, and she also has come through the qualifications, so I have tape on her and hit a one-hand slice backhand while she was playing at UCLA. She has a decent enough serve no Serena Williams but still can make it the low 100's, she will get her aces, and she is just as likely to double fault. She wants to play baseline to baseline, so here is the crazy strategy that I have for you that we are going to apply to see if we can shake her in the first few service games. Every time she has a second serve, I want you to simply hit it deep, it does not have to be hard, just deep, and then come to the net to play the next shot. You have a great net game, and we will see if she knows what to do, she likes to dictate from the baseline, and we want to steal time from her to be set. On your serve I want you to serve at about 80%, and serve wide, you will then get to the net or if you must stay back you know she is going to go crosscourt so then you can either change directions or charge the net and make her do a perfect shot down the line. She can win a few points, but she will lose 2 out of three because you are going to make her uncomfortable and she is going to panic."

I simply responded, "this is extremely aggressive and not my normal game so why are we doing it."

Paul just said "because it is not your normal game and I want her to be freaked out by a completely new attack she was not expecting. Unlike great counter punchers, she has no idea of what to do here and we will get through on her inexperience. If the match goes as we plan, she will basically give you the first set, then she will make the adjustment and start to go down the lines except in the second set, you will do your normal game and be ready at the baseline and send the ball crosscourt and have her on the run immediately. One other thing, I want you to lead the first few games with the slice one-hand backhand and not use the 2-hander until the third game, between the two she is going to face things she has never faced before, and I think we can freak her out. Remember Marianne has never been in a main draw of a tournament this big either."

"Paul, you really have been watching the tape on her a lot, so let's see if this strategy can work. As crazy as it appears it might just throw her off enough."

We arrived with our Uber at the entrance reserved for players and coaches. We had 2 checkpoints that we had to go through, and we showed our credentials. I checked in at the players locker room and then Paul and I went to the practice court where he was warming me up, a male player Lorg Johanson, asked if he could hit in later, he was needing some extra net practice as he was playing both men's doubles and mixed doubles. Paul and I hit for the first 30 minutes, and then Paul and Lorg did some hitting. Lorg asked me how come he had never met before, and the answer was simple, never had a ranking high enough to get invited to the qualifications, and just came through qualifications beating three opponents all ranked above me.

Lorg commented "your strokes look as good as anyone playing the WTA regularly. He then wished me good luck today. Lilly Jarman, I think you will be back after today."

Paul agreed, "we need to keep this going, this can be a lot of fun and for the next round you win it is like at least $40,000, in prize money. You already are guaranteed like $80,000, plus the qualification money, so if we get past this round, you will really have enough money for the rest of the year. If you can get to the third round it jumps by another $60,000. But today, let's show everyone what you can do. It is one point at a time and one game at a time, if we come through today, we can figure out what is next."

With practice finished, time to go to the locker room and get some bicycle time in before showering and then getting dressed in the new clothes and getting a lunch. We arrived at the locker room just after noon and by the time I finished my shower and got dressed in my new blue and pink Lacoste outfit, it was about 1 PM and the men's match on court 4 was just being introduced so it was time for more fluids and then a lunch. I checked my e-mail account and while a whole bunch of e-mails wishing me good luck today nothing that was important except, I was going to get a wild card to a women's 125 in Thailand if I wanted to play, it would be the week before the Japan open, so I knew where this had come from. We had to travel to Ashe stadium for the players cafeteria, that took less than 5 minutes to get from the locker-room. The lunch available at the cafeteria was exceptional and Paul and I sat at a table together, with my salad and a chicken salad sandwich on a croissant roll, it was great. A banana and more fluids completed the lunch. I think Paul decided he would have French fries and a cheeseburger.

I got a text from mom saying Dad has landed and was just getting his luggage but would be there by 2:30. Larry texted me also saying he was still on for being there leaving the office at 2:30, the firm is getting him a limo to get to the stadium, I guess they are thrilled his girlfriend is playing. Jake Willis said the club is wishing you the best today. All I could think of is that without the debutantes not wanting to be near the Eurasian girl, I would never have had as much time to practice, no parties for the odd girl out.

We just sat and talked until 2:30 PM, when they said that we were likely one set away from being call for court 4, so I went out to the bicycle again for about ten minutes to get ready and then some jump rope to get the legs ready. Dad texted he was just outside the gates of the stadium and would be waiting for me on court 4. Then it hit me I was playing the US Open, I had only watched it on TV, played at least 50 ITF matches and never played a 125, much less a major. Life in the minors is so different. We play for a prize money on 10,000, for the week, with the winner getting $1500, if it was not for the $100,000, I know that I would not have played in this tournament.

A text came and said match is about to end get ready to be on the court in ten minutes. I noticed the time was 2:48 PM, so we will be starting the match in the heat. I hope Marianne loves the heat and humidity of New York in August; this will be a tough match. I am packing 2 shirts for the match; I expect I will need a change sometime with this heat and humidity. I could see Marianne on the other side of the room, hard to miss her, only like 1 of 3 African Americans in the room.

Paul interrupts my thoughts, "it is time to go, and your dad is already in the player area of court 4. Larry is at the stadium and should be at the court somewhere near the second or third game. Let's go and let's talk about your mental readiness for this match."

As we walked to the court, which takes about ten minutes, we talked about just staying in the lines in warm-up and doing just what we have done for any other match. I told him except this would give me 45 points in the rankings enough to make the top 200 with the 25 for qualifying. The most I had ever won in a single tournament was 25 points, so this is already huge, I get 10 just for playing today.

We arrive at the court and the I am told that even though I have the higher ranking because Marianne is the NCAA current champion, she will get to be the second player to be introduced. Plus, she is the American here, so we like to introduce the American players last, so they get the proper attention.

Court 4: Introduction

I would like to introduce our players for the WTA first-round match this afternoon. Representing South Korea, Lillian Jarman. Lilly as she wants to be called recently won the Sea Colony Open in Delaware and is currently ranked number 255 in the world. Lilly played collegiately for Longwood University and was a semi-finalist for her university at the NCAA's. A very light applause came afterwards except for a guy in a suit running to the court yelling go get them Lilly. By now you know it was Larry.

Now her opponent, Marianne Jackson is our current NCAA champion from UCLA. Marianne has been a semi-finalist at the Australian juniors. Marianne plays for UCLA where she is completing her junior year. Her ranking is currently 450 in the world. Most of the audience applauded her a great deal more than my audience.

I could see my dad and Larry with a notebook, they said they would write the story of the match so no matter what happens in the match I will have a written account for the rest of my life.

Warm-ups at the tournament are 10 minutes, a couple of minutes at the net, a few at the baseline, then a couple of volleys and then serves. Prior to that we had a coin flip for determining who would serve first. I called tails and the coin was a head, so Marianne chose to serve, I had her facing the sun as much as possible.

First Round Match Court 4:

Hello this is Larry, I am writing this section of Lilly's story, her dad is sitting next to me in case I miss something, he will augment. If you have not been to the US Open, this court is probably the smallest at the stadium, it is next to the road and maybe has room for about 500 fans. The court has like six rows of bleachers that are just next to the court, plus you can see the match from other courts and a few others scattered around. Paul is in the corner so he can coach Lilly, he has his nice Lacoste shirt on. Marianne's coach from USTA and UCLA are in the other corner, so all the boosters are in place and the match is about to begin. I am taking off my suit jacket and putting away my tie, I will not put on the Lacoste jacket a little too warm for me. The temperature at the time of the match is 87 Degrees, about 30.5C. Very little breeze coming from the East maybe a couple of MPH, in other words it is a lot like DC and Virginia in the summer.

Marianne started the match serving and proceeded to double fault the first point, and then served up an ace on the second point. On the third point Marianne tried to serve again down the middle of the court and Lilly was expecting it and hit a one-handed backhand deep to the backhand of Marianne, who hit a forehand and Lilly was waiting at the net and proceeded to volley on the other side and won the point. The next point Marianne served wide, and Lilly hit a slice backhand down the line and again Marianne ran it down, Lilly approached the net and finished it with a forehand volley. Rattled, Marianne proceeded to double fault a second point for Lilly to be up 1-0. The two then changed ends with a pit stop for water.

Now it is time for Lilly to serve, and she had a reasonable first serve, and with a long rally of 22 shots, Marianne went for it and the shot was wide. Up 15-0. Lilly served a wide serve and Marianne hit it into the net. Now up 30-0, Lilly tried a kick serve and Marianne simply banged down one of the lines to crawl back to 30-15. Lilly again served a wide serve and again Marianne hit the ball into the net. Now Up 40-15, Lilly again tried a kick serve and again Marianne hit a big return down the line to close the gap to 40-30. Lilly served wide again, and this time Marianne was able to get the shot near the baseline and Lilly was able to return it to the corner. Lilly approached the net and finished the point off with a forehand volley. Lilly then was up now 2-0.

The third and fourth games while close Lilly managed to break on another volley at the net. and then hold for a 4-0 lead.

Marianne, then was focused on keeping Lilly away from the net, so she proceeded to serve down the line for 4 straight points and Lilly was unable to win any points so after she held, Lilly was still up 4-1.

Marianne appeared to have a new intensity and was able to get her first break point and lead 30-40. Lilly hit a slice serve wide it probably was only about 80 MPH, and Marianne hit the return into the net.

Marianne looked frustrated and then proceeded to hit wide on the next serve and Lilly serve again wide came to the net and finished off the game. Lilly was now ahead 5-1 and you could hear Marianne's coaches chirping at her to get her head in to the match and not allow Lilly to come to the net.

Marianne has a big serve and proceeds to do 2 straight aces and then led 30-0. Lilly was able to hit a forehand down the line to be down 30-15. Another serves and another ace by Marianne. Marianne was up 40-15 and Lilly barely got to the next serve and Marianne won the point and was now trailing 2-5.

During the changeover you could see the red light on the TV camera going live, so I guess ESPN, was watching the possible last game of the set.

Lilly quickly got up 30-0, when she served wide and then came in and finished the points off with volleys to the net. Marianne blasted 2 returns that Lilly could not return so the game was 30-all. Lilly hit a big serve at Marianne and all she could do is to pop the ball barely over the net which Lilly proceeded to put in the other corner and was now up 40-30 and had her first set. A repeat of the last 2-points and again Lilly was ready for the next serve. Ken tells me Barbara says this is on live ESPN, has just went live with her match and she is watching it on her computer and live. Lilly simply placed a slice serve wide that Marianne again put into the middle of the court and Lilly finished the point and the first set. She won the set 6-2.

Ken said that Lindsey Davenport was commenting that Lilly is on a run, and now Marianne is going to have to dig in to keep the Lilly away from winning her first WTA main draw match. She repeats, this is correct Lilly has never played a main draw of a WTA match so now she is a set ahead in the US Open. Let's see if the reality sets in for the rest of the match.

Marianne took a bathroom break after the first set and came back with a new shirt on. Lilly was looking around the stands and then she saw the 2 from Elijah's bagels yelling at her, let's go Lilly.

With a five-minute delay, the second set started, and Marianne was playing much better and held immediately. Lilly had a much harder time holding her serve and it took 4 deuces and one break point opportunity wasted by Marianne, before Lilly Held to make it 1 all. This appeared to be the pattern for the second set, Marianne was preventing Lilly from getting aggressive to the net by pounding down both lines. Lilly was having to grind and went to deuce on every serve she also avoided three break points and Marianne just did not appear to be able to handle the pressure situations.

At 4 all, Marianne was serving. She aced Lilly on the first serve leading 15-0. Lilly hit a return winner cross court to make it 15 all. Lilly hit another cross court forehand winner to go up 30-15. Marianne then hit a 115 MPH serve for another ace making the score 30-all, Marianne and Lilly went on a long point Marianne had Lilly in a corner and all Lilly could do is to hit a lob back to the same corner. Marianne tried to finish the point and blasted a forehand down the line that was just long. That resulted in Lilly having her first opportunity to break in the set. Marianne sent the serve wide, and Lilly hit a backhand back to where Marianne was standing. Marianne then proceeded to hit a thundering forehand down the line and Lilly must have guessed what was happening and with a running forehand that just made it inside the line, and with that she screamed and was now up 5-4 and serving for the set.

At the changeover, you could see Marianne's team trying to calm her down, she was upset that a match she thought was going to be easy was slipping away from her.

I could see the camera's lighting up the court and getting ready to show the possible end of the match. A call from Barbara confirmed what we thought. Paul was simply trying to get Lilly to keep-up what she was doing.

At love all, Lilly hit a wide serve that Marianne netted, and this put Lilly up 15-0. The next serve was one of the rare aces that Lilly had right down the middle of the court, it may have been inside by 1 to 2 inches. Now-up 30-0 Marianne was not going to go away easily, and she returned the next shot hard to Lilly's feet and all she could do is hit it way out of the court. At 30-15, Lilly hit a wide serve and decided she was going to the net and a serve and volley. Marianne fed it to her well and Lilly hit a backhand at the net down the other corner for the 40-15 lead. Again, Marianne was not going away easily and hit another unreturnable shot to Lilly. Now Lilly had one more chance leading 40-30. With Marianne guessing that Lilly was going to try to hit another wide shot, Lilly hit it down the middle and Marianne could just barely get it over, Lilly hit the open court for the winner.

With a scream that probably could be heard probably all the way over on the other side of the grounds. Lilly came over to Paul and jumped in his arms, I would say I was jealous, but Paul was right on the court, and we were 4 rows up. Lilly almost forgot to shake hands with Marianne, but rushed over to her and made sure that she shook her hand.

You could hear Lilly say to her "Good Luck" You will have a great career you have the tools.

Because we were on court 4 and not one of the big courts, the person that introduced her simply said congratulations Lilly. No questions or anything else to acknowledge her moment in the sun. Then he said expect the final match of the day to start in 15 minutes.

Lilly gathered her stuff in her bag, and signed at least ten big tennis balls, and a couple of scrap books. A week ago, nobody would have wanted her signature except when she was charging something on her credit card.

We went towards Lilly, and she came over and hugged both her dad and me. The phone rang and Ken handed the phone to Lilly. Mother Jarman was crying and then so was Lilly. Paul was calling in to Radford and the entire junior camp yelled on the speaker, way to go coach.

ESPN Sports booth:

Lindsay Davenport and Patrick McEnroe are live at the US Open.

Lindsay says, "On the outer courts I have been told that a scream from court 4 could be heard all the way over here. For those that like the underdogs, Lilly Jarman has just won her first WTA main draw match over the current NCAA champion, Marianne Jackson. She has been playing sparingly on the ITF tour until now. The 70 points she has won this tournament will move her up in the live rankings. For those that don't know how she got here, Lilly won an ITF tournament that gave her a wild card to the qualification tournament here. Lilly won three matches to qualify here and now will be on to the second round."

Patrick asked, "can we get her to come up here and talk to us for a moment, I think some of the tennis fans would like us to speak to her?"

Lindsay, "I have been told she is off the court and on her way to the players locker room hopefully we can get cut her off on her way to the locker room so we can do a short interview while we wait for the next match up on Ashe."

Outside Locker Room:

This is Kevin Plackman, I am an assistant for ESPN for the US Open. "Lilly, I have been asked if you could come quickly over to the ESPN booth for a brief comment and interview. "

Lilly responded, "I would rather take a shower and go home, but sure if they don't mind that I have not had time to get clean. With that she was on her way to the booth as requested."

ESPN Sports booth:

Patrick said, "welcome to the booth Lilly."

"Lilly smiled and simply replied to him thanks for having me over kind of surprised that you want to talk to me."

Patrick asked, "many players your age and achievements would have given up on your tennis career, would have retired and gone on to do something else, so can you explain what was going on"?

Well to tell the truth, "I have been working as an assistant coach at Radford University and elsewhere to get enough money to travel and enter the ITF tournaments, so I could have easily retired and moved on from tennis, except for the win late last year in doubles of an ITF last year. I won like $500, for that win which paid for my expenses there. Truthfully, I may have only been able to play a couple of ITF tournaments had it not been for my main sponsor this year, Hyundai motors, who gave me enough money to enter the tournaments regularly. I will cut off the next question you will ask, how am I playing for South Korea, with my nice southern drawl. The answer is two-fold, I have never had any real sponsors until Hyundai offered me this money for entry fees and travel and they are a South Korean company. My grandmother Dea is from South Korea, so I agreed to play for her and the sponsor country."

Pam Shriver came into the booth to ask a question. "Lilly, what does this match mean to you, and we both played in the Mid-Atlantic area juniors? "

Lilly responded, "wow, I have enough money to try to play full-time, and have already been given a wild card in the Japan Open later this year and another ITF 125 in Thailand. I will get my first trip to Asia this Fall."

Patrick ended the brief interview, "well Lilly thanks for coming in and good luck in your next match."

Pam jumped up and gave her a handshake and a pat on the back. Lilly just waved and you could see tears forming in her eyes.

Lindsay said "I told you that Lilly would win the match today, well she was a major underdog according to the sports bet and came through. She has a couple of days to get ready for what will be her second ever big-league match."

Lilly quickly went away from the set and left for the locker room to get a shower and change clothes. On the way she signed 2 more balls for people. After 20 minutes, Lilly emerged from the players locker room, having showered, and put on a fresh pink Lacoste shirt and jacket. It was nearly 7 PM, so we decided to go to Ashe stadium player cafeteria.

By the time we finished dinner, the 4 of us Lilly, Ken Larry, and Paul, we discovered who Lilly would play on Wednesday. The match just finished, and it took three sets and just under 3 hours to complete. Maria Schindler from Brazil had upset the number 12 seed in the match meaning my next round would be a primarily clay court specialist instead of the all-court player we expected. Paul when given notification said, "we will get tape on her and review on Tuesday prior to practice with Mike Finley. You have a 30-minute session for mixed doubles practice Tuesday, and we will follow it up with our own practice. We won't know until practice is over when you will play Wednesday and I know that your first round of mixed doubles will be on Thursday, so no practice that day, just play of the mixed doubles match in anticipation of your Friday singles opponent. I just laughed and said Friday match, that is really pushing the envelope."

With the dinner over, we were provided a limousine by Lacoste to go back to the Hilton Garden Inn for everyone but Larry. Larry said, I have a full day on Tuesday, so I'm taking the subway back to Manhattan. Larry gave me a hug and kiss and whispered enjoy your time you deserve it. I kept it together and gave him a bone crushing hug.

We were welcomed by the staff at the Hilton, and we have been told that your rooms are now extended until at least Friday. When I got back to the conference room converted to my room, they had put a sign, "Lilly Jarman tennis center". I laughed at the sign. My dad laughed and said it has been a long day for him, so with that Ken had his room key, and went to the elevator to call my mom again and then go to bed. I think he is staying the week because Radford won't be in full swing until next week, apparently someone is covering his classes on Thursday and Friday, I guess he was excused by the University from listening to the whining freshmen.

Paul excused himself and said to me it's nearly 9 PM, I have some work to do tonight and then to make sure that your doubles practice time of 1:15 PM is still on for Tuesday. Paul reminded me that the mixed doubles will start on Thursday, and will either be early on one of the show courts or late in the afternoon elsewhere, they are only about an hour with the no-ad scoring so let's not worry about it at this time. I then proceeded to look-up my e-mails on then my Facebook account to see if there was anything I needed to respond to. An ITF in California just gave me a wild card if I want it, and a WTA 250 to be indoors at the end of the year has stated they would like to consider coming to qualifiers. I responded yes to the ITF at this point, now that I will be top 200, I can soon get in these tournaments directly, so not sure I will need the wildcard. For those that don't know what a wildcard is, it is a direct entry into the tournament without having a ranking sufficient for a direct entry or not having to go through qualifying. I got a lot of congratulations and so many are from people that I knew in Radford area. Funny that they are congratulating me, when growing up all they could do is to keep their debutantes and baby rednecks away from me as the odd smart girl who plays tennis like a guy. I remember my senior year in high school, I was thinking about going to the prom, when one of these girls said, what's her name of your date for the night. Implying that I was a lesbian. I remember asking Michael Frederick, who played number 3 on the men's team. We were just friends, but he wanted to go to prom and had just broken-up with one of these debutantes. I remember with my heals on I was taller than him, but we danced a few dances together and we had fun nothing more than a dance for me, nothing romantic either. After running down memory lane, I thought it was time to try to go to bed and texted my brother thanking him for the good thoughts from earlier today. Finally, I sent an e-mail to Jacques thanking him for arranging to have my father at the tournament it was so fantastic.

Who would have thought at age 29, I would win my first round at the US Open and it was overwhelming. It took me 2 hours watching movies to finally chill enough to go to sleep. I kept thinking if I had never played tennis how lonely and ugly my life could have been. It got me to thinking about when I was competing as a kid, and how weird it was as the only girls from my area to compete. I was thinking about when I started competition and how it was being the outcast from country Virginia and how mean it was with the girls from the DC and Baltimore areas. They Just assumed they were better because they had the expensive cars, the outfits, and the big-name facility.

Chapter 7

From the Beginning to High School

You heard previously how my life started and how the debutantes in Radford, VA, never played with me and were not my friends. Well let me tell you elementary school was never going to be a picnic, but what I did not understand was that tennis was just as catty as were the hicks in Radford.

My grandparents were great though with helping, my second-grade birthday gifts and holiday gifts all were around tennis. From tennis outfits, always in pink tops and blue bottoms, or buying me a new pair of sneakers, or finding a way for me to do work for them and earn some money they would pay for my entrance fees to tournaments. Since I had long blond hair, also tennis themed berets for my hair. I don't know where they got them, but they were all my trademarks in the 10 and under competitions I played in, I always had them in my hair. Well, I will say that I was about to turn 8 I got to play a local tournament in Radford, and while the wealthy kids from the Country Club all expected to win, the little girl on a professor's salary, managed to play her second tennis tournament and made it to the finals. I lost to a ten-year-old from Blacksburg, Pauline something I don't remember her name and she quit tennis when she was 13. I upset the number 2 seed in the first round, winning if I remember 6-2 and 6-3. The second match was against a 9-year-old from Radford, that I just destroyed 6-0, and

6-2, I remember her crying to her mom and saying that odd girl hits like a boy. In the semi-finals I beat another 8-year-old from Roanoke, and she was the three seed, I remember it being a tight match I think it went three tiebreakers, but that was a great match. As I said earlier, I lost in the finals to a much more experienced and older player, but I still got my first tennis trophy, and my dad was so proud as I came over to show him. They took our picture, and it was in the local newspaper the following week. My mom has it somewhere in a scrapbook.

My second grade at Riverlawn Elementary School was not different than my first grade. My grades were good, and it was funny because of tennis, I had a lot more in common with the guys than the girls which did not help my social status, as they would let me play sports that the girls were not as good as me. I played kickball and soccer with them, and sometimes touch football. I think I was invited to one birthday party and that was a friend, Bob Kratz, while the little girls were all dolled up, I was wearing sweatpants and my pink tennis top. The little girl's kind of laughed at me, as the tomboy, but the guys all talked to me because they just cared that I liked sports. Did I tell you because we were rural Virginia, we were Redskin fans, and watched them whenever we could as a family. The rest of the year I missed parties not because I was playing tennis but because I simply was not invited. Since, I had a summer birthday our family rarely did parties anyway, but it would not have mattered none of them would have come to the party anyway. I got all A's in school except a B in writing, I just was not that good at my writing, did not have enough imagination, I guess. The note says, Lilly can do anything she wants, it's a shame she does not concentrate and achieve more. If I was getting mostly A's, what did they want, my dad just would laugh, don't worry there will be time to get ready for college.

During the summer, I got to play tennis at Radford University summer camps. I played one tournament at 10 and under at Hollins College, near Roanoke. I was able to win 1 round before losing to a girl from the DC area, I think she played five days a week at a tennis club in Northern Virginia, but I was just not as competitive as some of the girls I just liked to hit the ball and sometimes forgot that you were supposed to make sure your opponent just could not hit it back. As an 8-year-old I was lucky if I could get a serve in on every point.

For the summer I did not have private lessons or go to the country club that was reserved for winter. On the weekends we went to church every Sunday at the local episcopal churches either in Radford, or Farmville or a couple of times at Blacksburg. The community of Blacksburg seemed much more open to our family than that at either other city, so I kind of liked going to see my grandparents.

Third and fourth grades were similar, my education showed all A's and a B normally. My social status did not change other than I now had a friend in Frances Oliverio, she moved into Radford from the DC area and was a good swimmer and runner, so again the non-debutantes got to get together. Neither of us were invited to parties with the girls, and we were invited to fill in for soccer with the guys no touch football, my mom said no on that one. I was only allowed to play a local tournament as my parents did not want to travel with a young child, and the costs would have prevented much anyway. I do know that we got our second car while I was in 4th grade an 8-year-old Chevrolet Impala, which we would have until I finished high school. We went to a lot of tournaments in that car with the big trunk. The DC people came in BMW, Mercedes, and Lexus SUVs, so you could tell who was from the DC area and the Norfolk area, they all came in with these expensive cars. As far as tennis, I continued to do the summer camps at Radford, but they moved me up to playing with the twelve-year-olds, which meant instead of 3 hours at camp, we could do 6 hours with an hour for lunch. In the Radford Open I played my last year as a ten and under and won the tournament easily. The coaches asked me to start playing the twelves, and I ended up losing to a much older girl from the area who was getting ready to enter middle school. I was developing a reputation in the area, as the girl who could hit two types of backhands a one-handed and a two handed which I used most of the time. In the meantime, as I was getting taller, I was able to now get a serve in on most occasions that the opponents had to work to win the point. I again had my picture taken as the champion of the 10's at Radford tournament which Dea cut out and put in plastic. I continued to play at the country club, but now we started in October and played there through April. I was also getting some free extra hitting with the pro's since they knew my family did not have a lot of money. I did play a couple of tennis tournaments over the winter and so much longer than the outdoor tournaments due to the lack of courts. I never got past the semi-finals, as the DC kids were much more experienced in tournaments. The farthest we went was Charlottesville, VA and we even got to stay at a motel because I won 2 matches on Saturday at the 10's and the semi-finals and finals were on Sunday. I lost the first match and so my mom said let's get to a church, I think the Episcopal church starts services at 10:15, and we can go. I went in my sweats while the local girls were at Sunday school in nicer clothes. Bob Kratz continued to be my friend, and I will give you a little hint, Bob and I went to one prom together, nothing sexual Larry, he continues to be a great friend. Bob is now a practicing accountant in the Radford area, just completed his CPA. He is not married and has been a dating a girl from his college time at Wake Forest. I suspect that within a year I will be going to the wedding and introduce Larry at that time. I was invited to his birthday party every year, and while I thought we may date, we never did, and he will always be one of my true friends I could trust but you will hear about that later. That is all I can say I remember about the third and fourth grades.

So now at age 11 came the Fifth grade representing a new world. I was finishing up at my elementary school, entering tennis tournaments about every 6 weeks, and starting to travel as far away as Richmond, Virginia. We were starting to see where the boys and girls were in groups, but I only had one friend that was a girl and spent most of my time with the boys because I liked to talk Redskins, and other sports including Virginia Tech football, since my grandparents were there and worked there. A few boy and girl parties started, and I was not invited to. I was I the outsider Eurasian, but I was also growing early and at 11 was already 5 feet 3 inches so I was as tall as most of the boys, I guess that was intimidating. Truthfully, I had more fun talking sports with the boys and then an incident occurred that I probably should have known was coming. Jenny Franklin, an auburn-haired girl, and

I were in the bathroom, and she was talking about a party coming up and said something to me, well don't expect you to come to the parties with girls and boys.

"I asked why?"

"She said because you are gay!"

"I said what do you mean?"

"Jenny said we know you are butch and gay."

"I commented what would make you think I am gay?"

"Jenny said everyone knows you are a guy. You hang out with the guys, talk sports, and play tennis like a guy. we get you are like Martina Navratilova, so we don't want to invite you."

I left the bathroom, got on my bus, and started to cry. I talked to my mom, that afternoon and asked her was I butch, and she said who would tell you that, you are a little girl. I was told I was butch by one of my classmates because she says I talks sports with the boys. You are just 11 years old, and yes because you like sports you have a lot more in common with the boys than the girls have nothing to do with your life, don't let people tell you what you are, be what you want to be. You are a lovely girl who is athletic, and since your dad played college football and your grandfather works at Virginia Tech, of course you talk football.

From that day on I got that I was different, athletic and a girl, and that those little debutantes that were cheerleaders wished they got to travel on weekends had good grades. I guess when Larry and I are making love I should ask him if he thinks I am a guy. I think he would laugh.

I wanted to now talk about the tennis side. I never knew anything about rankings etc, but this was the first time my coaches talked about ranking in the Mid-Atlantic region and because I had only won 1 round as a 12 and under, I had no ratings. My first match was at Richmond at an indoor court called Raintree. My match was scheduled for 10:00 in the morning on Saturday, and there were 8 girls in this tournament. We stayed Friday night with my grandparents at Farmville, and mom and I left early the next morning for Richmond. I looked at the draw and noticed that I had to play the number 1 seed in the first round. She was from Richmond, and her name was Rachel Stone, of course she was blonde. I guess she was a little overconfident or because I had no ratings, she did not take me seriously. I'm sure she was told just get this match done fast to be ready for the semi-finals this afternoon. The only problem was that I was used to playing boys and when she served it was nothing special, so I hit forehand down both lines and kept her from pushing me around the court. In about 90 minutes I won my first round in a high regional tournament. I think the score was like 6-4 and 6-2, but don't trust my memory. Later that day I had to play another higher than me ranked player, this time from the Fredericksburg area closer to DC. This match went very long as she did the things, we call moon balls on every shot. "Moon Balls" are shots hit high into the air from the baseline when nobody is pushing you at the net, the player does this so that they don't have to be as accurate and it usually very successful. The match took well over 2 hours and somehow, I won 7-5 and I think 6-4, I know that we had very few breaks of serve and some of the points seemed to go forever. I had never played this long and with our limited funds had to drive back to the grandparents' house in Farmville and come back for the finals on Sunday morning. My mom washed my tennis outfit because we did not bring a second one with us. A mistake she would never do again, we always had at least 2 changes of clothes after that. Additional socks were in the back seat with an additional pair of sneakers. I would like to tell you I won this tournament but up against the 2 seed, a girl from Alexandria, VA, I lost 6-1, and 6-1. Truthfully, I had no energy courteously of the moon ball match, never ran so much the day before and nothing in the tank on Sunday. I was told by my grandparents who got the Richmond newspaper that a photo of us was in "The Richmond Free Press", although we never got a copy. I wanted to take the trophy to school the next day, parents thought better of it and glad they did in the long run.

 I played a couple of tournaments in the 12's before the Christmas Holiday, one In Blacksburg, and one in Roanoke. I did not make the finals in either tournament, or I also never lost in the first match of the weekend either. My dad took me to the tournament in Blacksburg and we stayed at my grandparents that weekend. I won 2 matches on Saturday and lost in the semi-finals in two sets and a tiebreaker, my first of my life, they had to bring a parent that knew the rules on to the court. Although I lost, I have to say it was fun staying in my dad's old room and looking at his football trophies. The other tournament as a higher-level tournament which also served as a low-level national tournament. Winning a match here got my first national ranking, I looked up after the weekend and I was number 1094 in the 12's. After that tournament I was now top 40 in the region given the few tournaments, I was happy. I made the mistake of telling everyone, and they said you dedicate so much time and you are only the 40th best player and 20th from Virginia, not very good. After that I never spoke of rankings until my senior year of high school, but that story is for the later years.

The holidays again were split between Farmville and Blacksburg, with Christmas in Blacksburg, and New Year's in Farmville, so grandparents time and presents all related to tennis again. Truth be known, my parents could not afford my outfits, so this was how my grandparents helped.

As for school I continued to have a couple of friends but mostly just stayed to myself to avoid being the scorn of the debutantes. My grades were good and Dea called me and told me she was proud of the way I was overcoming the debutantes and still such a wonderful young lady. I guess dad told her how the debutantes' families really shunned me because of my Asian looks.

In the winter and spring, I played three more tournaments, the first tournament was in Newport News, VA. We stayed at my Grandparents' house in Farmville, Friday night, and then drove down the rest of the way Saturday morning. For the first time, there was a number by my name, it said 8, which meant I was the 8 seed for the tournament, and all the girls were friendly with each other from the DC area, but nobody else was from my area, so again I felt alone. There were 30 girls at what was a high-ranking regional tournament, but it was also another low-level national tournament. I won again both my matches on Saturday, and we got to stay at a Days Inn which was great with me, we got some type of discount through Radford University, probably the only way we could afford it. With my fancy day 2 clothes, I was ready for the semi-finals, but the number 1 seed who was much more experienced and top 100 in the country, beat me with very little difficulty 6-3, and 6-2. A long drive with mom all the way back to Radford, a stop in Farmville, for a meal with the grandparents and a rest for mom. When we got home, my bratty brother asked where your is your trophy, and I said they don't do participation trophies like your sports. The next ratings, I cracked the top 900 nationally, and top 25 in the region. The next tournament was a lower rated tournament at the end of February in West Virginia, near Bluefield. There were only 6 girls in this tournament, and I was rated with a red one, so I got a bye Saturday morning. My first match was Saturday afternoon late, and I was able to win the semi-final. My mom had a friend from college who lived in Bluefield, and we crashed with her that night, mom on the sofa and me on the floor. Naureen was her name, and she made a big pasta meal for us, and I wondered where her roommate was and was told she left for the weekend. Since the townhouse had only 2 bedrooms, and it looked like one was an office I wondered where her roommate lived. A couple of years later, my mother explained to me that some women are attracted to other women, and Naureen had a longtime friend that she lived with. This was my first experience with a real lesbian, and truthfully, my mom and her got along, and I did not see anything different. The next morning, I went out and beat the girl from West Virginia who was the 2 seed, it was a tough match, but she had never played someone with a slice backhand, so while she hit harder, I could counter her moves and finished the first set 7-5 and won the second easier at 6-2. My mom took my picture, and then forwarded it to my dad, and both grandparents'. I again thought about taking the trophy to school the next day, now smarter, decided that was not going to be a great choice.

Since my parents insisted that I go to Sunday school, when we travelled for the weekends of tennis, I was given my homework a week early and often had to do this work while driving home, because mom would take it to church for the teacher on Mondays. This type of homework would go a long way to completing work later. I really don't remember the other matches I played that year; I know nothing was won or any finals, but right before I turned 12, I was ranked in the top 20 and 700 respectively regional and national.

I turned 12 over the summer and was invited to my first boy/girl party. While many of the people wanted to playthings like spin the bottle, I really had no interest except my best friend, Bob Kratz said it would be easier on me. When the bottle spun to Bob, he simply leaned over to me and gave me my first kiss. I think everyone was stunned that he kissed me, and it was on the lips and none of the debutantes were chosen.

Later he said to me, "I kissed you, but we are not boy and girlfriend, just friends, I don't like the girls picking on you because you are athletic and better looking than them."

I blushed and gave him a hug. It was the first time I had been told I was good looking, some of the girls were ahead of me in developing breasts I was not an early bloomer, and I was tall and skinny. After that incident, the debutantes left me alone, I guess Bob's action threw off some assumptions about me at least for a while.

Sixth grade was different in some ways, for the first time, I was at John Dalton Intermediate school, and for the first time instead of one teacher we had 7 classes and different teachers. While the debutantes were still with me, I found that there were a lot of other girls that liked sports and played them such as soccer, and volleyball. Since I was now 5 '7" tall, the boys were mostly shorter than me, but I was friendly to them and while we did not play sports together, I was at least not as singled out as elementary school. At this point, I got my first bra, my mother took me to the JC Penney in the area and purchased it right on the spot. She showed me how to use it and truthfully, I don't think I needed it, but all the other girls had them, so mom said I needed one also. I did not wear it for tennis at this point I really did not have enough to worry about.

I should mention that I was still getting a lot of A's and only B's in English, I just did not put enough effort in to the writing assignments usually finishing them late Sunday night before turning them in Monday morning.

As for tennis nothing was different really, we could not afford as much tennis tournaments as others but playing once about every 5 weeks, and using the grandparents' house, I finished the year 15th and

650th respectively. In the spring, I started to play the 14's because you're ranking from a lower age group died with your age, so you must initiate your next age group points so you can get seeded. I did not have a great amount of success but created a baseline so I could at least get accepted into the better tournaments. My training was different, for the first time I was training with the senior group at the country club, and at Radford, I sometimes would hit in with the college team at the end of practice. I think they thought of me as the annoying little sister that wanted to hit with them and truthfully, I probably was very annoying to them and kept asking a lot of questions. I would go to the home matches to see them play and learn things.

The next 2 years I went from a 12-year-old to a 14-year-old tennis player. I played every 5 weeks like before and I was top 20 in the region and because I only played in regional tournaments that were also national tournaments until right before I was going to turn 15, I did not have much of a national rating. They had a major National 14's at Virginia Beach and I put my name in and was accepted as an alternate in the 128 draws. A week before the tournament was to begin in June, I got an e-mail that due to cancellations I was accepted into this tournament.

With the news I was accepted, my dad said let's make this a family vacation, we can get an inexpensive motel, like Comfort Inn, and find a way to use coolers, and other ways to keep from it being expensive. James and Barbara were coming with us, so we did this as a family vacation they were going to drop us off for the matches, go to the beach and then pick up mom and me after each round. This tournament can take several days as there is a main draw and a back draw and double elimination. To win the tournament you need to play 6 rounds over a potential of 5 days as I remember. My first match was against a fellow mid-Atlantic kid and Sally was about the same rank I was but played like 2 tournaments a month. We played at 9:00 on Friday and the match took about 75 minutes with me coming on top in the clay 6-4, and 6-3. Meaning I advanced to the next round and received a boat full of points as this was a top level national. The afternoon match was played in the heat at 3 PM, and the poor girl from Mass, I think her name was Erica had not even played this season outdoors. While she was the 30 seed, I could play more easily in the heat and humidity. After a match that lasted two hours, I completed a very long match 4-6, 6-4 and 7-5. I had never won a match where I had lost the first set before. This created a scenario, where no matter what happened in my first match, I had made the round of 32, and with that came a lot of ranking points. We found an inexpensive pasta restaurant and we found one that was like a fast-food looking place and our 4 dinners were like $40, because we got a 50% off coupon in the players bag of goodies. The next morning, I was wearing my third and last tennis outfit and had the honor of playing the third seeded girl who was part of the national training center in Florida, named Maxine Rootes, a tall African American player. She was fully sponsored, so you can guess I was a little awed by the atmosphere of a major tournament. It took Maxine about 90 minutes to eliminate the country bumpkin from the winners' bracket and drop me off to the loser's bracket. Because of the other losers' bracket matches, my next round was not scheduled until Sunday. That gave my mom and me time to go to a laundromat and wash my clothes, I had nothing left to play with that did not stink and the men were complaining about the smell from the corner. I would like to tell you I made a great stand in the Sunday match but truthfully, I was overmatched on Sunday and a bit tired also, losing to a seed that had lost a first-round match and was now coming on strongly. She beat me 6-4 and 6-1, I just did not have enough experience to offset her academy experience and it took about another hour for me to be eliminated from the tournament. I played doubles, but my partner and I had never met, and we lost quickly on Saturday afternoon so great learning experience, but I was done by noon Sunday. I heard later that Maxine ended up losing in the finals, so I don't feel that bad. Just before I turned 15, I had my ranking rise to 175, nationally, with very few countable tournaments, and my regional ranking ended up like 15.

 At this time, I ended my growth spirt and was a tall 5"9" and barely over 105 pounds. You can guess the curvier debutantes use to call me a boy. I had very little frontal curves and really did not have the urge to chase the boys. My 32A cup did not have the boys running for joy and truthfully, I was not interested. Bob was still shorter than me, but for some reason he kept inviting me to the parties, we really were just friends but this way neither of us had to deal with the debutantes me because they thought I was gay and Bob because he for some reason was good friends with the gay girl, I think they assumed he was gay. Truthfully, we would find out later he tipped his toe in that pool, but he is getting married to a nice woman in Charlotte, NC next year, and that is another story. Bob is now a CPA and dabbles in real estate in the area, he does well with his personality and his fiancé is a nurse at the hospital. Janice Ormond, she knows he dipped his toe in the other pool for a while, and she loves him, and they say they want 3 kids.

So as I approached the end of my middle-school years, I had discovered that I was a pretty competitive tennis player, had played in a national tournament, discovered that those with training dollars that I had no access to were likely to be better than I was coming from a nowhere area of tennis, I was somewhat tall and thin, I had only a few friends and almost none in tennis or school, I was not popular with the boys because I did not have the boobs and shape that the debutantes did, and I was still able to get as good of grades as the brainiacs that is all they did in life. My family continued to be a source of support, especially with Dea my grandmother from Korea, she may have only been five feet tall, but she always seemed to know what exactly I was going through and found a way to make it better. My mother had taken a part-time job at the local bank now that we were grown-up enough to get by, she felt she could add to our money, and it did come in handy as we needed money to travel. My dad was now a full professor, it had taken a lot longer than usual as the university was trying to be cheap. With the full professor, came things like, tenure, which guaranteed his income and retirement benefits, so he would be able to retire at a normal age and not be worried that his job would end at any semester. Dad also had picked-up some writing assignments for local magazines and papers so periodically he would get a check for a few hundred dollars.

I was ready to go to high school and possible play high school tennis, they were not a great team, and it was a popularity contest, so not even sure they would let me play on the team. My coaches all thought I should skip my freshman year of high school tennis, so I could do a more robust tennis tournament schedule. I was going to the 16's next year and that was apparently the springboard they said to college scholarships, I had no idea what they were talking about I had never won a tournament of any significance and I thought this was nice, but I would probably go to school and get a business degree at Radford, the lower cost would save money.

I did discover that even a tall skinny girl could look better in a long dress and make-up. My mother told me I did not need it, but still took me to a friend of hers who was a Mary Kay dealer, everything pink, and learned about lipstick, eyeliner, and a few other things. I was a woman and it had been late, but I got my first period in 8th grade while others had already been for 2 years. Thank God it was not on a tennis court and my mom quickly gave me some tampons she had in her purse and then we went to the Rite Aid for my own supply. I also found out something now being a woman, the week of the period is very hard to play tennis matches, you are already uncomfortable and moody, and tennis did not make it much better.

Let's get back to tennis, I was able to win the tournament at Raintree as the 8th seed on the girl's 16's. I beat a girl from MD in the first round, another Virginia girl in the next round, then 2 girls from Richmond in the quarters and semi-finals. Then beat the 1 seed from Ashburn, VA in a match that had to go inside due to rain. That was my first tournament win in the 16's, as an eight seed I'm sure nobody expected me. The 2 girls I beat from Godwin High school I bet did not expect it. Over the summer I played one clay court national level tournament in the Richmond area and was able to make the semi-finals. With one year left in the 16's I was now top 20, in the region and top 200 all by traveling within Virginia. People knew that I played better than my ranking and was not distracted with boys so could concentrate on tennis.

For the first time we went on a real beach vacation, and of course we were able to rent a place near Virginia Beach. I was able to bike to the beach and with James we went to the beach for the first time. There were quite a few teens at the beach and one guy, Randy Parker, who was 17, liked to tease me. All week he would do things like hey tall girl you want to play volleyball. I finally had enough and on the third day, played next to him and kept my own, Randy was a little over 6 feet tall, and truthfully looked like a young version of my dad well-muscled, well-tanned and had dark brown hair, with dark bedroom eyes.

Randy said, "a bunch of the guys and girls are going to hang out Friday night before we all go back home, come on down and hang out we will be on the beach."

James did not go with me that night and when I got to the beach, I saw Randy playing volleyball, and he saw me and said Hey tall girl come join us for the next game. We played for about an hour and after that we all sat near the fire.

Randy sat next to me and said, "girl you are very athletic what sport do you play and why not volleyball."

"I told him I had never played volleyball except in gym class, he told me you should try, tennis may be fun, but you are tall enough and athletic enough to be a volleyball player."

Then he surprised me and put his arm around my shoulder and pulled me closer to him. Unlike any other time, for some reason I seemed to like the attention I was getting from Randy and felt very close to him. After a while he suggested that we take a walk, and unlike any other time, I reached out and grabbed his hand as we walked down the beach. About a quarter mile down the beach, we stopped holding hands and Randy turned to me, and our lips were the first things that touched each other. I had a towel with me and put it on the ground and sat down and Randy joined next to me. Again, we kissed and this time our tongues met. Randy then started to kiss me on my neck, and reached inside my bikini top and met me nipples with his fingers. They immediately bloomed and then we started a little more kissing and Randy started to kiss my nipples and then stood up waiting for his tongue to tease them. I untied my top so he could more easily reach both of my nipples with his fingers and tongue and while I had never really been with a guy before I loved the feeling with Randy. After several minutes, Randy started to run his fingers from my knees to my bikini bottom, and then reached my bikini bottoms and started to play within them. That is where I stopped anything, I had the talk and while I was excited, I was not going to have that kind of experience that night and forced Randy to withdraw his fingers and looked at him and told him it was not going to happen. He tried a couple of times later, but each time, I pushed him away. After a few more minutes I tied my top and kissed him one more time.

Randy said, "he had never had a relationship that far with a girl also, he had been kidded by his friends to go after it tonight. I really like you and I'm sorry if you never want to see me again."

"I simply said, I like you too, I'm not even 16 yet, so while we can play and kiss nothing else is going to happen."

He looked relieved, and just said, "so can I still hold hands and get kissed by the prettiest athletic looking girl here?"

"I said only if you don't try for something else."

"He laughed; you probably would be able to knock me out if I tried." I elbowed him and then we kissed and held hands back to the beach fire.

For the next two days, I played volleyball with the guys at the beach, and Randy and I played next to each other. We went to the beach together, held hands and even played a little bit up north, but nothing else was tried or even attempted by either party. We exchanged numbers because he said he would love to continue our relationship even if it meant a long distance. I realized the likelihood is that nothing would ever happen again, he lived in Springfield, VA and I lived just about as far away as possible. We would write each other but since he was up there, and I was way over the other part of the state other than e-mails and text nothing Randy played basketball and ran track in the spring to stay in shape. Both of us were busy and the only thing we did was text each other like very close friends. I will tell you we had one more date but that is for another story in my high school years. Both Randy and I left a couple days later and swore we would stay in contact. We did stay in contact every week, but only through texts and e-mails. Randy is now the lead auto mechanic at a dealership in Virginia, he completed several certifications and is the lead for all repairs from his dealership, not bad for someone just 30 years old. He only went 2 years to college and realized he loved to work on cars and went through numerous classes and certifications then the local Pohanka dealer just ate it up and hired him. I bet he makes a lot more money than some of those with graduate degrees, I saw his boat pictures on Facebook that he owns and not a bad thing to have. He got married about a year ago to a lovely girl from Georgia, and they are expecting their first child in December.

With tennis and romance all checked in I was all but ready to start high school at Radford, hopefully they would let me play on the tennis team. Randy is enough of a guy for me to keep in touch with, we both knew nothing more is probable. He was the first guy that said I was and athletic and that was attractive, and it really made me feel good. I had started to get more muscled and now was about 115 pounds. The debutantes may have had a lot more curves, but they did not have a great friend like Bob and admirer like Randy to help them. I would not give in to the teasing no matter how they tried to make themselves feel better.

Chapter 8

The Second Round

With a knock on the door, my breakfast from Elijah's bagels was waiting for me at 8:00. After eating what has now become my go to breakfast, I downed it with some orange juice and started drinking Gatorade to be ready for practice in the afternoon. I had to pinch myself, I was getting ready for the second round of the US Open, I have won more money than the last 2 years combined just by winning this one match. In the bag a note from the restaurant, we are proud of you, and we will have someone at your next match. I went to my laptop and looked for messages from Paul. He will be at my suite at 11:00, to look at strategy for the match against Maria Schindler on Wednesday, plus to show me the strategy difference of doubles with women and men on the same court. He also said we must leave for practice at 12:30 and we will have an Uber picking us up. He reminded me to wear the pink and blue Lacoste outfits, and the new wrist bands from Lacoste this morning that match the pink top, with the flag of Korea on it for the match Wednesday. I have no idea how Jacques got that done, but they will be fun for the next round. He also explained that we are having the new sponsor logos sewed in to 2 of my blue tennis skirts for Wednesday. This is getting so funny, having to talk about sponsors etc. I saw another e-mail from John Littleman, he has a potential additional tournament in Thailand that he has received a commitment for a wild card if I win

Lilly's Story

this upcoming match. It is a level 250 professional tournament with a minimum of $5000, for just showing up.

I got a text from Larry saying, work commitment today, will not be able to see you tonight.

(This is Larry here; I am inserting this piece into the narrative of Lilly's journey. I can't be with Lilly tonight; I am getting a diamond ring at the Diamond Exchange). My boss has made a few calls, and he is accompanying me to one of his contacts stores in the Exchange, I am looking for a diamond engagement ring, I am not proposing without it, and the office is excited to help me. If Lilly wins and has an interview with ESPN, the plan is to ask her to marry me at the end of the interview on ESPN, Pam Shriver is apparently a very accommodating person, and a romantic also.)

Paul arrived at my door and had his laptop out with footage of what we can expect from Maria. Paul explained that Maria is primarily a clay court player, so getting into long baseline rallies with her will not be beneficial to our cause. The plan is no matter what happens for the first three shots, I am going to rush the net on the fourth and make her get off the baseline. The strategy also says serve big like you are playing the 4.5 men in Radford, because we need Maria uncomfortable, and she has footage from the last match that shows you serve and volleying right away, we are only going to use that when you are at game points with a 40-15 or 40-love lead. These slight changes will give you a chance against this roadrunner. After we finished the singles match strategy, we talked about strategy for mixed doubles which will start on Thursday, reminder you are playing big and fast guys, so simply getting the ball back on a serve is a victory, some of these guys hit 130's and you will have to back-up and simply block the returns.

Time to leave and my dad said he was going to skip today as the heat was getting to him, so just Paul and myself went to the center. We got there early enough to get food at the players' lounge and just made the practice court at 1:15, for our reserved 30 minutes with Mike Finley. Mike has a big serve and at 6 "4" does not need a lot of room to make it to the net, looks like 4 steps. We played against Paul and Mike's coach to decide which player was going where and some basic moves. After talking to the coaches, they had an unusual line-up for us, I have a slice back-hand so I would take the second receiving side also called the ad side. Mike would take the aggressive neutral shots and we will try to meet at the net to win the points. This strategy is different than most mixed teams as the woman normally takes the deuce side. While we were going to be the lower ranked team it may take some time for them to figure out what was happening, and with the no-ad scoring games are going too fast and maybe we can steal a match and get some extra prize money. With the thirty minutes finished, Mike and his coach left, and we started on my practice session. It was nothing fancy but a good sweat and then it was over. I had a couple of people that wanted me to sign a tennis ball, I bet they thought I was one of the Europeans with my blond hair, they will look me up and say who is Lilly Jarman.

I went back to the players area and took a shower and changed into a fresh pair of clothes. Paul and I went to the players' lounge together where they posted the line-up for the next day. Familiar court, back on court 4 and third match on, the routine we did for the previous match will be the same for this round. We just have a different strategy with this roadrunner, we need to find a way to get me to play way above my ranking after-all she is a top 50 player in the world, and I'm like 215, I'm sure she is looking forward to the next round after beating me in an hour or less. Paul and I must somehow make that not happen.

By the time it was all over it was nearly 4 PM, signed a couple of balls for people waiting for players to come out of the lounge and then decided it was time to go back to the hotel. Dad texted did you know that the place had a pool? I responded not really,

Dad responded it does, and I have been here most of the day. Did you also know that Lacoste tennis shorts can be used as a swimsuit I have it on now and nobody knows the difference.

I started laughing so hard that I should not say it, but I let out gas and that made Paul laugh at me. Next was a text to Larry, telling him about the time for the next match. A response came back love you and I will be back to see the match taking ½ day of vacation tomorrow. I simply wrote back love you too, want a hug after I win. A smiley face came back in response. The last call was to my mom and telling her when the match will be.

I finally got her on the line, and it sounded noisy where she was, so I asked "where are you?"

"Mom said it was supposed to be a secret, but I am at the Richmond Amtrak station getting ready to board a train to DC and then another to New York. Jacques can be very persuasive; he said the company wanted both parents to be at my next match and I am on my way. I am taking the rest of the week off they understood when I explained that you were playing in the US Open. They may not be tennis fans, but they were excited that you were playing a big tournament. I will get there late tonight and will see you in the am I think I won't get into the hotel until near midnight."

While I was making my calls, Paul called Radford and the club is going to find a way to show the match live. The tennis team is excited at watching and they found a way to hook up a solution with a subscription to ESPN.

Paul told me that the club said," Lilly kick butt," but Paul told me that was the cleaned-up version. The junior girls asked wanted to know when they were getting their assistant coach back and we thought end of September probably.

Since it looked like nobody was going to be able to go out tonight, I asked the Hilton how they could help and they said we don't have a great kitchen, but we will order at one of my favorite restaurants and have enough pasta, sausage, bread, and salad for the three of us doing dinner.

Paul asked, "if it was possible to get some beer delivered", he needed something besides water and soda. The said they would pick-up some IPA's at a local beer brewery that was about a mile from the hotel. Dad got a scotch and water at the bar.

A knock on the door at 6:30 PM, and dinner was delivered. I called my dad at the bar and texted Paul. By 6:45, we all met at the conference table for dinner. I took out my Gatorade and water, the men enjoyed beer and liquor. I texted Larry but did not receive a response, he must have been in the subway somewhere.

With dinner finished Paul and I got together to discuss the strategy for the match tomorrow. Paul suggested no matter what happens, if you have gone 6 shots on your side hit it down the line and come up to net because even if you lose the point, we will be able to save energy and with this opponent saving energy will be key, she loves a baseline game, and we must make her uncomfortable. We warm-up at noon we get ½ court and this is just a warm-up so nothing crazy a few serves, a few volleys, and just relaxing hitting.

Dad said, "since the match won't be on until 3 PM, Barbara and he will sleep in and will leave for the tournament around 1 :30, we will get an Uber and be there with credentials for me Jacques has it for mom, and we will be at court 4 no later than 2:45. Ok, I am going to say it, remember when all people could say to us was that skinny blond girl has a nice game but she will never win anything. Keep that in your mind that you are here show everyone that you were just as good as I thought you were."

With that sentence tears came to both of us, I gave dad a hug and said "I will see you on the court tomorrow and will need you to help Larry take notes about the match. I also want you to yell like crazy at my introduction."

Larry finally texted back, I love you and will see you tomorrow. The next text was a little funny, "Lilly Jarman kick some Brazilian ass" I started laughing and showed the last text to Paul who simply said, "I agree what is so funny?"

Paul excused himself from the room and said see you at 11:00, if you feel you need it the hotel has a stationary bicycle, and you can do light riding for up to 15 minutes. With a fist pump the tennis time was over for the night.

My mom texted me she was getting into New York and good luck tomorrow. I then turned off my cell phone, read some e-mails, and then tried to go to sleep. All I could think was oh shit this is the second round of the fucking US Open. Excuse me mom but it had to be said. Turned on the TV and looked for a slow movie and tried to go to sleep.

US Open Day 3:

Today is the second round of the US Open, I will be playing Maria Schindler at about 3 PM. Maria is mostly a clay court specialist, but she is still very strong on hard courts. She is a top 50 player while my live ranking is about 215. She has played over a hundred matches at the tour level, I have one.

I woke up before eight and my breakfast was delivered from Elijah's bagels at 08:15. As I was eating, I looked at the schedule for Paul and me. We need to have the Uber here at 11:15, be downstairs with everything ready by 11:00. Warm-up on the practice courts was from 12 to 12:30 in the afternoon, shower and change to 1:00, meet at the lounge at 1:15 for lunch and strategy. Finish and get to players' lounge by 2 PM. Wait until called for the match and then play a second-round match at the US Open. A note was in the bag saying that Elijah's will have 2 employees at court 4.

I texted Larry to find out what time he would be there, and he said his plan would be to be on the court by 2:30, to make sure that we had our seat assignments for the player area, he will bring his laptop for notes. A "I Love You and Proud of You" came next and I started to tear.

Texted dad to make sure that mom had gotten there, and got a response at 8:45, we are both here and will be ready for your match, I will even make sure I am shaved this time.

My rooting section is complete, a boyfriend, a part-time coach, 2 parents and 2 employees from Elijah's. It will be like 250 to 5, you will be understanding if the crowd is Maria's, many more Brazilian fans than Korean fans here.

With a little time to try to relax I had time until 10:55, so just tried to relax by watching a movie for an hour plus. I then got a text from Mike Finley, he said that we were on the schedule for Thursday, we are in the upper half of the draw and all the matches will be on Thursday for the first round. He also stated remember only 32 teams for this event and we get like $5000, just for showing up, so I was like wow at the ITF that would have taken 3 tournaments to make that much money. With everything ready it was time to get the bags packed. (3 pairs of socks, 3 pink tennis shirts, 2 blue skirts, a change of undergarments, 10 wrist bands, and 2 pairs of shoes in one bag, 4 racquets in the other) I had packets of powder to help with electrolytes now ready and truthfully very nervous. I ended up going to the bathroom three times.

I met up with Paul downstairs and we were off, he had a change of clothes in his brand-new Lacoste bag. We started talking about how fortunate we were to be playing out on court 4, no crowds that we were not use to not much larger than the crowds at any ITF event. Paul then reminded me of the strategy today, six shot maximum rallies and then get to net and cut the points short. Don't make this a clay court like match which is what Maria wants long baseline rallies and a three-hour match, we simply don't want this type of match. Even if it goes three sets, we want it in less than 2 hours. Maria is in great shape and has no problem running points down all day long. The ride from the Uber seemed to take forever with New York traffic and finally arrived at the player's entrance. Unlike the more popular players I did not have to worry about fans demanding an autograph because nobody knew me or even cared. Well, I may just have something to say about that this afternoon. It took so long to get here; I know I am as good as these players just never had the opportunity to dedicate just to tennis. This may sound defiant but dam it, I want this so badly today I want to make it through at least one more round. The little girl nobody liked wants to prove she really belongs. Paul could tell what I was thinking as he saw me start to tear.

"Lilly, you belong here it just took a lot longer because you are from the country, and we did not have access to sponsors. Let's go out in style if this is our last singles match here fight until the end."

I hugged Paul and said, "let's go coach."

The next few hours before the match seemed to fly by, my practice went well, and I was hitting winners against Paul in practice and cracking my serves 5 miles per hour harder than I think I have ever done before. I took a very quick shower and changed into the game uniform still pink and blue with everything Lacoste. The extra sponsors on my blouse made it look like a billboard in my mind. We went over to the lounge and then went to get lunch. Everything seemed like a buzz I was getting so nervous that it was getting hard to concentrate. This was so unreal, Lilly Jarman is playing the second round of the US

Open, and then playing mixed doubles. I will win as much money in this tournament as I have won in my career. This is just getting unreal.

Then came the call from the court they were probably finished within the next 15 minutes. Paul could see the nervousness in my eyes and said, "Lilly just go out there and have fun."

I felt like my legs were heavy somehow, I was thinking I left my game on the practice court. Then came the call, 5 minutes until we must leave for the match. Now I am thinking God don't let me lose 6-0 and 6-0, they will say it was a nice one match run.

The call then came, time to leave for the court men's match is ending right now. Paul grabbed his stuff and then said to me, Let's go Lilly, and make a difference for those folks back home.

I make it to the court, and they are just ending the winner's interview, and I look up and my parents are there, Larry just came in as I was entering the court and then the introductions were ready to begin: The only fans I see that will support me were my parents and then I saw the two Elijah's employees, so I guess I am now up to 5 out of probably 500 plus fans. The grounds which in the first round were empty were standing room only, more fans here than I have ever viewed all of them with green and yellow flags and speaking in Portuguese.

Second Round match:

I would like to introduce the players for our second round match this afternoon. Lilly Jarman is playing in her first US Open and is currently ranked in live ratings 215. (Very little applause) Her opponent today, Maria Schindler, of Brazil is currently ranked 45 in the world, Maria is competing in her fourth US Open and made the fourth-round last year. Maria has three tournament trophies on the WTA. The applause and yelling from the Brazilian fans were deafening.

(Hello this is Ken Jarman, Lilly's dad, I am writing this piece for Lilly summarizing the match as it plays out) Larry is too nervous to write this today, if she loses, he needs to console her and if she wins, then he really has pressure on him.

You could see from the warm-up that Lilly was very tight, she was having trouble keeping the ball in play and kept missing her practice overheads.

The coin flip was won by Maria, and she chose to serve first. Maria's serves are in the 90 mile an hour range, not great but she knows how to place it. The summary of the important first game was that Maria was placing her serve well and Lilly hit the first into the net and the second out past the baseline. On the third point Lilly anticipated the serve wide and hit a hard forehand down the line for a winner. The fourth point was extremely long, I think it was a thirty-shot rally and Maria ended by hitting a drop shot that Lilly got to and hit the net. The next serve was down the line and Lilly got to it but hit the tape, Maria won the first game easily. Lilly looked frustrated as she went from her side to get ready to serve. She may have been nervous and then proceeded to serve right down the line for an ace to begin her service game. The rest of the service game was more to Maria's liking but at 40-30, Lilly hit a screaming return with her backhand and won the game to even the score at 1-1.

Maria figured out that Lilly was not as willing for long rallies as she was and proceeded to control the next three games to lead 4-1 in the set. Lilly fought back in the sixth game and after 3 deuces hit a screaming backhand to get back to 2-4. The rest of the set was not the best for Lilly and Maria held to go up 5-2. Lilly tried valiantly to hold off Maria on her next service game, but Maria kept extending long rallies even when Lilly thought she had won the points and after 2 break points Maria was able to end the set at 6-2. The very heavily Brazilian crowd started screaming for Maria with the flags waving and now the crowd was six deep standing and watching the match.

The second set was much more competitive for Lilly it was funny, Maria would have these long rallies on her service games and Lilly would have 2 to 3 shot rallies and a couple of aces along the way and at 5-6, Lilly was serving to stay in the match. It was at tight service game and when Lilly hit a backhand down the line just out Maria had her first match point. Lilly quickly eliminated that by serving wide and Maria hit into the net for deuce. Lilly served wide at deuce and hit a screaming cross court winner to get game point on her serve. I could tell by the red light that ESPN must have been showing the match at that point and the last point on Lilly's service game was quite different it was going long, then Lilly hit a deep ball down the center and rushed the net and when Maria hit it at her, she simply hit a backhand the other way for game point, which forced a second set tiebreaker. With no breakpoints through the first eleven points Lilly held a 6-5 lead with Maria to serve to stay in the set this time. I could see again the ESPN camera, and the point went through six shots each when on the next shot Lilly hit a deep forehand and came running to the net to put pressure on Maria, who hit the ball what looked perfect but Lilly with her long arms appeared to simply flick the ball just barely over the net and with that forced the third set.

ESPN Broadcast:

For you that like the great underdog story. Here is the second set deciding point on court 4. Lilly Jarman has just forced a third set by storming the net and with what we would say may be a little lucky, just barely got the volley over as it ticked the net.

Pam Shriver said, "I think the crowd at court 4 which looks mostly Brazilian, is stunned that Maria Schindler was unable to take her match point. I have been told by many fans you never want to let the underdog think they have a chance and now Lilly Jarman is locked in for a battle in the last set to make the final 32. A week ago, she was just hoping to make some money here."

Ken, here. I looked up and the crowd around the court is now like 8 rows deep standing and with the 250 seats around the court, the last 2 rows all look like they are Asian so maybe a little support will shift from Brazil to Lilly.

The match went as expected for the first 7 games, with Lilly serving big and easily winning her service games. Maria struggled with her service games but was able to through never giving Lilly a chance to break. So, with Lilly leading 4 games to 3, Maria served to even the set. At 30-all, Maria hit a wide service and Lilly did something I have never viewed before. Lilly hit a forehand around the net and it landed just inside the right side and the baseline, for a winner and her first break point of the match. The Asians in the crowd started screaming for Lilly, I'm sure my mother Dea was also screaming watching back in Blacksburg. The next point was going Maria's way when I see Lilly hit deep to the center of the court and Maria slammed it back only to see Lilly waiting for a volley at, the net, and proceeded to hit a backhand cross court for a winner. With the screaming of the Asian fans, Lilly was up for the first time in the match 5-3.

ESPN Broadcast studios:

Welcome back to Day 3 at the US Open. "Patrick McEnroe says to Pam Shriver do you have something to report."

Pam says, "Let's show the last point on court 4, Lilly Jarman just crashed the net and hit a backhand volley the crowd around the court most screaming for the Brazilian, but it looks like about 25 Asian Americans just as noisy for Lilly. Lilly will be serving for a chance to go 2-0 in majors. Since we are on hold on the major courts let's report for you. Let's go live on court 4 a court you hardly ever see."

Lilly steps up to the line and proceeds to hit a serve wide and Maria netted the return.

Ken here I can see that ESPN red light is on, and the place is now electric. Lilly is up 15-0 and hits another wide serve that Maria smashes a backhand cross court for the winner and it is 15 all. Lilly served a hard serve down the line and Maria hit it into the net now Lilly is up 30-15. Lilly hits the first serve into the net, and again hits a wide serve with not much pace on it and Maria hits a clean winner with her forehand. The Brazilian crowd is going crazy. Lilly again hits her first serve into the net, forcing her to hit a second serve. The point was getting long when Lilly hit a cross court shot and rushes the net and proceeds to hit another backhand volley for a winner. Lilly appeared to be taking her time and with the shot clock nearing zero stepped up and blasted a 109 mile an hour first serves down the line. Maria could only barely put her racquet on the ball. The pro-Asian crowd erupts in screams as my beautiful daughter won the match. Lilly goes crazy and screams at the top of her lungs "Yes", and then fell to the floor. She got up and ran to shake Maria's hand. We all started jumping up in the air and then realized what was going to happen shortly at ESPN.

ESPN Broadcast Studio:

Chris Evert arrived on the studio to get ready for the night matches. "Did I hear the loudest scream I have ever heard at the US Open?"

Pam Shriver then states, "you can guess that was coming from Lilly Jarman on court 4, she has just won her match 2-6, 7-6 and 6-3. Lilly has now won 5 matches in a row, and we were looking at her ITF record she has only done that once in her career and that was when she made the finals of an ITF tournament in Wichita, Kansas. Her win today places Lilly in to the top 200 of the worlds, with live ranking maybe 175. I thought I had heard loud screams before, but this was the loudest I have ever heard at a tournament. For the viewers we will get Lilly over here in about 15 minutes to talk about her come from behind victory. We also have a special surprise for the viewers during the interview."

Chris Evert said, "you have something up your sleeve I should know about."

"Pam just laughed you will have to wait and see."

Court 4:

Let's hear it for our competitors this afternoon. For the first time we heard applause for Lilly. She was in a zone and simply lifted one arm shaking it. The final match will start in 15 minutes.

Lilly came over to us after she had gathered her stuff and hugged everyone. Paul laughed damn "I must stay until at least Friday now. Lilly you may need to call and beg for my services through the weekend."

Barbara came over to her daughter and gave her a big hug. I did the same thing a minute later and everyone had a hug but Larry, who had left for the appointed place and time after the ESPN interview.

Lilly gathered her stuff, and we went off to the ESPN booth per the request of Brad Gilbert, who had been roaming the various courts for ESPN.

ESPN Booth:

Lilly was asked to take a chair and put a headset on. By then she had managed to brush her long blond hair and replaced the sweaty shirt with a clean one.

Pam Shriver said to Lilly, "welcome to the ESPN set once again."

Lilly just smiled and said, "thank you for inviting me."

Pam said, "You just won more money in this tournament than in your entire career put together, so others understand what this means, can you let us know what this really means for your career?"

Lilly simply responded, "I have three Asian tournaments that I have been invited to play in and I have never been to that part of the world. I can play ITF's without worrying about how to pay the entry fee or having to go through qualification every week. I don't have to have a coaching job to have enough money to travel. In addition, I have these fancy new clothes and Mizuno shoes to play with for the next 6 months. I used to get my shoes at the outlets or on sale because I did not have a sponsor, and I have most of my clothes from Walmart, to keep things more affordable."

Pam asked, "you have now won over $120,000 in prize money and you will get at least some money for your mixed doubles so glad to hear you are getting your break in tennis after all these years" Pam followed up, "who is with you tonight?"

"Lilly responded that both of my parents are here thanks to my sponsor Lacoste, and my friend and coach Paul from Radford Tennis Club and the University.

Pam then asked in a friendly manner, "I hear you have another friend that was here today, but he is not with you."

"Lilly responded yes, my boyfriend works and lives in Manhattan, but I did not see him after the match."

Pam said "Lilly, I would ask you another question, but you have a fan that is wanting to ask you another question." Larry came from the other side of the stage, and Pam said, "So this is your friend Larry, she gave him a hug and said yes, he is." "Pam went on to ask Larry, what do you think of your girlfriend's performance tonight?"

Larry left to be in front of Lilly and proceeded to get on his knee. "Lilly, I have the pleasure of being your boyfriend, and want to ask you if you would please be more than my girlfriend. Lilly Jarman, I want to ask you a question, will you make me the happiest man here in New York, by agreeing to marry me."

Lilly paused for what seemed like forever, and then jumped into Larry's arms and said, "you know the answer is yes". Larry then presented Lilly with the ring he had designed for her. The ring was a ¾ carat diamond, with 2 pink sapphires and 2 blue sapphires surrounding the clear diamond and was white gold, Lilly's favorite color of gold.

After Larry placed the ring on her finger and congratulations were all around, "Pam asked Larry why the unusual ring?"

"Larry said this came from Lilly's grandmother Dea and why Lilly wears pink and blue outfits. The blue is for athleticism, and the pink is for femininity. That is why Dea gave Lilly those colors and that is what she plays with, always pink and blue."

A cake then came up to the studio saying congratulations Larry and Lilly. A few pieces were cut, and Lilly proceeded to shove a piece into Larry's face and then he returned the favor.

Chris Evert then said, "so Pam you knew about this, and she smiled.

"I did and that is why I was so relieved when you won Lilly, so we could do this tonight."

Lilly was shaking and continued to hug Larry, then said "I wondered where you went at the end of the match."

The commentators all said congratulations you just got engaged in front of a few million fans. Pam then asked a serious question; "do you know who your next round match is."

Paul stepped in and said "we will figure that out later tonight, and Pam said Well they are on the court still, either Marci Frankfort the 17 seed of Germany or Wan Wang, of China. They are currently out on court 18 one set all."

"Paul just said we will look at the results later tonight because Lilly will be playing Thursday in mixed doubles in the late afternoon on a court 16, we will have time to figure out what is going on Friday. While I am here on TV, Radford I need at least a few more days up here in New York with Lilly if that is ok with you. I'm on loan for the duration of Lilly's time here, they sent me up when Lilly qualified, I coach Lilly when we both have time available, and the club is loaning me for Lilly's run here."

Pam said, "well coach you must be doing a great job because she is playing well. Everyone Lilly Jarman and team good luck in the next few days."

Lilly just said, "thank you," flashed the ring and kissed Larry before leaving the stage.

Lilly here now. After the ESPN time, I needed to take a shower before doing anything, so I went to the players' lounge but since most had finished for the day it was empty. What I did not realize is that on the third day of the tournament like half of the players here for the tournament are already finished so a lot less people here especially late in the afternoon. I got dressed in my final tennis outfit and put the Lacoste shirt on and from the locker room I decided I needed to make 1 call personally.

"I called Dea from the locker room because she was and will always be my greatest fan and source of comfort. When I called her, she seemed very tired, but she told me that she was very happy for me and congratulations on the engagement. I told her the ring you helped design was beautiful and I hoped you saw it. She simply responded you are always two worlds athletic and feminine. Larry respects you for both and he appears to be a very nice young man, you will make great children together. She said I am tired and going to take a nap, your match was exhausting. I hung-up and took my shower changed and met everyone outside the locker room."

I had several texts from John Littleman, he said we have a lot of requests for you to appear at tournaments starting later this month all the way to the end of the year. Your live ranking just went to 175, so now you get direct entry into every tournament and at least a qualification slot to the Australian Open.

I got another text from my younger brother James that he is coming to the third-round match. He is sharing a timeshare in Manhattan with a couple of tennis lovers from George Mason. I just told him we may have one slot left, so he may have to find a seat elsewhere in the stands. He texted back he understands, and he is staying until, Sunday after your 4th round match. Wow he is optimistic about my results.

I got another text from Radford they are so thrilled for me and understand they probably must find a new assistant coach, but they would still like me to visit them when possible.

I caught-up with my parents who said they are going to let Larry and me go out tonight and they would get meals near the hotel. Paul also said, I need to start planning and reviewing your next 2 matches Thursday and Friday. He also said no practice Thursday, the mixed doubles will be your practice session. Friday is the German seed Marci Frankfort, who won the match 7-5 in the third set and is playing ladies doubles on Thursday. Your match is last on court 16 on Thursday, so have fun tonight but not too much fun.

Since it was only going to be Larry and myself, I asked him if he wanted to eat at the players' lounge and he said not tonight. Let's go out to dinner, you can have 1 glass of wine tonight according to Paul to celebrate victory and engagement. The firm he works for apparently got a reservation to Grammercy Tavern. We had reservations in the dining room for 07:45 and it was now 6:45, so we need to get out the door to the limo right now.

I ordered a crab imperial dinner, never had that before, Larry of course ordered a steak and a stout beer. At dinner, we shared a glass of pinot, and for dessert we were in New York, so we shared a piece of cheesecake. The conversation went to what the heck happened today. Larry said, well I just got engaged to the very athletic and feminine Lilly Jarman, who has graced me with the honor of marrying me. Lilly also showed the world she belonged and made the third round of the US Open. So now the next question to ask regarding a wedding.

Larry assumed we would do a small ceremony in the New Year's Eve in Virginia. I said let's plan for a big wedding right after Wimbledon next year, I think we can do the second week of July after the finals. We both just laughed, Larry just said you may just be a little ahead of yourself Lilly. I called my parents and said can we arrange to get the church in Radford, for the third Saturday in July?

Back to dinner, I was all prepared to stay the night with my fiancé in Manhattan, when Larry said, we have plenty of time for that after the US Open, for tonight, I will hold your hand, kiss you passionately, and then send you in an Uber back to your hotel where you will rest for your match on Thursday and Friday. I just looked at him in utter disbelief, so you don't want to be with me tonight.

Larry made the perfect answer, "I will always be with you for the rest of our lives, but for these next few days you are Lilly Jarman, tennis player, and I am not letting anything get in your way. I love you and this is your time. By the way you may want to take off the ring before the match and secure it. It cost me a month's salary and I don't want you to lose it."

A little after 09:30 PM, Larry sent me back to near Kennedy airport in an Uber. I made it back to the hotel just before 10:30 PM. Got to my room and then checked e-mails from Paul and others.

Paul said we are not doing a practice, let's get together at 3 PM, for the mixed doubles match. He said he was studying tape on Marci and so far, it looks good, another player who has more success on clay than hard court, but this is a top 20 player in the world so don't kid us we are the underdog by far here we are going to be on a stadium court. I suspect grandstand on Friday, after the ESPN, you are going to have a few people rooting for you.

All I could think of is fans, never had any growing up in Radford, not even when I was playing number 1 my junior and senior years. The debutantes thought I was a lesbian; I wonder what they will say about my engagement on ESPN this afternoon. Larry is a quite athletic looking successful Wall Street guy; I think we will have beautiful children together even if they have my Korean cheekbones and nose features are prominent.

I could not sleep thinking about my past just remembering the isolation I suffered, no invites to parties, just a few tennis tournaments, even when I got to the finals nothing said in the school paper, they were just thinking about graduation. The quarterfinals at a national tournament and nobody recruited me until Longwood offered me a scholarship. Radford at that point said I could go walk-on, but since my dad worked for the university no money to offer. I did hear from a couple of division 3 schools like Christopher Newport, but they did not have money either so I could not afford to go with them.

I hit the pillow and fell asleep looking at my engagement ring. It took very little time to find sleep it was an exhausting day. I was thinking about my high school days and wow what a different experience today. In high school always alone, well except at Junior prom in Arlington, the debutantes would love that experience to talk about. I was the lesbian to them, and to my special friend not.

Chapter 9

The High School Experience

My parents said they only went to high school for 3 years; the freshman year was done at the junior high school level. Today, ninth graders as well as the other high school grades all went to one high school. The appropriately named Radford High School, was home to most of the students in the area. About 5 percent to ten percent of the people went to various private schools in the area or were home schooled. My parents could not afford something private anyway even though we were doing better with dad being asked to lead the department at Radford and the $7500, pay raise that gave him. Mom was doing better at the bank, and was making enough to support travel, a new car for us and vacations that all came from her salary.

For Ninth grade I would again be 2 grades above James, so we would be at different schools and different bus schedules. My personal protector would not help me here, and Bob Kratz kind of took that role on when anyone would tell lies about me or make up stories about me. Bob may not look it, but he is a real pit bull when it comes to protecting his friends.

Before I get much into my own story, I need to talk about James's story in his sport. With mom and me at a lot of tennis matches dad was often the driver for James in his meets. We always knew he was a consistent swimmer, but it was not until a swim meet in Richmond at the Briarwood, that we found out how good he really was. James was strong and swam a few events, but it was his first-time swimming in a fifty-meter pool. In his first event the 200 IM, he made the finals by swimming very fast and ended up as the fifth best swimmer going into the finals. I bet nobody saw that coming, we were not exactly well know names. He backed that up by then making the top three in the 500 freestyle, which there was no final for that event at night. In the 200, IM, from lane 2 he went out and took the lead in the first length, and it was not until the last length that someone caught him, he finished second, but that had a lot of people stunned. James was now a top 100 swimmer in the country, and nobody even knew his name. While a lot of good swimmers went all over the country in the elite meets, we had not traveled farther than Virginia and North Carolina. That was the last time my dad talked about him going back to football, he knew his son had a different destiny.

James would go on to star in Virginia swimming and won 2 events at the state meet again his 500 free and the 200 IM in his senior year. The University of Kentucky came running for him at that point and awarded him a half scholarship. The money was enough for my parents to be able to afford it with me getting a scholarship at Longwood and it being in-state tuition. He may not have been well known, but he was a late bloomer that a lot of schools wish they had waited to give him money. James would go on to make the consolation finals of the 500 Free twice in his career, and the finals of the 200 IM, his last three years, with a high finish of sixth, still very impressive for an honors student. Another swim event he made top 16 in NCAA. My little brother made all-American in swimming, He was gorgeous, smart, and tall and somehow escaped the clutches of the debutantes from Radford. I know he is dating seriously for the first time in his life, well in this case a lot of ladies want to date him and at this point nobody has come home to Radford.

Well back to my freshman year at Radford High School, I was taking somewhat hard classes having taken Algebra 1 in eighth grade, I was in advanced classes in science and not in English. World History and thought about an industrial arts class and thought better of it.

I had to take a gym class and a couple of other classes just for fun, home economics was not going to happen. I had no intention of being stuck with the debutantes every school day. I would like to say I was a dedicated student, but grades came easy and with tennis practices now 4 days a week and tournaments now averaging one every 3 weekends I did just enough to get mostly A's and then no more effort. Tennis was all on my own as the school tennis was in the Spring, and I was not interested in cross country. In gym class, when they had a tennis section, they kind of let me do half the class in coaching them, the debutantes were not happy that I was basically a teacher to them for those 2 weeks. The best result I had in the Fall happened at a tennis tournament in Charlotte, NC. They hosted a low-level national tournament, and as the 16 seed, I made the semi-finals, this boosted me to near the top 150 in the country, and since this also counted for my regional ranking put me in the top ten for the first time ever. Remember most of the ranked girls were 16 and I had just turned 15. I did win a couple of local tournaments in the 16's and was invited to a National Level tournament for thanksgiving, but that was not allowed to happen. I won a regional tournament for the first time and made a final of a local tournament in Blacksburg before the fall was over. Going into the Christmas holidays I was ranked 10 in regional and 145, nationally.

Randy and I stayed in contact with each other, and I was able to get my mom to allow me to play a tournament in Silver Spring, MD over the holidays. That tournament went the week after Christmas, and it was also not that far that Randy could see me play the tournament. I did not disappoint my ranking or my social by making it to the finals, losing my fourth match in three days in the final. The tournament results let me get 7th in the region and still probably nobody knew who I was. I got to hold hands with Randy a few times and we parted with a kiss after I won the semi-finals. Mom reminded me that while it was nice to have a friend like Randy, you need to stay focused on school and tennis, so you get a scholarship.

We spent Christmas with my mom's parents although her dad was now in bad health, he mostly sat in his recliner all day. James and dad went to Fairfax, VA for a swim meet and with us being in MD, we found a cheap hotel in Rockville, MD which became the center for the family for three days until we went back to Radford for New Year's.

A week later began the spring semester. Before we started tennis for our school, I played a local tournament in the 18's for the first time, and made the semi-finals, losing to the number 1 see a Lauren Douglas, who was a high school; senior and went to Rollins to play tennis the next year. Right before spring tennis began, my grandfather. Mom's dad had a stroke and passed away at the hospital a day later. This happened the first week we had tennis tryouts, and I was unable to challenge the other players for the top 3 positions going to the funeral and helping, as the coach said he was sorry, but those positions had already been won by others and I could play number 4 singles if I beat the others left. I won all the matches 6-0, but that did not matter the coach said I was stuck for the year at number 4. Our team was not that good, and we lost 6 out of our 10 regular season matches. In the regional finals, I won the number 4 position, winning 6-3, and 6-0, not many teams' numbers 4 were nationally ranked, but this was Radford, and the wealthy older kids, debutantes were given the high places never was I given a chance to challenge. The school newspaper had a small blurb about me winning the number 4 position, our team, season ended. Because I played number 4 the school did not want to pay for the cost of me going to Richmond for the state finals, so the season ended at the regional.

My USTA play was ignored for 8 weeks while playing tennis for Radford and the first tournament back I made the semi-finals in a top ranked regional tournament that was a second-tier national tournament keeping my rankings regionally and 125 nationally. I was now ranked 6th in the region in 16's and nationally this held my ground at 125.

If I had not explained the tennis rankings are a rolling 12 month of points from different tournaments, many levels for tournaments and they have different point levels. A few tournaments count for both national and regional rankings and some high ranked players only play nationally ranked tournaments and ignore regional rankings other than those that count as both. Those players mostly are academy kids living at academies and being groomed for professional tennis.

With tennis season over I had two weeks left in school, the first week was finals week, so I concentrated on tennis, and then the last week was clean-up week, clear out lockers and sign year books. Because I was not a popular person, I did not get any requests to sign yearbooks. I still had a couple of friends Bob and Frances that we would miss each other for the summer. Bob was going to be a senior camper at a bible camp in West Virginia. Frances was going away at a summer camp in the Maryland mountains, since her mom was Jewish, she was going to a Camp Louise, which was a long-term camp that was lower cost than most.

With Summer starting Jake Willis asked for a private meeting with my parents regarding tennis.

Jake said, "unless we get more tournaments and some more elite tennis practice, she won't improve her rankings. Lilly is a good player, so I was able to get her 2 weeks of tennis at the Stan Smith Academy in Hilton head, SC. If Lilly is as good as I think she is, she needs 2 weeks of preparation at the academy with the better players, and then we need to step up our competition level. To get this for free, I had to agree to host some elite athletes when they were in this area, so if an elite player is driving near us and they are staying over I agree to let them play here for a couple of days for free. All we need is your permission and transportation to Hilton Head right after the 4th of July, and then we will have her play a couple of national level tournaments one the end of July in Raleigh, NC, and one in Tampa."

My dad was perplexed, "I know I am not a tennis player, but Radford only let Lilly play number 4 this year why do you think she could be this good."

"That was a political decision, Jake said."

I packed and with my father went to Hilton Head, SC, about as far from home as I could remember. I was playing with the lower ranked national players and on most days holding my own. The year-round kids did not even practice with us, they were supposedly the elite. I called my parents every day, as it felt weird for the first time to be without them. While we had a couple of afternoons at the beach to relax, all I did was get on my bathing suit and read a book. My boyfriend was far away in the DC area he was a lifeguard at the local pool and I'm sure a few girls trying to get him out of his shorts. He was quite attractive and athletic.

On the last 2 days of the camp, we played 4 matches, I went 2-2 beating and losing one to the year-rounders and the same to the campers.

I did not think that was bad, but the coach Gene Coons, yelled "Lilly you can do better, stop letting them dictate play. I know you are shy and use to being an outsider, but you can't allow these girls to intimidate you because they have prettier clothes or are more popular. Once you figure out you can play with these girls you will."

That lesson took a long time for me to learn.

I was not able to do the national tournaments that they suggested but played a tennis tournament in West Virginia a high regional match and won the tournament. This put me fifth in the region but at least five girls were ranked higher nationally than I was because they had the time and money to travel. My family was not poor, but with 2 of us training and travelling, we could only do so much. I did get to the tournament in Raleigh, NC, got to the quarters that gave me enough points to just be outside the top 100 of the country. With that and a local tournament win in Radford I was ready for my sophomore year. No Randy time, he was in DC working and I was in Southwest, Virginia.

I turned 16, just before the school year began, my parents wanted to do a sweet 16 party, but I refused to have it. The debutantes had parties and I was never invited since they still thought I was a lesbian Eurasian, someone to be avoided to keep your social status. Bob tried to invite me a couple of times, but I simply did not want a pity date.

Sophomore and Junior Years.

While the classes were different, school was the same, I was in tough classes, played tennis, and had no invites to parties, dances, or other social events. My mother thought it was odd, but that was my life and with my weekly Randy text I had a relationship in abstention.

My sophomore year they let me play number 3, and of course qualified to Richmond and with my doubles partner we played number 2 tennis and won that regional also. Frances is a roadrunner and with me at 5'9" we had the run and gun and the put away. We went undefeated in league play, and regionally we won all our matches, so we qualified for small school states as a doubles group.

I never made it past top 5 regionally or top 100 nationally, just because we played no more than 3 tournaments every 2 months because of the travel costs.

In the state tournament, Frances and I lost in the finals and in the number 3 position, I beat all comers until the finals. I lost in three sets because I let the opponent take the initiative. She was from Godwin High School, came in a brand-new Audi SUV, and had a personal coach with her for the week. I did not think I could measure up to losing in the third set 6-2.

The school paper did mention I was a finalist in two events, took Frances and my picture but that did very little to eliminate the shunning I had with the debutantes. It also did not help that the guys would talk to me as an equal, because they respected my athletic ability. The girls here thought that was proof I was a lesbian and they thought Frances was my lover. Frances was actually a very popular girl, with dark hair and blue eyes, the guys had no trouble asking her out. I think she was dating every weekend at least one night and usually with different guys. Not saying she was easy, she just liked male attention and they liked her little 5'1" attractive athletic body, with her 34C she had things I did not have.

Between my sophomore and junior year, I turned 17, I had not grown since I was like 13, so many of the guys were now taller than me. That still did not make it any easier for a date as the debutantes had poisoned that. Truthfully, now playing a tournament almost every other weekend and taking an AP class. I had gone from a 32 A cup over this time to a 34B, mostly due to more athletic build, but I could fill out shirts a little better and had the attention of my male counterparts mostly as a friend. Bob and now James became very protective of me, and I know James took a guy and beat the crap out of him when he repeated that I was a lesbian, I'm sure that came from his girlfriend's mouth, just because they hated the fact that I was good at school, could talk easily to the guys, and really did not care a crap about the local gossip.

The tennis team now let me play number 2, and again I went undefeated in play, Frances and I easily won the regional tournament at number 1 doubles. Frances was now playing number 4 singles, and she was very hard to beat, she kept getting balls back and her matches were usually the last one done.

I was never challenged until the regional final, and had to pull out a 6-4, third set victory, that sent me to the state tournament.

At the state tournament I played in the number 1 and 2's in a new format that played the best 32 players rated as a number 1 or 2. Our number 1 did not make it, but I was invited to play the state tournament but as a low seed. In my first match I took out the 6 seed in an impressive third set 6-1. I then won the round of 16 match before losing to the 2 seed from Godwin in three sets, I think she won it 6-2. I was tired and playing a lot of 18-year-olds and super ranked national players.

In doubles, we were a deadly team together even as the last team in, Frances and I knocked off the top team from Fairfax right off. We ended up losing in the semi-finals 10-8, in the super tiebreaker.

We had gone further than any other team from Radford history. That had a few of the small division 3 schools sending me information about recruiting, but as my dad said state colleges are more affordable and division 3 don't have athletic money, so most of those coaches' data went into the trash.

I passed my AP US History exam a week later and again was not invited to the prom by anyone.

The first time:

This is not a section I would like Larry to read so somehow need to make sure he does not see this section. Larry is not my first lover, that was Randy and it happened at his senior prom while I was finishing my junior year. I had a tennis tournament in the DC area I could play in, and his parents said they would let me stay with them while I played in Alexandria. Randy asked me to be his date at his senior prom, and while he was in the other part of the state, I said yes, and we made it happen. I did not have to play until Saturday afternoon and his prom was on a Friday night.

I had received a text from Randy on a Monday night which was unusual usually he would send our weekly out on Thursday. It simply said, "Need to talk to you tonight, please tell me when you will be free to talk by yourself" I texted I will be free at 8:00, so give me a call.

Randy was on-time at 8:00, and after a few weird moments he asked, "hey tall girl, I know this is an insane question for you, but what would you think about coming to my senior prom up here?"

I had to think about it for a minute, and then said "if I can get my parents approval, I would love to come but how would I be able to do this I don't have my license yet, and I am sure my parents would go nuts if I tried to stay at a hotel. This is insane, I'm like 200 miles from you, and I bet a lot of ladies would like to be your partner at the dance."

Randy simply said a reply that would seal the deal, "Tall Girl, we may not have all our lifetime, but you are and will always be my first love."

I went quiet, but then the answer came easily, "yes Randy I will try to be you date, but we have things to work out like where will I stay etc."

Randy responded, "I know you can stay at my parents' house they have wanted to meet you anyway. They said a long-distance relationship for three years is weird, but you must be something special and I agree."

I waited a half-hour to go downstairs and gathered up enough courage to ask my parents about going to Arlington, VA, to go to a prom. This is going to not go over well.

Mom and dad, "I have been asked to go to a prom the week of May 7, which I know is a tournament weekend. The prom is not here but up in the same city as the tournament near DC."

Mom looked up and said, "you couldn't find someone here to go to the prom with."

Fortunately, James stepped in, "you know Mom I have a meet that weekend in Annapolis so we could drop Lilly somewhere, don't you have a friend that lives there.

"Yes, I will call Amy Lancaster and see if Lilly can stay there". And after 30 minutes it was decided that I would not stay at Randy's parents' house but would be expected back by 1 or 2 AM, to be back at Amy's house delivered by Randy.

My mother decided to take me to a store in Blacksburg, that was both a bridal shop and had dresses for formal events like prom. We were at the store being waited on by the owner, and she said to my mother, how high will Lilly wear in heals because with her already being 5'10", she should wear no more than 3 inch heals unless her date is tall. Randy is a little over 6 feet tall so that should not be an issue.

Dea arrived at the store and said to the clerk, "Lilly is a special girl and there is only one color that she should wear, and that is a pink."

There was a compromise, and it really was a dark coral pink instead of a normal pink, a little darker and muted. Dea indicated she would let me borrow her pearl necklace. She wanted something to show-off my neckline. I wanted a strapless dress, but my mother and grandmother did not allow that, so with my build I was able to get a plunging neckline, but it had to have straps to make me look like a proper lady.

The store owner said, "she would have the dress in a week, and congratulations on going to the Radford Senior prom."

One of the debutantes, Kara Dormant, was in the store and immediately said, "Lilly isn't going to our prom, none of the guys are going to invite her because she is a lesbian, everyone knows it just ask her friend Frances."

My mother looked at her and said, "I know all about you all, nasty little girls who will be pregnant next year, married to a drunk, and wonder why all your good years were in high school. I have viewed your type, and I don't care how much money you have you are a typical trailer trash I have known all my life." Then my mom, said, "should I show you a picture of Lilly and her friend from the DC area I think you might be surprised he is a good-looking guy they met in Virginia Beach, and have been on the phone every week. Both are athletes, and he wanted Lilly to be his date as they are both extremely busy and just because he is not one of your redneck friends does not mean that Lilly and Randy don't have a great friendship. Go tell your other debutantes that my Lilly is smarter, more athletic, and feminine than any of you. You are all just jealous because she is very comfortable around men and women as friends. Now go away from me or I will push my mother-in-law on you. Dea may be under 5 feet tall, but she will knock you silly if you talk about her granddaughter."

I was stunned at my mother.

One minute later, I started laughing. "Mom I would love to see her face when she gets back to Radford, how is she going to explain she just got her ass handed to her by the lesbian's mother. They are going to invent a story I bet that Randy is gay and you and I know her is anything but."

Barbara and Dea hugged, Dea exclaimed "should have told these girls and their mothers off a long time ago."

The owner said, "make sure that Lilly has the proper undergarments, no sports bra will work here."

The next trip was to JC Penney, where my mother took me to the lingerie section and said you are going to look nice so let's buy something special. After looking for about ten minutes I bought something that my mother said was lady like and appropriate. I thought they looked sexy and naughty, but I am a little early in the discussion of that. The slip was white, and the matching bra and panties were pink like Dea said I should always wear. I think Dea had an idea of what was probably going to happen, when she hinted that you are still a virgin right. I did not know what to say other than nobody ever wanted to date me before other than Randy and that never happened. She started to smile, and I think she knew what may happen in Arlington in 2 weeks.

Dea then said," just remember you are a beautiful girl, and you should never give away your beauty to someone that does not respect you."

Barbara said "I was going to buy you a watch, but I was given a beautiful bracelet that you can wear, and I have and a blue sapphire ring that you can use for the night. I want you to be as beautiful and feminine and show these girls what an athletic feminine girl can look like. I think you will look a lot like Maria Sharapova when she was young. I think that may be the only tall blond tennis player mom knew her name."

Dea came over to me and had already purchased a very mild perfume for the occasion.

So now the tennis player was all set to look like a tall princess for one night. All except my hair, which Amy knew a neighbor that would do something with my long blond hair for the evening.

On Friday the second week of May, I was dropped off by the men and went to Amy's door and she had a neighbor waiting to do my hair for the night.

Amy said to me, "you look a taller version of your mother when she was in college, a little Asian feature but the way you walk, and talk is pure Barbara."

It was 4 PM, and by the time my hair was done it was 5:15, Randy was coming at 6:30, and Amy then helped me apply make-up and change to my very fancy dress, my limited heels, and the pearls. She took numerous pictures for my mother; she will never believe her very tomboy looks this good.

You are so attractive, "you sure none of the boys in your town are interested, I just started to laugh."

"None I said".

Randy was going to pick me up at 6:15, and when he came in his charcoal gray tuxedo, Amy took pictures of both of us.

I forgot to say, what Randy said to me, "I wanted to say hello tall girl, and instead I am going to say the Lovely Lilly. He reached over and kissed me on the cheek, and said I am so glad that you can make it., nobody here thinks you are a real person. When they see you tonight, they will know I have a truly beautiful belle of the ball. He just said wow, you look so good I feel humbled to be taking you."

I put my hand in his and we walked to his parents' car, we were doing the prom right. We then drove to Randy's house on our way to Morton's Steakhouse, where they took pictures of both of us.

Randy's mom said, "aren't you that tall skinny girl that Randy is writing to every week. I recognize you from your pictures he has shown us, but in those pictures you don't smile. Tonight, you have a beautiful smile, not quite as skinny as Randy let on, a very athletic looking girl who will light up the room."

Dinner was very nice but truthfully, I had shrimp instead of a steak, and a good salad, and then we shared a brownie with chocolate all over it as a dessert. I made sure, that my dress was well protected, it was expensive, and I was thinking I could wear it again so wanted to make sure I did not ruin it.

We entered the school dance at about 7:45, it had been open since 7:30. Unlike back home, you could tell the area was much more diverse with students including Asian, African American, and Indian, all in one room and nobody seemed to care. It was so different than back home, and I felt much more welcome here than Radford ever let me.

I had my hand in Randy's, when an Asian looking girl came over to him, she introduced herself as Brenda Wang, she said she was a neighbor of Randy's and had known him most of his life. She gave me a hug and said, "so you are the secret girlfriend I have hear about. I see why your nickname is Tall Girl, you must be six feet tall."

I just laughed, "no I'm just 5'10', my heals which are killing me are making me taller."

Brenda said, "a lot of the Asian kids are like you from a mixed family, my mother is French, and my dad is Vietnamese, they met here in the states in college and apparently it was hot and steamy affair, as we have three kids all born within the first five years they were married. I started to smile I felt like I could relax with this group for the first time in my life. Brenda said something in whisper, "I think you and Randy look good together he is beaming, and I almost never see him this happy."

I walked over to Randy and gave him a kiss full on the lips, he was surprised but would not let my lips leave his for well over a minute. The next time I went to kiss him we let our tongues meet, it was like the last two years had gone away in an instant and the boy I had my first crush was holding hands with me and I loved it. I felt accepted in this area, and it was so different being with this handsome guy who just liked me for me, no judgements.

We danced several dances and then one slow dance and I thought we must have been the center of attention at George Washington High School, nobody ever looked at me as the weird one, but just as one of the popular boy's girlfriends. I suspect with Randy's looks a few may have been jealous also, from what Brenda told me, Randy had not done much dating, our weekly calls and texts were what he substituted for dating, and truthfully so did I. Frances had given me some protection in case the moment felt right and at this point I can tell you the moment felt totally right.

The dance ended just after 11:30, and while there was an after-prom at a local Dave and Busters, I had a tennis match at 1 PM, so we went to Randy's house so we could spend more time together. I guess we spent a little more time than I should have.

When we entered Randy's basement, he put on the local rock station, DC101, and we started to dance together. Randy started to kiss me, and then kissed my neck and behind my neck. I turned around and kissed him and helped him take his shirt off. I asked him to help me unzip my dress so could make sure it was not ruined, he just laughed as he slowly took the zipper down to just above my bottom. I went to the other side of the basement and took off my heals and my dress and made sure Frances's protection was within reach.

Randy was now only in his briefs came next to me and exclaimed, "I have always wanted you to be my first girl since the day I met you"

I grabbed him and kissed him and told me too. I let him kiss my neck and then he reached up and started to kiss my nipples which reacted to the reaction by standing up extensively. I unhooked my pink bra and threw it to the dress. Randy began to passionately kiss me and play with both of my breasts, and I could do is say please be nice to me. We fell to the couch me with just my panties on and Randy with his briefs. I started Massaging that area and his reaction was quick and I started to play with the bulge and pulled his briefs down so I could handle it directly. At the same time, Randy was fully engaged with my breasts, and they seemed to grow to play with his kisses. While I was handling his manhood, he started to run his one hand on my breast and the other up my leg and in to my now getting wet panties. I moved to one side of the couch and removed my panties and then came back to the couch to be with my lover. He reached from my long legs and my lower lips welcomed his touch and it drove me to groan in a low voice. I swear we stayed that way for a while with me on his manhood and him massaging my lower lips. I took the initiative and blew up that protection that Frances had given and shown me how to use. I placed it on Randy's manhood, as then I moved to the other side of the couch, and with little prodding Randy came to me where his manhood and my lips touched for the first time. My legs opened for Randy and within a minute we met each other's thrusts. I was having my first time with the boy I loved. We quickly took the towel that had been beneath us during our lovemaking and took it away as it was sweaty and wet. I went to the bathroom and cleaned myself up, including brushing my hair. Randy reached out to me kissed me from behind and rubbed my breast again and they responded again. I told him it was getting late, and we need to get dressed and get to Amy's house.

Ten minutes later, we were dressed and, in his car, driving to Amy's house. Randy put his arm around me and was smiling at me, I knew we were each other's first.

Randy whispered, "I knew have always loved you and know our distance may not let us be a true couple. You know more about me than anyone here. I want to say I do and will always love you."

I started to tear, nobody else was who I wanted to be with.

We reached Amy's house just after 1:15, Randy kissed me, and I opened my lips and sent my tongue to his. We met and kissed for another 5 minutes, then Amy turned on the lights and the date and my first time was complete.

My tennis the next day was adequate to get me to the Sunday matches, where I lost in the quarterfinals. I suspect my late-night escapades made me a little more tired than I could handle for the ranked girls.

My father and James picked me up on Sunday about 6 PM, and we got home right before 11 PM. My dad asked if I had a good time, and James gave me a look like I bet you had a good time, or that is what I thought he was thinking.

Four weeks later I finished my junior year and while I was known as a good competitor, I had received very few colleges inquires. I was now a woman in some respects, and still the outsider. I will say that Randy and I renewed our relationship for a week both of us were at Virginia Beach before he went to college, and I was getting ready for my senior year. Frances had an idea of what went on, so I guess you and I are not exactly poster lesbians.

So that is the story about what high school was like for the lone tall girl, not liked in her own community but accepted and loved elsewhere. My twisted story of how I ended up in Farmville, is another chapter I will relate.

Chapter 10

The US Open Mixed Day and Third Round Women's Singles

With a knock on the door, I heard my breakfast delivery from Elijah's bagels was delivered. It was 8:15, I had really crashed after the crazy night, a win at the US Open, and then the proposal on TV. I would love to see those debutantes in Radford, my engagement on international TV, they may have gotten a mention in the local newspaper after they paid for it. Like every morning, I had words of encouragement from Elijah's. I thought about it and decided to take an Uber to them on the way to the US Open.

I looked at my finger, and was like, did this really happen, did I win a second round at the US Open, and have the love of my life just propose to me on international television.

I was still sleepy, so just looked at my phone and Paul reminded me no practice today, we will take an Uber to the tournament at 3:00. I texted him back I need to go to Elijah's today, can we leave at 2 PM, so I can get there and take some pictures with the owner and staff. I think they would like to put a few up and want to return the favor to them. He texted back sure, let's have fun it is mixed doubles today.

I had to look up the rules for mixed doubles, I had never played it in my lifetime. Mixed doubles have no ad scoring, so deciding points were required at deuce. In addition, the deciding point is same sex received and serve. Third set is a 10-point tiebreaker and not a full set. A mixed match can take about an hour or maybe 75 minutes. So not much more than a practice time.

I went through the morning e-mails, skipped the congratulations stuff, and looked for what was happening with John Littleman. The morning was congratulations on the win, you won't believe the interest after your engagement on ESPN. I can tell you for sure, that you will have a designer dress for your wedding, I have an invitation for you to have a photo shoot for possible inclusion to the annual swimsuit edition. I am confirmed you now have wild cards to the four Asian swing tournaments in October, and finally my congratulations on your engagement, I could not have paid anymore for the publicity, your engagement ring story is going all over the place ESPN last night top ten, and papers all over the country athletic and feminine. I was out early this morning getting with Jacques, and they are now going to put out a blue and pink design with athletic and feminine on the shirt. We had to protect that saying this morning and the request was done and is now registered. This could be worth quite a bit of money for you and Larry as it is co-registered as the owners. I responded back that some of the trademark will go to poor folks in South Korea. Make this known, as it is Dea who came up with the saying. I also wanted to let him know I was to donate some money to the poor in Radford, VA so they can play sports, I guess this will be a private/public partnership. I want to donate $25,000 of my prize money so far and $10,000 if I win the next match.

A response came back, we can make it all happen, that is so generous given the journey you have been on and the sacrifices you made to get here.

The only other person I texted was Larry, and said "Love you my fiancé", with a response that was me also crazy working day some of us start earlier than others. Finally, see you tonight on court, may be late full working day.

I responded to others congratulating me on my win and engagement while I was eating and by the time it was over it was 09:45. I had not much to do so called my parents and they said they were going to skip today, so James could use the player pass and they would like to take both of us out to dinner and Larry also to restaurant in this area. I did not think Paul would mind not having to go to dinner with me.

I did say, "I need to be back by 10:00, I suspect Paul and I need to talk strategy against a ranked player like Marci Frankfort."

For a few hours I had time to myself, decided to put on my bathing suit, and for just an hour enjoy the pool and take some time to chill, it has been a whirlwind week. By the time I finally got to the hotel pool, it was noon, and by 1:00, I ordered a poolside pasta salad, a water and I went out on a limb and ordered a dessert just for fun. With lunch served it was time to get back to the room, pick-up my clothes at the front desk, some were dry cleaned and some more with all the logo's sown in.

Fluids started and then met Paul at the front desk where had already called for our Uber. Five minutes later we were on our way to Elijah's Bagels. We got there at about 2:20, and while the place still had a few customers most of the people had left for the day and one section had already been cleaned. I took several pictures with the staff, and even did a promotional statement with the owner, thanking him for his support and to try all the meals that they have for breakfast, least I could do for what they had done for me. I gave the owner a kiss to the cheek, and that was recorded by the employees for teasing the boss.

Paul and I jumped back into the Uber, we had to pay an additional $25, for the extra stop, but we really did not care, this was a fun trip and besides I have won a lot of money this week. We arrived at the stadium and by the time we went through security and got to the players' lounge we checked in on the status of the match before us, it was just getting on court meaning the 5:30 start time was likely.

Paul sent me out to do 15 minutes on the stationary bicycle, so by the time everything was done we were ready for the mixed doubles. Mike Finley and his coach joined us for the mixed doubles match, he told us he had won his first-round men's doubles match earlier today as the 16 seed over a wildcard team 6-2, and 6-4. Strategy is to somehow stay with this couple, Annette has a decent but nothing to worry about serve, and Max has a 130 MPH serve, just try to block his back.

At 5:15, we got the 15 minute or less for the match to be over, and it finished 5 minutes later. We walked the long walk to the court 16 right near the circular court 17 and way away from the players' lounge.

The last match today on court 16 is a mixed doubles match receiving a wild card Mike Finley from Britain, and Lilly Jarman representing South Korea from Radford, VA. Mike was a semi-finalist in last year's Wimbledon men's doubles. Then walking behind, us, welcome the 8th seeds who made the French open semi-finals, Max Schmidt representing Germany, and Annette Miletti, representing Italy. Max has won the Australian open in mixed doubles, and Annette was a semi-finalist in women's doubles also in Australia. Court 16 is a bank of four courts with stands on one side, the players boxes are alongside, so I looked up and James was in the box with Paul. Larry was not yet up from work, I guess the market closed at 4 PM and he had to change.

Good afternoon, this is James Jarman, I was asked by Paul to write in Lilly's iPad journal about the mixed doubles match. I had to look at the rules for mixed doubles because I had never viewed it with Lilly, even when I watched her play in Delaware at the beach it was always women's doubles so had to read the notes from Lilly regarding this type of match.

The German and Italian won the coin toss and decided to serve and after a five-minute warm-up began the match. Max had a massive serve that Lilly only was able to get back once in the three times she had it, so the European team won the first game of the match. Lilly was the first serve for her team and was quickly broken at 15-40, as she was having a tough time with Max's returns. Fortunately, Annette had similar problems and Lilly and Mike finally got on the board. Mike followed up with a hold and just like that it was 2-2. The set seemed to go that way until they got to 6-6, and a first set tiebreaker. Unfortunately, Lilly and Mike lost the tiebreaker 7-5 on an ace by Max. Mike and Lilly then switched service games and Mike won easily, and a break of serve was also easy that led to our team up 2-0. Max now had to hit to Mike first and then Lilly backhand, and the change in tactics and sides worked well, Lilly got the backhand to Max with a one-handed slice which he had a hard time doing anything but sending it to Mike at the net. The

Lilly and Mike team were up 4-0, before anyone knew what happened. Mike served and on a deciding point to Max, the team lost the first game of the second set when Max hit a screaming shot at Lilly that she could not handle. Now with Max serving down 1-4, he was able to get up 40-15, but Lilly and Mike won the next two points to force another deciding point. Mike pushed the serve back to Max's backhand and Lilly got on his side of the net and hit a volley right at Annette for a winner. Now up 5-1, Lilly served and kept hitting wide serves that Mike handled and 4 points later the match was tied at one set each.

Since the ten-point deciding tiebreaker is just like a set, Max was up and pounded an ace to go up 1-0, Mike then served a service winner against Annette and Lilly finished a point to go up 2-1. Annette's turn and she was able to hold against Lilly, and Mike won the point with a screaming return to lead now 3-2. Lilly was able to win the serve against the Italian and Max managed to win the point, so our team led 4-3, the next eight points went the same way, so our team was leading 8-7, with Max serving. Max again won his first serve, this time against Lilly to tie the score at 8 all. Max served to Mike who lobbed the ball over Annette, while Max got to the shot Lilly was waiting for it at net and hit Annette on the leg with her volley and created match point. Lilly was up to serve against Max, and while he hit the ball hard down the line, Mike was waiting for it at net and hit a great drop volley that neither Annette or Max could get to for the game set and match to Mike and Lilly. Afterwards all, four shook hands at the net, Lilly came over to us, and who came up from behind and the way he was yelling I could guess this was Larry who had just asked my sister to marry him the night before. Larry had been in the stands. It was obvious when he hugged her and gave her a passionate kiss.

All 4 players quickly left the stadium, and we met up after the match.

Lilly came from the locker room, and I returned the iPad to Lilly for her to write her story.

Lilly here, I quickly went to the locker room and took a shower and changed just as quickly. My dad said we are all invited to go out for a celebration dinner. Paul begged out indicating he had a lot of videos to go over, and we need to review at 10:30 tonight. He also reminded me, "one glass of wine and nothing more, because you have the first match up on court 17, which will start at 11:30."

Dad had made reservations at Magna Ristorante, that was recommended to him by the Hilton staff. In 3 Ubers 2 to the restaurant and one back to the hotel we broke up for the evening. We arrived promptly for our 7:45 reservation and were shown a back table that had been marked reserved. The wine was waiting for us, and Dad then toasted the newly engaged couple. I made a call to Dea, but she did not answer, I guess it was getting late. We had a great fresh pasta meal with a lot of meats and fresh tomatoes and cheese as an appetizer. I had to beg off on the dessert, but they gave me some ice cream while the others ate cheesecake, it was not fair. The evening ended at about 9:30, and dad refused to allow anyone near the check. This was on him, and he had no interest in anyone else even thinking about it. Larry looked at me and we decided to not argue.

We left the restaurant, and I received a very passionate kiss from Larry, and he said, "I am going to find a way to get to your match sometime in the second set, I need to work and have taken a lot of time off this week, I have a 9:00 meeting so will be rooting for you all the way. Don't reserve your ticket for me."

"I told him ticket six is his whether he comes or not. James was going to have to sit in the stands, I only had six tickets for the box, and with Mom, Dad, Paul, John, and reserving one seat for Larry, only 1 ticket left and that was apparently going to be for Allison from Mizuno shoes, she wants to be there she said to announce a new shoe."

The three of us left in the second Uber and went to the Hilton Garden Inn.

Mom and dad left immediately for their room saying they had enough excitement for the day. I left for my conference room and got ready for my meeting with Paul in 15 minutes. I know he will want to talk strategy, and will want me drinking the hydration fluids, they taste like hell but since we have an AM match need to start now.

Paul of course was on-time and arrived at 10:25, just to be sure. He came carrying his laptop. We have a chance, and this is how we do it.

"Marci has had 2 tough matches and played to the semi-finals last week in New Haven. My strategy is to push Marci with long points in the beginning even though she is a tough clay courter, she does not like this surface, but she is so damn athletic she can make up for her light serve at barely 100. I have a surprise for you to play but let's talk about it in the morning. Since the match is at 11:30, we have warm-up at 09:15, so we need to leave here by 08:30, make sure you have hydrated, and watch the sun and wear a visor to protect your service toss from the sun. Do that in warm-ups if you don't like it then toss it."

With it being 11:00 Paul let himself out, not before indicating for me to have a good night sleep, and not to worry will not have that many fans at the stadium. I saw a text from Dea she said very tired went to sleep early and I responded when I woke up.

Texted Larry before going to bed then crashed for the night. I can't believe I am going to play the third round of the US Open, if somehow, we can win it is worth 60,000 thousand dollars, a nice downpayment on a home.

Day 5: US Open Third Round Day

I woke up when my alarm went off at 7:00, and immediately started drinking fluids, it is predicted to be about 80 and humid when we start the match, it just finished raining so looks like the matches will be on-time. No breakfast yet, that gets delivered at 07:30, so a half-hour to run through e-mails. While I went through a lot of congratulations and other e-mails, I came upon one from Allison from Mizuno shoes.

Allison's e-mail said this is a mock-up of the next women's shoes that the company wants to design. I opened the attachment and saw an amazing shoe. The outside of each shoe was powder blue; the inside half was corral pink. The shoe had pink laces and the following, on the blue side of one shoe was athletic and on the other rear pink side was feminine. We are offering you $25,000, plus 5% of gross sales for these shoes. I responded back looks great but need to send to my agent. I then sent the e-mail to John, and he said ask for $35,000, upfront and 6% of gross sales. I sent the counter proposal to Allison, and she responded accepted will send paperwork to John this afternoon. Expect production in September with first shoes in November, you can play the last tournament of the year in October with them on. I realized that Larry had to sign because he was on the application so we had to include him on the compensation, and I will let that go between Larry and John, not getting into those details today.

I heard a knock on the door and the breakfast with bagels, banana, and some other fruit was delivered. Of course, there was a note inside saying someone from our store will be there to see you. Thanks for yesterday, already on the wall.

By the time I finished I had to rush getting a shower and then pack for the day. All new skirts, shorts, socks, wrist brands, and shoes. John's e-mail indicated he is working with Babolat to get a racquet contract for the next round and the end of the year. Not only will they provide custom sticks plus maybe $25,000, check also. I am going to have to hire an accountant or a financial person at least to keep track of all this plus what John gets as an agent. I think Larry can find someone here that he knows and can be trusted.

Well, the time had come to leave the room and get to the lobby to meet Paul for the match today. Like always, he was waiting for me, and the Uber had just come up. I had packed enough clothes for the match today and possibly interview afterwards as is required in the last 32 rounds. I suspect if I lose it will be a very quiet room that is getting way ahead of myself.

Paul said Lilly, "I think we have a good chance today. Marci has like 80 percent of her points from clay, and she must be tired with the long matches she has played. We try to play straight-up with her and force some long points by allowing her to run herself out of energy. Then, when I think the time is right, I will give you the sign of a "cross", and that will mean start charging the net serve and volley. I think we will have her tired and pushing to have to run to the net may be all we need to win this match. I want you to return service if you can first, so you get used to the crowd. I will be up in the stands as will be your parents, so you will know where to look for us. I'm sure your parents are leaving a little later because they don't have to be there until 11:30. We need to book it right to the practice courts. James is coming from downtown we have him in the stands and John will be in the second row of the box with a guest and then we will reserve the last slot for either Allison if she wants it or Larry, but I think he said he would not get here until after 12, so let's get him in the stands with your brother just to make sure."

We arrived and went straight to the practice court for 15 minutes to 20 minutes of hitting, and then 10 minutes on the bike. Marci had finished just as we were getting to the court, and just walked by me, she had no idea who I was and why should she has won tournaments and even a grand slam doubles at Roland Garros.

We went back to the lounge afterwards and I then went to the locker room and took a quick shower. We were getting close to time for the match by the time I got out of the shower and was dressed for the match. Paul and I waited at the lounge and my parents texted that they had arrived and were going through security and will be there in the box before the match. We got the 15-minute warning that our time on the match was coming. Then it was the 5-minute warning and then walk to court 17, which is the farthest court away from Ashe stadium.

As we walked out Paul said, "after this match you and I have some things to figure out as far as what you will want from me going forward."

I responded, "no problem I don't think you will want to leave Radford for the Asian swing anyway."

We arrived at the stadium; Paul handed me my bags "remember look for me for the signals we talked about."

We separated as we waited for the court announcement. Paul was so wrong I saw a lot of German fans and it looked like the bowl was already a quarter full of people walking in. Court 17 looks like a bull ring with fans all around, it is considered the fourth court of preference, Ashe, Armstrong, Grandstand and then this court. I handed my iPad to John who was waiting for me and said good luck, he said he will give it to my dad for entering the match.

This is Ken, Lilly's dad, I am going to be writing this for Lilly in her iPad, so she can have this forever. Introducing our players for this third-round ladies tennis match, from Radford, VA representing South Korea,

Lilly Jarman, this is her first US Open. Lilly walked in and a small applause. Well except for 2 ladies who had Eliajah's bagels T-shirts on. Now introducing her opponent, the 15 seed from Munich, Germany. Marci Frankfort, currently number 16 in the world rankings. Marci is the current holder of the Ladies doubles crown from Roland Garros. The mostly German crowd went crazy, and Marci raised her hand and the crowd got even more loud.

The two women, went to the net for the customary service toss coin flip, and when Marci won the toss, she decided to serve, which was good because I really think Lilly needed to work her way in to the match.

Paul commented, "look at the protection that Marci has on her thighs, physio tape she must be a hurting."

Ten minutes, later the 2 completed warm-up. Marci started the match serving, you could tell she knew how to place her serve but it was not a big serve, so the first game went to deuce before Marci was able to win the game with one unforced error and another by Lilly. Now it was Lilly's turn, and she immediately served wide and after what was probably a 12-shot rally Lilly won the first point on her serve. The second point went to Marci after another long rally. Lilly then won the next three points one with an ace and the others easy, leveling the match at one game each. This pattern of long serving by Marci and easy hold by Lilly went on until the match was 4-4 with Marci about to serve. Lilly looked up at Paul and he was making a cross sign, I had no idea what this meant but Lilly just shook her head in acknowledgement. On this decisive serve, Marci hit a wide serve and Lilly hit back to the server's side deep, Marci hit the ball and Lilly was waiting at the net and hit the ball with a volley. Marci held on to the next point and this went to the deuce point. Marci again served wide, and Lilly hit a forehand down the line, Marci got it back, but Lilly was again waiting at the net and finished the point to go up 5-4. After the changeover Lilly was serving for the first set. She must have had something in the tank and hit an ace at 115, the highest of the tournament and close to a Serena Williams serve. Marci looked dismayed when Lilly then served the next point as a puff serve which she hit right back to Lilly, and Lilly immediately hit the other corner which Marci hit into the net for a 30-0. Lilly must have the nerves and had her second double fault of the match. Now leading 30-15, Lilly jumped the intensity up and hit another 112 mph down the line which Marci could barely pop up and Lilly hit an overhead to get up 40-15. Lilly served a 105 mile serve wide which Marci pounded at Lilly who could only launch the ball into the stands. Lilly had one more set point. Lilly set-up to serve a big serve down the "T" but caught the tape for a let. On the next first serve Lilly hit it wide and Marci made the mistake of hitting the ball back to the middle because Lilly was coming to the net and caught the volley and Marci could not reach it. Lilly won the first set 6-4, and our box was screaming and a standing ovation. I looked up and the bowl was now almost completely full as the major courts had not started. I don't think Lilly had ever played with more than a few hundred fans and now the crowd was clapping for the big underdog.

ESPN Broadcast Booth:

Pam Shriver and Brad Gilbert had the first shift. Pam said, "If you all can hear the roar, I think we have some news from court 17." Hey Patrick, do you have something to report?

Patrick reported, "well gang, if the shouts of athletic and feminine did not give it away, Lilly Jarman just took the first set here with a strong net game. The noise is getting loud with the women saying feminine, and the men yelling athletic. If you are the seed and you see this, it must be weird that most fans are rooting for your opponent. Marci has about 500 German fans, but it looks like between the Americans and the Asian fans, we are seeing them change the nature of this match and the noise is getting insane."

Pam reported, while we are waiting on play to begin at Ashe, let's follow this match. Marci has taken a bathroom break and will be back in a minute. While she is away, she must be hearing the chants."

Marci came back on the court to a launch of cheers from the German crowd at the bottom of the bowl. Marci while not a big server is keeping Lilly from coming in by hitting very deep in the corners obviously, she has been coached not to let Lilly into the net.

Ken here, the second set finally started, and Marci looked like she was full of new energy to keep this unknown player off her game. It did not take long for her to hit into the corners and Lilly hit four errors in a row and Marci won the game. Lilly, not to be outdone served two aces and won two other points to hold her serve at love. Marci was up in the brighter side of the court and was having a difficult time serving, Lilly could see her inability to handle it with speed and proceeded to hit three winners and get up 15-40. Marci was able to serve very wide and Lilly came through with a hard shot to Marci who hit the ball down the center and Lilly knew what to do and put it down the line with a robust forehand that Marci could just touch, and the break happened. I have to say the crowd erupted.

For the next six games the server held not easily but no break points, the match was now 3-5, with Lilly ready to serve it out.

ESPN Studio Again:

Brad Gilbert reporting, "Let's get back to court 17, while we have a break. Patrick how is it going over there?

"You can hear it Lilly Jarman broke Marci Frankfort early in this set and now gets ready to serve to get in to the fourth round of the US Open. Let's stay here."

Ken here again, somehow Larry fought his way down here and is sitting in the aisle next to us. Lilly hit the first serve into the net and then the second went long, another double fault, yes, she looked nervous. On the second point Lilly went back to the serve and volley and won the point. Now even at 15-15, Lilly took some power out and decided to serve wide again and the point went about 12 shots before Lilly hit a heavy forehand into the corner that Marci hit into the crowd. Lilly next served down the line and came and won the point with a volley at the net.

ESPN coverage:

Lilly Jarman to serve for the match up 40-15. First serve into the net, second serve also into the net. She looks nervous and is taking her time before she serves the next point. Lilly reaches up and tries to go down the line and the serve was long. Now with her trying again to finish the match, Lilly hit a soft serve just to get the point started, and back and forth they are going, on the 21st shot in the rally, Lilly goes for broke and hit a smash down the forehand side. Marci hit it back to the corner, and Lilly came into the court and hit a strong slice backhand down the other line. The screams and erupting crowd, tell you what just happened. Lilly Jarman, welcome to the round of 16 in the US Open. Marci threw her racquet across the court to where she had been sitting. Lilly came sprinting to the net and shook hands. The boos at Marci are now being eclipsed by the sound of fans screaming the chant again Athletic and Feminine.

Brad Gilbert requested, "can you bring Lilly to you for an on-court interview." Well Lilly Jarman, I want to be the first to welcome you to the round of 16 at the US Open."

Lilly with tears in her eyes, simply said "to the fans thank you for coming to see me play, this means so much to me."

Brad again asked, "are you hearing the chant of the fans today?"

"Yes, and to my grandmother Dea, thank you for everything you have done. I must thank my coach Paul for helping me through this match and to my family, can you stay until Monday." Larry was released by security to join Lilly and came and gave her a big hug and kiss.

Brad yelled, "well folks let's hear it for Lilly Jarman," and again the fans stood and cheered.

Studio team discussion, "well what will Lilly do now that she will be in the top 125 or better when the live rankings come out? She will stop playing ITF's shortly and play only tour level matches. I had heard from her mother that the girls in Radford were mean to her growing up. I guess she will be popular when she comes back to town."

Ken again, our team walked out of the stadium and as Lilly left, she heard a major ovation, her story of country bumpkin to tennis equal apparently is popular with the crowd. As I left, I received a call from Dea's neighbor saying that Dea was not feeling well and they had to have her transported to the hospital, they don't know what is wrong she just complained that she was very tired and that her legs felt heavy.

"I said I understand and will fly to Richmond and then drive to Blacksburg in the morning. As much as I wanted to stay here, I had to go and make sure that my mom was in good hands. I left the group to plan to get DC or Richmond. I told Barbara what was happening and that she should stay here with Lilly, James and she could represent the family." I caught-up with the group and returned the iPad to Lilly.

Lilly here, now that the match was over it was early afternoon and I needed to sign a few autographs and found our way back to the player's area. I took a shower and changed clothes so that I could be presentable. By the time I got out and met everyone outside of Ashe stadium, it was almost 2:45. James had gone to other courts to watch the ladies in the stands and maybe a couple on the court. Larry said it was too late to go back to work, but he was going back to his apartment for a while, he needed to clean-up if he was going to be here. Dad told me he was leaving for Virginia in the morning and mom, and I would be up here. Both left in an Uber for the hotel and said they were going to go get some food together tonight since it was their last night here.

Paul was on the phone a lot before the match and after the match and we finally got some time together.

Paul said, "I told you I needed time together to talk about what's next for the both of us. I know based on John's e-mails that you have a lot of tournaments in Asia this fall, and not sure how we want to approach our coaching relationship. I have an offer at Van Der Meer academy in Hilton Head, to take over the junior development program for the year-round students. I have also been nominated to be the next head tennis coach at College of Charleston. My family is from there, and it would be a great spot for me. I have also been asked by a few professionals if I was interested in being a coach for a few of them. Lilly, I am committed to you for the rest of the year, but not sure we will be together after that. Like you I am getting married to my high school sweetheart. I know it has been 15 years since we graduated, and we both had different lives, but Ann and I are getting married when we get back to Radford at the courthouse. She has a six-year-old from her first marriage, and well I don't know how to tell you this, we are expecting a child together in March. She is a schoolteacher so if we go back home, she has a lot of jobs open to her, and with college coaching comes a lot of perks."

I just looked at him for a minute, and then hugged him. Paul, "you are like my big brother if I had one, and I respect whatever you decide. I am grateful for everything you have done for the last few years. Let's go out of this tournament in style, get you married, and then tour Asia. We can make some money for whatever you need to. I understand John has a contract for you for the end of the year, which will guarantee you 10% of prize money or $50,000, for the rest of the year whichever is higher. The money we have earned so far this tournament is just about $250,000, so you will get a check of just under $25,000 shortly after the tournament ends. I know this is just a downpayment, but I think with the money you get from here plus any travel costs will help you in whatever you decide to do. I know that I could not do anything like this without you."

Paul said "Lilly Jarman, I love you like you were my kid sister; I hope you don't mind but if we get a daughter, will you mind if we call her Lillian. This has been the thrill of a lifetime for someone who never got beyond number 3 at College of Charleston. I do have a degree in Kinesiology, I guess that has helped me get a few jobs offers."

"I told him if you have a chance to take over Van Der Meer, programs, that was where you could make the best and I could understand if you went home with your wife and child, and stepchild. I love you as a brother and this time will never be the same without you. Lastly, can you believe we have more time to play. The second week of a major championship."

Paul indicated he was going back to the hotel to start looking at strategy for mixed doubles on Saturday and watch whoever will be playing in the round of 16. With everyone gone, I was alone for the first time today. That did not last long as Allison texted me to get to the publicity tent.

Corporate area US Open:

Good afternoon, my name is Allison, and I am from Mizuno shoes. This afternoon we would like to announce our latest shoe that will be out in a couple months. The shoe was inspired by Lilly Jarman's engagement and this afternoon we came to an agreement for this shoe going forward. Lilly is our first signed tennis player, and here is the latest offering: Introducing our first new shoe, this is the "Athletic and Feminine" shoe, as you can see the color scheme matches Lilly's engagement ring and from the crowd this afternoon, you can see the women like this phrase. On the back of the shoes, one says Athletic and the other says Feminine. A few pictures taken and then a few questions to Allison."

By 4:15, I was free to go and decided that it was time to go back to the hotel I was exhausted. Publicity, tennis, and an engagement all in one week, and I still won't get to see Larry alone.

I got back to the hotel and instantly fell asleep, the next thing I knew it was 8 PM. I had a text from Paul saying we don't need to get together tonight, match is last on court 17, so we will not play until probably 5:30, the mixed doubles. I will see you at 10:00 in the morning. I walked over to my parents' room; they had finished eating and suggested that I call room service because they close in 15 minutes. I ordered a club sandwich, chips, and a salad. I asked for a soda, and they had a diet coke very cold they said available. Dad was almost all packed to go back to Virginia, he had texted me that his flight was at 8 am, so he was leaving before I got up, and will monitor with Dea and watch on ESPN+.

My dinner arrived back at my room, and after dinner did not even bother to look at texts or e-mail, I was just exhausted. After finishing dinner, I simply crashed thinking. I bet there are a bunch of debutantes that are crapping in their pants, I guess she really was not a lesbian. She was just in to sports and playing sports.

To those colleges that never recruited me, I guess you are wondering how I got here when you thought I was not worth recruiting. To my coach at Longwood, thanks for training me.

Chapter 11

The Recruiting Year

I could not do this story justice without talking about college recruiting. Because of Title IX, Women's tennis is at most universities that give scholarships so tennis and college can be a possibility for numerous girls even those in backwaters. The elite schools look at those playing national tournaments and ITF's, a low-level of tennis professional tournaments. Some elite juniors don't play anything but either of those two, then you get your top 100 that are rated in national tournaments. Add to that about a couple hundred foreign tennis players and you have the majority of the recruits for Division 1 and 2. Division 3, does not give scholarships and since most of them only give financial basis on needs I got some interest from a couple of the local colleges after making a run in the state tournament, but again the elite schools had the players they want already in the pools they desire.

    At the end of my junior year, I had taken my SAT's and did not do badly in the core section of about 1350, not bad for an athlete. I took the ACT's because the southern schools mostly used this test to get into college. My results came in the end of October and with 31's in three sections and a 29 in English, suddenly schools wanted to talk to me not about tennis though. While my grandmother Dea would not approve of it, I did not put Asian and my records as some schools required Asian students to have higher scores. Because my dad worked for Radford, that was always going to be a possibility, I could be a walk-on, and the school price was limited but I really wanted to be elsewhere. My grades and these scores got interest from schools such as Virginia Tech, James Madison, and George Mason, near DC. I even heard from a couple of schools in PA, like Indiana University of PA, and Bloomsburg University, both were Division 2, but expensive for me as an out of state student. We were doing better but not that good, and I really did not want a huge student debt.

As a senior I had one AP course because they simply did not offer much at Radford, and besides it was tough doing homework on the weekends and playing tennis matches. I entered the year 10th in the 18's and nationally like 200, mostly because I had not played much in national tournaments and very few knew who I was.

I was able to get 2 weeks of training in at the Stan Smith academy in August before school, but that did 2 things, no matches to help my ratings, and no time with Randy before school, so my magical night was the last time I saw my mythical boyfriend. I have to say here as he started his next journey we started to do less and less texting and calls. By November we had both drifted apart, and I realized it was over. Gene Coons had me play with the national kids because most of the summer kids had gone home or were on the junior national tournament. I was very competitive, and Gene said "I think we can make some calls for you to go to college. I am going to do the video and show them, you beat our best 16-year-old this week, and beat another girl who is committed to Ohio State."

To get some exposure, Jake wanted me to get in some regional tournaments, and they had a low-level tournament in Baltimore that I drove up to. Yes, I got mom's car and with my new license proceeded to go to Baltimore for a weekend. I stayed at Amy's because my mom said an 18-year-old should not travel and go to hotels by herself. Amy agreed to come to the tournament and drove me. I guess some of the other seniors did not need the points because this was a low-level tournament and I managed to reach the finals against mostly 15-year-olds. The next week, I looked and my ratings in this combined event got me to 8th regionally and 160th nationally. Two weeks later I won a tournament in

Richmond the last of the outdoor tournaments in the area, and when I looked up, I was now 6th in the regional and still hovering just under 160, as a guess a couple of people aged out.

With the win suddenly started getting invitations to come visit teams from the Pennsylvania conference, including Shepherd in West Virginia, Shippensburg, and Clarion. Clarion said they could not offer me a sports scholarship but was interested in providing me with a quarter academic money thinking I would qualify for a financial grant for another quarter. Shepherd said they only have one scholarship each year and that is committed but if I walked on, they would give work-study, that would pay a few hundred per month in expense money. Bloomsburg finally came back and said they could offer me a quarter scholarship for each academic and athletics but that still left a lot of money for my family to cover.

I need to side-track here, I was not going to go to Homecoming at all, but Bob insisted that we go together get a couple of dances in and Frances and her current boyfriend Kirk Swank, a football player insisted that I go with them the first weekend in October, I went to the Homecoming dance on the Saturday after the Friday night football game. I decided since nobody had viewed me in my dress last Spring, that I would save the family money and go in the same dress as the previous year. This was a casual thing with Bob and me and so nothing was going to go on other than a kiss on the cheek. As I stated he and James were always my protectors. Bob is only about the same height as I am so with my heels, I was very much taller than him. He did have a nice tuxedo on, and some people said we looked good together. Frances and Kirk were much friskier than we were and since Bob was driving, they enjoyed each other in the back seat slipping each other the tongue.

When Bob and I arrived he insisted to hold my hand and see the faces of the people here who both think we are odd fellows. Kara Dormant saw me and just turned away, she knew better than to say something to me. Her group and some of the jocks just stayed away from us knowing it was not going to go well for them. Interestingly, a lot of the jocks were people I talked to during the week. Amazing that when you support the Redskins and are passionate about it, how much easier it is to talk to the athletes. A lot of these women just had boobs and no brains. They were looking to get pregnant as soon as possible with one of these guys hoping the guys were going to get a college scholarship. It was so pathetic, that they put their worth in who they had dated, no self-worth and purpose at all. But those are the ways of the debutantes, a lot of them wealthy generational families that are there just to provide a next generation of debutantes.

The evening went well, Bob was a charming guy and we held hands as he stated on several occasions every time, we knew someone was watching. Frances told me later that the whispers behind us were funny. She said, some were "I can't believe Lilly owned a dress much less looks that good in one. Another apparently said, wow the tennis lesbian dresses up nice. Frances said that a couple of Kirk's football friends said, wow, never would have thought that was what she looked like without sweats, the girl is hot. Yes, I ate it up, and Frances just laughed, I think a few people are really turned on by you and that dress."

Bob said, my friend is my girl for the night, and I am getting a few looks, so that is why you have been friends with the tennis lesbian." Who knew she looked that good with those long-tanned legs.

Well, that was the end of the full lesbian talk at least to my face, and from then on, a few other guys even wanted to talk to me more than just sports. Bob prevented that too much and now he was protecting me from the players rather than the expose to the debutantes. Life is so different just from getting some make-up on and a good-looking dress. In the tennis world I have friends that are both straight and lesbian, and quite frankly they are just tennis players, and some are friends, and some are merely, what they are.

Well back to the recruiting, after now getting a ranking near the top 100, I got a few more people looking at me. Radford now said I could walk on, and they would guarantee me a top 6 shot, but now I got a call from the coach of Coastal Carolina, saying he would like to me to walk-on and if I did well in the fall matches could get a half-scholarship. Again, maybe's and not much else. My grandmother in Farmville called me and said, have you ever thought of Longwood University. I really had not it was not that high academically according to rating systems.

She told me they play division 1 and looking for local unknown talent. She sent me some information about them hiring a new coach, Mitchell Wilson, formerly of the Evert academy in Florida. (No, he is not related to Larry) I did not know anything about him and looked him up he had been the main junior coach for many second-tier pros.

In November I played another tournament that had both regional and national coverage, with the top 5 already college committed, I was the second highest ranked player here, even the girls younger than me were garnering college coach attention. The coach from Mount St Mary's, Md was there looking at one of his senior recruits who I beat in the quarterfinals, she had a higher national ranking than me. I then upset the top ranked region 16-year-old playing up, beating her in a close second set 7-6 in a tiebreak. The finals proved to be a little bit easier, winning in straight sets in just over an hour to another 16-year-old. After the match I was approached by a couple of men, the first was the coach from Mount St Mary's asking if I was a junior, because he did not have me on his radar before today. I said no, I am a senior at Radford, but I only play one tournament a month because of the travel costs.

"He asked if I was being recruited by Radford, and I said they would like me to walk-on, they could possibly use me as a number 6. He said go to junior college next year and let me know because my money is committed for this year, but I could see you as a top 3 player for us."

"A second guy very tanned came up to me and said I know you who you are Lilly Jarman, I was told by Jake Willis that we have this talented local girl that nobody has even thought about recruiting, my name is Mitchell Wilson and I represent Longwood University, I will be coming to the University next semester to lead the team and we are looking to improve. Lilly, have you ever heard of either Longwood or Farmville."

"I said yes, my grandmother lives there but not sure if the University is academically rated high enough for me. I know they are a middle hugging academically, and I am close to getting academic money by James Madison, where my dad played football."

"Well Lilly, I have the potential number 1 slot available for you if you want it next year, with my coaching and your natural ability I think you could make the NCAA tournament and chase some of the players from a big school. Lilly, remember I know you are interested in academics, and a degree from us and some notoriety from the local papers will be a good way to get to grad school in engineering at Virginia Tech."

"I just said thanks and will think about it and took his card."

How did you know I was interested in engineering, he yelled, "ask your grandmother, she called me."

With the win I made it to the top 5 of the regional ranking, and national number 95. I went to the tennis recruiting web site and noticed that I had gone from a 2-star recruit to now a flame that said 3 stars.

That was the month of November still no real offers. I returned to training with Jake and asked him what I should do with college. His advice was if I wanted to play in college, then you are going to have to convince people that you belong. The light schedule has given you very little exposure. Then again if I went to Virginia Tech, I could play club and probably be a very competitive player. You would be about the highest rated player in the country playing club tennis.

He said, "we just messed up we should have pushed to get your more exposure. Another alternative is 1 year Junior College and start this over properly."

December came and right before the holidays, I went to Alexandria, VA and made the finals of another regional tournament with national rankings. Right before Christmas, I was now ranked number 4 regionally, and made a new national ranking of 79. The next week the ratings showed me as a rising 3-star recruit, in other words I was a 4 star but not ranked that way yet. I looked and no school showed any interest, and I was the only one without a commitment or interest in the 3 stars. I also just received my national merit society membership. I was asked to put in academic at UVA, Tech, James Madison, and my grandmother said put an application in to Longwood as your safe school, so I did.

Due to academic work, I did not play another tournament until February, and made another final, only to lose to an academy kid who was home on break. My national ranking now was 75, but still, nobody really recruiting me. I was determined that it was not the end of my career at the end of high school season.

With that all done, I applied to a couple of other schools that gave financial relief, Dickinson, and Temple in Philadelphia. I got a letter from Rhodes college in Memphis, TN, but they were a small Christian school in division 3, and I was not interested in going there and let the coach know.

My dad tried to tell me, you know that if you went to a good junior college for a year, then a lot of the better schools will want a shot at you. I was so turned off by going to a JUCO for a year, that I found this like another year of high school, I had a 3.65, GPA, and an average of 30's on my ACT. Someone needed to take me on an academic scholarship.

February came and Radford High tennis started to get ready for the season. With all the debutantes gone, the coach tried to still have me play number 2, the top slot he wanted reserved for one of the more popular rich kids, a junior level debutante. I beat the freshman 6-0, and 6-1, so the coach and no other choice than to finally play me at number 1. Frances, on the other hand was not as fortunate so she played number 3, and we played together for doubles at number 1. My last USTA tournament went well, I made another final, and pretty much finished my USTA career at number 4, regionally and number 69, nationally. The recruiting news now had me as a 4-star recruit and without a single interest shown.

March came and the commitments to colleges were mostly done, only the second-tier schools, so I was prepared for one year at junior college. Hillsborough CC in Florida had a nationally ranked team, and the coach said he would love to have me there. The campus was Tampa, Florida, and with the Florida weather I would never have to play indoors again. I was rejected by UVA, accepted by Longwood, Radford, and accepted by Virginia Tech, but for the second semester, a weird new thing that would have me no college for three months until enough flunked out that there was room at the dorms. Dickinson accepted me, and the financial aid took the cost down to about $30,000, per year. My parents could only afford about $15,000, so I had to decide if I wanted to borrow 60K, for college and then play a decent but not great division 3 team. I was accepted into Temple, and that was becoming the best option, although my parents were not thrilled for me to go to Philadelphia. Of course, I was accepted into Radford, but that meant living at home and maybe getting a shot at the number 6 tennis player. The PA schools of IUP also accepted me and for the first time the coach sent me a letter of interest. I had put in a quick application to IUP 2 days before the last chance for acceptances just in case.

Hillsborough said they were going to follow my high school season, and see what they could do to support me if I wanted to go there, which could living at a family's extra room, and such because officially, they had very little money, so they were able to find community members to host his kids, and then work study, and getting a job elsewhere if needed.

The tennis season went better than expected, I went undefeated at number 1, Frances went undefeated at number 3, and as a doubles team we only lost once. The team with us at the top and the freshman holding her own, had us win our first regional title in school history. The school newspaper and then the local Roanoke papers had an article. Suddenly, I get a call from James Madison coach, would I like to come up there and see the program, we think you could be a candidate for number 6, and as an in-state student the money will be easy for you.

It was now May, and two things were happening, I went to the prom, with Bob and then came the regionals. The prom was no big deal, we just went as friends, held hands, and at the end of the night, Bob said, "I will miss you Lilly Jarman, you are a great friend, a beautiful, and smart girl, and someone someday we will be very lucky to be your lover."

I no longer heard from Randy; he had moved on.

I had gone on a couple of dates, nothing really happened and no chemistry, but it was fun to get some type of acceptance that I could be me and earn a little respect.

With a few options to continue to college and play tennis I entered the Virginia State tournament as the number 4 seed. Frances and I were the 3 seeds in doubles. The tournament would be played singles first Tuesday through Thursday, and then doubles Friday and Saturday. I was the highest rated tennis player on Tennis Recruiting that had not committed yet, and only interest on the report shown by Hillsborough, Radford, and Longwood. James Madison moved on when I would not commit as a walk-on, so the obvious was going to be JUCO.

The tournament had some of the top players from all over the state of Virginia, a couple from the Norfolk/Virginia Beach area, most of the others were from DC area or Richmond. The event was played at the campus of University of Richmond because it was an unfair advantage if Godwin hosted as they had 2 players in the tournament. The team event was the following week, and our team was going for the first time in the school history, but for recruiting this was the week that mattered. Well, I should say that the juniors this mattered because the heavy recruiting letters would start in July, the letters that I had never received. My first-round match was a sophomore from Fairfax County, Sally O'Laughlin, obviously an Irish girl with freckles and red hair. The match started off very even, but she could not handle my one-handed slice backhand. At 3-3 I really figured out that I would hit my slice backhand and simply push her around, she was getting tired of this, and I broke to go up 4-3, the next two games went easily to me, and finished the set 6-3. The second set went more easily I simply overpowered the girl with a powerful serve and return games to the corner. My mother then went out and got us a hotel room for the rest of the week at an Extended Stay. She chose this place because with a small kitchen we could save money by cooking and keeping things in a refrigerator.

The afternoon match was not much more difficult as the poor junior, Mandy Moore from Virginia Beach nice basic player, but she had no match for my more powerful serves, and I moved her around all afternoon, in just over an hour I had completed the win at 6-2, and 6-3.

That left 8 players in the draw, almost all the seeds were left only the number 7 seed had been upset. My mother said we are going to pick up a pasta meal and went to a nice local Italian restaurant. For the first time in my life, I saw my mother Barbara get a drink, she had chianti.

She said, "I needed something here, and your grandmother is coming Thursday if you make the finals on Thursday."

The next morning the four quarterfinals all were played at 10:00 I got the lucky draw of playing the fifth seed from Godwin, she was there number 2 player Leanne Lovely, you could not make up that name. Leanne was a nationally ranked and regionally ranked player with more matches than I did and I'm sure she was like; I can beat this country bumpkin. Overconfidence is one thing, but she had a huge cheering section that cackled every time I made a mistake. It got so bad that the referee had to be called to the court to keep it civil. Frances and my mother were the only ones cheering for me, our coach just stayed quiet, but then again, he was going to a college program at UNC Greensboro starting in September. At 5-5, Leanne was serving and at deuce, I hit a screaming backhand down the line for a winner. The rooting for Leanne was deafening, and the referee got them to quiet down Leanne left me an opening with a forehand that I put in the corner she just could not get it back in the court. So that let me serve for the set and with all the fans she had she was decimated as I hit 2 big aces down the line, forced a third error, and then proceeded to serve and volley for the set winner.

The second set was very close again and again at 5-5 it was getting crazy. This time I held easily and led the set 6-5 and forced Leanne to hold serve to force a tiebreak. At 30-all we had a long point, and her forehand was just long and that is what I called, the crowd turned ugly against me, but the referee said she could not overrule so it stood at match point for me. The crowd from Godwin started yelling obscenities and had to be quieted twice before Leanne served. I caught her serve and ripped a backhand down the line that she got back but I was waiting at the net and finished the point off. I raised up my hands and the boos and words from the Godwin fans were ugly.

The semi-finals were starting at 2:30, where I was not so lucky and had to play the number 1 seed, the top player from Godwin, Pauline Parks. Pauline was the number 1 seed, committed to Michigan State, this was also her last tournament she was told to shut it down for the summer and just practice. Godwin has a very good support group and Pauline had nearly 100 people rooting for her, I had three including my grandmother, Frances, and my mom. I would have liked to have dominated the match, but Pauline had other thoughts, I dropped the first set in a tiebreaker, but was able to force the action in the second set winning 6-3 and forcing a decisive third set. The set went to 3-3 all with Pauline serving the decisive seventh game. The crowd was really rooting Pauline on but somehow, I managed to stay with her, then at 30-all, she hit a double fault, and I had a break point that I jumped on her second serve hitting a strong forehand cross court. Now leading 4-3, I held my serve and was leading 5-3, and thought it would be quickly over. Pauline held on to get back to 5-4. With my last service game, I had to overcome 2 break points and finally managed to hit an ace to have my first and only match point. I hit a wide serve and followed it into the net and finished the set. I had upset the previous year's champion and was on my way to the finals, but this match was so tough on me, I had a hard time recovering having played 4 matches in 2 days.

On the other side of the draw, Romina Perino, from Fairfax County area, had won as the second seed, easily as she ended up playing the weak part of the draw and took her less than 2 hours on court while I had been on the court for 4 hours.

A couple of coaches handed me their card, one from Old Dominion said as a VA resident he wanted me to walk-on, and he was sure after one year playing like number 6, he could find money for me.

The coach from Richmond came over and said, "are you sure you are a senior, I could use you next year, but my money is spent."

He recommended I go to JUCO for a year and come to him in February of next year to see what his money looked like. All kept saying your just too late for us to recruit you, but wow you are doing well.

I was getting ready to leave when my grandmother looked over her shoulder, "hey isn't that the coach of Longwood? She waved him over and said, I want to introduce you to my granddaughter."

Mitchell said, " I have met her before; Lilly I want to say that Longwood is again interested in you, and I think we may have an opportunity that nobody else can give you. You know that we are in the same conference as Radford and other schools throughout South Carolina, and North Carolina, and we are a division 1 program. I have talked to your coach Jake Willis, and he says that if you come here, you will be either our number 1 or 2 by the end of your freshman year. Since you are in a state university, you can also get priority to Va Tech for graduate school. I also know that your grandmother would love to see you play at our home games."

All I said, "let me get through this weekend, I have the singles final tomorrow and then the double with Frances over the weekend."

He indicated he would get paperwork by the time I had finished the tournament for me to have money from Longwood.

I was so tired mom, went out and bought dinner of pasta salad and found some place that had nice meatballs to add to the dinner. She bought some garlic bread also.

I was so sore when I woke on Thursday, I had to take a shower for what seemed like a half hour and then used bomb to loosen up the muscles. No matter what I tried to do, I really came out flat and lost the first set 6-2. Romina who came from Romania as a child hit a big shot and was much fresher than I was. I managed to push myself after taking some Advil between sets and win a long set at 7-5, but there was absolutely nothing left in the tank. I lost the deciding set 6-1, and congratulated Romina on her performance.

After the awards and pictures for the newspaper, Mitchell came with my mother and grandmother to say congratulations on a great tournament. Mitchell said "I have been showing this to your mother and grandmother and been on the phone with your coach and father this morning. I know you can go to junior college next year and probably could then get recruited by some conferences, but that causes you to lose 1 year, and I have developed professional tennis players, and you can get a division 1 experience through the Big South Conference. I am offering you a pretty good deal, the school based on your outstanding academic record, and ACT, is willing to provide you with Virginia rural academic scholarship of half of your tuition. The Athletic department is willing to pay a full half of your entire expenses here. So basically, all your parents would have to pay is the other half of the dorm space and food. Because you will be close to your grandmother's location, you will have family support anytime you need it. I know your dad was worried about you going to Temple because it is in the city. I have printed out everything I just said in duplicate, let me know what you think and if you accept it, call me and I will pick it up. If you say yes, we will also need to get you to Longwood for publicity over Radford, Richmond, and the conference. Did I tell you I already have signed 2 other freshmen in the top 150 of the country, but your talent still is as good as any of them?"

Later that night we had a family call, and it was my brother James that had the best argument. "Lilly thinks about it you get to play NCAA division I, get dinners at grandmas, and you will be close enough that we can see you play. I want to see you win the conference and that will be easy because Radford will be hosting the tournament. Junior College is a glorified high school for you. Your coach knows how to train junior champions, you need that type of intense coaching we could never get anywhere else."

So even though Frances and I did well in doubles winning the tournament 8-3, playing 8 game pro-sets, my weekend was full of thinking of what was next.

On the last day of May, we called Mitchell that we wanted to talk to him. My dad and brother joined us in Farmville, and we went over to Longwood. Before a few people and a reporter from Roanoke and another from Richmond, I went through the signing ceremony at Longwood. The question that both reporters wanted to know was simple, given your national ranking and finishing the finals of Virginia, why is it that so few schools wanted you in division 1.

My answer was simple, well coming from Radford, I did not get the tournament time regionally as most of the tournaments meant hotel stays and money was tight. Same issue with travelling to national tournaments, I did not have a sponsor so the costs were more than we could afford especially with my brother James being such a great swimmer and having to travel also.

With that signing I just ended a very short recruiting scenario. I e-mailed the coaches from the other schools that I had made a commitment over the weekend. Only one school e-mailed back, and they said sorry we did not have the money for you this year and good luck.

Sunday night I went on my computer and changed my status to signed Longwood University, I was the last senior with 3 stars or above to sign.

Tuesday at Radford HS was so funny, the publicity had come out on Sunday and the high school athletic director posted the article online in our athletic section Monday afternoon. Bob came over and gave me a hug. Frances came running and told me she was now recruited and signing at Hollins, as she wanted to get a degree in journalism and writing, and the Hollins coach liked her as a double's player for the team. Wait until she finds out that it is almost all women there.

The debutantes still did not speak to me, but the guys gave me a high five and congratulations. Three weeks later I graduated and walked with all the honors. Bob received honors for his tremendous amount of community service for disabled, and Frances surprised everyone, when she was given an honor of most academically improved student, having gone from a 2.0 her freshman year to a 4.0 her senior year. They announced it and gave her an additional sash when she got her diploma. Because her dad and mother were not in the audience my parents came over afterwards and hugged her. Frances was raised mostly by her grandmother as her father was in prison for dealing drugs and her mother had a new family. Ken and Barbara, they wanted to make her feel just as welcome as I was and took pictures of the two of us, she has been such a good friend. We both cried when we realized we were not going to be together anymore.

Frances graduated from Hollins with honors and writes a political blog for the Richmond Times today. She is still adored by the men, but the ring on her finger last month and the swelling belly I saw last month I know that she will be a mother next year in the first few months.

So, this is the story of my brief recruiting I sent an e-mail to Randy. A week later I got a simple congratulations back. It was over.

Goodbye to Radford and hello Farmville. Grandmother Miller for Sunday dinners.

Chapter 12

Mixed Doubles Second Round

On the sixth day of the US Open, I am still in the tournament. I woke-up at 07:30 and ran e-mails for a while until breakfast was coming. Today was an interesting day, nothing to do early this morning. I called up my mother and said, "mom, can we do some shopping this morning? I really want to get a nice dress or two, I'm tired of just wearing tennis stuff and at the end of the tournament would like to have a real date with my fiancé."

Mom said she would like to do something now that dad was on his way back to Virginia. She came over to my suite for breakfast, ordered room service and told them to deliver to my room. I was not going to deviate from my morning routine, it had worked so far. Yes, athletes are superstitious. Mom got to the room just as my morning breakfast was delivered, hers would come shortly.

I closed my laptop, and then had breakfast with my mom, we had hardly had one the last few years. She wanted to talk about wedding plans, and we talked about when, and we decided it would be mid-July, after Wimbledon. Then the location, was something that we wanted to talk about. Where, and I was thinking a Manhattan wedding, and my mother said no way. We then thought about Larry's family near DC, and ours in Blacksburg and Radford. Then we discussed an alternative, since you went to Longwood, and Grandmother Miller still lives there, what about a compromise that is closer to the DC area, our Episcopal church in Farmville. I thought about it, "said it is a possibility, but don't you think we should do it in our home of Radford."

Barbara said, "the witches and nasty women who shunned you and me for so long, I don't want to give them the money this wedding is going to provide. I want the money to go to the community that accepted us and where my family has roots for 5 generations."

I called Larry about the possible location, and when he heard what my mom said about Radford, and about Farmville, he agreed that this was a nice compromise, plus it is only like 2-hour drive from his home as opposed to Radford which was almost 4 hours.

He then asked, "do you know when also?"

I screamed out, "the second Saturday after Wimbledon ends in July."

Larry's response, "so the girl that was in the minors for years now wants to plan her schedule around the biggest tournament in the world. I think that will be a great time, but can you at least call my mother about the details before you finalize them?"

Larry's mom had met me a few times and I had her number on my cell. I dialed her number even though it was 8 AM on a Saturday morning. I put it on speaker so my mom could also be on the call.

"Hi Jean, Lilly and my mom Barbara are calling you to discuss our initial thoughts for the wedding. We know that Radford is like 4 hours away from your house in DC, so we are thinking a compromise. Not Manhattan, although I understand my agent would love it here, we were thinking about my mom's hometown of Farmville. The church that her family has gone to for over 100 years, I'm sure we can get it through my grandmother who is a church elder, even if someone has a Saturday night, we will be able to get it earlier in the day and then have the reception at Longwood University, they have a nice spot that I am thinking of. I would think I have some friends there that can help us out."

Jean simply responded, "that makes sense, and we were thinking about it based on your lives being away from Manhattan makes sense for the wedding, and from what Larry tells me about your life growing up, I would not want to honor the city either."

We also want a summer wedding, it will be probably July 20th, after Wimbledon, and we want it indoors, nobody wants a 90-degree heat outdoor wedding.

The only thing that Jean asked, since we are methodist, wondering can we have part of the wedding by our minister? I thought about that for a moment and said what a great thing to do.

"Jean asked how many bridesmaids you are expecting?" Well, I have one brother Larry was talking about his brother Brian as best man, so I am thinking three to four at this point.

Agreed, was all we heard, Lilly welcome to the bigger family, Barbara I want to thank you for the girl you have raised, she is such a sweet girl. We will get together to talk about other things as we go, Lilly will be travelling a lot this Fall, so we may have to do a lot of the planning. The children will probably be very tall, Lilly is taller than me, and Larry is about 6'2".

I reminded them they were a little ahead of themselves and said thank you. Jean simply responded go and we will see you before you go to Asia. Larry says you have been invited and the money is good.

The wedding plans were started.

We had three hours to shop and with an Uber ordered we went to several stores including the original Macy's, Bloomingdales, and Prada because I needed some very fancy shoes. After spending a lot of money, I had 3 long dresses, 2 skirts and 2 blouses, all on sale at Bloomingdales. I spent $750, on 2 pairs of shoes, "On Sale", that was insane one would be for my wedding weekend, and the other was to be for the travel in Asia.

We had to rush back because I needed to get everything together for leaving by 2 PM for the tournament. It was time to get back to tennis player. Future bride had spent over $1500 of her prize money.

Mom went back to her room to check on dad and Dea. I rushed to get on my tennis gear and pack my tennis bag with all fresh stuff. I called Paul and he said the Uber is coming at 2:30 so get your ass in gear. I ran to the elevator and met him just as the Uber pulled up.

Barbara here, I have the responsibility of using the iPad for the match today, but here is what I found out by talking to Ken. Ken said his mother was not very well and may have had a stroke, but she was able to talk and communicate, she just said her legs felt very heavy and that she thought she had a headache. Of course, she wanted to go home, but Ken demanded that she stay. He was going to stay at the family house. He asked me not to say anything to Lilly so she could concentrate on her matches. Ken had flown directly to Richmond, and then drove to the hospital.

Lilly and Paul were at the US Open, but I did not leave until 4 PM, for the match now scheduled at 5:30 PM on court 16. James was leaving at the same time picking up Larry along the way. Only the three of us plus Paul in the box this afternoon for the match.

Lilly and Paul did a light warm-up at 3 PM, and then went to the players area. James, Larry, and I went to the court and as soon as the previous match was over, we started to go down to the court 16.

At 5:25, the previous match was over and at 5:30 the introductions began. Our final match this evening is a mixed doubles match between the wild cards Lilly Jarman and Mike Finley, representing South Korea and Great Britain. Their opponents this afternoon is the 4 seeds Beatrice Berg, of the Netherlands and her partner Johan Smythe of South Africa. Our number 4 seeds were semi-finalist at the Australian open and Wimbledon tournaments. The bowl was only about ¼ full as matches on the show courts were still going on.

The other team won the toss and chose to serve. I will tell you that I am not as good in reporting as others so you will have to live with the results. Johan was a very tall guy 37 years-old and about 6'7" so they had a big server. As good as a server he was he was not very good returning, so all the players appeared to have weaknesses and strengths and the points did not take long, the set went to a tiebreak. Beatrice is almost 6 feet tall herself and looks like she is strong. The strategy appeared to use their power against them wide easy serves by our team finishing at the net. At 6-all in the tiebreaker, Lilly served a wide shot to Beatrice, and she tried to hit it down the line, but was about 3 inches wide. Johan served a big shot to Mike who managed to hit the ball back while Beatrice slammed the ball directly at Lilly, who could simply put it in the air on the other side of the court. Johan hit the ball and Mike was waiting at the net and ended the point and the first set. (8-6).

The next set seemed to go similarly but at 5-all, Lilly was broken when Johan smashed a shot down the line that Lilly hit into the stands. Beatrice was serving for the set, and the points went back and forth until they came to the first deciding point of the match. Lilly returned the shot with a strong cross court that Beatrice hit, and Mike was waiting at the net and finished the point forcing a second tiebreaker. Again, the tiebreaker went in a pattern with the men holding both serves and the women only holding when they hit to the other woman. This time the tiebreaker went to 9-all before anything happened, and with Johnan serving he thought he had an ace, but it was called a let. His next point he went wide, and Mike was anticipating it and hit a winning forehand to the double's alley. Lilly then was up to serve, and with her slice first serve, put Mike in perfect position to take the ball at the net, which he did, but Johan managed to get the ball back. Lilly came running in and hit a slice down the line and Johan simply could not get to it. Set and match to Mike and Lilly, quite an upset at the time., and another $5000, for each player.

Lilly here, I have iPad back from my mom. With a handshake and a hug, we ended the match. I had to text John, that we made an upset and were going to be in the quarterfinals on Monday against the five seeds. I suspect it would be on Grandstand as the juniors started taking the other courts on the grounds. I also texted Allison and my dad that we had won.

By the time the match was over it was almost 7 PM and after taking a shower it was 7:30. We went out to dinner at Parkside Restaurant that was recommended to us within a few blocks of the facility. Mom took her phone out and went to text dad that Mixed quarterfinals will be early Monday probably around noon, on Grandstand.

Mom said," dad says congratulations on the win, and hopeful for the second week."

I started laughing, wow second week of a major, I was just hoping to qualify.

Larry and James left for the subway to take them downtown, mom and I left to go back to the hotel. I knew Paul wanted to meet me at ten PM, to discuss the strategy against the 2 Seed Mariana Alexandrova, from Russia. The schedule says the match is second on Armstrong, so only going to be like ten thousand people possibly at the match. I also must tell him my fuel tank is getting empty, between 6 singles matches and 2 doubles matches, getting engaged and all the other distractions' I was so tired I was not sure how we were going to keep it together anyway. I knew that Maria is a huge server and had a big shot with forehands just under 80 miles per hour. Mine were barely 72, and I thought I hit big. She has a serve that averages between 115, and 120, my maximum was about 116, so on paper everything I do she can do better, and she is 22 and I am just turning 29. The strategy session with Paul is going to be fun.

I called Larry to just to make sure that James and he had made it back and just because I wanted to make sure that my fiancé was the last person I spoke with tonight. Well other than my coach talking strategy.

At 10:00, Paul came in and started with the schedule. "We are number 2 on Arthur Ashe after a men's doubles match. The program says start no earlier than 2 PM, so expect that warm-ups will be at 01:50. We will warm-up at 10:30, for about 20 minutes, I suspect you are getting tired with all the matches you have been playing. Talk about a tough match, this is going to be it. The only weakness I see with Mariana is a lack of patience. She has a big serve, is tall and can get into the corners very well. She has won doubles titles, and that mean she has an effective if nor beautiful volley game. The only way I can think of winning this match is to serve at her body, have long points, and somehow hope she is off her game. She has won a grand slam and been a finalist at Wimbledon, you need to just somehow shake her up a bit and if we can steal a set then you never know what else can happen."

"I asked him what she would think about me", and his comment was that she would say that your run is about over, you have had an easy run mostly with clay courters, and you have never been on this stage and will be awe struck. I really could not argue with that assessment and really hoped he was going to say sure we have a way to do this and here it is.

Paul finished, "the only assessment that made sense was that maybe she will be overconfident, and we have a chance." Paul told me next that he has a way for him to join the Asian tour after this. What he will do is resign from the club as soon as we get back and provide 2 weeks' notice. Then he will be with me until after the Asian swing season ends. Once that happens, he is going to take the job in Hilton Head, to help push the academy back to the lead academy in the USA. This will mean travelling to tournaments recruiting juniors along with coaching. Coastal Carolina has also asked if he can come up once a week to assist in coaching, a long drive but he loves college coaching, and they are division 1. Paul also asked if I would attend his wedding in ten days as one of the witnesses at the circuit court judges chamber."

I accepted and said, "I want to make sure that you will attend my wedding next July in Farmville. I am assuming your wife can travel by that time or you will be allowed to travel to Longwood. With tears in my eyes, I said let's go out and try to win this for all those that never had the opportunity. Hey if nothing else, I can say I played a major grand slam winner in the US Open. Nobody will ever believe me twenty years from now."

Paul got ready to leave the room and put his arm around me, "let's go out and have some fun."

The day was just about done, my head was spinning thinking about my Longwood University teammates might be saying, wonder if any of them will attend my wedding, we weren't great, but we did get a team championship my senior year. I know the captain Lucy Swisher, will be watching me and said I told you she was good. I had not heard from anyone lately, but I would like to reach out to Coach Wilson, he is now the head coach at Florida State.

Now to ponder playing the number 2 player in the world, how the hell do you beat a machine if she is doing well? I guess you hope she needs some oil. Turning off and going to bed everything is off. I looked at my ring and thought of Dea, she was such a great force for my life.

Chapter 13

The First College Years

Now that High School was over and I had signed with Longwood, it was time to initiate the next chapter of my life. After walking at Radford HS as a National Honor Society and the word that I had been given a major scholarship to Longwood even a few of the debutantes congratulated me. My regrets were mostly that Frances, Bob, and I would not be together. Frances at Hollins, me at Longwood, and apparently Bob did not want to tell us where he was going, but I heard later NC State. He never said publicly. I guess he was ready to move on and did not want everyone to fuss over him I did not see much of him that summer, but I guess that could be expected, we had helped each other out for so long and we both felt it was time to expand our horizons. Yet, no matter what he does, where he goes, he will always be a true friend of mine. He only saw me as a friend and we really enjoyed each other's company, nothing sexual, but just so completely free to be ourselves with each other with no judgement. As I think about it Bob and Larry have some of the same qualities, it may be interesting if Bob gets to the wedding, do I introduce him as my high school sweetheart, or simply my best friend.

Since I was already signed, sealed, and delivered to Longwood, I really did not need to play USTA anymore as a junior. Instead, I played the open tournament at Hollins college. The draw had 16 women in the draw that looked like many my age, to a few women in their forties.

Since I did not have an adult ranking the poor number 2 seed had to play me, in the first round. After a 6-2, and 6-2 win, she said where are you going to school? I told her that I was a late signee and was going to play at Longwood. She said, I played at Virginia Tech, you should have been signed by one of the ACC teams, man you can serve and hit hard. The quarter finals, I got the honor of playing the number 6 player at Virginia tech, and dispatched her 7-5, and 6-2, on Saturday. I stayed with Dea on Saturday night and got ready for 2 more matches on Sunday if I won the semi-finals in the morning. The first match was against the 3 seed, the number 2 player at James Madison, she was an upcoming senior. The match was even but I managed to break and hold to take the first set 7-5. The second set went my way early and held on to win it 6-3 and get my way to the finals. My opponent, Melissa Andreov, from Bulgaria, who is number two at Virginia Tech, and the number 1 seed from the tournament. Melissa had won most of her matches the previous year at Virginia Tech, and I looked her up, probably the number 1 player this season as she was a rising junior. She had won all her matches easily. With a crowd of about 50 watching us, we played a very hot and long match, I won the first set 7-6, in a tiebreak. Melissa won easily the second set 6-1, and while I held on to make it 4-all in the final set, I proceeded to lose the final two games. I forgot that this was a prize money tournament and for making the finals, I had won $275, it was the first prize money I would make, I was given the NCAA form so I could apply the winnings toward my training expenses. I had my picture taken with the champion.

Melissa asked me, "why Virginia Tech had not recruited me given that you were from the area."

"I said they never approached me I guess I did not have the national ratings."

"She said to me do your freshman year at Longwood, and call me about being a transfer next year, you have a very good game, just need to be with better players to get to that next level."

I heard that Melissa did well in the minor leagues in Europe and then went to medical school and gave up tennis.

I played one additional tennis tournament in Richmond, and made it to the semi-finals and won $100, for making it there.

That was my tennis competition for the summer, I mostly was teaching and hitting at Radford. I made enough money over the summer teaching group lessons and a few private lessons, that I had enough money to buy a used Chevy Malibu, not the one I have today but it was a purple car and was dependable transportation. The great thing about the malibu, which I named Marvin, was I could get everything for my dorm in one trip.

James continued to impress people and made the finals of an 18 and under national event in the 200 IM. Not bad for a 16-year-old that nobody had ever heard of. Obviously, he was the number 1 swimmer at Radford for his entire career. While he finished last in the finals, we were all proud of him, and that began his recruiting a bit earlier than mine. My little brother was now like 6'1" and still growing, he would end up 6'3" when it was all over, muscular, and smart. The debutantes wanted him, but we had trained him well, he was not going to let one of them near him. Frances had a younger sister, Michelle, and I think my brother and her had gone on a few dates. Unlike Frances, Michelle was nearly 5'5", and really a beauty with dark hair and blue eyes. Like Frances, with a head on her shoulder, she may like guys, but she was not going to be a tramp like some of the debutantes, we were all fine with James dating her. With his travels and school schedule though these were going to be very few.

I thought I was going to go to school at Longwood by myself, but what I thought apparently did not happen. With Mom and me in the Malibu, and dad and James with us in another car, we all went to Longwood on the last Saturday in August. They would stay with my grandmother, who I had been assured would make sure that I had a place and a person to support her.

The three-tennis freshman were assigned the same dorm, Register Hall, along with Tiffany Junker, a returning sophomore on the tennis team were assigned a quad set-up. Normally freshmen are not allowed cars on campus, but because I was an athlete, I had an exception. Marvin the car and I were the first of the four to check in. Amber Zag was the next to come here. She was from Taiwan and was already 20 years old. Amber had been in the country training in Florida and flew into Richmond. The school met her at the airport and brought her to Longwood. The final freshman, Janice Williams, was from Britain, and flew to Dulles airport and Coach Wilson drove there and they came in at about 10 PM. Tiffany would not come in until later, Wednesday just before classes began. I had thought we would have come in earlier, but coach said since our conference was spring that we would have practices only when the NCAA allowed it, he had assumed we would train all the way until we got there. Funny thing is we started to train on our own, as a team without the coach for the first week. The family left on Sunday after we all went to Granny Miller's house. Mom was crying all the way to the car as they left to go back to Radford.

Freshman Year:

Longwood has about 4500 students of which a little over 3400 are undergraduate. The Freshman class is usually about 1000 students. Initially I was a general studies major, which I would later change to business marketing, the other tennis players tended to be business majors, except Janice decided to major in communications, she wanted to be a broadcaster back in England. The school was typical of this area majority of white students, but at least a quarter were minority. I identified as multiple races and Amber was like the 1% that identified as Asian. All these numbers still represented a much larger number than at Radford High School, and truthfully so many were also in athletics, that the race issue was silly. Our tennis team had 2 foreign players, 1 African American player and me who was multiple, and we realized that none of that mattered, we were the Longwood University tennis team.

The first two weeks were tryouts, it was obvious that our captain was our number 1, Lucy Swisher, she defeated everyone and had been a top 50 player in the US, but had not done well on her SAT's, so she chose Longwood. The proverbial big fish in a little pool, nobody looked like they would challenge her. Coach Wilson had a week where we went through 1 set challenge sets. I had assumed I would be like number 6, but coach had me challenge last year's number 5, Brittany Boreman, who was a senior. I dispatched her easily 6-1, and that moved me to number 5 as we only had six girls and that is what you needed to field a team. The next day, they had me challenge Amber and the set went my way 6-4. That moved me to the number 4 position. The next day, I played Tiffany Junker, last year's number 3, and the match went easy, 6-3, so now I am looking at a possible number 3 position, and that was fine with me. I was surprised on the fourth day, that I was asked to compete with Janice, she had international experience and was in the top 5 from Britain. This set went 6-6, and in the tiebreaker, I manager to get a breakpoint and won 7-6. I was very surprised that made me the number 2 player on the team, I never challenged Lucy for number 1, she was very good and experienced, and you did not want the novice as a number 1. Coach said that I would play number 2 or 3, depending on the match-up. The next week, coach worked doubles combinations, and after a week, it was funny. The two seniors played together and were going to be number 1, Tiffany and Janice were to play number 2, "Blond Team", and then number three was Amber and me, "Mutt and Jeff Team". So that was the end of the tryouts and with September ending, we were now getting ready for the season.

The tennis season goes both semesters, the fall is mostly ITF tournaments and then a couple of matches to get the season started, we must finish by a certain date in November, after that NCAA say it is a no go. That is good because it gives you 4 weeks to get ready for finals.

In my first ITF, I played the second tier and was able to make the second day of the tournament undefeated but fell twice to players with more experience. Our doubles team, Mutt, and Jeff won our lower tier flight. Nobody else made the second day. While I had a big serve, Amber was very good at the net, and after I hit a couple of people with overheads, that seemed to make us do better. Our team finished 4th out of Six teams, so we were not that impressive, but Coach Wilson said he was happy with the results.

We played Liberty University and defeated them 4-3, the deciding point won by the Mutt and Jeff team. We played UVA and lost 6-1, we were not ready for prime time, but the Mutt and Jeff team still managed to win against them, thus for the Fall season I went over 500, and our doubles team at number three went undefeated.

As far as school was concerned nothing was overly hard, I had an English class and that was my only B at midterm, the other classes were as easy as high school in my opinion.

Unlike others, I had family in the area, so when we were not travelling, I was expected to come to dinner with my grandmother. Truthfully, it was good to see her get a nice meal and for a couple of hours just be Lilly Jarman, not tennis player. On a couple of Sundays, I took one of the two other freshmen with me for a nice meal. Janice with her very British accent and Amber with her very distinct brand of English from English teachers and Chinese family.

Socially, with Randy no longer in my life, Bob gone off to college, I was on my own. I went to a social thing but absolutely had no interest in dating anyone. The other tennis players were a little more man friendly, and a few asked why I never dated. They all just said she misses a guy from high school. It was a good excuse, but they knew I was just not interested in dating and did not through that entire year. I will say the tennis team were my friends and that was all I needed. I was not the odd-looking outsider as I was in Radford, but still very protective of myself.

With the Holidays coming I went home to Radford and was able to see everyone including Bob home from NC State. John Unger who I knew from school, asked me out on a date. Funny, without the pretense of the debutantes in high school, John asked me out on a date, and while I knew nothing was going to happen, we had fun. He was an engineering major at Virginia Tech, and he said the girls here, just were not for him, he had not realized how weird they were until he left. While we did not date much over the next few years, we did keep ourselves as a line to Radford without the debutante experience.

Three weeks after coming home for the holidays I returned to school this time as a business marketing major. I thought about a science major, and it would have been impossible with all the travel and extra work, so I made the compromise. Plus a few people said with my lean and lanky look, I could do well in business. I had to laugh, a year ago, I was the lesbian that wanted to be a guy according to the debutantes.

The team started practice 2 weeks later, with our first match against George Mason in Mid-February. While George Mason won the match 4-3, it was a sign that we were going to be better than the last place finishes the previous year. The next weekend, we played Georgetown, and we defeated a major conference team for the first time in a decade, our 4-3 win was predicated on the Mutt and Jeff team, winning a tiebreaker for the doubles point, and then the three freshmen all won, with me playing number 3, Janice at number 2, and then Amber at number 5. All four points from the freshmen players. The next day we went up to Baltimore to play UMBC in Baltimore, and this time we won 5-2. I played number 2 this time and managed an easy win.

The season went competitively, and while we were last the year before in our conference, we ended the season in fourth, which allowed us to make the conference championships, because we were the last seeded team, we had to play number 1 Charleston Southern, at Charleston, SC. They had beaten us in the regular season, 6-1, I had won doubles with Amber, but the other 2 teams lost. This was one of only two singles matches that I lost at either number 2 or 3. Tiffany had upset a player in a tiebreaker serving as the third set.

This time Coach Wilson, had us prepared and flipped me to number 3 due to my lack of experience. In the doubles, our seniors upset CS and with the Mutt and Jeff team, we managed to take the doubles point. The coach at Charleston did not appear worried about it though and sent out his line-up. In singles, Charleston managed to win number 1, 4, 5, and 6. Janice managed a win, and I was leading 5-2, in the third set when Charleston clinched. Even though I had only lost 2 matches because I played number 3 about half the season, I did not receive either a first team or second team all-conference. I was listed as honorable mention all-conference. Charleston Southern obliterated Radford in the final, 4-0.

At this point I will tell you I did play number 3 against Radford at Radford. It really felt funny being rooted against in my hometown, but that did not keep me from beating a senior in her last home match 6-4 and 6-3. My parents were able to watch the match, as did Dea who was staying with my parents.

I did go out on a couple of dates and of course it was one of the tennis players, Jonathan Quick, a nice guy, a little romance between us, but nothing serious, and we parted for the summer and never dated again. He transferred to James Madison over the summer.

My grades for the year 3.8, not bad for someone that really hated to study and was travelling. Lucy continued her academic ways with a perfect 4.0, as captain she was showing the way. Lucy, I kept on saying was a senior because she graduated in May, but had only played 3 years, so she decided to come back and play the next year while she was in graduate school. Lucy had been awarded second-team all-conference and wanted a shot at number 1 the next year.

Sophomore year:

The summer was long as I chose to work at the Country Club as a junior professional. Which meant the only thing I did was be a hitting partner for the elite tennis juniors so the coaches could watch without hitting. For the camps I was responsible for attendance and making sure that everyone was accounted for at lunch and getting ready to go home. Between those two, I would also get a little practice time in myself. I played Hollins tournament and again made the finals netting another $275.00 for training costs.

James was getting ready for his senior year, and he heard from so many schools that it was funny. Frances came back and we went out on several evenings together. John Unger and I would hang out and a few nights of hand holding but nothing ever happened that summer, he was working out and was going to try to walk-on at Virginia Tech, he tried out over the spring and made the cut for the summer squad. He was hoping just to make the team he realized that as a safety he was not likely to even get on the travel team. He did tell me he suited up three times for the home games, when someone was injured but he never saw the field except for one extra point, when the team was leading 56-7, over Duke. I did not see Bob he stayed at college for the summer, and I think this may have been when he experimented with an alternate lifestyle.

Brittany Boreman had graduated from school, and Tiffany decided to leave to go back home to New Jersey. The three now sophomores agreed to stay together, and then coach asked us if we could get Kiki Sullivan to room with us, she was a lower tier player from the Netherlands. She was already 21, as a freshman and she was a shade shorter than 6 feet, so I was no longer the tallest player. We also got a Junior transfer from George Mason, she decided to transfer when the coach left for a higher division 1 opportunity. She was from Annapolis, MD, and had been a very decent player that was top 10 every year in Mid-Atlantic from age 10 to 18. Kara Thomas assumed she would be number 1 or 2, that was an assumption she would not attain. We got a second freshman who was our number 7, she had played well in the Roanoke area, never made the top ten regionally, but was a good doubles player, Susan Snider, was a nice girl about 5'8", but was not very fast. She had good volleys so ended up playing doubles every match and then we were able to rest other players to just play singles that day.

Longwood did not have a long season in the Fall, and as the newly minted full-time number 2, I played the ITF in the toughest bracket and managed to get to the quarterfinals, the same as Lucy in the other half of the bracket. In doubles the Mutt and Jeff won the tournament at the number 2 slot, yes, we went to the number 2 slot after going close to undefeated the previous year. The big schools probably were asking where the heck is Longwood University, and when did they get better. We played 2 West Virginia schools and held our own with the improved lineup, we beat Marshall 4-3, and lost to West Virginia University 4-3, they won only because they won the doubles point. It was a very successful show of our improvement.

I was asked to a couple of sororities, but with tennis and taking 18 credit hours, I simply did not have enough time to pledge, plus it felt a lot like the debutantes all over again, so I simply said thank you too busy. That did not hurt my going out though, I went up to Hollins College the week before Thanksgiving to see Frances, who set me up with a Bill Shaker, a Junior at VMI. Bill was from Kentucky and his southern accent was even worse than mine. Bill and I clicked, and we went out twice again before holiday break and both of us going home to our families. Unlike before, when Randy and I simply texted, this time we were close enough that we found a place to meet and have a date. (Staunton Virginia, about an hour away for both of us). Yes, we even stayed at a motel one Saturday evening, I won't provide any more details than that.

We did a few dates before tennis season started again. I only had 15 credit hours this semester. Our first match was also a conference match against UNC-Asheville, and to our surprise we won 6-1. They had been third in the conference the year before we almost blanked them, only Amber, playing number 6 singles was beaten. We then played Wake Forest on our way back and came close to knocking them off losing 3-4, primarily because our doubles teams were still not set at number 1 and 3. I had not dropped a set the entire season in singles, and we were undefeated at number 2 doubles. The season went on and we did not lose another conference match, and ended the season 6-0, in conference, and 13-3, overall, including 3 out of 4 victories in Myrtle Beach over Spring Break. I had only 1 loss at number 2, the entire season.

Bill asked me out for a formal dance at VMI the week before conference, and Granny Miller went out and helped me buy a dress. It was good the dance was Friday night, and then I stayed at the motel with Frances that night before we both drove back. This was a military dance and funny thing, but Bill did not have a pass to go off campus, something about being written up for telling off an instructor. He was allowed to go to the dance but was restricted to campus thereafter. Frances may have had a room with me, but she spent no time in it other than to take a shower the next morning and then leave for Hollins in the morning. The more time I spent away from Radford the more I realized that the debutantes did not represent most of the world. Most people accepted me with my Eurasian looks, and southern accent.

The conference tournament was the next week. We as number 1 seed, Charleston Southern, Radford, and Campbell made the cut. Our first round against Campbell we won 4-1, with three matches 4 through 6 incompletes. Charleston Southern also won by the same score, setting up a first for our school in a long-time showdown for conference championship. In the championship on a Saturday, the tournament which was in Charleston, SC, our team looked very tight and nervous. While we had beaten Charleston 4-3 in the regular season, they took the doubles point 2-1, and we each split our singles matches with our team winning 1,2, and 4, and the others going to Charleston Southern. Before the match Lucy was awarded a first-team all-conference and I received a second team all-conference. Apparently, they were not going to let a number 2 player make all-conference first team. Our team was crushed at the loss, and coach Wilson said look 2 years ago we were not even invited, and this year we were basically a tiebreak away from being conference championships. We had just missed out on an NCAA berth, and it really stung.

We had a banquet for the first time for the end of the season. Walker's Diner hosted the event with the seven of us plus our coach and the athletic director came to the event. The team bought Lucy a very nice bracelet with a tennis charm, as she had been our captain for the last two years. Coach Wilson was also given a present by the team, but his biggest present was a new contract by the athletic department. At the end of the presentations, Coach Wilson came over to me and said so for all of you our unknown star is our own Lilly Jarman. Lilly, you, and Amber have been invited to compete in the NCAA doubles championships in Florida next week, only a few numbers 2 teams have been invited, and you 2 are the first by Longwood in over a decade. I also want you to know that the team has selected you as our MVP this season, undefeated as number 2 doubles and only 1 loss at number 2 singles all season. I had voted for Lucy and could not believe it when much of the team had voted for me.

Coach Wilson then said "OK, quiet girl, I think it is time that you step-up here and accept your award."

I was asked to talk, not very good at public speaking, and Coach Wilson encouraged me to talk after reminding me this was a friendly group.

I stepped up and said, "thank you to the girls on the team. We had a good season and I think we will continue to improve and next year win that additional tiebreak. I also thanked Lucy for being our captain for the last 2 years. I then concluded by saying I guess the other schools that did not want me might be starting to regret it.

Coach laughed, "I bet they are."

A picture of all three of us Coach Wilson, Lucy and I were taken by the athletic director, and posted in our school newspaper the next week. I will say that Amber and I lost in the first round of the double's tournament, but it was a great experience for both of us. One week later, school had ended, and I had a 3.7 GPA, and a cumulative 3.75, not bad. We thought that we would not see Lucy again, but we would find out that she was our brand-new assistant coach, an unpaid position that she had as part of her graduate studies scholarship.

I would go to see Bill at VMI as it was on my way home. We had a date and a romantic evening before I had to go back to Radford. For some reason, I applied for a position at Radford as a coach for the summer and they had turned me down, so I went back to the country club to teach juniors and work-out with the other coaches. I was later told that Radford would not support me because I had turned them down in favor of Longwood and they were not going to help me out financially. So funny how history and the truth had so changed. They had told me to be a walk-on, and maybe I could play number 6.

I did not compete in any tournaments that summer, no time, and frankly after the hard season the last year I wanted to get my body fully healed. I had a nagging thigh injury that finally healed by the end of July. I was doing a lot of weight work and by the time school started I had added nearly 10 pounds of weight mostly in my arms and legs. As far as seeing Bill, I did get up to VMI while he was doing summer school for a couple of dates, I am not sure we were getting serious but at least it was fun having another guy to be with and liked me for being me.

Junior Year:

The team was going to be so different this year, Lucy was no longer on the team, but we would hit with her as an assistant coach this year. This also left a void in the captaincy and the top position. Kara Thomas was frustrated that she had not beat me out for number 2 and decided to leave for another school, her third in three years. We had two positions in the top to replace and in came 2 more foreign players to our mix. Alexandra Dominguez, from Mexico City, and Anna Dimitrov, from Bulgaria. Both were excellent players that were 20-year-old as freshmen. Then came the vote for captain, coach Wilson had nominated Janice Williams and others had nominated Amber Zang, both juniors and would be likely a two-year captain.

Coach Wilson pulled me aside and said, "look Lilly, I could have nominated you also, but you are going to have your hands full, I have not told the others but unless someone really impresses me, you are going to be my number 1."

I shook my head isn't that the position you want the captain to be, and just said no, you have more talent than anyone here, but I don't want to put double pressure on you. The team voted Janice as our new captain even though she had dropped down to number 4, due to the increased competition.

With this improved team I would be the only American in the top 6, Susan Snider was still our number 7, and this meant she was our spare for lesser teams to rest players.

Number 1: Me
Number 2: Kiki Sullivan upset others.
Number 3: Anna Dimitrov
Number 4: Janice Willaims
Number 5: Alexandra Zhang
Number 6: Amber Zhang,

This team had no seniors, three juniors, two sophomores, and 2 freshmen. All seven were as good as any team in the conference. Maybe some of the better conferences with so many languages, from Spanish, Bulgarian, Chinese, Dutch, and British English.

Because I was going to play number 1 for the first time, I was getting a lot of extra playing time with Lucy and coach Wilson, when he introduced to me for the first time to serve and volley. His coaching was with my speed and stride, I could shake things up by using this occasionally, scaring the big hitters they will have no idea what hit them.

The Fall season consisted of the ITF regional championships this year at UVA, and we were thrown in with all the Virginia teams this time plus WVU. I was included in the topflight with 16 tennis players and unseeded. I then proceeded to knock off the number 1, from WVU, 4 seed for the tournament 6-4 and 6-3. In the quarterfinals, I defeated the number 2 from Virginia, and that took more than 2 hours. The next day, I lost to the number 1 at UVA, who was ranked as the 5th best player in all the NCAA. She had beaten me 7-6 and 7-5, and then went on to win the championship.

The coach from UVA then came over to me and asked where I had played my tennis, when I told him Radford VA, he just shook his head, how the hell did my assistants miss a local kid with this much talent. Yes, I got a little swelled head. I played with Amber for the last time in the doubles bracket at number 2, where we upset the UVA number 2 team to win the second level bracket and as a team Longwood ended up third overall, beating WVU and VA Tech, and just about taking out Richmond.

In the 2 matches we played Coach Wilson jumped up our competition, we played Richmond, and beat them 4-3, then beat Old Dominion 5-2. I went undefeated in these 2 matches, but doubles split at number 1 with Anna as my doubles partner. Amber was playing number 3 with Susan and doing quite well, our number 2 team usually was Kiki and Janice. Alexandra was usually the odd one out and then won all her singles matches so the combinations were doing well.

Coach Wilson came to me after our last match," I don't know how to tell you this Lilly Jarman, look at the national rankings, you are 40th in the NCAA's. I want this to sink in that I promised you would develop with me as your coach I am so proud of you. This is early but you can't hide anymore, nobody is going to play with their line-up you are going to get everyone's best."

Bill and I were unable to get together with his obligations in his senior year and my obligations for the team until November, when my season was over, and he was able to get off for a weekend. The date went well but you could tell something was off, finally he looked at me, and said I am nervous about going to the Army right after I graduate. The reality of what was next, was hitting him, and mostly we just talked about how we could keep our relationship going with him being away. Very little romance went on that night just a lot of talking.

I must stop here. I want to brag about my nationally ranked brother, (James) his first NCAA match he set a team record in the 200 IM and qualified for the NCAA's. He told me his school made qualifying time for the 400 free relay; he was the only freshman on the relay. He called me that weekend and said I am coming home for Thanksgiving, and I want to see my big sister I said I was planning to go home to Radford for a couple days, and then had finals coming up within 10 days. James had travelled a lot of last summer now that he was a top 25 in the country and had all sort of people trying to recruit him. Still don't know why he stayed near Virginia, he could have gone to Texas, a really great team.

The holidays were at our house, the K brothers all came in with Dea, and then off to the Millers, so many people in our extended family. No time for Bill, but quite a few questions about him from my mother and Dea. Dea was like, you may not want to live the military wife life, so keep that in mind before you commit to this boy. 5 Months later when he asked me to marry him, I thought about it and ended the relationship, I was not quitting school to be a camp wife. Bill wanted me to marry him, and asked me right before his graduation, and I said no I will not commit to leaving school and following you at this point. Basically, at that point it was over as he was mad because it was a big tradition among the VMI guys to get engaged right as school ended. I just had no desire to do this and was not sure I was that into him enough to marry him at that point I was just 21, and I was not like the debutantes not here just to have babies and give up the career.

Three weeks later we returned to school for the start of the season. We all had made great grades, and everyone had returned so this was going to be an interesting season. The pre-season rankings for the conference came out and we were a consensus number 1, so much better than my first year. Our first weekend of tournaments was going to be a North Carolina swing of three matches. We upset nationally ranked

Wake Forest, 4-3, despite losing the doubles point. We lost to Duke who was top ten in the country 5-2, and then beat North Carolina 5-2. The following week the national rankings came out and after going 2-1 I was now ranked 35th in the country and the team was rated 45th, our first ever top 50. The team went down to Hilton Head and won all three of our matches, University of South Carolina, University of Illinois, and then University of Kentucky. The matches were 5-2, 4-3, and 5-2, nobody would have expected it. When the next national ranking came out, I was now number 30 and the team was down to 40th, this was going to be an interesting season for conference. Since we had to play Charleston Southern in Charleston, SC, our coach also arranged for us to play College of Charleston, so we could justify the expense. We dispatched our main rival 5-2, and then the next day we beat College of Charleston 4-3, I had a rare loss I was tired I had a three setter the night before and lost this one in a tiebreak 10-7. I slept on the van the whole way back to Longwood. The next weekend we played UNC-Asheville winning it 6-1, our number 6 match we decided to default as two girls had small injuries and they were playing Radford on Saturday evening.

I was very hesitant about playing Radford, dad said they had a really good player that had come from India, (Tamil Punjab) and they basically had me out as a traitor leaving Radford for Longwood. Such a lie, yes you invited me to walk-on and maybe be the number 6. Now that I was coming in as the number 1 player from Longwood, and we were the team to beat in the conference it was not going to be a fun match. At least Mom, Dad and Dea were there for me.

In doubles, we changed things up for this match, I was partnered with Janice at number 1, Kiki and Anna at number 2 and Susan and Amber at number 3. We knew that Alexandra had been nursing an ankle strain, so this let her do more warm-up on the out courts. The doubles point came down to number 1 and needed to go to a tiebreak with an audience of about 75 watching, it was a pro-Radford group, but much to their disappointment, our team won 7-5 in the tiebreak, when Janice hit a forehand down the line that Tamil could not handle. Because the number 1 players had played later than any of the other teams, we were sent out after about a ten-minute rest last of the courts on. We were on the main court, I can guarantee that I had played on these courts a lot more than Tamil, but after warming-up I could see she was very accomplished. The match had already been decided when we got to the third set, Tamil won the first 7-5, and I had won the second 6-4, the match was now in the third hour, when we got to the tiebreak to decide the match between us. I took a quick lead on serve 2-1, and the match went to 6-all. I double faulted on my next serve and handed Tamil a match point that she took served to me and all I could do was to hit it into the net. The team had won 5-2, but I had lost a conference match for the first time as the number 1 player. The Radford crowd was routing heavily against me, I felt like the little girl all over again. I hate Radford, and I let this get to me, I swore after that I would never let the thought of the debutantes impact me again. Coach Wilson said to shake this off, you just found out that many teams have a really good number 1, it is depth that will get our team through.

The next week because of the loss, I dropped back to 45 in singles, but the team was marching on to now 39th, people were starting to take notice of the little school in the farm area of Virginia.

We had four more matches before the conference tournament, we won all of them either 6-1 or 5-2, some of the 6-1's is because we decided to rest a player.

The week after was a major dance at VMI, Bill and I were attending Frances did not go this time from Hollins, she had broken up with her date several months ago. I had a nice rose-colored dress and with heals was as tall as Bill. He pulled me aside and said after the dance is over, we need to speak.

It was at a bar, that he got on his knee and proposed to marry me. It was also at the same restaurant that I said no, I am going to complete my junior and senior years at Longwood, I am not going to follow you to OCS, and then be a camp wife, and by myself when you go overseas.

He felt insulted and said to me, "if you don't want to marry me, then we are done."

I stood up, got in my Malibu, and drove back to Longwood that night. When I got back to the room, Janice looked at me crying and said, "it's better for you to say goodbye now, you are not the camp following type. You may have the nice southern accent, but you are independent and given your grades what was he thinking, good for him and did not think anything about you. Cry tonight, but give me a hug, and I will get some coffee and we will talk a while."

We talked until 4 AM, when I finally fell asleep. I never thought of Bill again, just told my mother that it was over and then called Dea around noon repeating it. Dea said, "I told you need a better guy than your little soldier boy." Ok, Larry, I guess you got Dea's approval, so you must have something going for you.

After a couple of days of depression, I had to get ready for our conference tournament. This year Radford was host, so it would be great and horrible at the same time. We were playing them in the first semi-final as they slipped in as the 4 seed, while we were the number 1 seed. UNC Asheville was the number 3 seed and playing Charleston Southern. We were first up and this time we had the top line-up with everyone now healthy. Our doubles line-up included Susan and Amber at number 3, we had lost at number 2, and they clinched the doubles point. So, with a 1-0 lead and being used to the boos now, I went out on the court. This is where Coach Wilson said I want you to take on the serve and volley and see if she can handle it. I won the serve and proceeded to hit big serves and come in right behind them and finish the point 4 points all mine for the first game. In the changeover you could see Tamil talking to her coach trying to figure out how to counter the charging rhino at the net. 4 Serves and 4 points later I had broken Tamil, and the first set went quickly with me winning the set 6-1. The crowd was not happy and let me know it. The second set I was told to play traditional, and it was a solid set with it getting to 5-5, before I got my first break point. I decided to charge the net for the first time so after my return went in the corner, I was waiting at the net for the winner. Now up 6-5, for the first time, I simply hit the serves out wide and waited at the net each time, five points later, the set and the match were completed. I raised both of my hands up in the air and screamed at the top of my lungs "Yes". All the years of abuse by the debutantes and their parents came out. What I did not know that was the 4th and decisive point for the match we won 4-1, and the other matches simply were told to stop.

UNC Asheville had pulled and upset and won a 4-3 decision over Charleston Southern. The finals were scheduled at 4 PM, James was down for the finals as were both of my grandmothers and my parents. Somehow Bob and Frances were there and both yelling, show them Lilly. I started to tear-up as I thought about the taunts and the isolation, I was subject to as a kid.

This time our team did not fail, we won the doubles point easily and then proceeded to win at number 3,4, and 5. I was 2 points away but that did not matter, they just yelled at me, we are conference champions. The team came together on Kiki's court, and we all started screaming and crying. After the team was awarded the championship trophy, the other awards were announced. Player and Freshman of the year went to Tamil Punjab. Coach Wilson was named as coach of the year, and Kiki and I were added to the first team all-conference. Anna and Janice made second team and honorable mention. Coach came over to me and eased my pain you know you should have been the MVP, and your performance was the best this year and you are 12 positions ahead of Tamil. This was a political decision; they don't feel we belong as the champion.

One day later the latest rankings came out I was listed at 30th in the country, which meant, that I was invited to play the singles tournament after the team play was over. As winners of the conference our team gathered for our first NCAA selection show: Our region was the UVA section, we got the honor of playing the number 2 team in the country, the other 2 teams were UMBC and Old Dominion. I will tell you it did not take long for UVA with the second and tenth best players in the country to knock us off. At least I did not finish my match against them, so it was not a loss. I'm, not sure that the team was upset, it was the last week of May and school ended 2 days before the NCAA's. I had to fly to Georgia in the next week with Coach Wilson to play the NCAA's. I was like one of three from small conferences everyone else was from major conferences. My reward for being from the small conference was playing the number 4 seed, from University of Texas,

Lauren Muster, her team had just finished playing the quarterfinals where they had lost, but they had played a lot more matches that we had. I don't know if it was the style of play, or that she was tired, but she ended up losing to me 6-4, and 6-3, a big upset apparently. I did not have that much luck against the Notre Dame number 1, she beat me in three sets for my first experience at this level.

Coach came over to me and said, "give me one more year Lilly Jarman, and you will be here for the final weekend, and then we can watch you play in the pros."

I thought he was kidding, but he sent me an e-mail of what we were going to improve for the next year.

Because school was out by the time we got back from the NCAA's, we just had a dinner at the Walker's Diner where Coach Wilson announced the awards for the team. I received MVP for the team, and thanks coach for taking a chance on me when others did not. He just reminded me you better come back next year, Virginia would love you, but we want you more. Come back and lead us to another NCAA bid before you go professional. Amber was our academic athlete and we all had gotten together to get Coach Wilson a gift. He was nominated for NCAA coach of the year but that went to the Stanford coach who won the NCAA championships. Our dessert was heavily discounted by the Diner and the local paper came to take the picture of the team all dressed up.

I had hoped to go back to Radford but again they turned me down for a summer position, so I ended up going to summer school staying with granny Miller and working part-time at the school teaching and taking lessons. I never heard from Bill again, and quite frankly that was ok. Frances was still at Hollins, and she had been playing number 6 at the school and enjoying the area. I promised to visit her when I played the tournament and she said I could stay with her at her apartment, and asked should I fix you up for a date. I laughed; I don't think so the last one wanted me to marry him.

It was only after this year, that I realized I was able to play at or near the level of these players. I did not need a man that wanted to control my life, and I was really doing well academically, only Amber was doing better than I was, so at least I did not have to worry about graduation, nor any academic athlete awards, Amber had that tied up. Wow from unwanted to now in the tournament, it was an amazing ride. The next year was going to open a lot of eyes, but that is a different story.

Chapter 14

The Fourth Round

With a knock on the door, I woke-up to a breakfast from Elijah's Bagels waiting for me. A note was enclosed saying Lilly Jarman go out there and compete today, we appreciate you. I opened my laptop and looked for times from Paul, he said we are number 2 on Armstrong Stadium, men's match before us starting at noon, could be anywhere from 2 PM to 3 PM, for us to be called, so let's do warm-up at 11:15, for up to 30 minutes. We can stay at the players' lounge after we get some food and rehydrate.

I received texts from dad that he will be watching from Virginia with Dea. Mom will be getting to the grounds after church, and probably 2 PM. James said he and Larry are getting there around 1 PM and will be at the box.

I read the e-mails from John and Allison saying they are truly grateful for our new relationships and expect financial support for the next year to be overwhelming. John said you will be able to take this money and have a great life no matter what you want to do. When you get married, Lacoste is going to provide a French designer for your wedding dress, just a thank you from the company. I just laughed, oh my next July I am getting married. John's Memorial Episcopal Church will be so decked out and with the friends coming from DC and the Northeast, Paul and family from Charleston, and a few other crazy things the city will never be the same. Longwood is finding a suitable hall for us to have the reception. I called Lucy and although she is still single, she has a date coming with her for the wedding. Amber says she is going to try to find a way to get there from Taiwan and Janice said no way she will miss this, so the Longwood contingent will be there. Wait until they see that the minister is a woman, I bet that will be different. I think the only ones I would invite from Radford would be Frances and Bob, but mom and dad may have some other ideas, with neighbors surely none of the debutantes will be invited.

Back to the present and not the future, I am getting with Paul down the lobby in 2 hours and we will take an Uber to the stadium. I had an idea that will get me in a lot of trouble, I am going to go over to the stands and get a passionate kiss from Larry before the match begins, that should shake things up a little. ESPN may have a little fun with this.

The truth of the matter my body is so slow this morning I had to drink coffee. 8 matches in the less than 2 weeks, in a typical month I might play 5, I don't know how much is left in the tank. I am playing the most accomplished player I have ever viewed, in a stadium I have only visited as a fan, this is going to be a hell of a day.

I finished breakfast and started to look at more e-mails, decided that was enough and closed the PC and packed for the day. I did call mom and check on her as this was going to be another long day. She was doing fine, and said dad was down with Dea, she was doing better than yesterday.

I tried to relax by looking at a movie while I packed, 3 sets of tennis clothes, 4 racquets, 10 tennis wrist bands, and two pairs of shoes. Packed my water bottle with Gatorade and ready to go.

At 10:30, I left for the lobby. Paul like always was there ready to go, he put his arm around me, "Lilly Jarman, let's have some fun today. He then said, we are lucky, won't be as much coverage on us as the big matches on Ashe. Just so you know we will be expecting about 8,000 to 10,000 people in the stadium at the time of our match. Don't let the noise bother you, it is just another tennis match. Yeah, and by the way you are playing a grand slam champion instead of the normal top 250 we normally play, she is faster, hits harder and is crazy dedicated to winning. I would say obsessed, and if you can stay with her the crowd will turn to your favor, so let's stay with her and have a lot of fun. No matter what happens today, it has been one hell of a ride. Who would have thought a month ago that we would be here?"

At 10:45, the Uber came, and we were on our way. We got there just in time to make our half of the court and Paul had me do a light work this morning knowing I had played 8 matches already here so we just hit. The practice went well but I have to say it felt like I was still sluggish, I guess I really was starting to feel the total matches on my body.

Practice went well, and afterwards, I heard a request from a tennis fan, Lilly can I have your autograph on this tennis ball. I asked her name, and she was from Buffalo, NY and her name was also Lilly. I signed the ball Lilly Jarman, and then added athletic and feminine. I added what she asked, she said you have no idea what that tag line from your grandmother means to a lot of us, it is ok to be athletic and we can still be feminine. I signed three more balls before going to the players area, taking a quick shower, and then got into the match gear. Paul changed his sweaty t-shirt for a Lacoste polo style shirt, we need to keep the sponsor happy.

I received texts from the core group. All of them were on-time, and then got one from dad saying that he and Dea will be watching from the hospital, Dea is proud of you.

Lunch at the players' lounge, I ate a sandwich with some pasta, and we started hydrating, so many fluids, someday I will be glad when I don't have to drink a couple of gallons per day. Paul said our strategy is to hit a baseline game for about four games, if we are 2-2, or better than you get to surprise her and mix in some serve and volley. I called Larry and told him to be at the first row today, wanted him as the thing I saw when I was getting a little frustrated. The reality is I wanted to be able to give him a kiss before the match.

I noticed at the locker room that a ton of the players had left already as we entered the beginning of the second week. From 128 in singles, they were down to 16 men's and women. The doubles were similar as 2 rounds had been completed taking it down from 64 teams to 16 teams left or 32 players. The mixed had started at 32, and was now down to

16 people, and some of the people left were in multiple events like my doubles partner. The juniors had started but they really don't get the privileges that the touring professionals get.

It was now 12:30 and the match on Armstrong had begun, I just started reading a book online to get my head out of the match that was coming. I also read the notes for the match that Paul had for us. He went out to talk to his fiancé about the next few weeks. The plan was that he would get married on the second Friday after we got back, I would be one of his witnesses. He will be great back home, and we should have fun going through the Asian swing.

At 2:30 they indicated that they were heading for a fourth set ahead of us, so went over to the bike and went on it for about ten minutes. At 3 PM, they sent us the 15-minute notice that the match was going in to a fourth set tiebreaker ahead of us. Finally at 3: 15, we got a 5-minute notice, and it was time for the short walk across the plaza to the Armstrong area to be introduced, I gave the iPad to Paul to have someone record the match summary.

This is James here, Larry and Mom said they were too nervous to record the match and I think Paul was way too busy, so this is the best you get when a swimmer comments on a tennis match.

Introductions:

I would like to introduce the players for this afternoon's women's fourth round match. From Radford, Virginia, representing South Korea, Lilly Jarman. This is Lilly's first time at the US Open. Now introducing her opponent, number 2 in the world currently, has previously won the Australian open three years ago and was a Wimbledon finalist last year. Welcome from Russia, Mariana Alexandrova, who was a quarterfinalist last year here. Lilly made a quick run over to the stands and planted a big kiss on Larry, and then ran back to the court. The fans went ballistic, and then chanted two or three times, (Athletic and Feminine). I am sure that Lilly did this on purpose to get the stands on her side versus a much more accomplished player.

They flipped for the serve and Mariana won and chose to serve, Lilly made her look up in the sun, as the roof was open.

It was getting cloudy, and getting windy from the southeast, no rain was due for another hour, so the match was started with the roof off.

Both players warmed-up very well, and you could tell that Mariana was the less nervous player. When they were practicing at the net Lilly did not hit one in the court while Mariana simply just did them like she was a machine.

A large crown here at least 10,000 fans watching the match. I think the crowd was divided between Russian leaning fans for Mariana and almost as many for Lilly. Paul said to everyone, let's just enjoy today, how many tennis players get to the fourth round of a major. Lilly will fight to the end.

Finally, they called for the end of warm-up and the players went to the bench, took fluids and Lilly took out a granola bar. The match was going to be tough. Mariana had a tough serve that was very flat, so Lilly was able to read it well, and she won two of the first three points. Mariana then hit a big serve at 115 down the middle for an ace to even the score. Lilly guessed the next serve and hit a screaming forehand across the court for a winner and had a break point. Mariana tried the same serve down the middle, but Lilly guessed and blocked it back, Mariana hit a forehand down to the corner and Lilly then went for it and hit a forehand down the line for a winner and broke the first game for a 1-0, lead. The crowd behind us went off in applause, obviously not the start Mariana desired or wanted. Lilly served wide and came in and charged the net and won the very first point with a backhand volley. The rest of the service game went the same way and Lilly won the game easily and led 2-0. The next 4 games each server won easily, so Lilly was up 4-2, and we were thinking that this could be an easy set. That was wishful thinking, Lilly double faulted the first point, and Mariana hit a winner down the line for a love -30 game. Lilly did manage to win the next point to trail 15-30, when Mariana hit it into the net. The next point Lilly hit wide, and Mariana punched it down the line, Lilly netted her shot, so now it was a breakpoint. Mariana broke back one point later when Lilly hit the ball long.

Mariana then evened the score with an easy hold, and the match was tied at 4 all. The two then served easily the next four games, forcing a first set tiebreaker. I will say at that point the clouds were getting darker, and Lilly used to less than good conditions at the ITF level seemed like she was picking up a new gear.

ESPN Broadcast:

Let's do a split box, Armstrong court. We are getting into a tiebreaker between Lilly and Mariana. For those that though this was going to be an easy match, Lilly looks like she wants to belong here. Folks, to let you know rain is within ten miles of the tournament site according to radar. They are already putting the roof on Ashe, and we have been told that after the tiebreak, they will do the same for Armstrong.

Lilly serving and serves wide, and Mariana delivers a hard forehand down the line, Lilly barely gets a racquet on it and sends it to the other corner, a forced error by Mariana wins the point for Lilly.

Since we are at a pause on Ashe, we will continue with this court only. A double fault and now Lilly has a mini break. A serve up the line, and Lilly can barely get a touch on it, and it is now 2-1 Lilly. Lilly serving and again goes wide and is waiting for the shot at net and wins on an easy volley. Lilly serves again, and Mariana and Lilly went back and forth in a long 20 shot rally before Mariana hits it long. Lilly now stands at a 4-1.

James here, the clouds are getting dark and Mariana knowing she is going to get a thirty-minute break hit 2 service winners and now Lilly leads 4-3. Lilly not to be outdone, proceeded to hit a 115 down the middle for a winner and then an ace wide, to lead 6-3.

ESPN Broadcast:

Lilly Jarman is at set point and the crowd is getting very loud and New York unruly. Mariana hit a great first serve again Lilly can't do anything with it, and Lilly is at her second set point. Mariana knows that she needs to force Lilly to win this outright and hits an ace down the middle at 118 MPH, her highest so far this afternoon.

James here, Lilly hit her first serve into the net, so she has one serve left to win the set. Lilly simply puts a kicker in the corner where Mariana can only hit a short ball back to the middle, Lilly lines up her forehand and hits a tremendously hard forehand to the corner where Mariana could not get it back in play.

ESPN Broadcast:

Listen to that crowd, Lilly Jarman has just taken the first set off the number 2 player in the world. You know what the pro-Lilly fans are yelling, "Athletic and Feminine" Lilly Jarman, Brad Gilbert says "Lilly is playing 100% in the zone, and this is her seventh match of the championships, I wonder how much more she has in the tank. We will be taking a break from this court as the roof is rolled on."

Lilly and Mariana quickly are grabbing their bags as they go back to the locker rooms. On the outer courts plays has finished as it has begun raining on the outer courts and so play will begin in Ashe in about 5 minutes and with Armstrong, roof is getting closed just in time.

James here, I just got a call from Dad, Dea is not doing well and looks like she may have had a heart attack again. Dad says Dea saw the set end, smiled, and then went into cardiac arrest, she has been revived but they are taking her to CCU right now. Paul left to go back to the locker room with Lilly, so when they restart the match, she will be ready. Paul indicated to me before he has left, Lilly looks spent, I don't know where she will get the energy to finish this match against such a great player used to this type of pressure.

Larry said to me, "no matter what happens today, think of what we can say to our children and show them the tapes of the victories here, nobody will believe us."

ESPN Broadcast:

The roof at Armstrong is now totally rolled on, and they are making sure that the lines are dry for the players to play. This delay must favor Mariana, as a power player she is going to love finishing the match indoors, the ball does not travel the same indoors, and without the wind slices and some of the other shots are not going to be as effective. Mariana also got 15 minutes to take a quick shower change clothes and get ready for her next higher gear to even the match and take it to a third set.

James here, despite taking a shower and getting a fresh set of clothes on, you could tell Lilly was running on fumes. She looked tired and did not give off the sense she was ready to make the US Open quarterfinals.

The match resumed after a very long roof roll and checking for water on the court situation. A few women were yelling to Lilly "Athletic and Feminine" I think they were trying to motivate her. The air in Armstrong was a bit stale, it was taking quite a while for the air conditioning to take over. Mariana looked very determined, no smiles, just a very blue-eyed blond stare that looked evil. Mariana began the set serving and was amped up, her first serve was an ace at 119 MPH down the center. Lilly had no response and looked frozen on the next 2 serves. Mariana lost a point at 40-0, when Lilly guessed and simply hit it down the line before the Russian could track it down. Mariana was not deterred, she simply hit a 120 MPH ace again to end the first game of the second set.

Lilly was set to serve after the change of ends, and I thought she would respond quickly like I had watched her so many times before. This time she just did not look herself; her serve was just under 100 MPH and Mariana could sense she was not as strong as the first set and hit it as hard as she had all game across court for a return winner. The second point did not go any different and you could sense the set was not going to be easy. 2 More serves and the first break of the second set was completed. Mariana could sense she had a weakened Lilly and started to serve the third game. She hit a ramped-up first serve down the center again and Lilly was able to get a shot back Mariana just finished the point off and that started the pattern for the service game. The game was captured by Mariana for a 3-0 lead and poor Lilly called for a medical time-out. Lilly appeared to get something from the trainer, it ended up being Pepto Bismal, apparently, she had a very intense stomach ache. After the five-minute medical time-out Lilly tried valiantly to get back into the game and after getting the score back to 30-all, Mariana showed her experience and finished the second break of serve to now lead 4-0. Mariana pushed her serve but at least Lilly was able to get to 40-30 with a great backhand down the line. Marianna just hit a great serve wide that just ticked off Lilly's racquet, for the game lead of 5-0, in the set. The set was slipping away, but Lilly must have started to feel better and ramped up to a 108 MPH first serve and Mariana hit it into the net. The second point went similar, but this time Mariana hit it long about 3 inches over the baseline. Lilly proceeded to hit another hard serve down the line that Mariana was unable to get over the net getting Lilly a game point for the first time in the set. Lilly jumped on the opportunity and hit a great wide serve that Mariana could only hit back to the middle allowing Lilly to finish at the net and at least save herself from giving up a bagel in the second set. Paul started to clap to Lilly, let's get back in this match, and Lilly tried to win the game, but at deuce Maraina was able to hit a very good shot into the corner and Lilly netted the return. The next serve was another very hard serve and Lilly was able to get it barely over the net and Mariana was able to hit it into the corner for set point. The match was now tied at 1 set all.

ESPN Studios:

For anyone that thought that Mariana was not going to fight for her chance to get into the quarterfinals just had a jolt. Let's look at set point here, Mariana is ramped up and just hit a 115 out wide, and Lilly could just block it back while Mariana hit the ball into the corner. Brad, does it look like Lilly has any chance for the third set. It appears that she was suffering from something medically and took something during the time-out. She looks like she is recovering but let's remember this is her first time at anything like this.

James here, Mariana took a medical timeout to go to the bathroom after the set point. She came back in a dry shirt and a new skirt. Lilly took the time to change her socks to dry socks from her bag. When Mariana came back, she was welcomed by a chorus of "Athletic and Feminine", she did not smile at that chanting. She looked very pissed that the stands were chanting for her underdog Korean opponent.

The set started with Lilly serving, and it appeared she had more energy, whatever she took during the medical time out looked like it was working. Lilly proceeded to have caught her second wind, and ripped her biggest serve down the center line just in and signaled this was not going to be as easy a set as the last one. With an ace she delivered it was just the beginning of an easy hold. Three points and Mariana was like this is not going to be so easy and said something to Lilly as they passed by. Afterwards, Lilly smiled, I will need to find out what she said to her. Mariana was in for the fight and put a big serve down the middle and again al Lilly could do was block it back with Mariana finishing the point with a wicked hard forehand in the corner that Lilly could not even chase down. Second point went Lilly's way when Mariana had to hit a second serve and Lilly smashed it down the line for a winner. Mariana shook her head and yelled nice shot very much dismissive in the way she said it. Mariana then proceeded to win the next three points easily and evened up the set at a game each. Lilly proceeded to serve a big game and six points later she held to take a 2-1 lead in the set. On the crossover Mariana was muttering to herself and her box started to give her encouragement since the instructions were in Russian, I can only tell you it looked like they were encouraging her.

Now behind, you could see that Mariana was very focused and won the next game with 2 aces one double fault and 2 forced errors by Lilly. Lilly still looked determined to stay in the match and like Mariana won with an ace 2 service winners, and then Mariana won a point before Lilly was able to win a long exchange that went over 20 times across the net.

This time Mariana's team was jumping and encouraging her. Meanwhile we heard a few "Athletic and Feminine", fans rooting for Lilly. I heard Mariana say to Lilly, you're not the only one that is athletic and feminine, pretty much a disdainful expression. Mariana continued her dominant serving and won this time with 4 straight points, an ace and two service winners and a forced error, the set was now tied at three games all and Lilly was getting ready to serve. The decisive seventh game was waiting to be served, after the first six points the game was tied at deuce, Mariana took a second serve of Lilly's and hit it down the line for a winner. With break point ahead of her, Lilly hit an ace down the "T" just barely in and Mariana requested a video review of the point. The game went another 12 points similar until Mariana hit a cross court winner to have her second break point. Lilly tried to hit another ace down the "T", but this time Mariana was waiting for the shot and hit right back to the feet of Lilly. All Lilly could do is hit the ball up in the air and Mariana hit a tremendous overhead that was just inside the baseline for the winning point. Mariana was now in the lead for the first time in the set and the match.

Lilly looked frustrated in the changeover, Paul was encouraging her to fight on and make her earn it.

With the end now in site, Mariana stepped up to the line and proceeded to hit three service winners in a row. Lilly did manage to win the next point on Mariana's second serve with a heavy topspin forehand in the corner. At 40-15, Mariana hit another 120 MPH serve down the "T" and all Lilly could do is hit it out of bounds, leaving Mariana to have a lead of 5-3.

ESPN Studios:

Let's go out to Armstrong, where Lilly Jarman is serving to stay in the match. Brad what's going on out there? After a very tight first six games, Mariana has broken Lilly and then held herself and is now up 5-3.

James here, Lilly needs to hold to extend the match and they have now been playing for over 2 hours and 15 minutes according to the match. Lilly proceeded to double fault on her first serve, and then aced on the next serve to even it up at 15-all. Lilly won the next serve when Mariana hit the serve long. Lilly missed the next serve long and

Mariana then pounced on the second serve that Lilly hit up in the air and over the baseline. Now at thirty all, Lilly missed her first serve as it tweaked of the net and went long. Mariana came inside the baseline for Lilly's second serve and pounded a return that Lilly could not handle and had very first match point on Lilly's serve. Lilly again was unable to get her first serve in and Mariana thought she had won the match when she hit a hard forehand that all Lilly could do is put it up and over and somehow it managed to land on the line giving her some hope for the match.

ESPN Studios:

Brad, can you take us through the match on Armstrong. Lilly Jarman just pulled a miracle lob over Mariana to stay in the match. She has been having trouble hitting her first serve in, and just hit another long. Mariana is now inside the baseline waiting on the second serve and hits a massive forehand across the court for a winner. Now match point number 2 for Mariana. Lilly hit a slice serve down the "T", and Mariana and Lilly are going back and forth, no real advantage until Mariana hit a strong forehand down the line. Lilly was able to get there but just barely, and her shot was about 6 inches too long, giving the match to Mariana, 6-7, 6-1, and 6-3.

James here, Mariana yelled something in Russian at the conclusion of the match and Lilly looked totally drained as she walked up to the net to shake hands. Lilly simply went to her chair put a towel over her face. After about a minute, she took the towel off her face and started packing her stuff. The crowd stood up and gave her a standing ovation as she started out of the stadium, so many women yelling" Athletic and Feminine". Larry ran over to Lilly and gave her a hug at the railing before she exited the stadium. Just as she was about to leave the stadium, the stadium announcer said let's hear it for Lilly Jarman, the stadium started clapping and she received a standing ovation. Lilly had to put the towel to her face as we could all see she was in tears again. 7 years of trying and never making it to a big event and receiving a standing ovation she was overwhelmed all of us came out and she just started sobbing all the way out of the stadium.

ESPN Studios:

Let's go to Armstrong and interview, Mariana Alexandrova, getting back to the quarterfinals. Brad Gilbert on the interview, "Congratulations on a very tough match over Lilly Jarman."

Mariana was excited and simply said with her deep Russian Accent, "thank you Brad, what a tough match, Lilly made me work for everything, just shows you some people just need an opportunity. I want to congratulate her on a great tournament, and yes, I was glad we went indoors, it helps my serve not to have the ball flying around. Mariana said OK everyone so Lilly can hear it, let's yell it "Athletic and Feminine". The stands erupted one more time as Lilly was leaving the stadium."

Back to the studios:

Lindsay Davenport was just coming in for the later matches and spoke. If you don't think Lilly Jarman made a difference for people in this tournament, you only had to hear the chanting for her as she finished her match. Now that she is ranked in the top 200, let's see if she can move forward. Did you see her emotions after the match, you know she has been fighting to get to this place playing in the equivalent of the low minors and making the top 16 of a grand slam. Remember all her points were ITF level 100 and below, and now she has a ton of points from here that she gets to use for a full year. Let's see what this result allows her to do.

James here, we let Lilly go to the players' lounge and take a shower, she needed time by herself. She spent an hour in there and then a meeting with Paul, they needed the time to talk about the week. I told everyone I was leaving tonight to go back home and gave my sister a hug and told her I was proud of her. I gave Larry a hug and said you better treat my big sister with respect. I handed the iPad to Lilly to continue the journey.

Paul announced to the group, that he was leaving Radford University and will travel with Lilly in the Asian swing before he leaves for Hilton Head and Charleston, SC, as a head for junior player development and as an assistant head coach with the College of Charleston. He also told us he was getting married at the courthouse in Radford a week from Friday. He said Lilly and Larry have agreed to be the witnesses for the wedding. The rest of the group was stunned, and he said by the way we have at least one more match to play on Monday.

Barbara said that she has been here long enough and is taking the train tomorrow afternoon to Richmond, and then another train will take her to Blacksburg, and then she will meet up with Ken, to take care of Dea.

Larry just grabbed me and hugged me and said your doubles match is after the market closes so I will be here in your box with Paul.

I called dad to see if he got to watch any of the match, he did not answer but texted back. I am at hospital with Dea, watched what we could but only a few minutes on ESPN. Another text, come on home and rest I know you must be exhausted after travelling all summer and the matches at the US Open. I suspect that a few at Radford are waiting for their coaches to quit before the Asian tour and you and Paul need to say farewell.

What dad did not know that not only was Paul accompanying me to Asia, but he was quitting also.

Since I was done with the singles tournament, I wore a basic white Lacoste shirt and this time, wore a green tennis skirt. One girl recognized me anyway and asked that I sign her program, which I did quickly. I realized that it was almost all over.

Everyone got together for one last meal before they went home, I got to eat a steak and had a bite of cheesecake from Larry's dessert, hey I still had to play mixed doubles late afternoon on Monday. Then we decided to go out with a champagne toast. Barbara said to the glorious week that we all will remember for the rest of our lives and to the new couple. Larry and I stood up and kissed, then someone from the New

York Post was snooping around and took our picture. The picture was on the third page of the paper the next day, from nobody to somebody to nobody, in 10 days. Good luck to Larry and Lilly.

Larry told me he caught a lot of crap from his peers Monday morning, and when he said I guess you are marrying the new debutante, he simply said to them never call Lilly a debutante, you may not last the night.

I thought it was going to be the end, I was back to a world of being anonymous, but it was going to be different now. With the launch of the shoes and T-shirts, Larry and I were going to have to do some publicity for products now. "Athletic and Feminine".

All of us broke-up and Larry said, see you in the evening, gave me a kiss, and said to Paul take care of her for at least one more day here.

When Paul, mom and I got back to the hotel, they had a banner printed, thank you Lilly Jarman. At least two more days here, Mixed doubles and then away you go back to Virginia and the quiet life until we leave for Asia. I simply closed my lap top I did not want to see anything talk to anyone. I was exhausted and just simply wanted to hear from Granny Miller, and hope Dea was coming home soon I want her at the wedding. I was thinking of what Coach Wilson said to me to get me to stay at Longwood for my senior year, Lilly Jarman gives me one more year and you will be in the final weekend of the NCAA's and then go professional. I guess it was good that I spent the last year there, made All-American and put Longwood on the map at least for a short period of time.

In one week, I had won nearly three hundred thousand dollars received well over $50,000 in endorsements, and a new product line and T-shirt were going to be launched with Larry and my wedding as the focus. I took out my engagement ring on and then proceeded to crash, my body was racked and exhausted. With the Asian swing I could win enough money to fund it and now I will get a direct entry in to the qualifications in Australia, and Roland Garros.

It was time for the next chapters of tennis and my life and all I could think about was last year at Longwood, my opponents will never believe it.

Chapter 15

Senior Year at Longwood

Most of the team from our championship stayed with us to the next year. Anna Dimtrov was the lone transfer, she went to Indiana to play for IUPUI, in Indianapolis, she wanted to be at a larger and colder city, I guess Bulgaria and Indianapolis must have something in common. We picked up two freshmen, a DC native Sierra Johnson, from just outside the DC area, she was an African American player that had gone to the JTCC at College Park and was a top ten in Mid-Atlantic. She came to Longwood because she needed a year to get her academic performance aligned with what major conferences would want and she was a top 100 nationally when she played 16's, she had not played that much in the last year after tearing a calf muscle why some of the big schools had passed on her. The second freshman, came from Estonia, Pauline Asomonova, was a decent player not highly ranked but for sure she would replace Susan Snider as a double's specialist and number 6, for this year. Unfortunately for Amber, she was now the number 7 player for her senior year, that meant she would play sparingly, but since she had decided to change her major a year ago to Nurse practitioner, she was not going to be available for some of our matches anyway with hospital duties.

So here we were:

Number 1: Me, SR
Number 2: Kiki JR
Number 3: Sierra FR
Number 4: Janice SR
Number 5: Alexandra SO
Number 6: Pauline FR
Number 7: Amber SR
Number 8: Susan JR

Now that we were a conference champion and top 40 in the NCAA, a lot of the teams that we were used to playing refused to play us in the Fall so we had to travel quite a few more miles. When we travelled to Louisville, KY, and then to Lexington, KY, Amber was unable to join us, it was the first time in over three years she would not travel with us, and she was such a good doubles player despite her height. We beat Louisville anyway, 5-2, taking the doubles point, and then only losing two places, both our freshmen lost, but they forced the matches in to 10-point tiebreakers. The next day we beat the University of Kentucky, and we won again 5-2, this time losing the doubles point with different combinations that we were testing, and only Kiki lost in singles.

The ITF tournament was going to be hosted by University of Virginia, so for our team, we were lucky after each day and went home, plus Granny Miller came to the matches and brought me a sandwich for the first day. Eight teams this year, Radford, UNC-Asheville, and Longwood from our conference. Virginia Tech, UVA and Wake Forest from the ACC. WVU from Big 12, and Georgetown from the Big East. This was not the low-level tournament we were used to competing in. A couple of other schools sent a player or two but not a complete team. I was the third seed, with UVA player and Wake players seeded 1 and 2.

The top singles draw consisted of the number 1 and 2 players from the 8 schools and 4 other players. The top 12 players received a bye in the round of 32, Kiki won her match, and her reward was an afternoon match playing the number 1 player from UVA, where she was not able to stay with her and lost 6-2, and 6-2. Sierra did not play the second tier of singles instead, we put her in the doubles group as our number

1, with Kiki. Coach Wilson did not play me doubles saying you are going to have your hands full, and this does not count for conference, so our second doubles team was Alexandra and Janice, at 12'1" they were not going to lose with a lot of lobs. The others played singles and doubles in the lower slots which did not have as much pressure as just more match time.

My first match was against the number 2 at WVU, she was a pretty good player but just wanted to bang at the baseline, I just outclassed her with a lot of slices and blocked returns and let her hit enough unforced errors to make it easy. I won 6-2 and 6-1 in just over an hour leaving me the quarterfinals the next morning without much effort expended on the first match.

On Saturday, I was playing the quarterfinals I was the lucky one to play the number 5 seed, the second ranked player from UVA. So just like playing at Radford, everyone was going to be rooting against me. At least I had Granny Miller rooting for me, and Coach Wilson. My opponent Debbie Harrison was an accomplished top 50 junior who had made the semi-finals of the Orange Bowl, the national major tournament. The match was a tough one, she had more match experience than me despite only being a sophomore, but she had played ITFs at the professional level making a couple of quarters. I won the coin flip and decided to serve. I think she was expecting the counterpuncher she saw yesterday, but my coach said play big and proceeded to hit 2 aces and 2 service winners. Debbie did not expect me to be able to return her big serves, but I had no trouble she telegraphed them, and I simply was waiting. Before she could change anything to be more competitive, she was down 5-0. She held but I was just as relentless and ended the first set in 30 minutes 6-1. The second set went to a to a tiebreak, and we were 5-5 in the tiebreaker, when I hit a winner down the line setting up my first match point. I only needed one, as Debbie proceeded to let me line-up her second serve and hit it in the corner for an upset victory, if you were thinking she was from a power conference and should have won.

The rest of the team was being competitive, our number 1 doubles made the quarters on Saturday and our lower players all won at least one match putting us in a tie for second with Wake Forest. I bet a whole lot of people were wondering who the hell is Longwood. Sunday was the semi-finals of the singles matches and the doubles had both the quarters and semi-finals, none of our doubles teams made the finals on Monday. This pretty much made sure we were not going to be any higher than third for the weekend.

My opponent was the number 2 seed or the number 1 player at Wake Forest, her current ranking was 20 according to the NCAA, what she probably did not know or cared about I was number 25. The start of the match was delayed about an hour after weather produced a light shower and they had to dry off the court, so the match started at noon and the clouds prevented the sun from being a factor in the match. I don't remember much about the match except I looked up the score and I won 6-4, and 7-5. I asked a couple of the players, and they said my opponent Sallie Jenkins, just was not able to get started early and I had broken early in both sets. I was going to be a finalist against the number 1 seed Diana Fossey, she was a sophomore at University of Virginia, currently ranked number 5 in the NCAA. Diana was from Britain and had been the number 1 junior ranked player in Britain, has played the Wimbledon juniors making it to the semi-finals.

With the team pretty much finished on Sunday night, only the finals were still going on with University of Virgina in each one of them. Coach Wilson and I were the only ones that drove from Farmville to Charlottesville, the match was going to be at 2 PM. Coach Wilson asked if I was ready to take on a really good player, I thought I was. At the end of the day, while I played most of the match well, Diana was much more consistent and won 6-4, and 6-4, for the title. I was somewhat disappointed with the loss.

Coach Wilson reminded me that I was getting experience where all these other players had the experience I needed to get. He reminded me that I had come from practically no background, and I was getting comfortable at this level. Basically, now you are playing the best and you are mixing it up with them."

The next week, rankings came out for the NCAA, and I was now up to 19, the highest of anyone male of female in Longwood's history.

The Richmond-Times Dispatch had a picture of the finalists of the ITF that Granny Miller cut out and sent to my parents. The article said University of Virgnia player Diana Forsey won the ITF and lead the University of Virginia to the team title. I was in the picture; they did not even mention me in the caption. I was mentioned as the finalist in the small article in the Sports Section. Longwood did make it in the article as third place finisher for the weekend.

The team had one more weekend set of matches to finish the Fall season, we went up to Towson State in Baltimore, and won 7-0, and then went to UMBC and won 6-1. The only loss was at number 6, when we played Susan Snider and she lost in a match tiebreak. What I realized was that our team was very good, and we were starting to get some recognition. In the team preseason rankings, we were now rated in 24th in the NCAA.

With all this action on the weekends you would be correct in assuming I had like zero social life. Nobody asked me out to any dates, and I really did not have time for them. One sorority asked me to come to a homecoming party, which I decided to do, had a nice dress and one of the sisters set me up for the night with a guy that was at Virginia Tech, he was a senior engineering student, and like me was Eurasian. His mother was from Vietnam, and his father was a GI, like my grandparents just one generation later. He was a shy guy we did not dance much, and we never saw each other again. That was my social for the semester and my academics were fine at a neat 4.0, for the semester, because I was doing so well in many of my classes I only had one final and stayed with Granny Miller most of the week. I helped her paint a couple of rooms that week, and I loved all the home cooking, I think she enjoyed the company. We went to church together, and I swear she tried to set me up for a date, but I was able to bail out of it. After looking at my records, I only needed 9 hours to graduate, so for me to be eligible my last semester, I took a 3-hour graduate level course on statistics in case I went for my MBA.

I should tell you that my brother James was a pre-season All-American, he had barely made the NCAA consolation final heat his first year, but he was doing really well anyway. He was big too now, like

6'2" and just over 210 pounds, I think he should have been a football player like dad but that was not his calling. I got to see him for a couple of days at the holiday, his team went training in Miami, tough time, I guess. James left the day after Christmas, we had to come back from Blacksburg, and he met up with his team bus in Richmond. On the way back the three of us went to see Granny Miller, and we stayed for dinner, she was happy to make it and told my parents that I am being a good girl and that we went to church together quite frequently.

Since we had three weeks off and I did not want to stay at campus with nobody there, so back to the Country Club and the junior tennis players. None were as good as my teammates, but a workout was a workout. I even started to play with one of the pro's Manuel Oritz. Manuel had played Davis Cup for his native Colombia, and he said let's play a match I want to see you at your full out best. The match was scheduled New Years Eve, after the kids had finished for the day. Manuel said that let's make it worth it for me, if you win you get my salary for the day, if not you have to go on a date with me before you go back to school. Unfortunately for me, even 2 years removed from the professional circuit, he still managed to beat me 6-3, and 6-3. I agreed to a date on the 2nd of January at Sharkey's, weird that we were going to be at Radford the site of so many of my torments, on a date with a good-looking Latin tennis player. Fortunately, the date was free of debutante sightings, and frankly it was just nice and to go out and be free to be me. I even laughed when Manuel talked about his international tennis travels and some of the exploits, he, and his friends on the challenger tour. At the end of the date, he said something to me that was insane, I expect to see you next year on the tour. All I said was nice joke, and after giving me a good night kiss, he said you have no idea how good you really are. Manuel and I went on a few dates on my last semester at school, and I would hit with him after the semester ended and prior to doing anything professionally with tennis but way ahead of the story.

I returned to Longwood for my last semester, 3 easy courses for my undergraduate degree and a master's class on Working Capital Analysis my first class in graduate school. My roommates, came from Europe and Asia three days after I arrived, 2 of us for out last semester here and poor Kiki would be back for another year. We had been through the wars together and we had one semester left. On our first night back, we went over to Granny Miller's for dinner she invited us all over, and she went all out with pasta, sausage, garlic bread, and salads for everyone. She said one thing to all of us, enjoy your time together, you will remember this year the rest of your lives. What great young women you have become, going to change the world in the next few years.

Due to NCAA regulations, we did not have our first match until late February, we went to Marshall University and then WVU on the weekend and won both 6-1 and then 5-2. I lost my first regular match in dual meets to the girl from WVU, I had played a tough match, traveled 2.5 hours, and then played at the indoor courts near WVU. My opponent was simply there for both days waiting for me. I dropped to number 25 in the next ranking, but the team was squarely in the top 20 for the first time. On the way back from WVU, coach Wilson reminded me that everyone guns for the number 1 player and even the split had helped the team.

Our season began in earnest 1 week later we had another weekend away, first to UNC-Asheville, and then to High Point on the way back. We again won both matches 6-1 and 4-3. I won both of my matches easily, and we would have won more easily if we had played our top line-up, but we played both Amber and Susan at 5 and 6 after we had already won the match. Coach wanted to save some of our players as he knew it was a long season. The following weekend we hosted Charleston Southern, on Friday afternoon and won the match 5-2, and again we only lost the last match because we decided to do our last match as an exhibition, no sense in running up the score. Our second match of the weekend was against Garner Webb, out of North Carolina, a complete decimation our first conference 7-0 in a very long time.

We were now at our Spring Break, where we went to Orlando, Florida to have four matches in the week. Our first match was a loss to the University of Florida, where I lost a tiebreak to the then number 4 player in the NCAA's. The team lost our first dual meet 3-4, still not bad considering we were playing the champion of the SEC conference and a finalist in the team competition. We played LSU from Louisianna next and won in an upset 4-3, this was despite losing the doubles point forcing us to win at least 4 singles matches which we did for the upset. The other matches were against teams in big conferences but not that highly rated, Syracuse which we won 5-2, and then finally Northwestern from the Big Ten, which we won 5-2. The team was doing very well and despite my one loss here I moved up to 16 in the nation and our team went to 17, this was going to be an interesting season.

We returned home to knock off both Charleston Southern and Radford at home, and both were 6-1 scores, our team was going to be seeded number 1 again at the conference tournament again at Radford. Unlike the previous year where we were hopeful of winning the conference, this year we won both matches easily even though I lost in the third set of my match against Charleston Southern the second day, my monthly period made me very uncomfortable during the match. The team won our championship 4-1, once we had reached 4 wins we were done. Coach Wilson received his second Coach of the year award, and while I made first team all-conference the girl from Charleston Southern won the MVP, in fact I was third in the voting as KIKI had an undefeated season at number 2. Coach Wilson came over to me and said don't worry about the vote for MVP, we all know you were the best player, but you did not come in with a lot of fanfare.

While we were waiting on our NCAA bid for the year we received our rankings, team 15th and my personal ranking remained at 16. My personal ranking would allow me to be a seeded player when the singles tournament took place, the lowest seed, but that was still better than risking playing a top ten player right off.

One of my sorority-based friends asked me to go to a formal that she was going to at Gamma Psi formal dinner and dance and needed a date. Michelle Lambert was someone that had been in business classes with me and knew that I had time off from tennis. Michelle was a member of the Phi Mu Delta sorority, and while I was an independent, she still wanted me to be the date for a friend of hers Bernie Smith, a nice guy not athletic but he was now a graduate assistant, but since he was at the University his brothers had wanted him to come to the party as being the former vice president of the fraternity. Grudgingly on the one weekend that I had off from tennis, I had agreed to go to the formal dinner. I went to JC Penney and then to Macy's to get a dress and shoes to match for the night. I also went to get new lingerie for the evening, I needed something other than a sports bra at least.

I met Bernie at the formal, Michelle had driven to the event with her boyfriend, and we all met at the front of the fire hall. It was amazing what they had done to it for the evening. Bernie had gone all out and bought a corsage for my wrist. He met me for the first time, and said, "seeing you took my breath away, you look so nice." He looked clearly nice and was just about my height a little shorter than me with my 2-inch heels. I had never met Bernie formally before, but you could see from the moment we met that we had something together, and in the bathroom, Michelle said to me, "will you be coming back with me tonight or will Bernie drive you back to school."

I did something that I have never done before and giggled, well maybe late tonight. The dance was over at 11:PM, and I drove over to Bernie's apartment with him. We made love that night in his apartment, and I returned to my room at about 6:30 AM. Kiki was awaiting, so the Ice Princess had a little extra fun tonight. I went to bed and did not wake up until 1 in the afternoon.

I did hear from James that he had made the finals of the NCAA in both the 200 IM and the 200 free, his highest finish was 4th and that was the best for his team. So, he was officially the first All-American in our family. His team had also made the finals of the 800 free relay, ending in 8[th,] and helping the team to a top 25 finish. My parents were in Michigan at the NCAA's, and they recorded it for Granny Miller and Dea to see later.

We all went to the field house for the NCAA selection show. There were 16 teams designated as home teams, and we thought we would be not one of them, and then we kept waiting for the seedings and where we were going to go to Charlotteville as they were the number 2 seed. When they called the 4 teams for the region, we were not one of them. After 30 minutes of getting nervous about where we were going, we heard the sub-region in Radford Va, with Virginia Tech, Eastern Kentucky, East Tennessee State, and then the host team will be the champions of the Big South Conference, Longwood University, from Farmville, VA. The selection committee had us as the 12 seed in the tournament. When they talked to Coach Wilson, he said we appreciate it and want to see Lilly Jarman's hometown come out to support her in their last chance to see her before she ends her career at Longwood as the highest ranked player in school history. They panned over to me, and I have a high five to my coach and said, we feel like the little engine that could. Wow 4 years ago we were the worst team in the conference and now we are going to host a weekend with the NCAA with some very great teams.

The tournament would be played on Friday and Saturday of the next week, and I got a call from my mom, she wanted to host the team Friday night for dinner after we had won our first-round match. I told coach Wilson and he said that would be great, that way he could save some money and have a team building event. Our match was scheduled against East Tenn. State at noon, and we did not disappoint, we won the doubles point, and then proceeded to win at 2, 4, and 5, and while I was at match point, they stopped me and said that Longwood had just won the match 4-0. Kiki had won easily at 6-2, and 6-1. At 6 PM, after everyone had changed, we went to my house, it felt so weird introducing everyone to my proper southern parents. I wondered what the debutante parents said, when the local television station came over as we entered the house. I was being interviewed as to how it felt to be back at home in the first 2 rounds of the NCAA's when I was so lightly recruited. I basically gave the credit to our coach who saw potential in me when nobody else did. The team started to chant Lilly, this had to piss off the debutante parents when they saw this, the girl they shunned was getting press. The next day, we played Virginia Tech from the ACC, they had finished fifth in the conference but truthfully, they had more fans that Longwood did. After we finished the doubles point, we went back to singles play, while Virginia Tech won the first two points (3,4), and we were down 2-1, Alexandra won at 5 and Kiki won at 2 to get us back up 3-2. Pauline lost in the third set and so the match had come down to my court and after losing the first set 7-5, I had won the second set 6-3. With both teams rooting for both players I broke on the seventh game of the third set and then held to take a 5-3 lead. My opponent was not yet done and held for my lead and service game to serve for the match and our first ever sweet 16. I had a match point at 40-30 and hit it long and it went back to deuce. I served a slice serve at probably 90 MPH at the "T" and my opponent hit it into the fence. This time, I had match point and proceeded to serve and volley and while the shot ticked off the net, it bounced twice before my opponent could manage to hit it. The team came over to me and started screaming and hugging as we had made it to the sweet 16. Our team had never even won a match much less a sub region. My parents and grandparents were all at the matches, even my grandfather was able to travel with Dea to the finals. His ailing health he had not been travelling much anymore.

I got a call from Bernie later that night that he would like to see me again when I got back to Farmville. I texted back, NCAA second weekend next Thursday through Sunday, how about a Monday afternoon date. I got a heart response and yes, I will pick you up at your dorm.

Meanwhile school was getting ready for finals week for seniors which was a week ahead of the others. I only had a single final this week of the three undergraduate classes and to complete a paper for my one graduate course. I was going to get a couple of dinners with Granny Miller, Amber joined me for one night given she was going to get the collegiate academic athlete award and wanted to practice her speech she came along.

The remaining 16 teams were invited to Orlando Florida to compete for the title. We were slotted as the number 10 seeds, meaning we had the opportunity to play the number 7 rated team, which was the University of Illinois. The match was slated for Thursday at noon, hot temperatures for both teams, but where we had played most of our season outdoors, they had played indoors. When it was all done, we managed to win 4-2, Amber, Janice and I had won, and we won the third doubles after splitting the first two for the doubles point. Only Kiki's match was unfinished. Our reward for beating the number 7, team was now in the final 8, we got to play University of VA on Friday.

The Friday match was played at 10:00, we were the first on for the quarterfinals. UVA, jumped out to a 1-0 lead when they won the doubles point. Kiki lost her first match in a very long time, and at number 6, Pauline won putting us back in the match 2-1. Sierra won at number 3 and put us even. My match was going to go three sets as were the slots at 4, and 5, behind me. Janice lost at number 4 very quickly, putting UVA back up to 3-2. My match went long, but in the end, I managed a 6-4 come from behind victory to tie the match once more this time getting the best of Fossey. Alexandra, managed to get to a deciding tiebreak, but unfortunately, she lost the tiebreak 7-2, and UVA advanced to the semi-finals. The entire team, just dropped to our knees and started to cry, our miracle team season was over in just a flash. No other small conference team had made the top eight, but unfortunately, we came up just short.

We had the day off on Saturday before we flew back on Sunday, so we went to Universal Studios who was giving free entry to all the 16 teams. While we really enjoyed the place especially the Harry Potter area, Coach got a call regarding the individual tournament. Longwood had been given 2 slots in the 32 tournament that would start on Monday. Kiki was unseeded and I received the 7 seed, the first time we had ever received a seeding. I had to call Bernie and tell him that our date had to be delayed as I was staying in Florida for the singles tournament. He understood but clearly, he was bummed. I said the singles tournament will be from Tuesday through Saturday and for sure we would be back Sunday afternoon. To make all-American in tennis you must get to the quarterfinals, Kiki was slated as the 18th best player.

I did manage to call my parents and tell them the results of the team competition and that I would be staying for another week. The team flew back to Richmond with Lucy leaving Just Kiki, Coach Wilson, and myself to compete in the singles tournament.

"Janice said you better get back to school Sunday because graduation ceremony is a week from Monday. She said I am going back to the UK on Tuesday leaving from Richmond, and Amber was leaving the next morning from DC and was leaving Tuesday night. We need to have at least one night together after our four years, before you will be in the states, I am in Europe and Amber leaves for Asia."

The next two days went by quickly, nothing to do but practice with Kiki and find about my first opponent that I would play on Tuesday. I was playing Sarah O'Connor from Notre Dame, in the first round. Kiki was playing a top player from LSU. Coach Wilson was split between the two of us, Kiki started at 08:00 and my match was starting at 09:30. Kiki split sets by the time I started playing Sarah, so no coach while Kiki was in her third set. I had a pretty good serve going and managed to take the first set 6-3, I broke at 3-3 and won the set 6-4. Just as I was getting ready for the second set, I saw Kiki and Coach Wilson coming with smiles to my court, I had assumed that she had won her match. My second set was tight again but this time at 4-4, I broke and served out the match. Sarah threw her racquet at her bag in disgust, I guess she thought she would win the next match.

The advantage I had over Kiki by being seeded, was I did not have to face a seeded player in the second round, but Kiki had to play the 4 seed from Florida State on Wednesday. I was playing Pauline Evans, the number 1 from Boston College on Wednesday. Since we were down to the final 16, the matches did not start until 10:00, Kiki got that one, and my match started at 11:30. Kiki tried hard but was beaten 6-3 and 6-2, she was done for her junior season. Ten minutes later I started my warm-ups. I was thinking about Boston College and how much tennis she was playing outside in practice, I guess she only was doing outdoors when she played the teams in the south because it was barely above 50 in Boston still. We had a good steady wind from the west, so poor Pauline had no idea of what to do in the wind, where we played in windy conditions all the time. The match was not as hard as I thought it would be and after just over an hour, I had won the match 6-2 and 6-1.

Coach and Kiki came over to me and congratulated me on the major win. Coach Wilson then said to me, congratulations to our first Longwood All-American, I promised this to you. I called my parents and James was already at the house. I said, "put it on speaker, I am in the quarters of the NCAA's tomorrow which means I am already an All-American."

Mom was not there, and I asked where she was, and Dad laughingly said, "she is on her way to the airport in North Carolina, she will be with you for your next round, she wanted to see your last match and I said we have enough savings just do it. She has a hotel tonight near you at the Holiday Inn, and comes back Saturday night, and then will get home about 2 AM, Sunday so go ahead she is there all the way to your finals."

James reminded me that he got his ahead of his big sister, I simply said yes, but everyone expected it of you, and nobody wanted me or expected it. They said they would tell Dea and Granny Miller, although I guess that the local papers in Farmville will let her know.

Thursday morning practice and Kiki was my practice partner against the number 2 seed from the University of Central Florida, obviously Jacki Thomas was used to the limelight, she has trained in Florida, so not going to be any advantage. Coach said that she played in a very tough conference in the ACC with Duke and UVA, and she was rated as the number 2 player in the ACC, while the team was not as strong. To understand the difference in our junior background, Jacki had played the junior Australian Open and Wimbledon before she committed to UCF instead of turning professional. She had placed second in the 18's in the Orange Bowl, while I was not good enough at the time to even get an invite.

Coach Wilson knew her and said she is about 5'3" and a road runner who can often run a player off the court. He had coached her for a while in junior tennis before she had a private coach travelling with her. He indicated our strategy is clear, she has played 2 long matches, and this is the third day in a row that she is playing, so serve and volley her or simply go for it we don't want a 3-hour match that is what she trains for. The longer the match the more she will want to go for it, plus she plays in the big conferences we have the advantage that she won't have any video on you other than word of mouth from here. My mom got to the courts just as I was finishing warm-up with Kiki, and I gave her a sweaty hug. I had 20 minutes to change into my Longwood uniform, and I was out of clean clothes.

With the quarters we started at 10:00 on 2 courts, my match was second on court the number 1 and 2 seeds were the second pairs of matches. I think everyone thought I had been lucky to get where I was and that this was going to be an easy match for Jacki, but there are times when a big serve and net game can throw off the baseliners that was what we were counting on.

Jacki won the serve and held her serve but it was not fast in the mid to upper 90's but she anticipated the returns well and was able to win the points easily. My serve was just about 100 MPH, and wide, I think Jacki was surprised that I was waiting for the return at the net and won all 4 points easily. Now it was my turn and I started just going for it down the line on her soft serves, and was up 15-40, and then broke her immediately with a backhand down the line and then I was waiting for it at the net. Now up 2-1, Jacki and her coach were in a huddle, thinking I would keep up the wide serves but instead hit a hard shot down the "T" and received my first ace. I hit three more big serves and very quickly went up 3-1, surprising everyone watching. Another Jacki service game and another break, which put me up 4-1, Coach Wilson said don't get cocky she has some experience and will be able to counter what is happening, let's just steal this set and move forward. Jacki and I traded games and eventually it went to 5-2, and Jacki got back to 5-3, before I held on for a first set victory of 6-3. Now the crowd was buzzing, and you could hear my mom yelling go Lilly. The second set was not going to be that simple, and the set ended up at 6-all and forced a tiebreak to decide. I only remember the score the rest was a buzz, at 6-5, I simply hit a slice to the wide side and came in and won the point when I hit a volley at the net. Coach jumped up in the air and Kiki and my mom came running to the court, I had just upset the 2 seed, and was going to go to the semi-finals, on Friday.

I could not believe I had made the semi-finals of the NCAA and that made me a first team All-American. I would lose the next round 6-3, and 6-2, to the number one from UVA, Diana Fossey again, the second time this year but I had made it where nobody ever expected.

On Saturday, I had to play an eight-game pro set to determine the third-place finisher ahead of the doubles and singles finals. I ended up winning the match over the Stanford number 1, 8-6, and received a trophy indicating third in the country. The trophy went to coach Wilson and is now in the Longwood athletic awards case. He had a small plaque added stating, Lilly Jarman, Longwood first All-American female tennis player.

My mom left for the airport immediately after my match before the awards ceremony. We had checked out of our rooms already and Kiki and Coach waited for me after I took a shower. Lilly, I promised you I would get you to the top of the NCAA and this is your legacy, he said he would have hugged me but not in this world, simply gave me a high five. I told Kiki this will be you next year and I know that she made it to the top eight the next year, her All-American year.

Our flight from Orlando, got us to Richmond by 10:00 PM, and by the time we got home it was 1 in the morning Sunday. Kiki and I collapsed and went to sleep, the next thing we knew it was Amber and Janice yelling at us to get up. They said we are going to the diner for an impromptu season ending awards banquet. What I did not know was that this was being done for the Richmond Newspaper, while Fossey of UVA finished second, they wanted to know about the local girl that finished third. Nobody had predicted this ending and with the trophy I had the team MVP award, they took my picture and interviewed me. The team picture was taken and appeared in the Richmond paper on Monday with the feature the underdog team and their trophies. Our conference trophy and my awards were all there plus Amber's award for Academic Athlete.

Coach Wilson with a tear in his eyes yelled, "Lilly thanks for being my first All-American, and when are you going to start playing the ITF's?"

"I said can I get through graduation on Monday first?"

"He laughed and said sure, just let me know."

Monday came, and with that the end of my college tennis and my degree Suma Cum Laude, along with Amber. Janice graduated with a 3.6 average for Magna Cum Laude, the three freshmen had done it. We walked in our different schools and then found each other after the ceremony.

My parents took pictures of all three of us and sent them to Amber and Janice's parents. I was going to miss them; Amber was accepted into Medical School right off. I saw them off Tuesday and we all cried as we said good-bye. I knew for the first time I had been fully accepted and no longer worried about the debutantes.

Bernie and I got together for our date on Tuesday night, I did not leave his apartment until Thursday morning just in time for me to pack up and say my goodbyes to Kiki and then to Coach Wilson. This time I gave him a hug no matter what the protocol says and thanked him for believing in the country bumpkin. He started to tear-up and said just make sure you tell them about me when you get to the US Open. I had not done so yet in the tournament, but that would be on my new blog that John indicates I should start.

While Bernie and I were very comfortable with each other, our time ended after that Thursday morning, he stayed at Longwood, and I went back to Radford and then to my next journey.

Chapter 16

Mixed Doubles Quarters US Open

Most of the team were either gone of leaving. I got my last breakfast from Elijah's and took it to Mom's room to see her before she left for the train station. She was going to take a fast train to DC, and then another all the way back to Blacksburg, VA. She would get there around midnight so poor dad would have to leave from the hospital, go to the train station, and then take her to my grandparents' house.

She gave me a hug and said, "when the week is over come home before you go back on tour, we want to start the wedding plans together."

The talk went to kids, and I immediately said don't you think that is a little early to talk about that, just starting to make some money, as is Larry, and I am going to try to get in to the Australian Open.

After about 45 minutes, we finished breakfast, hugged, and she told me, "I want to see you and Larry back in Radford before you leave. I miss you and Granny Miller will want to see her favorite granddaughter."

"Mom, there are only two granddaughters, and one stays in Florida, so not sure that is a real thing."

Back in my room, I opened the laptop and went through e-mails, now back to normal, mostly ads, not the popular person having lost. John Littleman's e-mail indicated your Asian tour is all set now, you will play three tournaments, Seoul South Korea, Hong Kong, and we have you at least in the qualifying of the Japan open. You are entered into the 125 in California, the last week of September, and fly from there. Paul will be with you in Asia, but you will be without him in California, apparently, he wants to take a one-week off to move to South Carolina and have a little bit of a honeymoon. Paul will meet you in Seoul, and finish the swing, then we will figure out about the next year. Allison said production of the shoe is imminent and the first pairs will be with you in Hong Kong.

I looked at the e-mail from Paul regarding our match today. The mixed doubles match was scheduled fifth on court 1, all doubles match ahead of us. Estimated time will be 6 PM, so mostly under the lights. The e-mail indicated will warm-up at 3 PM, for 30 minutes, and then chill until we were ready to go. The next line went like this, something that I was afraid to admit myself, I know you are wanting to just leave and end this, but you can make an additional ten thousand by winning today, so let's just have some fun and get some rest. Lastly, I am going to the pool at noon, let's do lunch there, if you are as tired as I am from the last week, we need some chill time. If this ends today, then let's at least think about this implausible run, nobody would have thought this was possible a week ago. I am so proud of what you have done and the future you are building.

I did not have any additional e-mails. I did receive a text from James saying he was safe in DC, and to have fun today. I then texted Larry about the time of the match this afternoon. The text back, I am at the gym, needed some workout time been sitting a lot lately. Another text came in with a heart and said are you ready for the rest of your life? I started to leak from my eyes, a whole different world than I had ever thought was possible all from a few tennis matches and a wedding proposal, all in a ten-day period.

Enough of the e-mails and texts, I was hoping to hear from dad on Dea's condition, but he was probably in the hospital and busy. I sent him one anyway saying I was coming down to Virginia this weekend and taking a couple of weeks to decompress. It was a little reflection time and time to get some wedding plans and see the people from my part of the world before going to Asia.

For 7 years from my graduation to this week, I had been playing sparingly on the professional tours. Three weeks after graduation I won $500, back up at Hollins winning both the Women's double with Frances and the singles tournament. That paid for the entry in to my first ITF qualifying tournament. I made the tournament main draw and lost in the first round, my check was $125, from the tournament unfortunately the $200 entry, and the $250, in expenses told me this was not going to be an easy way to make money. The one thing I knew was I could not afford a full-time coach like many of these women, I had no sponsors, and Coach Wilson was able to help me through tournaments in Virginia over the summer, but I did not have enough money to play full-time. While I had made the NCAA's top three nobody came looking for me, I did not know how to reach out to these corporations for sponsors. I did manage a small sponsorship with a local restaurant, that basically gave me up to $250, per month in travel expenses. My parents gave me $4000, as seed money for the first year. I was at Radford University practicing and was introduced to the new assistant coach, a guy named Paul Manford. I thought I had an accent but his was much deeper than mine, he was from Charleston, SC, and was working as an assistant coach for the women's team and the second coach for the elite age group tennis players. Paul had played collegiately at a second tier apparently, but his mind was very good in how to manage a match.

We struck a deal for the next spring, I would be a hitting partner and extra coach when they needed it at Radford, in return, he would provide me hitting/coaching sessions at Radford. In the interim, I was able to get into some ITF's and a Challenger 75, level. The reward for the Challenger 75 in Charlottesville, VA, was I got a check of $1400, for getting to the semi-finals, but the points in singles and then the doubles points with Frances at least got me invites to other ITF's. The ITFs basically made me a couple of thousand dollars for the year and cost as much in travel costs and entry fees, so no real money in the bank account.

For six years I would basically fall into this trap, I could get enough points to get invited into the ITF's and an occasional Challenger but never had enough points to get direct entries to the Challengers and the ITF's paid at most about $1000, even when you won. I was still getting about $20,000, per year in prize money and when it was all said and done, my costs were not that far from it even with driving and staying with free benefactors arranged to eliminate hotel costs. I finally consumed the seed money and was getting ready to move on and finish my MBA, I was already admitted to James Madison, and they were going to let me reduce my tuition by being a hitting partner and part-time coach for the Women's team. Coach Wilson had remitted a recommendation, and it did not hurt that dad was an alumnus. It was time to move on and I had begun dating Larry, so I thought tennis was going to be over in the next 9 months.

Last year, I was at a Challenger and entered with a player from Britain who knew Kiki as a kid and was a pretty good player. Top 300 in the world, Sara Blanker, was her name and she had stayed in Europe and then to the states working on her ranking. After the week we had won the doubles, and I made the quarters of the singles. That was when things changed when Kia approached me after the tournament and said they wanted to be my primary sponsor for the next year. So that is why you see Kia on my bags, and we put a Kia logo on all the Lacoste shirts. Maybe I can get them to give me a program car and retire the Malibu once and for all. Sara found a higher ranked partner for this year.

I was now able to enter the low-level challengers that would give me enough points to get into some of these directly. I entered the Challenger in Delaware at the Sea Colony Tennis and Pickleball resort. I barely squeaked into the tournament without having to qualify. I had done a week of practice after the season had ended for Radford and it really helped playing with the girls and getting coached by Paul. After a week of matches on the clay, I had somehow won the tournament and they had a little kicker, the winner was awarded a wild card entry into the US Open qualifying tournament. The money I received for winning the tournament also made it I could play another ITF 125, in Cancun, Mexico. I got to the quarterfinals there and it paid for the trip and somehow Larry found a way to make it to Cancun, not only did I win some money and points, but I also got to see my boyfriend at the end of the tournament. We also enjoyed the use of the hotel together.

I could tell stories about how I had to basically beg for people to practice and to stay with, but nobody wants to hear about the bad times more than I spoke about already, needless to say, it would have helped had I been more known as a junior and able to secure sponsorships. If it had not been for the arrangement with Paul at Radford, I would have had to give-up a long time ago, but that lifeline gave me cash and coaching where I would never have been able to afford it. No more whining can't change the past, but it was so fun to finally get to play in the big tournament and maybe a tournament or two in Asia.

It was Labor Day, so it was going to be busy at the US Open, we are on a popular court the second week. Most of the team was gone home, Kia representative was going to be in the box today as will be Jacques from Lacoste and Paul, the box will be about half full this evening. With lunch at the pool completed, both Paul and I had sun time and then he said to me you need to get out of the sun rehydrate and be ready for a muggy match tonight. Because of the holiday be ready to meet me at 2:15, we need some additional time to get to the stadium today.

At 1 PM, I left the pool, went back to my room, chilled out, got my clothes for both warm-ups and for the match and we completed the possible last day at the US Open. The match was still worth $19,000 for the team or $9,500, for me if we can win today. That would have been three winning tournaments at the ITF level, just put it in perspective. Just think I can always say, I played the quarterfinals of the US Open Mixed Doubles as a wild card entry with a partner I had never met before.

I met with Paul and got ready for our Uber to the stadium, I wonder how many more times I would be with Paul, but for 7 years he has been the backbone of possibility. As we were walking to the practice courts, I put my arm on his shoulder and said to him "let's have some fun today."

"His response, of course, no pressure this is fun tennis."

At 3 PM, we were on our half of the practice court when Mike Finley and his coach had arrived. Mike had won his next round of men's doubles earlier in the day, and after his shower and a change of clothes, was ready for our hit today. We were on one side and the coaches were on the other side. They were hitting at us as hard as possible to get used to the power Alex Popov would send our way later this afternoon. His partner Varvara Romanoff was also a very big hitter, so we had to be always ready at the net. The next things they had us do was to practice our lobs so we could get them running and moving away from the net, they were big hitters but not as fleet of foot as others I have played. I played Varvara a couple of years ago at an ITF event, she beat me in three sets, but I learned she moves well side to side but has a problem forward or back.

We went back to the players' lounge where I took a quick shower and then a change of clothes to the Lacoste uniform and proper shoes. I even had the South Korean sweat bands already to go. The eighth day of the tournament and a lot less players here, so we were able to chill out. Larry texted he was at the court and as soon as the current women's doubles is over, he will meet Paul at the court.

Ten minutes later we had a notice that court 17 was in the third set and to expect it to be 15 minutes. Then came the notice that it was time to leave and go to court 17, it is a long walk, so they warned us early to give us time for the walk. I handed the iPad to Paul and told him I think Larry can handle the duties today. Then as we got to the stadium, I left for the players entrance and Paul left for the stands.

Larry here, I will be doing the notes for the match today. The Russian team were also unseeded and for some reason they chose to introduce the team first. Welcome to our last match of the afternoon, introducing our players, from Russia, Varvara Romanoff and her partner Alex Popov. Varvara is currently ranked number 20 in the world for singles and top 50 for doubles, Alex Popov is currently ranked number 10 in doubles and still a top 100 in singles. Now introducing their opponents, from South Korea via Virginia Lilly Jarman, and from Britain Mike Finley. Mike is number 8 doubles player in the world and Lilly is a first-time player here. The stands started with a chant of 'Athletic and Feminine", this is going to be fun, for the first time in her career, the stands are in Lilly's favor. The Russians won the toss and decided to serve.

You could tell from warm-up that Alex had a huge serve, somewhere in the upper 120's and thirties. The only thing that we could see it was almost always flat, and predictable. Alex began the serve against Lilly, who was only able to block the ball back, but it landed over the baseline. Mike was more fortunate and timed a screamer down the line with a good forehand, Alex could only watch the ball down the doubles line. The third point Lilly blocked back over Varvara and Alex hot the ball to a waiting mike who finished the point off. A second serve by Alex and mike hit a thundering shot down the middle that Varvara simply framed up into the stands. Now with a break point Alex served and ace to Lilly and then had to face Mike with a second break point and on a second serve, Mike hit a very hard forehand directly at Varvara who hit the ball into the net. The crowd went crazy rooting for Mike and Lilly. Mike held serve easily, and Lilly was able to get to the deciding point on her serve. Serving to Varvara, she hit a 94 MPH serve wide and when Mike poached to her side of the court, he put the ball away, so with that result our team was up 4-0, before Alex was able to turn it around and hold his serve. Mike held to get a 5-1 lead, and this time Varvara forced the set with a deciding point. Lilly hit a tremendous backhand that Alex hit cross the corner, Lilly was able to chase it down and hit a backhand in the double's alley for the winner, and the first set went to Lilly and Mike. Again, we heard the chant we were starting to get very familiar with and it seemed to disturb the Russians.

The second set did not go as easily, and at 5 games each Lilly was broken to set-up the Russian team to serve for the set. Varvara was serving at 40-30, when Mike hit a tremendous shot to steal the set point away from the Russians. The deciding point was served wide, and not very hard, Lilly hit a forehand around the net pole that landed just inside the line to equal the set at 6 all. The Russians did not go away easily, and they were leading 5-4 and serving when Mike hit a screaming return that Varvara was unable to do much with and as soon as it popped up Lilly hit a forehand at the double's alley for the winner and evening up the score. On the next point, Lilly simply did a blocked shot up and over Varvara and out of Alex's reach. Mike simply went to the line and hit an ace for the winning point. Mike came over to Lilly and gave her a hug, the team would face the number 1 team in the semi-finals. They won an additional $19,000, as a team for making the semi-finals, $9,500, for Lily, was as much as she had earned in some of her years in the ITF.

Of course, the fans that were at the court started screaming, "Athletic and Feminine", I could not have asked for more publicity. Jacques and Allison said, we are going to use these fans in our advertising. Larry, you should be getting some nice royalty checks as a part-owner of that saying. I handed the iPad back to Paul and waited for them to come out of the locker room after Lilly had showered again. Both teams left the court, and we knew that the semi-finals would be Wednesday probably on the stadium court this time.

Paul said to me, "it's late Lilly, I am heading back to the hotel, and we will not have a practice session until 4 PM, so enjoy yourself tonight. I want to talk to my own fiancé and the parent of my stepchild; she is getting lonely with me here so long."

Larry said, "so I can take Lilly out for a date tonight", and Paul agreed simply shook his head in agreement. I knew she had to back as she was still in the tournament.

"Larry exclaimed Manhattan tonight."

"I told him if I can stay the night, I'm tired and really want a glass of wine. Can we call in a dinner rather than going out tonight, I don't want to be seen in my tennis clothes tonight."

Larry knew an Italian place so when we got down to Manhattan from the Uber, we placed an order, and he bought a bottle of rose at the store next to it. After waiting about 20 minutes, we picked up our dinner and went to his apartment on the 32nd floor. It is small but only 5 blocks from his office, so he can walk to work. We had dinner and I had a glass of wine, before anything could happen romantically, we sat on the couch, and I fell asleep. The next thing I knew, it was 1 in the morning, and I had a Redskins cover on me and had been asleep for almost 4 hours. I simply got up and went over to the bed and lied down next to Larry and out my arm around him. I did not wake-up until 730, in the morning. I had fallen asleep for nearly ten hours.

After waking up Larry and taking a shower, I knew where we should go for breakfast, but Larry reminded me that he had to be at work at 8:45, for the trading day. He yelled, "you will be on your own today until at least 4:30."

"I told him I had to leave at 3 PM, had a hitting session at 4 PM in Queens."

With a kiss on the cheek, Larry proceeded to go into the shower and get ready for the day. I felt a little naughty, proceeded to take my clothes off and meet him there. I think we both got a little cleaner than we anticipated, but I was on my own with a few thousand in the bank from yesterday, and a desire for nice clothes, Sak's seemed like the target for me. By 1 PM, my wardrobe had changed a bit, new jeans, skirts, and tops, of course the majority were on sale. I would have to wait for a couple more nice shoes. The credit card said I had spent like $1000, but I don't get to New York with money and time like anytime, so yes, I did splurge on myself, it has been almost eight years since I got to spend more than twenty dollars. I left a message for Larry, that I was on my way back to the hotel and then to practice. I would meet him at the Mets stadium after he was finished with work.

After I got back to the hotel, I texted my mom to make sure she had made it to Blacksburg, to be with dad and Dea. She texted back, she was at the hospital with both, Dea is in PCU, which is a step down from ICU or CCU, but at this point they have not found anything other than she appears to be anemic and underweight. They are going to give her a unit of blood, and fluids to make her feel better. I asked if I could talk to her, and mom said not a good idea at this point. I asked her then to wish her my best and that I will come to see her as soon as the tournament is over. Mom said I will tell her, and you know she is so thrilled for you and Larry, she was happy to see your engagement ring on tv. I closed the phone and wished I could be with them, but at least one more day of tennis awaits.

I gathered my clothes for the warm-up and let Paul know I was in the hotel and would meet him at 3:15, for our practice session.

"Paul said good to have you back and will meet you at the lobby. It will be just the two of us, as Mike has doubles match this afternoon in men's doubles, so we have a court with limited players in singles left and most doubles are playing between 2 and 6 pm, so they don't want to warm-up in 90-degree weather. I know you love that weather but most people with common sense are avoiding it."

I met Paul and we both were Lacoste outfitted to make Jacques and John happy. The shoe company had 3 more new pairs of shoes for the next two days, they said they had a better shoe for me to try-out at warm-up and if I liked them to use them in the next round. John came over to us as we were getting to the court and wanted me to know that everything is set for 4 weeks in Asia with both Paul and me. I had direct or wild card entries in the four tournaments and the ITF 125, has also accepted me based on my new ranking which when it comes out next week, will have you in the 140, range, so you will have five tournaments after this and before the season shuts down. There is a late ITF 125 in November, back in the states, but only if you need it to get in the top 100 to get you a direct entry in to the Australian Open.

Larry texted me that he would meet me at Mets stadium at 6:30 and then we could go out for dinner near the stadium and call it a night. I texted back, that I will move from the hotel on Thursday unless we have a miracle, so may need to park my car near his apartment. I called the desk regarding my car and possibly needing to leave it while I was visiting my boyfriend and they said for you Ms. Lilly, we can make the exception, leave the car here and let us know the license number so we can take care of it. I then texted Larry that the car was handled, so after the Wednesday match I will be free to move out Thursday and come to his apartment leaving the malibu at the hotel. I am thinking I will go to Blacksburg first to check in on Dea, I am hoping she will be out of the hospital this weekend. Going to leave Friday morning, and it will take most of the day to get to there, hoping it will be done by 8 PM.

(Lilly's Dad here) I am writing this after the fact but what Lilly did not know was that Dea was gravely ill. They were giving her transfusions, and fluids but she was not responding well afternoon, they did a blood test and it revealed that she had stage 4 cancer that was pulsing through her body. They believed it started in her uterus and has now spread throughout her body. Typical of my mom, she never complained, and let everyone think she was alright. The three K brothers were all together for the first time since our dad passed, and it did not look good for Dea, and we just were not sure how much to let Lilly really know. Barbara had rushed here talked to Dea this morning. All Dea could talk about was her granddaughter and her experience in New York. She wanted to hear the wedding plans of Lilly and Larry; Barbara just gave her the highlights. Granny Miller drove up this afternoon to see her friend Dea, they often communicated after my grandad passed away.

Paul and I went to the US Open, you could tell it was Tuesday of the second week, so many juniors around the courts and so few matches left to play. Quarterfinals were starting for the singles competition, and so would the doubles for the men. The women's doubles are a day behind. Now it could rain because for the professionals' courts were only on Ashe and Armstrong, and they could fit doubles in if they had to. The Grandstand court would be where we will play on Wednesday, if the rain holds off or we could get pigeonholed into Armstrong, of the singles matches go early, they will use the mixed doubles to keep the crowds happy.

Paul got the text that the schedule for Wednesday, we were going to be number 2 on Grandstand court. Expected playing time was 1:30 in the afternoon. That will mean that our box will be empty, even Larry won't be able to make this event. I then thought of Lucy Swisher, she was close to the area, and I saw her in the stands for one of the matches. I looked at my phone, and texted her, need someone in my box on Wednesday have a slot available if you can make it here. Just as practice had ended, I got the text back, give me the details, I will be there. I texted her the details and how she would pick-up her credentials at the "Will Call" area. Lucy said to me have you texted Susan Snider, she lives in Philadelphia, and here is her number. A few minutes after I sent the message, the response came back with a heart, and she would be honored. I made a request to both, if they had a pink top, I would appreciate it if they would wear it and the texts came back yes. While I would not have anyone other than Paul and John in the box from the team, I would have a couple of the Longwood gang.

The box would have enough people now to make it look like someone wanted to be here.

Larry joined me as we started near the Mets stadium. Paul went back to the hotel to look at strategy, get some dinner delivered and then have a video conference with his fiancé and future stepdaughter.

Larry and I went out to dinner at a restaurant nearby and we shared a pizza, and I got a salad. While Larry, got a nice beer, I was stuck with iced tea, match day on Wednesday. We did not finish the pizza so they gave us a box for later, I thought Larry would be taking it back to his apartment, but he said, he was too tired to go back to Manhattan tonight, so we took an Uber back to the hotel. I reminded him no fooling around tonight as I had a match tomorrow, and he just laughed, I'm too tired to even think about it.

After we got back to the hotel, I texted my mom to check in on Dea. She texted back me that Dea was still very weak and tired, but she was happy about my engagement to Larry. I then texted James to check in on him, and he responded that he was on his way to Blacksburg to see Dea. That had me wondering what was really going on with her, I started to worry but nothing I could do from here. I told Larry about Dea's condition and my concerns. I started to sigh, and Larry just hugged me, and said we will deal with whatever happens together. We sat on the couch, and both fell asleep very quickly, at 1 AM, I then left for the bed, and put a blanket on Larry. I saw a text from Paul that we were getting together at 8 in the morning to plan the day. I texted him back with ok, and his response a little late to be texting people, good night. I realized I had not even showered after our practice hit and changed to my pajamas, it was going to be the last full day at the hotel, all set to check out Thursday morning unless something happened in our match Wednesday.

US Open Semi-final Day

I woke-up to my alarm at 7:00 and shook Larry awake. He said oh crap and took a quick shower and headed out to get his clothes and go to work. He gave me a kiss and said good luck today, I would love to be there but need a day in the office with meetings I will be there in spirit, plus now you are going to have the Longwood connections, I don't want the interrogation from your former teammates. Paul said he was picking up breakfast of a good bagel and lox from the closest bagel store, a banana for me, and coffee for him and a cold Gatorade for me, competition body. I noticed it had rained overnight, and then looked up the US Open site and it said that all outdoor courts were in a thirty-minute delay as they were drying off the courts.

At 8:00, like clockwork Paul entered the room to talk about strategy today. Our opponents were the number 1 seeds and accomplished in both singles and doubles and had won Roland Garros in the mixed doubles. The woman was from Argentina, Caca Capo, a very beautiful woman with dark hair, and a very long and lean look. Her partner was from Australia John Langway. Both had won doubles majors both with same sex partner and in mixed. Rumor had it that they were more than just a tennis couple. Neither of them was playing singles much as they were top five doubles players and now that they were in their mid-thirties making enough money in doubles that singles were not required for them anymore to keep sponsors and make money. Mike and I have nowhere near the resume they have and that is going to be an issue with communications. I can hit a bigger serve than Caca, but she is very good at the net and can win points easily. I remember seeing her win an ITF doubles match when I was just beginning, and she was a really good player at net. Paul chimed in and her partner is a big server with limited range but will be very hard to get over as he is 6'5" and has a strong overhead. A strategy her will be simple, hit down the lines and push the middle.

Get yourself together and we will leave for the Open at 10:30, and you will do a hit with me prior to the match, we will get lunch at the player's lounge and then wait for the match. The first doubles match is now scheduled at 12:30 and we should be on the court at 2 PM, hot and humid conditions, keep drinking fluids. They say the effective temperature will be in the mid 90's.

After Paul's meeting, I got my stuff together and then texted mom. She answered but said she would call me back from a quiet place later.

I answered the call when she was somewhere outside the hospital, and she indicated that Dea had a tough night last night, she was doing better this morning, but she was still very weak and tired. James was there with her and going to stay at the family house with the three K brothers who are all there. I asked her should I come there now, and she said if Dea knew you left the US Open to see her she would probably kick us out of the room, and get home to meet you, so please we will tell her you called and that she will see you next week.

(Lilly's Dad insertion here) Dea had a very rough night, she had a cardiac event that she recovered from with the aid of drugs in her IV bag, we were nervous, and it was confirmed that she had the cancer we thought and soon she will need chemo treatments once we can get her anemia fixed, and she is getting a transfusion now. She did wake up briefly this morning and smile at the three brothers and went back to sleep shortly thereafter.

I met Paul at the lobby, and we were off to the semifinals of the US Open Mixed doubles, it was a cloudy and humid day, I was used to this weather, but it can be tough to handle, and vision was going to be in and out with bright sun and then clouds.

We did a short warm-up at the open and then met Mike and his coach at the lounge while we ate our lunch.

ESPN Studios:

Pam Shriver speaking, "I have just been told something that has me remember that this is a sport and sometimes real-life barges in. Lilly Jarman is about to walk on to the court for a semi-final in mixed doubles on stadium court. I am not sure how we got this news, but sometime today and she will find out that her grandmother Dea, has just passed away in Blacksburg, VA. I don't think anyone will tell her before the match but certainly no matter what happens today, life will be real today and not the fantasy of our tennis tournaments. As many of you may remember it was Dea that chose Lilly's colors when she was a child. My sympathy to the Jarman family for the loss of the matriarch of the family."

As I was going to the court, I finally found Lucy and handed her my iPad. She would take notes for me regarding the match.

Susan then came running up to both of us and gave me a huge hug and said, "I knew you were a lot better than others said you were, wow." I introduced them to Paul, and they asked so where Larry is, and I had to say all the days this is the one he must work. They said any chance we can meet him later, you hardly dated in college and now you have this whirlwind proposal on ESPN.

"I said maybe."

Hello Lucy, here, I am taking the notes for the upcoming doubles match. The announcer introduced the upcoming match will be the first semi-final for the mixed doubles match. Please welcome our players, representing South Korea and in her very first US Open, from Virginia, please welcome Lilly Jarman. And now her partner, on this wild card team, Mike Finley from Great Britain. Their opponents, From Argentina, and winner of several doubles' crowns and mixed doubles grand slams, Caca Capo. Her partner also who has won numerous doubles titles and mixed grand slam titles, from Australia, John Langway.

Ken Insert here, Dea was very sick, woke up this morning and said let me know how Lilly does. She then had a stroke, and we lost her within an hour. The doctor said we all needed to say goodbye, and we did just as she stopped breathing with the ventilator. At 11:45 AM, my mother Dea, the strongest woman I had ever known crossed over to be with her true love, my father. I decided to hold the text for Lilly to call me until she was finished with her match, Dea would have haunted me if I had. The three K brothers were all here to see our mother pass, and with us was Granny Miller, James, and Barbara. Even if she had survived the stroke, she was very ill with her cancer, and it would have been not very long when that would have taken her, so we were glad that she did not suffer. I am suffering with the loss of my mother.

Lucy, here, the team of Lilly and Mike lost the serve and John started the serving. Mike has extremely hard serves and won his serve with 4 straight points. Lilly then started for her team, a strategy that most would not do, but Mike's strength is the net, and he proved it winning 3 straight points. Caca held serve more difficultly after getting to deuce she won the deciding point. Mike won his serve easily, and that is the pattern that would take them to a tiebreaker to decide the first set. When the tiebreak got to 5-all, it was Lilly's time to shine and served to Caca, and it was right down the "T" and curving away from her, Caca could barely touch the ball. Caca then was serving to keep her team in the set, and unfortunately, she double faulted the set away, and the potential upset to the finals was becoming real.

Ken here, once someone said that ESPN had announced that Dea has passed away on the air, I texted Paul so he could let Lilly know at the end of the match. I did not want to do it, but she could be possibly interviewed about it at the mandatory press conference, and I did not want her to suffer like that.

Lucy, again, the second set showed why Caca and John were the number 1 seeds. They won the first 5 games of the set, and Lilly was able to avoid the set loss by holding serve on the deciding point. John then proceeded to go to deuce and won the set 6-1, when Mike could not handle the deciding point hitting it long. After two sets, they were tied, and the match would be decided by a ten-point match tiebreaker.

As the team sat down, we heard with the bowl about a third filled, "Athletic and Feminine", a cheer that made her smile as she downed fluids for the match tiebreaker. Sarah and I started launching the same cheer trying to rally our friend and teammate.

I wish I could say that our team won, but at 7 all, Lilly was broken, and the other team was serving at 8-7, and proceeded to win both points with overheads ending the match and Lilly's run at the US Open. As she stood up, the entire bowl gave her a standing ovation, and the chant of "Athletic and Feminine" was probably heard all the way to the ESPN, studios.

As the team was heading to the tunnel to leave, Paul stopped Lilly and showed her his cell phone and the text read. We watched Lilly read the text, "Dear Paul, let Lilly know that Dea's final words were how was Lilly doing. Dea passed away this morning after a stroke she will be missed by all of us."

Lilly pulled a towel over her head and started sobbing loudly as her favorite fan had just passed away.

ESPN Studio:

We are showing you the raw emotions of Lilly Jarman, she was just told that her grandmother has passed away. You could hear her sobbing and the towel over her head, let everyone know that she was hurting. Lilly was hugging her two former teammates here to support her, and her coach is also in tears, he knew Dea and the journey.

Post Match Interview:

Lilly was late to the post match interview that was required as part of the press availability to the players. Mike had been talking about the run that he and Lilly had made when Lilly finally stepped in and sat down. A reporter then asked Lilly a question, "What is it that you would like us to know about your grandmother that passed away today?"

Lilly responded, with tears in her eyes, "When the debutantes in Radford, would pick on me for being Eurasian, and not invite me to their parties, one person was always there for me, and even when nobody was recruiting me, she said you will get your opportunity and then Coach Wilson offered me a scholarship, and then I made All-American, only one person was my greatest fan. In absolute tears, my greatest supporter and the person who told me I could be athletic and feminine, passed-away today. Her final words according to my dad was how was Lilly doing."

Lilly started sobbing and left the room, even the press clapped as she left. Mike gave her a hug and said next year I want your promise that we will be on a team next year.

Somehow Larry had appeared at the door just as Lilly was leaving, she ran to him and hugged him, and the weeping began again in earnest.

Lilly quickly went to the players locker room and changed her clothes. She called her mom who was at the family home in Blacksburg, she told Lilly not to worry about getting home tonight, no plans had been started for the funeral.

Lilly came over to Paul and said, "I will make sure we are there for your wedding, I think you are getting back this Friday and then you are getting married next Friday. I suspect the funeral will be on Saturday in Blacksburg."

"Paul said, Lilly it has been my honor to be a part of this run, gave her a hug, and said are you ready for me to be with you on the upcoming Asian tour in October?"

"Lilly started crying again, her world had changed so much in the last two weeks."

I handed the iPad to Lilly, and said I have everything written down. Lilly thanked me for coming at the last minute and then hugged Susan and told her you too. Susan and I left her there with her coach and fiancé and we then went home to our respective cities, telling Lilly we want to be there for the wedding in Radford. Lilly said not going to be there, going to be at Farmville, and Longwood, Granny Miller is helping there.

Lilly here, all I could do is look up at the ESPN studio and think had this really happened and then Dea would have loved to be here, wish she had been able to come before she died, but dad said she did get to watch me on tv.

Larry picked up Chinese food and we went back to the hotel to plan the next week. I was still a mess, but Larry said she died as she was independent and proud of her family.

I fell asleep by 9:00, when I woke up Larry had gone to work to get ready for taking plans to be with me next week at the wedding and funerals. I had to go to Paul's room and say my goodbye, as I got ready to leave for Blacksburg. I checked out of the hotel at 10:00, got in the Malibu and finished packing, with all the clothes I had I barely could fit it all in.

Jacques, John, and Allison called to wish me the best with the family. I knew I would call Larry about noon from the Jersey side of the mountains, I was going home through New Jersey, and then south to Pennsylvania, and then to I-81, all the way to Blacksburg. It was a very long drive, and I would have a lot of time to reflect on what had happened and on my grandmother.

I called Elijah's bagels and thanked them for everything for the last two weeks, I was done with my New York experience. More adventures to come and a wedding to plan, but first a funeral to be at, and time to heal.

ESPN Broadcast Studios:

"Pam Shriver speaking, we showed you the conference with Lilly Jarman after losing her match and her grandmother yesterday. We want to wish her and her family the best during this grieving period. I want to say to Lilly thank you for being here with us over the last two weeks, your story was so fantastic, and we look forward to seeing you again. For those that say dreams can't come true, wait until the rewards for Lilly come to her over the next few months."

I just received a call from Kia, stating they wanted to give me a car to use when I get back to Radford, and before the Asian swing. They said we can't have one of our people forced to drive a very old car from another company. The car was going to be delivered to Radford by September 11, and it was likely to be a Telluride, so I would have enough space for clothes and equipment. One additional perk but I would not own it, I really do need to get a tax guy now.

Chapter 17

Beginnings and Endings

With the US Open behind me, and many miles of driving in front of me, I had time to reflect on the last two weeks before the reality of what was coming ahead this month. I will get to Blacksburg in time to see the family the three brothers will all be there, Ken, Karl, and Kevin in Blacksburg. My mom, brother and Granny Miller will all be there also. I will stop by and then go to Radford Saturday.

So, everyone does not get worried, I am stopping at the various rest stops to enter my thoughts on my iPad, not going to get killed with the traffic on the Garden State, going through Pennsylvania, and then I-81, all the way down way too much traffic to be stupid to read and write on the iPad. It was a little after noon when I stopped at my first stop to get some fluids and at a Roy Rogers at the rest stop in New Jersey. I got a burger with ham on it, sounded good, (Double R Burger), French fries and a diet coke all in my plate. I added several condiments, I was cheating on my diet, and was enjoying it.

Two weeks ago, I was a completely unknow athlete, now in the ratings will be top 140 in the world, moving up over 100 places with the points from the US Open. From now on I can get into ITF's and Challengers without going through qualifying. I got invitations to go to Asia and play up to four tournaments. Oh yes, the man I truly love, asked for my hand in marriage on live TV that all my friends from college saw and were yelling for me. I got to launch my first line of shoes and now the world will used the term Dea started for me. "Athletic and Feminine", shoes T-shirts, and apparently from what Jacques says a sweatshirt with blue on the back and pink on the front. I look at my engagement ring with the blue and pink sapphires and the diamond and realized this is real. I won more prize money in a week than I had my whole career, and based on the clothes in the Malibu, a couple thousand was on my credit card. Who would have thought a pair of shoes was over $300. Next week, the Malibu will be put to rest, it has taken me so many places, and now it will be replaced by a fancy Kia for the next year. The Malibu will be saved just in case everything goes poof again. I have finally put the debutante's world behind me, and now it is time to move forward.

Then there is the coaching from Paul, without it I know I could not have been ready. A week from now, Larry will come to Radford, we will be at the courthouse, and we will watch him get married to his childhood sweetheart. "Ann Chidester", I have met her before, and then he will meet me in Asia to coach one last time through the swing. If I somehow get into Charleston, SC next year, I am going to have him sit in my box for any matches, oh shoot, that is clay, going to be no fun.

I'm now at a rest stop just north of the entry in to I-81, needed gas so figure I would stop and take 15 minutes, to let the malibu rest and to write a little bit in the iPad. My thoughts are around my grandmother, and every time I think about her passing, I can't stop crying. When the debutantes would not allow me to be with them because I had Asian features, Dea was there to let me know I was special. She was the one that started my clothing colors, and when the guys I brought home did not measure up to her standards for me she told me. I guess Larry must have made her standards because she helped him with the engagement ring. I'm looking at it and it is gorgeous and unique, kind of how Larry describes me to his friends. I can't believe he and I will get married next year by this time. I want to visit Farmville before the swing and see the areas for the wedding with Granny Miller. I also have been told to have time to visit the team at Longwood, not as good as when I was there but the new coach, Jonathan Kindman, is trying to recruit some better players and he says he has a couple of recruits that would like to meet me next weekend.

I'm now stopping at I-81 near James Madison, needed a bathroom break, and driving over to see where dad played football while I am here. Not going west to see mom's little school out of the way. I had to stop because the traffic was heavy on I-81, with large tractor trailers and I'm getting tired so dropped by McDonalds and got some coffee, so off my tennis habits. I received a call from dad saying to meet me at the family house he was clear of the hospital and the family was all over the house in Blacksburg. I'm not sure how to react, I am so thrilled to see my uncles and we will be burying my greatest fan. Mom says we need to also work the Radford issue.

Mom says that Radford wants to honor me for what has happened over the last few weeks, and truthfully not sure what I want from Radford. I am thinking not the town but maybe the college but need to think this out, so many bad memories eliminated, but the debutantes will be in attendance and will try to be my friend now. I don't want to do this just to show them that they were wrong to push me away from the community, and the moms also. If we do something it should be to get others to reach for their dreams and not let others kill them.

I'm just outside the exit for Blacksburg, and it is just starting to get dark, I am taking a few minutes to write here before seeing the family, hopefully I can get some food here but knowing my family there will always be food. I really want to hug my dad and uncles tonight, I feel bad but can't imagine how it is to lose your mom, that was so dedicated to her children. Granny Miller will be there too, want to see her also, to plan on being at Farmville, later this week.

Jarman Home, Blacksburg, VA

At just after 8 PM, I made it to the house in Blacksburg, I knocked on the door and Uncle Karl opened the door. He yelled to my dad, Hey Ken, there is someone that wants to talk to you, says she is related to you, but she is way too tall and beautiful, for her to be related to us.

He then proceeded to hug me and then said welcome home superstar, surprised you came in that old jalopy of yours.

"I laughed and told him what Kia told me; the new car will be delivered to the Radford Jarman home on Monday. Uncle Kevin then came over to me, and gave me a kiss on my cheek, and started to cry, so Dea's favorite is home from the US Open.

"Where's your trophy, I thought you won the tournament according to your father."

"Sure, I ended up getting beaten in the semi-finals of the mixed doubles, they don't have a third and 4th place trophy like when we were kids."

"Kevin just said I wish Dea was still with us to see you come home and she would have wanted to see that ring on your finger. He then lifted my hand, wow I only got to get engaged privately, you had to show up the entire community by doing it live on ESPN. So where is the lucky guy?"

"I told him later in the week, he must do some work and I blew a lot of his leave up there in New York at the open."

Mom and Granny Miller were the next to come greet me, they said James will be back later this week. They cried as they saw me and again said I wish Dea was here to see you come back to us, she really was your best fan.

I asked where I could stay for the night and was there anything to eat. Mom indicated that Karl's old bedroom was shared by Granny Miller, and they can make space for you with a blow-up bed, and as far as food, look at the kitchen. Between the members of Christ Episcopal Church and your friends from tennis we are well covered, you name it we have it as far as cold cuts, fried chicken, salads, and several grit recipes, take your choice of meals. We have everything to drink from water to hard liquor for you to drink. I took a water and then some cold cuts, there was something that nobody was eating, and I asked what it was. Dad said that it was corned beef tongue, and I gathered it with some coleslaw and made a sandwich. They all looked at me oddly, I just responded this is a New York city delicacy, just go to any deli up there and look for corned beef tongue. I bet this came from ESPN, and yes, I looked at the card and it had. My family is going to give me poop about being a celebrity. (15 minutes of fame)

Friday: Blacksburg

The world has changed, my dad and Uncles met with the minister at Christ Episcopal Church and then the Storke Funeral Home coordinator, about what to do with Dea's funeral. The funeral would be a week from Saturday with Viewings, on Thursday night and Friday night, apparently Dea was well respected in the community, so they asked for 2 nights and then a very formal funeral at noon Saturday. I am being asked to prepare a presentation about my life with Dea and the type of person she was. The service will be about 75 minutes and then internment at the cemetery. After that we will all meet as a family at 4 PM, for the reading of the will, and early family dinner to memorialize Dea.

Larry is flying into Roanoke-Blacksburg airport, and I will pick him up there next Friday and then we will drive together to Radford for Paul and Ann's wedding at the courthouse. We will stay at my parents' house in Radford, and then go to Blacksburg, the following morning.

At 1 PM, I received a call from Paul regarding the plans for the fall. He gave his notice to the club and college this morning, they were disappointed but understood his new positions and his upcoming marriage would make staying here impossible. He did tell them he needed to leave in two weeks for his 1-week honeymoon, and then to meet up with me for the Asian swing. They had thought about calling me to take over as the assistant coach, but he told them likely that I was going to be full-time on the tour so not likely to be available. Paul said there is a plan for me to come to Radford College tennis practice on Tuesday afternoon. I would then see the juniors their afterword, to sign autographs, tennis balls, and to talk to the juniors.

The house in Blacksburg was extremely crowded and people kept coming over and giving us food, so there was so much food we really did not know what to do with it. I was able to go up to the room and take a very long nap from 1:30 to 4 PM, I guess everything was catching up with me.

By the time I got up and was able to take a shower and change clothes it was almost 6 PM and had to call Larry to make sure that he was aware of everything and apparently Paul had already kept him in the loop for the wedding, and he was going to work through Thursday of next week so he can do the wedding and the funeral. Since the wedding was going to be at the courthouse no formal attire just a suit and tie and a dress for me.

A lot of stories about my grandmother but very little else going on: Saturday:

The women's final was going to be on TV, but truthfully, I had no interest in watching it. I had my dream, and the mixed doubles was being played also and all I wanted to know is who had won, only to find our opponents were the winners, so I don't feel as bad about losing, we gave them a go.

I got a call from the country club and from Radford University about Tuesday. Paul was being invited and I know Ann was coming with him. Jake Willis had a reception for me at the Country Club all planned around lunch and then on to Radford University women's practice, and the junior practice so it was all set.

I thought about picking up a tennis racquet, but thought about it some more, and decided it was too early, and with the family here not appropriate. My body was still healing from the last two weeks I could still feel my legs were sore and my right arm asked not to be serving yet.

Sunday:

I left Blacksburg for Radford with the promise to be back Thursday and then back to Radford for Friday and back Saturday. When the neighbors saw the Malibu, they came over to see how the family was doing and if they could do anything for us. I had a few said they were rooting for me at the US Open, some of them I knew were the mothers of the debutantes so all I would say is thank you, never asked about their daughters, I had no interest, and they were doing this to look good in most cases not really cared about me or my family. I looked at the fridge and the pantry and saw I needed to go to Food Lion for food. After what seemed forever, I bought enough food for when my parents returned. I cooked a pasta dinner with sausage, a salad, and some garlic bread enough for at least three nights for myself. I bought a bottle of wine and had a wine cork to keep it for a couple of days. I think Mom was coming down Tuesday, so I may have to cook something for the two of us.

Tuesday morning:

This is the day I had been dreading, all the glad handing I would receive accolades at the Country Club at noon and be around for a little over an hour before going to Radford. I knew I had to get dressed in the pink and blue combination and all decked out in Lacoste gear. I had a box of sweat bands to hand out and at Radford, a whole bunch of shoes were going to be waiting to be handed out to the juniors. Lacoste had tons of T-shirts with the Lacoste logo for me to hand-out at both sites. Unknown to me, mom and dad were coming to the country club and then going home to Radford to get clothes and be away from the preparations for a day.

At 9:00, I got a text that a driver was coming to my house in the next ten minutes with the Telluride, it was so big and powder blue with white interior and trimmed with pink accent stripes both in and out. I loved it, and will keep the malibu around, don't know how long I will have this car. By the time I got all the paperwork signed it was 10:00, and time to go to the Country Club to be there by 11:30.

I rolled up to the club, and saw the sign saying, "Welcome Home Lilly". Inside another banner read Lilly Jarman's junior tennis roots. I loved it, and waiting for me was Jake Willis. He went to give me a hug, and I said this must be a hug and I want to give you a kiss. There must have been fifty ladies at the club, and after speeches about this is where

Lilly learned tennis and we need to support more like her, it was my time to talk.

Good morning, I am assuming that based on the banners you were expecting me this morning. I appreciate the happenings today and have my wrist bands for everyone here. I would not have been able to make it to the US Open without the support of the club. Jake Willis helped us when we did not have much money, and so many of the junior professionals helped me learn the game. Without Paul, who has been working here, I would not have made it past the first round. The colors you see me wearing tonight, are the colors from my grandmother Dea who passed away last week.

The speech was interrupted: "Athletic and Feminine."

Yes, that was her doing, and if you have not looked at my ring before, you will notice she helped design my engagement ring.

I would have loved to come back here with a trophy from the US Open, we made it to the semi-finals, the team that beat us won the tournament. I want to thank you for being very welcoming to me here, I learned a lot and all your families were so welcoming to our family. You never know what happens when you work towards your dreams. I don't have to say that here, many of you have been very successful in business and local charities and it is one thing you all know it is easier to pursue the dream with hard work.

My new sponsors will be donating clothes and shoes for low-income people throughout the area, so they have a chance to learn and play. Larry and I are donating a portion of our proceeds from "Athletic and Feminine", to this area.

Thanks again, and let's cut the cake and get this party going.

A little more than an hour later I was on my way to the next stop back in Radford.

As I got to the courts, I saw the sign in pink and blue lettering. Welcome Home Lilly Jarman, our coach and friend. This one made me cry, and my parents joined me here. Since this was for the College Team, I could not give the girls anything as it would be a violation of the NCAA rules. I could though practice with them and then I saw

Paul and Ann hand in hand, coming to the court. The tennis team all had on pink tops and blue skirts, not exactly Radford colors.

I did make a speech to the team about pushing forward when others said you have no chance or that your pedigree was not right. I also wanted to thank the girls for letting me be a part of their team, and that they will do well going forward without me there to practice with them.

Paul was asked to come and talk about his leaving. Paul said, "if you saw Ann over there, well we are getting married Friday, we were childhood sweethearts that went in a different direction and now we are coming back together with a move back to our beloved Charleston area. I will be working at Hilton Head most of the year and then working College of Charleston. I will be a first-time dad next year and a stepdad all in the next year. Oh, I will continue with Lilly through the end of the year, somebody thinks she could be a top 100 ranked player and getting her in to the Australian Open. Now, I want to say you will be in good hands I understand that you will have a new coach shortly, Sierra Johnson has been hired to replace me. She played at Longwood and plays locally as a regionally ranked professional, she was on Lilly's senior team and has been teaching tennis in DC with her boyfriend being here she wanted to move to this area. You will be in good hands with her, and I want to hear that you worked just as hard for her as you did for me."

We could not give the girls anything directly, but we could give it to the college and if the girls happened to use them, I could not control that, so the remainder of the first box of wrist bands was placed at the outside of the locker-room.

We hit with the girls on the team for about half an hour and the local paper was taking pictures for the morning edition Wednesday.

At 3:30, PM, the age group team started to come in. I handed each of them a T-shirt and a pair of wrist bands. One little girl, who is of mixed parents, but identifies herself as African American, came to me and gave me a hug. Miriam Jackson, who was ten, said to me, Lilly I am so glad that you told your story, I also get that I have two worlds and the little girls here don't always want to play with me. I gave her a high five and said, so just go out and beat them. I stayed around for another hour and as promised the shoes came to our facility; each girl received a pair of Mizuno shoes. I called Allison and left a message thanking her for the shoes. The boys received a Lacoste windbreaker, this was a cost on me, a case of them that Jacques said would come from my first commission check, oh well. The reporter for the Richmond Times came over to interview me for a puff piece, I got Miriam to shake my hand for the picture, we who live in two worlds share a bond. The questions were mostly around my tennis at the US Open, and then about Dea Jarman. I told them she was my greatest fan, but Miriam here will have to be my main fan going forward, we share a bond, and I did not elaborate on that bond."

"Miriam smiled and said yes, we do."

Finally, they took a picture of my mom and me together with a few of the tennis kids and then of me coaching them and practicing with them, not sure what they will use, but it will go back to Lacoste and Mizuno for publicity. Then just as fast as it began, everything was over, I realized that was probably me, a moment in time of the US Open and then it will be over.

Mom and I decided to go to Sharkey's for the fun of it for dinner. We both got ribs which was a mistake, I had to clean my hands so many times as people came over to shake my hand or get a picture.

"Mom said so how does it feel to be a celebrity, I stated laughing it will be fifteen minutes of fame. Finally, mom stood up and said, we love the ribs here, please give Lilly 15 minutes so we can eat our dinner before coming over to ask for a picture."

I was stunned that my mom would basically say leave us alone to finish dinner.

The big day of return was over. I know they wanted to do something in the Radford city areas, but I had no desire for a big event like that, this was all I wanted back with my tennis people.

Thursday:

Today was the beginning of the funeral services for Dea in Blacksburg. Mom left early and I was going to leave later. I had to go get a second black dress one for the funeral was already here, needed one for the viewings at Storke Funeral Home. After shopping for an hour, I was able to purchase what I needed and then packed a lunch and closed the Radford house.

The viewing was scheduled from 7 to 9 PM tonight, I would get there about 5, get some dinner and change. On the way I confirmed all the arrangements with Larry and meeting him at the airport at 9:00, and then get to the house in Radford, change and get to the courthouse. Stay for the wedding until about 2 PM, change clothes and get back to Blacksburg in time for part of the viewing for night two. I went back to the bedroom shared by Granny Miller and myself for the night, knowing I was leaving early Friday.

Friday: New beginnings and then Goodbye.

I had the alarm at 6:45 and took a quick shower before others got up. Such a crazy day ahead, pick-up my fiancé, go to a wedding of my coach and friend, and then start to say goodbye to my grandmother. I had to get on my nice dress and then pack away the dark dress for later tonight. I think we were possibly having to go straight to the funeral home so needed to be prepared. I proceeded to text Larry who was already at the airport waiting for his flight to take off. I was rushing to get to the airport, he won't have a long time getting his stuff off the regional airport. Sitting at the gate by 9:00, waiting for Larry, I was anxious to see him, it had been a week and I really wanted to see him to help me get through tonight. At 9:15, I spotted him, and a minute later got a kiss from Larry that was both passionate and excessive for a public kiss. He proceeded to give me a hug that I thought would crush my ribs, apparently, he was very happy to see me. Larry was looking for the malibu in the parking lot when I told him look for the powder blue Telluride, with pink accent stripes, and he saw it and laughed, we are going to live with pink and blue for a lot of things now. Well, at least for a while, and it will pay some bills and pay back some communities that supported me in the dark times.

On the way to my parents' house so Larry could change his clothes. I will say that we were somewhat romantic that morning, and I needed to take another quick shower before we went to the courthouse. After blow drying my hair, I proceeded to get my fancy dress on and do make-up for the first time in a week. The advantage of being Eurasian is that with my features and ability to tan, I did not have an issue with looking too pale. Larry was handsome in his suit, and I helped him with his tie, he always had a habit of it being too loose. He could use a little more sun in my opinion, too much Wall Street time.

Courthouse, Radford Virginia

    I thought about driving the new car, but it would not be appropriate for my relationship with Paul. We chose the malibu, starting to rust but it was the car that Paul knew me from. I was asked to meet the judge at noon, Amy Conklin, the first female circuit court judge for the area was going to perform the wedding. It turns out that Amy was a 4.0 tennis player and played league tennis in the area. She had a pink tennis top that she wanted me to sign. She said, "we women with brains and athleticism need to stick together, then she said I'm not quite at your athletic level, and with my three kids, I have a great partnership with my husband so I can play at night."

    I signed her top and of course added, "Athletic and Feminine", I guess that was going to be my tag line and just had to get used to it. She had a sandwich for me, and asked what I knew about Paul and Ann, and I let her know what Paul had said to me.

    "They were childhood sweethearts, and both married and divorced someone else, and now they are getting together and will have a baby together in about 6 months. I know that Paul had gone home for a holiday, and when he came back said he had a blind date arranged for him, and it turned out it was Ann. Apparently, they have rekindled their relationship, and both are ready to be with family and friends back in Charleston, SC. Ann has a daughter by her first marriage, and she will be at the wedding as a flower girl. I know Paul already has a good relationship with his future stepdaughter and I know that Paul and Ann are very committed to the blended family. I guess I should not have told you that Ann is pregnant, that should be something they should have told you."

Judge Conklin laughed, "I already met the couple, and they already told me that she was pregnant, one of the reasons they wanted it now before she showed much. I signed the license earlier this week, so they are ready, and you did nothing wrong."

1PM: Court House

The simple wedding that Paul and Ann had planned was going to be just that. The couple would walk in together, and Paul and I would be sitting where the attorneys normally sit. Paul came in a dark suit first and was in front of the judge's bench, then Ann's daughter, Paula came in, she was so cute holding the basket of flowers. Ann then came in wearing a grey skirt and white blouse, she was not in a full wedding dress both second marriages, and they were saving money for a new house in Charleston area.

Judge Amy came in front of the bench, and proceeded to do the wedding ceremony, we had Ann's daughter with us, so it was easier for Ann. When the section of the ceremony came does anyone object to this marriage, it was totally quiet. Judge Amy had each provide vows to each other and then proceeded to have each other give a ring in exchange. Amy then declared them man and wife. Both Larry and I applauded at this, and then Paul kissed Ann. We came over to them and shook hands and hugged the wife and groom. With that done, I then presented a check for $10,000, to Paul, this is a downpayment from last week, waiting for the final check as they are taking out Federal and New York taxes.

The rest of the money will be transferred to your account next week, and then to finish the agreement for the rest of the year. First, you and Ann need to drive to Charleston, take your honeymoon as Mr. and Mrs. Nolan. I will meet you in Asia, as we get ready for the next step in this journey. Since this was the court chamber no alcohol is allowed, we went to the front steps and popped the champagne that Larry had brought with him. We only had plastic cups with us, but I thought it would still be good enough for the occasion.

Paul pulled me aside and let me know, go be with your family, and memorialize your grandmother, I will be busy, and you need to get this behind you, you won't be any good until this is all complete. I'm not saying get over it, I am saying until you have closure here you won't be able to do anything new, so go be with your family and take your time to honor Dea, and then as she would want, please move forward. I looked at him, and understood what he was saying, and it was going to be a tough couple of days. Before we left, we did somehow manage to spray "just married" on Paul's car in spray soap I had purchased at the grocery store on Sunday. We will get you ranked high enough to get a direct entry in to the Australian Open, just think about it entry in to 2 majors in a few months.

By the time we left the court grounds it was getting late in the afternoon, we barely had time to change our clothes and change to the newer car. I put on my first dark dress as we were going to go straight to the Storke Funeral Home, I bought subs at the closest Walmart because we really had not eaten much for lunch and I did not want to wait until after we finished the viewing and arrived at the Jarman House. Larry had already reserved a room for himself at the Holiday Inn Express in Blacksburg, I would drop him off after we attended the viewing. The family would not find it funny if I stayed with him tonight, and besides we already had a romantic session today. It only took about 45 minutes to get from Radford to Blacksburg, and another 15 minutes to get to the funeral home. We got there just after 7 PM. Nobody complained that we were a few minutes late, just a lot of hugs from everyone. I forgot that almost nobody in the family had every been introduced to Larry, most of the beginning of the time was introducing my fiancé Larry to the family. None of Dea's Korean family was here, she had very little contact with her three siblings and their families, from the day she left Korea with my grandfather. My uncle Karl pulled me aside and said he looks a lot taller in person than kneeling next to you on ESPN. We did not even know you were dating anyone seriously and then poof right there on TV, my niece is getting engaged, and only your grandmother would have helped your fiancé design the ring.

"I hardly had any time and then my uncle Kevin came over to me and said did you or Dea approve of your fiancé, because Dea could be a bit controlling, something you probably never saw. I can tell you she had a mean streak and I'm sure she probably chased away a few of your suitors because she did not approve of them. Probably to please her in controlling who was allowed to marry you much more than just looking out for your best interest, but that is how I knew my mother and not the grandmother you experienced."

I simply responded that Larry had called Dea for her blessing, along with my dad before he popped the question to me. Dea suggested the pink and blue sapphires added to the diamond ring because that is how she saw me as "Athletic and Feminine". Since I look like Uncle Karl, with Asian features, she probably knew something about what I had experienced as a Eurasian child in a mostly white European neighborhood, never quite fit in. For me, she was and will always be my protector. Always strange how people appear differently to others than to yourself, all based on experiences.

We had a lot of people at the Funeral Home from about 7 to 8, mostly people that knew Dea from the church and from the University that knew her when she had done some volunteering. From about 08:30 to closing it was mostly family with a few cousins coming in some I had never met before, but we probably had 50 people on Friday night and about 75 to 80 the night before. The talk about how Dea was forceful was different depending on who was talking, some said she was a leader in getting things done for the community, while others described Dea as almost a bully in getting things done the way she thought it should be. A lot of people came up to me and told them how much Dea was proud of me even before the US Open for pursuing my dream and overcoming prejudice in Radford. Some said based on what they had heard about my life in Radford, it was no surprise according to Granny Miller that the wedding was going to be in Farmville and at Longwood University. A lot of the people saw Larry and told them that he was marrying up, I had to tell them it was going to be an equal marriage, except I will be having the children, Larry has not figured out how to do that yet. There were lots of stories about seeing me and Dea when I was a kid and how much she was thrilled to have a granddaughter after having three sons, they thought she wanted to spoil me, I wonder about that never thought I was getting anything that James did not get. The night was pretty much over, so Larry and I got in the new car and drove him over to this hotel and then I returned to Dea's house. Granny Miller was not there but she asked me to call her as she was going home to Farmville.

The call was all about Larry, and the wedding plans. First, she said she also approved of Larry, but she had wished that he had called me before asking him to marry him, if Dea had that honor. I apologized for not having had Larry call her, and knew that she would have approved of Larry, not as tough as Dea and I remember a previous boy that Dea had said was not good enough for me. Granny Miller was much more trusting, and I did not think she would have been upset about not being asked prior, but again I was wrong and tried to make it up to her. She then said with you travelling all over the world, it would be up to Barbara and her to complete all the wedding plans and she was willing to do it, and it will be a big event for the town. The call ended and I said to her, I love you Granny Miller, and without your dinners not sure how I would have made 4 years at Longwood. The girls loved your dinners also. I returned to the Jarman home and took up the room that I had previously, I knew it was going to be a long day on Saturday. I texted Larry the timelines for Saturday, we were going to be on our feet a lot, and I need to finish my speech for my time to talk about Dea.

Goodbye to Dea:

I woke up at 6:45, and there was all sort of pastries waiting for me downstairs, my mom had made everything from bacon to sausage to scrapple for meats, and I saw some bananas, so I grabbed one even though it was a little unripe, oh well. I took some fruit salad that a neighbor had brought by and took a few pieces. I had finished my speech something like midnight, so at least a few hours of good sleep, well at least it was sleep. I had to pick-up Larry at 11:15, and apparently

James was staying at the same hotel, but he was coming on his own, he had to pick-up his suit at the dry cleaner beforehand. James had been in DC all week and was just getting here for the funeral. Mom was not too happy he missed the earlier events, but James had missed some time at the US Open, so he only had so much leave he could use, grandparents were not in his company's bereavement policy.

Granny Miller called me and said she would be at the Church no later than 11:30 AM and suggested that I get there early also as it could be packed, and to make sure I practiced my speech."

"I told her understood, and then she said no fooling around at the hotel, no time for that today. I did not respond to the last one, was not going to get into an argument this morning." I sneaked in for a quick shower at 8:30, before everyone else rushed in, and I'm glad I did because my mom was waiting as soon as I got out of the shower for her time.

"She told me dry blow your hair in the room, not enough time for her to wait."

I finished the hair drying in front of the mirror and then proceeded to get all my clothes on so I could leave by 10:00. I got to the Holiday Inn to pick-up Larry before 11:00 and we were at the church just as Granny Miller was getting there. The parking lot was almost full when I found a parking place, this was going to be a huge funeral. My uncles and dad had already met with the pastor Thomas Freeport, the priorities and timelines were all but completed at that point. Dad told me I was number three of five tributes to Dea, preceded by him, and Uncle Karl. After me was Granny Miller and then Uncle Kevin.

At noon, Pastor Freeport said we will be about five minutes late, we have so many people we are letting the people who parked across the street make it inside. The service did not start until 12:15.

Pastor Freeport began the service. We are here today to celebrate the life of Dea Jarman, Dea came from a hard life in South Korea, met her love of her life and was a war bride. Dea who never had a high school diploma eventually received her degree at 50 years old from Virginia Tech while raising the boys. Dea had three boys from her marriage, Ken, Karl, and Kevin, and of their spouses only Barbara is here today with us. In the last few years of her life, she befriended who we call Granny Miller, Barbara's mother, and she is with us today from Farmville. Two of her grandchildren are here today, James and Lilly Jarman. Lilly, I was expecting you to be wearing a pink and blue combination, but glad you are here today with your fiancé Larry, and we want you to show the famous designed engagement ring later. Larry, you must have made a great impression on Dea, without meeting you, she approved of you as Lilly's potential husband. Many in the community can attest, that it was not always easy to get Dea's approval. Dea touched many people's lives in this community, while some said she was hard to deal with, she also was a great leader for education possibilities for our young people and especially for those without financial means making sure they had enough school supplies.

At 12:45, the service had moved away from the traditional Episcopalian service to the tributes to Dea. The two brothers finished their speeches, and then it came for me to come up to the alter, Pastor Freeport said to the audience we all know by now the saying that Dea had for this young lady as does appear to be now the entire world. Introducing Lilly Jarman, 'Athletic and feminine", a phrase that Dea gave to Lilly, and represents so many of the young ladies today who like sports and still like to be true women.

I stood up and went to the podium, and fortunately I had written my speech because I started to tear-up immediately. For those that do not know me, yes, I am Lilly Jarman, I am Eurasian, and I play a little tennis, Dea was my connection to my Asian side of the family who I have never met. Growing up in Radford was not easy for me, having Eurasian features, as my mother can state, the old-line Radford, was not accepting of me because I looked different from them. When things were rough for myself, Dea would remind me that I was a special child from two worlds representing the best of them. The old Radford families, which I nicknamed the debutantes did not like me for simply looking different and having my sites on career and athletics. It was Dea that made things easier for me, and when girls laughed at me for developing a little later than they had, Dea coined the phrase you are both "Athletic and Feminine". Being 5'10" at 14, and gangly at the time, I never felt better than what Dea told me I was. Later in life when boys wanted to date me, and one even wanted me to marry him, Dea said he was not serious enough for you, and she must have been reading my mind because I ended it the same week. Larry only had two conversations with Dea prior to getting engaged and she gave him the blessing for us to get married, apparently before I knew he was going to ask me. The ring I have on today is how Dea saw me, "Athletic in the blue sapphires, and feminine represented by the pink sapphires". I guess according to Larry, I must be the diamond. Even when Dea knew she was not long for the world, she asked my dad how I was doing at the US Open, always my biggest supporter. Sorry Mom and Dad, I don't include you as you were my parents always there. When nobody wanted to recruit me, Dea said someone will and then Longwood came, she must have known something. I am also sure Granny Miller here also had something to do with it. So, I am here to celebrate my grandmother Dea, still my biggest fan she will watch me from heaven, and then bless our marriage next year.

Fifteen minutes later the tributes to Dea were complete, and I was a real mess. I was in tears and sobbing, Larry had to help me as we left the church. The internment service was done at the cemetery at the rear of the church with chairs for the immediate family. Pastor Freeport held another brief prayer for Dea, and then my dad and uncles all placed some dirt on the coffin as it was lowered into the ground. She was buried next to her war hero lover and husband Ken Jarman; my dad is Junior just in case I confused you with names. People started leaving the church parking while I stayed to say thanks to Dea privately. In our lives we all need someone like Dea who supports us unconditionally and protects us from the bullies in the world, Dea was that person for me, and I guess she knew to pass that on to Larry as she knew she was gravely ill and never led on. Granny Miller hugged my mom and me and said she was going home before it got dark, she was afraid to drive I-81 and I-64 in the dark. She patted my dad on the back and then departed.

The family drove back to the Jarman house and waiting for us to get there was Julian Askew, ESQ. He was going to handle the estate and had been a friend of the family. The family gathered for the reading of the will around the dining room table with Julian add the captain's chair at the end.

While nothing was surprising that all the property and any cash and other savings were to be held equally by all three brothers, with my dad Ken as the executor. There were a series of individual requests to others in the community and family and then it came to James and me. James was given her car, which he needed anyway her Mercedes was better than his Chevy. Finally, the request came to me. Dea specifically bequeathed to me, an amount of money ($3500), to have me meet the Asian side of the family in Korea, and the family China plus a few pieces of Waterford crystal. A letter was enclosed for me, the name and address of Dea's nephew and niece in Seoul, plus the address of a younger sister, Lilly, who now lived nearby in the same city. I told the family, given that I was already going to Seoul for a tennis tournament, I would not take the amount of money for the trip. I was told that the paperwork for that must be signed so nobody or myself could contest it. With the signature on a drawn-up piece of paper printed out and signed by me, everything was over. Kevin and Karl packed up and left to be with their family. Mom and dad left for Radford, while James returned to the hotel and was driving back to DC to sell his current car and come back for the Mercedes in the next week. I left for the hotel and stayed the night with Larry.

Larry and I drove to the airport early Sunday, we had a very passionate kiss at the airport, and I knew I would not see him until late November after the Asian swing. We had been good at the hotel, well at least we did not get very romantic, it would have been an insult to Dea's memory. On the way back to Radford, I called Paul, and left him a message, that we want to have a great Asian swing, and enjoy his next two weeks.

With my car leaving Blacksburg, the Dea portion of my life was over, and I felt like something would never be the same.

Chapter 18

Asian Swing

I spent time in Radford and worked out with Paul before he went on his honeymoon, and I needed to go to Silicon Valley, for the 125 tournaments. This is the first of four tournaments away from the East Coast and America. I have never been to any of these countries, much less see my Aunt Lilly, and my cousins Juwon, and Woong Jongro, in Seoul.

One week after the funeral, I said my goodbyes to my family, mom drove with me to Richmond to begin the next journey, and then took the vehicle back to Radford. We went by Farmville first to see Granny Miller, and make sure she was doing okay. John had arranged my travel and for the very first time in my life, I was travelling business class in the front of the plane, first Richmond to Dulles airport and then a direct flight to San Francisco. I had several packed bags to pick-up and others were delivered to the hotel in the valley directly. The tournament will be held in San Jose, with 32 total players. I am the 8 seed for the tournament and have been told that I will be first on Monday, noon west coast time, and it will be on Tennis Channel as a filler before the men play the Laver cup. The tournament hotel was in north San Jose, a Hyatt and the rate for the players was $100. I was booked for three days, and we could extend as required to make the next connection. I did have a tentative flight from San Jose to China, and then to the tournament city of Nanchang. John had been very good at making the travel arrangements at the WTA 250 tournament. Beyond that week, I had to look at what John told me to do. Paul would be joining me in China, and with me in Tokyo, and Seoul.

Four weeks to get my ranking to the magical 94, to get a direct entry in to the Australian Open. This is going to be tough, never travelled this much but the sponsors are footing the bill, and hotels were better than the Motel 6, or the basements of sponsors in the ITF world. My current ranking will only get me direct in to the ITF125 and with wild cards I can get into 250's and 500's. Not high enough to even try to qualify for Mexico the 1000 level.

But for now, it is time to enjoy the San Francisco Bay area, win some money, and get some points. Paul was being replaced for the week by Paul Goldstein the head coach of Stanford, so I would have some coaching anyway. I am paying him 10% of my prize money or at least $500. John was connected to Paul through his time on the tour and through the Bryan Brothers so he was available, and his assistant would cover practice for the team.

At this point I need to explain the rating systems for tournaments. Grand slams have up 2000 points for the winner, 1000's is the best after that, 500's and 250's are lower-level tour pro tournaments with the top number of points to the winner either 500 or 250. Finally, you have where I have mostly played ITF levels 125's, 100's, 75's and 50's. Those players inside the top 100 rarely will play one of the ITF's tournaments unless they are about to lose points from the last year and want a quick fix to get the points back. At this level you get a lot of former college graduates or early professionals fighting to get ranking points to get on the main draw tournaments of 250 and above. Many people like me never get above this level like those in Class A ball to AAA for baseball. I was one of those players until the magical ride in August and earlier this month. On a good run I use to get into these tournaments and now they are a base that I just won't need any more well at least until the US Open points expire next September.

I checked in to the hotel, and it reminded me what the world of the touring pros and then here. I will be sharing a room with another player as the tournament requires, I guess it saves money for the tournament and the players, only $70.00, per night per person, so it saves money until that person leaves and then they charge you $100.00, per night until you leave. The Hyatt provides breakfast as part of the deal, many of the players never get to the breakfast especially if they have the evening matches.

Sunday:

I met Paul after taking an Uber to Stanford and he had one of his top players as my hitting partner for the morning hit. Amber Payne, a very good ball striker, that forced me to run in to the corners and take on a lot more motion that I really wanted to do. Paul reminded me that I would have been a qualifier for this tournament last month, so remember what it took for you to get here one tournament does not make a career, you are seeded here but don't get cocky any of these players had higher rankings than you did a month ago, just put that into your mind. After an hour we finished the practice and the rust from not playing for almost three weeks came off and by the last 15 minutes I was holding my own. Paul described his career on the circuit, mostly challenger victories, and eventually made it mostly on tour, but he got married, had children, and accepted the coaching job at his alma mater. He told me to relax and know that every week from now on steal some points and get your rankings higher, you have enough money now to stay through these tournaments, take advantage so you can get into main draws of WTA tournaments. In fact, also learn to be able to talk tennis, you can sometimes get side gigs when ESPN or the tennis channel need additional commentators.

Paul was more a mental coach than a physical coach and he said, "I can help you stay in the games this week mentally, I'm not here to change your game, but we can have a little fun."

After getting back to my motel, I texted Larry to see where he was and what he was doing. He texted back, dinner with friends remember I'm three hours ahead of you. Then I got a heart back, and "I Love You",

I forgot how lonely these tournaments can be in the minor leagues of tennis.

I checked in on James and my parents, all were doing well. Mom said James apparently has a new girlfriend he is dating, met her at the US Open, and she lives in DC, but he has not driven with her to our house yet. I so much wanted to check in with Dea it was still hard for me not to have her with me anymore. Granny Miller texted me to say good luck in the tournament. I felt so alone, travelling with nobody, staying at a hotel with a stranger, I had forgotten how bad this is at this level. I made a declaration, not going to play these anymore after this tournament, going to get rankings up and play main tour from now on.

Monday:

The tournament was in the first day of the main draw, and a couple of qualifications on the second and third court. I was playing Linda Faust, a recent college graduate on the rise. I don't think she was thrilled about playing a noon match. Some tennis players don't get up until noon because matches are often in the late afternoon or evening and by the time, they get ready for bed it is after midnight. I think she should have stayed in bed, by the time she woke-up I was already up 4-0, Linda won her serve and was behind 4-1. I did not let her back in the set and was up-5-1 very quickly. I broke again on her serve and finished the first set at 6-1. I looked at the stands, there were maybe 50 people in the stands including both Linda's and my coaches. The second set was not as easy, at 4-all, I was able to get a break point and hit a screaming forehand down the line, and then all Linda could do is barely touch the ball sideways into the stands. I simply served it out and finished the match 6-1, and 6-4 in a little more than an hour. I was not signed-up for any doubles so had the rest of the day off and would not play again until Wednesday.

The next day, I did something I had never done before, I took most of the day and explored San Francisco, I had never been a tourist with money before, and found that I was still too frugal to spend money here. I needed to take a cable car and go to Fisherman's wharf to take pictures.

Paul had me practice after Stanford, so went back to the hotel in the afternoon, and went to Stanford for my hit, and then to look at the second-round schedule. I was playing a Chinese player, Zhu Chan, and I knew nothing about her other than she was ranked 250 in the world. She has played all ITFs in the Far East and was up here getting points and lost in the first round of the US Open qualifications. Paul G had looked her up and said she was a very nice player, nothing spectacular but can run everything down. She is only 5'1", so her serve was also not very impressive.

The match was not any more attended on Wednesday than the Monday match, I guess 2 PM on a Wednesday means only seniors and students could watch the match. It did not take long for me to know how she got her points, I often had to hit what I thought were 2 winners to get the point, and after a full hour I won the set 6-4, this was not the type of match I wanted. The second set was not much different other than we went to a tiebreaker, and I won it going away at 7-1. I looked up and the match had taken 2 ¼ hours for two sets. The next round was the quarters, but I had an upcoming issue, if I made the finals, I would not make it to China and be able to play in the tournament, they were a day ahead and I would miss the tournament. Paul said he has had that issue when he was touring and losing a match here was not as bad as missing the opportunity for a tournament with double the points. I really did not have to worry very long, on Thursday I lost the match 7-5 and 6-4, to another NCAA recent graduate from Texas, she was the number 1 seed, and she was going to stay in the USA and play these 125's and get her rankings from winning multiple lower-level tournaments the 80's and 100's. Paul told me that is a lot harder way to get your ratings, you must make the semi-finals almost at every tournament which meant driving several hundred miles on a Saturday and hoping your next match was not on Monday. I bid farewell to Paul G and was ready to go top Asia for the first time. John told Paul G that he would have the check for $500, for helping me out shortly, as he would cut the check.

Paul N had texted me that he was leaving from Atlanta on Friday afternoon and would be in China late Sunday morning, I was going to meet up with him late Sunday afternoon for a hitting session to get the travel off our bodies, we were traveling across the world.

I must mention that I was daily texting the home base and waited each day for the responses. Nothing was new with my parents and Larry just seemed to be waiting to see me In November when I could come back to the states. James did send me a picture of his girlfriend, a very nice-looking girl who is bi-racial from DC.

The rankings came out as I was flying to China, and through the planes Wi-Fi, the quarterfinal points had moved me up to 135, in the world, still needed quite a few more points to qualify.

The flight seemed to take forever. We got to Beijing, and I went through customs as the first entry point into China. The next flight to Nanchang, took a while so when it was all done it was late Sunday night when I got to the airport. A car was waiting for me to take me to the hotel. I had a message at the hotel desk from Paul, saying he would see me in the morning. I proceeded to switch my sim card out, and texted Mom that I had landed safely in China, and to let everyone know that I was in China. I checked the WTA web site. I was first playing an unseeded player in the first round, and I was not on the Monday schedule. That meant I could sleep in until the afternoon, we would practice in the afternoon on a side court.

Monday noon, I was awake with the ringing on my cell phone. I had no idea why someone was calling and missed the call. I looked at the number and it said Alllison, so I called it back. Allison picked-up the phone and said welcome to China. I asked what the call was about this morning, she was very excited and told me that the Lilly Jaman version of the shoe was going to be delivered to me at the South Korea, Kia Open next week. The shoes are ready to hit the market the next week, but wanted you to have them for the tournament, since as a Korean player, great place for the launch. I was taken back, I had always thought of the US Open as my home country and forgot, I represent South Korea now, I had to remind myself I was now in Asia, and they won't accept me either as only a ¼ South Korean. I met Paul at the tournament venue, and then we went to the side courts to practice. The rust from travel was a little heavy and I was hitting awful until about the last 5 minutes, Paul said Hey, the ball hits the same in China as it does in the US. That comment let me finally laugh it was the first time since Dea's funeral that I had laughed, everything for the last three weeks, seemed like I was ghost just going through the motions. I wanted to be with my family but knew that this is where I had to be for my profession. Paul said he missed being away from Ann, but realized it would be only 1 month, and then he would be with her and their children in South Carolina. He also said, when you play in Charleston, I should be a new parent, but you better leave a space in your box for me. I was wondering, why won't you be coaching me at Charleston, and without any hesitation he said because I will be coaching College of Charleston, and you will have a new coach arranged by John after the swing. I told him, then you better be there, I will want to see the baby and I think from my talk to Ann, she would be mad if I did not stop by. Paul conceded that I was probably right, and it was time to get back into our current tennis mode for the next three weeks.

I was lucky to stay at a British hotel, they had good food that I could figure out what it was and had fish and chips for dinner. Paul joined me in the combination pub and restaurant and discussed my first-round match due second on the second court. I was playing Ashleigh Pyang, an American whose parents had left China when she was a kid, so I suspect if there is any crowd, she will have the crowd behind them.

The 250's were much like the ITF's, a few spectators, for this my court looked like it could handle 500. I walked on to the court and the very brief introduction was for me and my rank of 135, and then Ashleigh who was 95 in the world. The first round in these tournaments is the round of 32, and it takes 2 days to play and thereafter the play is everyday usually with the finals on Sunday.

Our match was supposed to be the big hitter versus the retriever, I took control early and did not look back in the first set until I finished the match with a wide serve and finished it off at the net. The second set was exactly what they thought it would be, but I managed to win it 7-5, the match was just under 2 hours. The only real coaching Paul needed was making me be prepared to look for my opening and just finish it off. The next match was going to be against the 6 seed, Diana Chang, at least that is how her name looks like in English. She was from China and played enough of the tour to keep her in the top 40, she did not do a lot of the clay season in Europe preferring to stay in ITF's than Europe.

Paul verified the time for the next match, and it was scheduled for third on. I was asked to play doubles, but Paul said not with all the travelling you have done the last two week, so we honestly turned it down, the focus was to get ranking points and win some cash. By winning the first round I already had won $6000. I would get another 8,000 dollars if I won the next round. Paul would get a nice piece out of this as would John. With the discounted hotel costs, we were barely break-even though for the week even if I made it to the quarterfinals. Routine, for the week was to do dinner here at the hotel at a player's discount, and breakfast was free for everyone. Because there were other tournaments for men and women all over the globe no TV coverage for this one until the semi-finals, I could play without my family seeing it so I would send them an e-mail with the results. My communication with my fiancé was limited to sending him an e-mail and hoping for a response when he was awake, I was like 12 hours ahead of him, so we were awake and asleep at different times. I have heard people that do business with Asia work odd schedules so they can align with them for at least a part of the day like working until 8 or 9 PM.

Diana was very much like my last match at about 5"2" she could chase everything down, her serve was limited to about 95 mph, so I could align and win many points. I won the first set 6-3, having served first and breaking her serve right away. The second set was bad for me, and I lost in the tiebreaker 7-5, after I had a double fault that gave her the advantage. The third set was tight until I broke at 4 all and then served it out for a 6-4 advantage.

Paul was impressed with the performance though, he said, "in the past when you had those players and tried to go for it way too early, I guess you are finally taking the coaching of waiting for the opening and then winning the point."

The match had taken just under 3 hours, and I was going to now play the number 3 seed in the quarterfinals. My opponent was number 20 in the world and someone I had played against in mixed doubles,

Varvara Romanoff. A lot of the Russian players preferred the Asian swing, as opposed to the European tournaments. We were going to be third on the main court on Friday, and nothing to do between this evening and practice in the morning.

Paul and I met at the dinner pub, and again I ate while Paul talked about the match and our opponent he had been scouting. Paul explained to me that she is a big hitting Russian, who can hit her way into a match and out of a match just as easily, let's just extend the points and see if she can blow herself out.

I said, "I will try but she has a big shot, and she can hit winners from anywhere."

My life was the same after that, take a shower do some stretching, and then sit down and e-mail my family and fiancé and at least once a week to James to see how my lawyer brother was doing plus, I was starting to inquire about his dating the same girl for over a month, that was very unusual for him. I wanted to know more about her, but that was never going to be a direct question he was going to answer. Granny Miller said that the wedding was all set at Farmville, with the wedding at the chapel, and then the reception at a building in Longwood. Longwood was donating the facility, and they were going to make sure it is being catered with a local company, the cost is going to be more affordable than expected. Oh well that is next July after Wimbledon, ha-ha, who would have thought that was going to be a possibility. The country bumpkin planning on playing Wimbledon, that was still not possible, I would get at least an invite for the qualifications.

The morning of the match, I followed the program, hydrate, and hydrate some more, then stretching, and finally breakfast. We had a light workout at noon, then just in and out waiting for the match to begin just before 5 PM, local time, about 7 AM, back home. When the match was finally called, we were playing in colder weather, temperatures about 60 and going to drop throughout the match. After this tournament Korea is going to be an indoor tournament.

The match went well for the first set, with Varvara donating points all over the place, and I was able to win 6-2. The second set she was much more dialed in and managed to hit a ton of winners and won the set, 6-3. The last set, she continued her power game, I tried to keep up but, in the end, I lost the third set and the match 6-3. I realized that in my first two main draws I had been to a quarterfinal and a round of 16, I may not be better than many of these players, but I was just as good they just have a lot more experience than I did.

Paul and I met to discuss our travel plans to Seoul, we would leave on Saturday and get there Saturday night. John was making the reservations for everything, and this was going to be an emotional journey for me, meeting my aunt, and cousins for the first time. When we looked up the live rankings, the 60 points I had received had just moved me up to number 128, still way too high to get into a main draw of the Australian Open, but even now I would get seeded in the qualification tournament, so at least I was going to get a red number.

When we got to the hotel, a package was waiting for me from Mizuno shoes. There were three pairs of shoes waiting for me, the first ever "Athletic and Feminine" shoes, in my size with a note, do your new shoes proud this week. The shoes were going to hit the market the last week of November in the states, they were originally estimating about 5K by year-end but now have advanced orders of almost 10,000, at $2.50, per pair, we would get $25,000, for this quarter alone.

I guess we were not expected to do as well in Seoul, because the hotel was a Holiday Inn, about 2 miles from the indoor courts. Because there was a 500 the next week in Japan, and a 1000 in Beijing to end the season, I noticed that this tournament was not that highly rated, and I got the 8 seed, so my wildcard was not even required. Many Americans were getting points in indoor tournaments in the states, so the players here were mostly Asian and European. I was the only American in the draw, but I was playing under the South Korean flag, so I wonder what was going to happen. I had the address and phone numbers of my great aunt and 2 cousins Juwon and Woong Jongro. I had sent them a letter last month that I would like to meet them, and they had in turn provided me with telephone numbers. I nervously called each one of them to invite them to my box on Tuesday and dinner Monday night. All three accepted the invitation, I was going to get my connection to my Asian roots for the first time.

I received specific instructions from dad to say hello to his aunt, and to get pictures because he had never met any of them and did not even know that they had existed until the funeral, Dea had never spoken about her family in Korea. Even James was curious about the side of the family that we had never met and wanted me to send him pictures and why they never looked to contact us previously.

Sunday was a typical off day from tennis, sleep until 11:00, but this time I did some sightseeing in Seoul as I had nothing to do, Paul had called off practice to let our bodies heal. I traveled to the Gyeongbokgung Palace, I had never been to a palace and this one was very impressive the tour took me almost 2 hours to complete. I went to a couple of markets and ate Korean Meatballs and kimchi in a box, well it was at least interesting, I was surprised that I could get a diet coke at the same stall. By the time I got back, Paul and I were ready for our dinner meeting, he had ordered some food, and assured me it was not dog, but he kept kidding me it was.

"Paul said I have looked at the competition here and the number 1 seed you would meet in the quarters is a clay court player and just like last week in China, 2 Chinese and Japanese players both shorter and less powerful than you. As I see it you can get to the quarters just like we said and then a clay courter from France in the quarters, we will figure out the semis and possibly the finals later. I know that you are going to meet your great aunt after Tuesday's match and some cousins and I want to remind you to keep your mind on what we are here for, get you to number 94, in the world, and we get a direct entry to Australia. We have practice Monday at noon on a side court, for 45 minutes, we only get half the court. I declined you to play doubles this week, but be prepared John has a request that you play doubles next week with Karen O'Grady, another of his clients that will be in Asia, she is an Irish player the highest I can ever remember number 80 in singles and 50 in doubles."

Practice went fine and we were at the tennis facility, and they let us know that the match we were playing was number 1, noon Tuesday. I was not on the show court but the second court, so it was going to be a very quiet court, or at least that is what Paul and I thought. What I did not know was that Kia Motors, had purchased a lot of tickets, and with them as a sponsor and me playing for South Korea, I was told to expect a full stand of about 500 people for the match, the capacity of the court.

When the match began, it was not supposed to be on the Tennis Channel, the number 1 court was supposed to be, so I did not worry about it. I knew that they had cameras on the court, but the number 1 seed was playing at the same time, she was featured. Then I looked up and 500 Korean men in suits were at the court and politely clapping for me. The came the introduction first in Korean and then in English. The introduced my opponent from Japan, Lorinda Kobayashi, then they introduced me. Her opponent this afternoon, representing South Korea, and recently a top 16 finalist at the US Open, Lilly Jarman. All 500 men stood up and started clapping and then yelling "Athletic and Feminine".

Tennis Channel Studio:

Chandra Rubin here for the first matches this evening, midnight US, well they have just introduced Lilly Jarman, and you can hear from the main court the cheering for her home country she is representing. Look at the shoes Lilly is wearing, these are the first we understand of the new line that comes out next month, The "Athletic and Feminine shoe" by Mizuno. It only took three weeks for Lilly to get hers and we understand the shipments come out shortly, the shoes are normally made by Mizuno in China, but they have leased space in a South Korean factory that will be the main factory for this shoe. Now we will get back to the main court, but we wanted to show everyone the applause that Lilly is getting. We are also coming with Lilly later today when she meets her great aunt Lilly, and cousins she has never met before.

Paul here, the poor girl that was playing Lilly realized that this was going to be a tough match, everyone in the stands was rooting for Lilly, and then just as we were about to start, in my box came a grey-haired Korean woman and 2 other people about 30 years old, this apparently was Lilly's great Aunt and her children. This was going to be an interesting day for Lilly.

Fortunately, Lilly was in good form and managed to take the first set from Lorinda in about a half-hour. The next set was more difficult but, in the end, Lilly took it 7-5 and the box was extremely happy about the results and stood up and cheered Lilly.

Tennis Channel Studio:

Lilly Jarman had just won her match 6-2 and 7-5, the representatives from Kia are all applauding as they leave the stands. We are staying here, in Lilly's box is her great Aunt and 2 cousins she has never met. Lilly has presents that she and Paul were waiting to give them as is custom in this area, and the tournament is asking all of them to come to the court. The elder Lilly was asked what she thought of her great niece, and in Korean. Lilly senior, who was about 5 feet tall, came over to Lilly and said, I am so proud of my namesake in her tennis, I want to talk to her tonight about her grandmother the stories and her love that had her leave Korea. She then proceeded to kiss Lilly, followed by hugs from her cousins all of which she had never met before tonight. The cousins said we want to meet our cousin who is tall and wears our flag on her sleeves. Lilly has tears in her eyes, she said Aunt Lilly you look a lot like Dea, and she was so special to me.

Paul here, we were done for the night, I told Lilly let's get back to the hotel and change before you go out to dinner. I was not going with her, but knew she had to go through this to move forward. I knew Lilly needed to change and try not to be recognized, so she had purchased Korean clothes for the evening, the only problem is she is 5'9" tall with dirty blond hair, she may have Korean features, but she will be recognized in her adopted country, thanks to Kia plastering a billboard, welcome Lilly Jarman to Korea, both in Korean and in English. I am worried that Lilly will be so emotional that she will not be able to play Wednesday in the round of 16.

I went out to a restaurant to meet my great aunt and cousins for dinner after quickly showering and putting on a more local appropriate dress. Because of my height, no heals, I didn't need a lot of people that could recognize me. I had written instructions on how to get to the restaurant, and the name and address of the restaurant to give to the taxi driver. It had been a little over an hour after we left the tennis center that I was in the cab waiting to get to the restaurant. Wooraeok was the name of the restaurant, it was famous for Korean barbecue, and apparently a good bar to go with it. I was not going to be able to drink anything with alcohol, tournament match again tomorrow.

They were waiting for me when I got to the restaurant and the waiter took me to our table, before I could sit down, I had someone put out their hand and asked for my autograph, I promptly gave it to them, and laughed nobody wanted it 4 weeks ago. We were seated at the and I brought pictures out of Ken and his brothers. Only 1 had Asian looks. I then showed pictures of Dea at a later age, with Lilly and James. My cousins had never known Dea when she was alive just stories about her leaving Korea.

I showed pictures of my mom and Ken, Junior, with dad having the very dark hair. We ordered drinks, and then I asked," Aunt Lilly about Dea and how hard it was to move to the USA after the war.

Her response in broken English was somewhat surprising, "Dea was always a head strong woman, and wanted to travel the world when traditional women of Korea would stay home get married and have Korean children. Dea went to work at the military base not because she needed the money, although it was good for her, but she wanted to learn about other areas of the world and learn English, which our father forbade. Dea was obstinate and then fell in love with a foreigner and left the country. Our Father was not upset he knew Dea could not be a traditional Korean daughter, so when she left, he cut her off without a letter or take any correspondence until he died. Even when Dea sent letters to him, he ripped them up and said he had 1 daughter and this Dea person was not his. He knew she had 3 boys but never wanted to meet any of them as they were not true Koreans with a white father. While you are here representing South Korea, you are not one of us, you are mostly white blood. I was friendly with the cameras, but we don't want any contact with you or your family after this week. Dea was my sister and turned her back on Korea, you are just a white blooded Korean, and we don't need your kind here."

I was stunned, and had nothing to say, I had hoped the day would end better where I could find out things about Dea, but this Lilly cared nothing for her sister, and looked at us as nothing but European pretenders. I ate dinner and talked to the cousins and never said another word to great aunt Lilly, the rest of the meal. I paid for the meal, flagged down a taxi, and told my great aunt, I'm so sorry that Dea could not be here tonight because she was so loved in her community, it is a shame that even 50 years later you still have a cold heart about your sister. I was hoping to find out more about my family and invite you to the wedding in Virginia next year, but I am glad I found out now that you are still cold hearted after all these years, I loved Dea, and you would have been honored to know her as a pillar of the community. I got in the cab and was so mad I thought I would punch the car but refrained. I responded to my family met great aunt Lilly, she and the family don't want to know us, glad it is over. I honored Dea and the cousins were at least cordial, but her sister is an evil wicked bitch, I don't want to talk about her ever again. Best thing Dea ever did was to leave her family behind in Korea, they are not people that are welcoming. Any letters she sent over the years were apparently destroyed before anyone read them. Now I know there were 2 worlds that disapproved of me, the white debutantes, and the Korean family, so glad I will be living in an area where multi-cultural children are accepted.

I got back to the hotel and called Paul, no more involvement with family, they rejected me as a half breed, so they are not to be invited back to the tournament. I started to cry, as they were so hateful just because I was not all Korean, just like the debutantes at home, because I was not all white. I was stupid and still picked-up the dinner bill, should have let them do it.

Paul and I got up this morning to discuss strategy and he wanted to make sure the events of last night would not impact my play this afternoon. The round of 16, and I was again playing Diana Chang again, this sometimes happens, you play the same person as the same women. Because I was in the same side of the draw as the number 1 seed, again they put me on the second court and out of the limelight. Diana had learned a little about me and refused to let me just overpower her, between delaying her serves until the last second, and slice after slice she was not going to get blown off the court this time, but with the newly designed shows on, and using my anger form last night, I was able to stay with her and won the first set 7-5, as she was serving to get the set to a tiebreaker. The second set went much easier as I think Diana was really rejected when I broke to win the first set, and I was up 4-0 before Diana held and then broke me to get one of her service breaks back. Diana was able to force the set to 4-3, before I righted the ship and held for a 5-3 advantage. I was able to get to another break point when Diana double faulted the set and match away, I was very appreciative as the match went less than 2 hours.

The quarterfinals were going to be an interesting affair, Mary Garcia was from France and known primarily as a clay court specialist, but she was also number 18 in the world and the number 1 seed for this tournament. She can drive a player crazy by hitting winners all over the court and has every shot in the book, her one liability, she was not that fast, and you could get her on hard courts stuck out of position. I think she is probably being coached that Lilly is just a big server and can't do much else, but I like to slug out points also.

The match was on a Friday, and we were the first on the main court, it was going to be an interesting match. Mary won the serve and chose to return; my serve was hot early and proceeded to get 2 aces on my way to winning the first game. Both of us held until it was 6-5 with my serve, Mary was not expecting this match and I was able to take the set at 7-5, and Mary cursed something in French and looked at me with disgust. I think that was my motive to play even bigger and I won the set 6-2, a major upset of a top 20 player. I was told the tennis channel showed a couple of the highlights, but I was going to be in the semi-finals against the 4 seed from the Ukraine, Maria Koval, a big striker like me and another top 50 player in the world.

Nothing for me to do at night so I simply was good had dinner with Paul and then went to bed at crazy early time of 9 PM, I was not going to let this day go by without a chance to win it.

Tennis Channel Studios:

Chandra Rubin, we have a full schedule for you today, from Seoul South Korea, we have 2 semi-finals, the first featuring Maria Koval from Ukraine, and her opponent an upset winner Lilly Jarman, who upset the top seed in the quarters.

Paul here, I have the iPad to record the match here, I did not want to put pressure on Lilly, but this is her second semi-final in singles of any type in like 3 years. We warmed-up and just spoke about what was going to happen in Japan. Lilly was supposed to be in the qualies, but because she is still in South Korea, she was given a direct entry in to the tournament. WTA has an exception that we are taking because the earliest we would be able to leave Seoul is Saturday night and qualies will be in the second round it also takes one of the spots from those playing this weekend.

Maria is a tall girl just about six feet tall and reed thin, she has a buggy whip forehand when it works it is great but when it is off, she donates points. She has a big serve but it mostly flat and predictable. Lilly stayed with her the entire first set, neither was able to generate a break point, but with the tiebreak at 5-all, Lilly blocked a serve back and Maria hit the forehand long, setting Lilly up at 6-5 and served an ace for the first set. The place erupted in applause for Lilly. We heard the phrase again. The second set went again to a tiebreaker where Maria started spraying the points and Lilly finished it at 7-2, with an ace down the middle. She screamed "Yes", and the phrase was being chanted by the crowd. After a handshake I realized that Lilly was playing in her second final of any kind in like four years.

A month ago, she was trying to get in to her first main draw of any WTA tournament and now she is in the finals of a WTA 250, of her adopted country.

Lilly here, I had to do an emergency laundry at the Holiday Inn, most people had left for Tokyo or other tournaments, but I needed clean clothes for the final. While others were traveling, I was doing laundry, apparently Paul had already done his. Ranking points for a win was 250, and for just making it here was like 150, a great deal of money. Paul was going to like his share if we win $85,000, and $50,000 if we lose.

Sunday morning and it is raining in Seoul, glad the match is indoors. The match is on Tennis Channel, but it starts at like 3 AM Eastern time, parents said they were going to watch setting an alarm. Paul is telling me that this is just another match and to relax and have fun. My opponent went through a grueling match winning in more than 3 hours and three full sets, and was unseeded, she was also just 18, from Spain, Gabriella Gonzales, on the tour known as GG, she was a recent junior Wimbledon champion and moving up the rankings quickly. GG was not overly tall at 5'7", but has a great forehand, and a nice slice backhand, great for grass.

Introducing from Spain, Gabriella Gonzales, a recent junior Wimbledon champion and her opponent, representing South Korea, Lilly Jarman, the crowd is going crazy, nobody representing Korea had ever made the finals.

Tennis Channel:

Both players today are looking for their first title, so this could be quite interesting. Lilly has the advantage of being sponsored by Kia and is representing Korea, so this is going to be like a Fed Cup match for her. Chandra Rubin and Paul Annacone calling this match today. Lilly has won the toss and chosen to serve.

Lilly immediately serves a wide serve and came in and finished the point. This is what she must do to win today.

Paul here, Lilly is on fire this afternoon, her serve is clocking wide 105, and down the line 114, poor GG has nothing for her and Lilly breaks GG on her serve. It did not take long for Lilly to be up 5-0, before GG held serve. Lilly simply won 4 straight points on her serve, and the first set was hers. GG took a medical time out after the first set, and changes clothes at the same time, I told Lilly to do some serves and run in place a little while she was waiting. GG was able to hold serve but you could see her laboring. Lilly proceeded to take the next 4 games with GG laboring, when she called a medical time out again. After ten minutes, she came over to Lilly and shook hands, and the match was over 6-1, and 4-1 retired. Lilly just won her first tour level tournament, and the crowd erupted.

Lilly thanked everyone at the tournament, she had her first trophy in the WTA tour. She was smiling and happy. The pro South Korean crowd kept yelling in Korean "Athletic and Feminine", it was amazing.

We ran back to the hotel and then after Lilly and I showered, off to the airport, this time with a trophy in her hands, off to Tokyo, after winning a boatload of money and a lot of points.

On the airplane, we look up the rankings, and with the 250, Lilly was now Number 98 in the world, even if she wins no other points, she was going to be the top seed at the qualies. My share was like $8,000, for the week, and it will be a great downpayment on the new house.

We arrived in Tokyo, at almost midnight. By the time we got through customs and checked-in to the hotel it was 2 AM. I told Lilly that no practice today, we will figure out who you are playing and gave her back her iPad.

I received congratulations from tons of people and then put my iPad down and went to bed. I tried to call Larry, but it went to voice mail. Fortunately, there was American Fox news on the TV, it was boring enough to put me to sleep, except they showed the end of the match in Korea and showed the fans screaming for me. Wow this was such a weird week, the highs of the win and the lows of the family, at least we got closure, they were not a part of the family and we put them out of our minds.

I woke up Monday morning well I thought it was Monday morning only to find it was noon. I texted Paul and saw that Larry had tried to call me back, now it was near midnight in New York, so I just texted him that I missed him, and two more weeks on the road and back to Virginia. A text came back with a heart, I missed him so much especially after the disappointment in Korea with the family.

I was at a Hilton hotel in Tokyo and called Paul and asked him if he wanted to spend a few hours sightseeing. We were going to see the Zojo-ji Temple, and then go through the town and then the Imperial Palace, we both went and enjoyed ourselves.

I had played three weeks in a row, and I was exhausted. I managed to win my first round on Tuesday, and then lost on Wednesday. Paul and I were done for the week, and we started to fly home on Thursday. He was going to Atlanta, and I was going to DC, and Larry was coming down for a few days before going back to New York.

On the United Flight between Tokyo and San Francisco the stewardess, asked me if she could take my picture and then announced on the overhead, we are honored tonight to have with us Lilly Jarman, "Athletic and Feminine".

By the time I got home to Radford, it was Saturday morning and by the time I woke-up it was late Saturday afternoon. My trophy had just arrived from Japan and was added to the trophy cabinet.

On Sunday Paul called me and said, "we have 1 more ITF tournament to play in Michigan in two weeks, this was the insurance points."

I looked up the rankings later Sunday night, and with the points from Japan I was number 94, in the world, and a direct entry into Australia. The reason for the last tournament was to make sure that the year-end would keep me there.

"Paul said no tennis practice for one week, four weeks on tour you need a week off, simply do some running and some stretching and get a massage".

I went back to sleep and woke up with nobody in the house, they were all working, and I was alone at the house. I was just waiting for Larry to come to Virginia this Friday, the years of hell of the little tournaments and working to get entry money was over. I have won over a half million dollars in prize money and payments for sponsorship.

It hit me, I was a touring professional now in the top 100, I was engaged, and people now accepted me.

Chapter 19

One More Tournament

Two weeks off from tennis competition, and only one more tournament for the year to go. That would mean 6 weeks off and some hitting with the women's team at Radford before going to a new adventure, Australia. The time off was fantastic in a time of healing, I was sore everywhere, four weeks in a row and so many matches and travel, the body needs time to rest.

Larry surprised me and came to Radford for a long weekend, it was the early November in Southern Virginia, beautiful with the trees changing colors, I was home with my family and my fiancé, and then a surprise came home it was my brother James, and of all things he had a girl with him. He had been dating her for only 5 weeks, since the US Open, and the first girl he had taken home, "Olivia Johnson" a marketing professional for a telecommunications company in the DC area. They came in holding hands, obviously they were getting along well, she was a graduate of Howard University, and she was biracial. She later explained to me that her mom was African American, but her dad was white. I told her I understood with my Asian features down here, I always felt like I never quite belonged, she related stories about her childhood, and I swear she was living some of my life. The person I can relate her looks to was Madison Keys, but Olivia was about 5'6" not almost six feet like Madison is. If they get married, I wonder which gene pool will come through, Asian, European, or African American with any children. James would kill me about speculating already, but again he has never brought any girl home to meet my parents.

James came to me and wanted a private discussion. I was like uh oh, what did I do wrong. He said, "I have not told Olivia I am a mixed-race child."

Well James, that cat is out of the bag, Olivia and I talked about being multi-racial, and I'm not sure why you hid yours, but how were you going to explain me when she met me.

"James just said, well it had not come up, and I had not thought it through."

"Well James, that will be an interesting topic for you on the way home little brother."

He then punched me in the shoulder and said, "you had to open that can of worms."

"Yes James, if you are serious about her something that would be apparent as soon as she met me, and an uncle."

James responded, I really like Olivia, and I guess it had to come up sometime, this time you are protecting me. What do you think of Olivia?

I told him "I approved of her, but if you are talking that way now, you are utterly and completely smitten."

"James just smiled and kissed me on the cheek, saying you are probably right."

The rest of the weekend was talk of my travel next year and the wedding to be the weekend after Wimbledon completed, the plans were all made. I had thought about wearing the Miller's wedding dress, but the women are like 5'1 or 2, and I am 5'10" so that was out of the question. I asked Allison, from Mizuno as she was in the industry, and she said, give me your measurements, both Lacoste and Mizuno are going to get your dress from a French designer, and don't worry about the cost, the publicity for this wedding is going to be worth it. Well, that was going to help in the budgeting $5000, or more was no longer needed. I wonder how my accountant was going to handle that? Did I mention that John had helped to get an accountant from a regional

CPA firm in New York that specialized in artists and athletes. He recommended that Larry use the same one for this year with checks coming in for "Athletic and Feminine". The shoes were hitting the market, and pre-orders were now more than we had dreamed, over 25,000 pairs of shoes, and I think our commission will be something like $10, per pair or a quarter of a million dollars when they are sold, John would receive quite a bit of it, but Larry and I would get at least $100,000, each before taxes.

Larry left for New York on Sunday evening, I drove him to the airport, and he said I will be here for Thanksgiving, but we are expected for Christmas dinner in DC, you will need to come as my family have not met you formally, but obviously they know who you are and have viewed our proposal. I hugged him and teared that I was going away again and would barely see him from the holidays to our wedding. I really don't know how this is going to work with me travelling and Larry here.

The Radford season was just about over for the fall season, but I worked out with the players on their individual workouts. After 10 days of no tennis, I was able to move again fully. The girls were great as I was listed still as an assistant coach, I was permitted to work with the team. It felt great to be back on my original courts.

I finally called Paul about the following week in Michigan, he was flying from Charleston, to Detroit, and to Lansing on Saturday. The only place he could get us was an Extended Stay hotel, at least they had a kitchen in case we could not find a decent hotel, especially since there was a home game. I checked my flights from John, I was to drive to Richmond, then a flight to Detroit, and then rental car and drive to Lansing, about an hour and a half. They were getting me a Kia Sportage, enough space for all the stuff I needed.

I had three more days to go before leaving for another week and used my time to practice and to spend time with my parents it had been a while since I had time to do this. Larry and I also were starting a real estate search in the DC area, his Wall Street firm was going to let him transfer to the DC office next year, and that, was going to make seeing him easier if we shared a place there as opposed to one of us in

New York, and one in rural Virginia. We decided on a condominium townhouse complex near Tysons Corner, VA. I was not crossing the border to Maryland taxes were too high.

With a hug to my parents, I was on my way to another tournament, the last of the year for me, it was another 125, but needed to protect myself from others playing through November. I was the number 2 seed, which meant until Sunday afternoon, I would not know who my opponent was going to be, that would be decided on qualifications over the weekend and Monday, my first match was to be Tuesday.

I met up with Paul late Saturday night, and we discussed the week and the strategy, was to try to win as many matches as possible, to move me up in to the low 80's if possible and be totally protected, that meant basically getting at least to the semifinals if possible. He was going to watch the qualifications for my potential opponent and wanted me nowhere near the tournament except for practice at the courts, the hotel had a stationary bicycle, we would use that, for aerobic, it was too cold for me to run outside.

Monday night and Paul discussed my first-round opponent, Katrina Ferguson, a nice player good skill, but beatable, serve was adequate, and nothing more than a very good player in returns. We saw that per our request, the match was the first one on Tuesday.

Poor Katrina never really got in the match, before she knew what hit her, she was down 5-0, and then lost 6-1, the first set, she played a little better in the second set and was at 2-2, threw in a double fault for me to go up 3-2, and did not win a game afterwards, the match barely took an hour. Paul made me do an additional 15 minutes on the practice court with that easy win.

With a day off, not much to do In Lansing, MI, so simply reviewed wedding plans that mom and Granny Miller were doing, everything was in place, I had a couple of decisions to make, like I needed to look for a Maid of Honor, and those that would be in the wedding. I wanted it to be some of my friends from Farmville, but they were international and needed to contact them early. I sent an e-mail to Kiki Sullivan and asked her to call me, we were like six hours behind them, and at noon she called me. I asked her if she would like to come to Virginia in July and wanted her to be my Maid of honor. Kiki told me she had just gotten married in September and would have to talk to her husband about it as it was going to be expensive. We had not even talked about the size of the wedding parties, and when I asked mom, she said three each way is good. She also thought if things continue with James, it might be nice to include Olivia in the wedding. I was trying to think of the third, and thought about Susan or Sierra, Sierra was in the area, but Susan and I knew each other a lot better.

Wednesday night and Paul asked to get together for dinner, he had ordered pasta from a local restaurant, and we would eat it in the hotel while discussing, the match. I wanted some wine, but a strict no alcohol during matches week policy. My opponent Patricia Kim was an American opponent, 17-year-old and playing in her first professional tournament, had won her first-round match in three sets. Paul said just serve and volley her right off, fast, and easy win.

Just like Tuesday, the match went my way very quickly, this time broke the first time she served and held on for a 6-3, set win, and the second set was even easier, winning 6-1, apparently Patricia had never gone against a serve and volley approach player. The match allowed me to get done quickly, and the points were driving me to a closer to guarantee for Australia. Another night and another pasta meal to discuss the match on Friday, this was boring, with a few minutes of work. My opponent Marta Mazetti, of Italy, like me she was not young, and she needed points to get back into the rankings, she was the six seed here. She was a seasoned veteran never higher than 75 in the world but had made a living staying right in the top 100. My match was the last one on Friday, which meant a start time about 7 PM.

Hate waiting all day but that is the world of tennis, the match was the only one in the evening so I knew exactly when it would start, our warm-up was at 2 PM, went back to the hotel and got back to the courts at 6:30, time to stretch and be ready.

The match started as we had expected, and I served and held the first game, Marta holds her serve and there were no break points through the set and so the set was decided on a tiebreaker. The tiebreaker was tight, and I held on to make it 6-5, and then Marta missed her first serve hit a soft second serve. I hit it down the line and Marta could barely return it and I finished the set at the net. The second set was 3-all until I double faulted and fell behind 3-4. Marta was just as unsuccessful as I was, and I was able to even the match all 4-all. My next serve went easier and led 5-4. Marta and I battled her serve until I was able to get a break point. Marta then proceeded to double fault, and I walked to the net as the winner going to the semi-finals.

By the time the match was done it was late, and we were lucky it was Friday, because the local pasta place was open until 11 on Fridays and Saturdays, and we ate spaghetti at the restaurant before going to call it a night.

"Paul said the semis are not starting until 2 PM, let's call it a night, I want to call my wife and see how she is doing. We are second singles so expect it to be right before 6 PM, when we must play, we will do a very late lunch together then get to the stadium, and a warm-up at 3:30."

Back in the hotel, back to the routine, e-mails to the parents and to Larry, I know New Yorkers don't get to bed this early. Larry responded at bar, miss you, and VA is coming along. Looks like I will transfer to DC office in April, and then a house in Tysons Corner needs to be found. James called me and said his relationship with Olivia was getting intense and he was wondering if I could speak with him after this tournament. I said sure, I will have six weeks off from tennis so other than some practices at the country club and family time I should be good.

I was getting updates from John, on dollars and sponsors and stuff, while it was great to know, it was not very fun to read. I knew that shortly, we would have enough money that with 1 great season, I could have money enough to do anything I wanted. They were making sure that any commissions that we earned were not going to hurt us, I did not understand it at all, but John assured me the taxes were best the way they had it figured out with Allison.

Saturday morning came and I went across the street to the coffee shop, and they had bagels, I figured I would eat one, boy was I wrong, it was a roll with a hole, and not a real bagel. I did get my bananas and decaf coffee, just not the same. Paul asked to get together at 10:00, and we met in the hotel common space, they had breakfast until 10:00, but after that we were good to meet. Paul said we are playing the Canadian, Pauline Pratt this morning, she is the five seed, and prevailed in the match that was on just before us. She took out the four seed in straight sets and is a pretty much a younger version of us here. She is 5' 10", has a good serve and will match you shot for shot, what she does not have is an ability to serve and volley, you won't get a lot of opportunities, but we can get some quick cheap points here and you never know, she may let us get her in trouble. If we can get through, one more final for you to play, and then it hit us, one more day together and then we part our ways. It got real at that point.

Paul here, I am writing this one for Lilly, the match went on at 5:30, good we had a late lunch before otherwise the energy drinks could only do so much. Pauline was a very good ball striker, and she broke Lilly early in the first set, and went on to win it at 6-4. The second set was very even, and there was not a single break point opportunity the entire way, Lilly got to deuce twice but no break points, Pauline got no more than 1 point on any of Lilly's service games, so when it went to the tiebreaker. Lilly, fell behind 3-1, and then reeled off five straight points. Pauline came up big to save off two set points, on the third Lilly served an ace to force a third set. Both big servers were forceful and again nobody got an advantage for a break and after 2 hours on court, a match deciding tiebreak was required. Lilly was strong this time and got up 4-0 before Pauline was able to get a point. They both held serve from there. Lilly had match point at 9-7 and was ready to serve. Her first serve went into the net and the second serve was ripped by Pauline down the line, Lilly was able to put her racquet on it and the shot went down the line for a match winner. Lilly screamed, yes, came up to the net and shook hands. I handed her back her iPad, and then we decided to order a pasta meal and we brought it back to the hotel so we could talk strategy for the finals.

Lilly here, we looked up the live rankings and I was in the top 90 now at 86, but could end up as 82, if I won on Sunday but either way, we had done what was needed, picked up $5500 in prize money but it was the points that was the goal for this week, Australia was secure.

Larry called me to tell me he watched the match online, kind of grainy but a great match, three weeks until Thanksgiving weekend and I will be there with you. I have a flight out to Virginia booked but for now, it may be time for you to enjoy your coach for another day.

It hit me like a ton of bricks, I would not have Paul after the match as my part-time coach, we would always be friends, but the world will be different without him as my primary coach and mental trainer. He was like having a big brother, I could always come to him for issues. I know he will be at the wedding, but it won't be the same. When I come home from the tour, he won't be at Radford.

Sunday morning: We ate breakfast together at the hotel, we wanted to talk about the number 1 seed. Lydia Poe, she was from Hong Kong, and was a rising star, at 19, she was ten years younger than me, energetic, and unlike most people opinions of Chinese she was my height, fast as a cat and was now entering the top 80 of the world and if she wins top 70, she won't stay there long, she will be top twenty by the time she is 21.

My flight from Detroit through BWI to Richmond would be at 7 PM, tonight, Paul's flights from Lansing was at 7:30, the discount airline went through Detroit, but he would be in Charleston with his wife by early morning.

"Paul asked me how I was recovered from the match last night?"

"I was frank, there is like nothing in my tank this morning. I hurt everywhere, it has been a lot of matches this Fall and not sure what I have left for this one."

"Paul then went on that it would be nice to win this match and we are fully done with the objectives for the week."

Then the talk was to what's next, and then both of us started to bawl our eyes out. We know this is the last day, we will be together as coach and friend, and mentor. I know professional tennis players change coaches all the time, but Paul was more than a coach, he was a big brother, he had helped me when nobody else was able to. When the world told me to give-up Paul said your dream is not over, and when we achieved things, nobody thought possible including a tour win, and a round of 16, in the largest tournament of the year, Paul was there.

Paul here, I have the iPad for the match summary of the finals. Nothing could be harder than doing this match, Lilly has almost nothing in the tank, and when it is over, we are done also. Lilly never got into the match, she had no movement, and the serve was not even close to her best. The match was over in a little over an hour, and Lilly had lost the finals 6-2, and 6-2. We went back to the hotel to pack and leave for my airport and then hers.

I packed my bags and waited to meet Lilly at the hotel lobby, we completed our bill for the week, and it was time to go. Lilly simply grabbed me and hugged me, and started crying, then I started crying, our match was over and so was our time together.

Lilly drove me to the airport, and as I was getting ready to leave, she told me "We have 2 more events, you better be at the wedding next summer, and if I qualify for the Charleston clay courts, you better be in my box." Lilly gave me a big hug before I got my bags out of the car. It was time for me to go home and be a father, husband, and a coach to a whole lot of people, my family was back there.

Lilly here, after I dropped Paul off at his airport, I was trying to drive the car and had to stop. I started crying and could not stop, I never realized how much Paul meant for me and now when I am back in Radford, I won't have Paul to talk about the matches, how to finance my next entry, and life in general.

The travel back to Radford was depressing, and when I got home, I ran in to my parents' arms, and said I love them, and I gave them the finalist plate from earlier today.

I was now a touring professional, and it was time to move on, Australia coming. In six weeks from now, I would enter the tournaments for the first time as a top 90 player, with a new coop coach, and a guarantee to get in to my second grand slam tournament of my career. Now it was time for family, fiancé, and conversations with James, he had been dating Olivia for 2 months now.

Chapter 20

Home and Then Australia

The second week of November and no tennis matches until the first of the year, time to heal, celebrate the holidays, and practice at the country club with numerous junior coaches when they were available. The leaves in southern Virginia had fallen for the season, and the tourists that followed them had gone. Radford is primarily a college town, with dad working at the university, and mom working at the bank, there was little to do during the day.

I owed a trip to Longwood, not only to see the college girls but to also see Granny Miller. I called coach Kindman at Longwood and asked if he wanted me to call any of his potential recruits. He gave me the number of Sally Argento, a senior in the New York area, looking to play a lot and who did not have the grades for schools like Duke, so she was a potential candidate for Longwood. I made the call at 8PM, on Thursday, and after a few minutes of talking to her parents, I got Sally on the line. Sally said she thought she could make it to the professional ranks being top 75 in the country and wanted to know about the life of a professional. I was honest with her that I had struggled my first seven years on the tour and only this year was making money, but if she went to Longwood she could get a degree, get some good contacts playing division 1, and you never know. Longwood would allow her to show off her talents and play some of the best teams in the country, like

UVA, and Duke. I hope that helps and I told her if she was coming in this weekend, I could come up to see her.

I needed to see Granny Miller and went to Longwood the Saturday before Thanksgiving. The girls welcomed me at their private workouts, and I hit with them that day for about 90 minutes wearing my official uniform, and then took pictures with the team, and the Richmond papers. Granny Miller was happy to see me, and we had dinner together and talked plans for the wedding, she asked about Larry's family. I told her I had not been to their home, but it was in Fairfax, outside of DC. Larry was one of two children; he has a younger brother who is a senior at Christopher Newport University. His name is Chris, so I am assuming that Larry will want him at the wedding party, and I will ask that James be there, leaving Larry with one more decision. He has no sisters, so I need to fill in the party for the ladies, awaiting response from Kiki and Susan, and well depends on something with James, but that would do it.

I called Larry and asked him who was going to be his best man, and he said his boss at his firm, Victor Singer, would be his choice and has already asked him and he said yes. He confirmed his brother Chris and figured I would want to invite James and let me do it not you Lilly. I stayed the night, and received an e-mail from Kiki, we would be proud to be with you for your event in Virginia. I will be flying into Dulles airport, and then getting a rental car for the week. If the wedding is on a Saturday, I will be there the week before to have a hell of a shin dig for you as you call it out there. 2 Conformations for the wedding, and I let Granny Miller know, and went back to Radford after breakfast.

My mother was having the Thanksgiving feast this year, Granny Miller was doing the pies and would bring them with her the night before. James was coming down and Olivia was joining us for the weekend. I called Paul to wish him a happy Thanksgiving before I left to get Larry at the airport, his boss gave him off for Wednesday so he could get an early flight to our regional airport. I had not been with my fiancé since the funeral in late September, it was time for me to renew my relationship. We decided that Larry would stay at a hotel, not much space in the house with James coming in and me staying. Uncle Karl was coming in for the day, so he was staying with James in his old room, so not much space.

We checked in to the hotel and we went up to the room and we fully reacquainted ourselves with each other, afterwards I needed to shower and look normal when I got back to the house, because the rest of the family would be there shortly. James and Olivia came in about 9:30 PM, the traffic was terrible on I-66 getting away from the city. James had his arm around Olivia when they came in and she was going to stay with me in my old room.

Thanksgiving was somewhat crowded; Dad had invited 4 international students who could not go home for the holidays, so we had like a dozen people for the meal. My responsibility was corn stuffing and then traditional giblet stuffing.

James though asked me to talk to him for a few minutes. I stopped my preparation and went outside to talk to him. James said to me, "ok you know that Olivia and I have been dating since August and we are now very close. Do you think it is too early to ask her to marry me?"

"I looked at him, and said you tell me what Olivia thinks, and his thoughts came through."

Olivia said last month that she had never loved someone as much as she loved me but is it too early to ask her to marry me, I'm only like 28, and she is 29, so are we just too early. "James 2 things, only you and Olivia know if it is too early, and second nothing says you must get married for a while both of you get your careers off the ground wedding can come later. My wedding is being rushed and we have 10 months to plan it."

The Thanksgiving party went well, and we delayed dessert for about an hour when the family came together again, James got down on his knee next to Olivia at the table and proceeded to ask Olivia to marry him. Olivia while surprised said yes and jumped into James's arms. Olivia indicated later that he asks again in front of her parents, to finalize it.

I had a weekend with Larry exploring areas of my native Virginia including the Natural Bridge and Luray Caverns, all areas Larry had never been to. We stayed the night together and went to the hotel in

Radford on Saturday night, Larry and I spent the night with romance in the hotel before I drove him back to the airport on Sunday.

The next four weeks were away from Larry and with the family working, I worked out in the gym every day, and with the Radford women and junior pros in the area. On December first I received a call from John regarding Australia, and introducing my condo coach Johan Christian, who had played for South Africa on the Davis Cup and would be coaching three of us in our Australian swing. I was only able to get in to 1 tournament before the main draw of the Australian open, a tournament in Auckland New Zealand. The problem with my ranking is that only 250's being held at the same time as the Hobart gave me enough spots to get into the tournament. Otherwise, I would have had to play in the ITF's in Australia. I would play this the first week of January and then 2 weeks later the Open, it will be weird for the first time without Paul. I received a call from Johan welcoming me to the team, and he sent me practices he wanted me to do and certain skills he wanted me to work on in practice with the junior pros.

I understand that James met with Olivia's family and the engagement was made official. They were waiting almost 2 years for the wedding, and it was to be at a church in DC. They had to reserve the Saturday afternoon that far in advance. They were planning on moving in together when both of their leases were up and to give time for roommates to get another renter.

Larry and I did not see each other during this time, he was preparing for his transfer to DC in April and was starting to do an active search for a 2 Bedroom condo or a small townhouse near Tysons Corner. His parents knew people in the industry, and they were trying to find something suitable, what I did not know was that Larry's family was wealthy. They wanted to do something different for the wedding, they wanted to have a fancy dinner at the 4 Seasons in DC, for the family the weekend before the wedding, and they would do the night before the wedding In Longwood with the families. I told them don't be surprised if some of this is filmed by ESPN. We either called or texted every day though.

On the 15th of December I texted Olivia and asked her would you like to be in the wedding party as a bridesmaid.

She called me back and wanted to know if I really wanted her when she barely knew me, and I said sure I want you especially now that you could be part of our family the June after. She texted back in an hour and said she would love to be a bridesmaid, but she lived in DC and the wedding is in Farmville, so anything would have to be on the weekend.

I told her the Maid of Honor is coming from Denmark so that won't be a problem. I still had one slot left even though I had asked Susan, she had declined it because she was in Philadelphia and the trip was going to be expensive and at this time, she could not afford it.

I was finishing training when I got a call directly from one of the three players that was going to be under our coop coach, Anita Krantze, was a German player, currently number 125 in the world, and only 22, she had played at LSU for 2 years before she turned professional. Anita indicated she would meet me in New Zealand she was in the qualifiers for the event and hoped to be in the main draw. She also asked if I would sign-up with her for doubles and said sure, just dollars for both of us if we get in. On the next day, I got another call from the third player, from Spain, Isabel Garcia, a top 100 player, who had been on the tour for about five years and was still only 23, so I was the eldest of the three players, but again I would figure that, I spent 7 years in the minors before the miracle in New York.

John sent me the financials since we had started in late August the amount I had made and the endorsement money I had received less charges for Paul and himself, the number was staggering at a half million dollars and climbing with every T-shirt and shoes under "Athletic and Feminine" branding. He said we have the endorsements ready for next year and they are now $250,000, for the year, so I was going to be a wealthy woman, and Kia was handing me the title to the Telluride. That was going to be a 52,000, taxable event, so we are at nearly $300,000. The tennis shoes, shirts, and now skirts and tops by Lacoste with the alligator is going to make you and Larry well over $150,000 each without my cut. You are going to be a comfortable woman for the rest of your life.

So, with the financial side of my life now much better, I decided to donate the malibu to a church, to auction it off for a donation to supporting poor families with food and medicines. I understand they got $7500, for it and it will make someone a nice used car.

I celebrated Christmas with my parents early, I know James and Olivia were coming after Christmas to spend a few days with my parents and Granny Miller. My Christmas was going to be with Larry in Fairfax, VA. To make sure things were on the real, I was given a room to use for the next three days. I drove up to Fairfax early On Christmas Eve, so I could be there without driving at night, and they were calling for a chance of freezing rain, I was not going to get the Telluride hurt and me also, so I hugged my parents and drove the 4 hours to Fairfax, Virginia. I drove up to the house which was listed as Mclean, and it was huge, it was like three of my houses in Radford, and it was only the medium size in the neighborhood. I had my clothes for three days, and lots of presents, many of which were from crafters in the mountains, I like giving presents not from department stores and online is good for toys for the kids, but for adults, hunting at craft events is more fun for me. I brought all my stuff and knocked on the door. I heard the dog barking, and the door opened and both Mr. and Mrs., Wilson welcomed me to the house, they said I got here before Larry. They asked me not to be so formal with them to call them they said either call me mom and dad, or if that feels weird, Jean, and Albert will do for now. We have set you up in the last bedroom on the second floor, and welcome to our home. I simply said thank you for having me here, your house is so beautiful and large.

Jean insisted on getting a hug from me, she was about 5' 4" so I was a bit taller than her. "Larry will be here in about 20 minutes, he is coming from National Airport, and has an Uber from there to here. Look at "Athletic and Feminine", what a great tag line, I am hearing it everywhere and Larry is buying me a pair of the tennis shoes for when I play tennis. I know that Larry and you met when you were at a tennis event at College Park, not sure why he was there as he played soccer, but I heard that he asked you out after the quarterfinals, and at first you said only if I make the finals, and you then proceeded to lose in the semifinals. He apparently still wanted to go out and you guys starting dating almost 2 years ago, with your travel it is the first time we have been in the same place. Welcome to our home and I guess the family. How long will you be her?"

I had to tell her 3 days, after that travelling to New Zealand and then Australia, going to play the Australian Open. Jean indicated she wanted to meet my mother Barbara and your grandmother who are planning the wedding.

"We will need to find rooms not sure how far from Farmville we will need to go to get 35 to 50 rooms. I understand the plan is for 150 people, and I told her it had to be that size due to the size of the church."

"I then told her that my sponsors asked for ten slots so each side got 70 total spaces each, and that don't be surprised but this may also have ESPN cameras." I then took my stuff up to the room assigned only to see that the room had powder blue sheets with a pink comforter, my colors are now everywhere.

Larry and his brother Chris both came within about 5 minutes of each other, Chris looked a lot like Larry, but he was just under six feet, about 2 inches shorter than Larry. Larry approached me, and despite his mother being in the room, proceeded to give me a very passionate kiss.

"Chris said I will kiss you on the cheek, I don't want to make Larry jealous because I am the better-looking brother."

We all went to midnight mass as the local episcopal church, and about 8:30, in the morning we all came down for breakfast. I had already called my parents; they were up and wished me a happy holiday. I helped cut things up for the five of us, and they had a full buffet ready to go by 9:00. After the breakfast came present time. I'm not sure how much they enjoyed my presents, but they at least said thank you. Jean then said, this will be our last Christmas without a daughter, Lilly, welcome to the family we can't wait until we see you and Larry get married in July.

While Larry and I could hold hands, we had to behave and for the most part we did as this was his parents' house, and we were not yet married. I survived the inquisition from uncles and relatives the day after Christmas, apparently the Wilsons got together the day after

Christmas, but only the cousins, aunts, and uncles, about 20 people. I guess they were at spouses for the actual holiday. I survived the questions from all of them and had one normal day with Larry before we both had to Leave. I went home to pack for the next 6 weeks, New Zealand, Australia, an ITF in Hawaii, and then Austin, TX before I would be able to come home.

We did get a little frisky in Larry's old bedroom before we left, I drove him to the Metro and then he said see you in six weeks, I will be losing sleep watching you.

A practice with the professionals in Virginia and then off to New Zealand. It was going to be an experience and I had never been to this part of the world. Professional without Paul's support, a new world was coming.

I had to fly out the 29th of December to New Zealand and what a flight, I drive to Dulles airport and my car was going to be there six weeks and found an extended parking place to reduce costs. The flight went from Dulles to Los Angeles, 2-hour transfer, then to Auckland, New Zealand. I had no idea of what day it was and time when we arrived, I knew it was daylight, and we were in the warm air, but when they finally said, welcome to Auckland, I found it was noon on December 31st, I was like 12 hours and a day ahead of Larry, I simply sent him a text him on my local phone that I purchased, it came back who the hell is this. I told him this is my New Zealand phone for the next week. The text back was happy new year good luck, and I am going back to bed it is like 2 am.

When I got to the Hilton hotel, which was the tournament hotel, I sent e-mails to my parents saying I was safe and have a happy new year. Then I went to sleep and the next thing I knew it was 10:00 and hungry, glad they had room service. I ordered a BLT, French fries, and a soda, they were done for the night with full dinners, this was about as good as it could be done. The rest of the world was getting ready for new year's, I had 5 days to get accustomed to the time zones and be ready to play tennis. I ate my lunch/dinner and went back to bed and slept through the new year. The life of the tennis professional holidays and other things were rare with family just a bubble.

I had a note waiting for me from Johan, tennis meeting at noon and practice at 12:30-, now it hit me, I was in another world, New Zealand. I doubt I will see much though other than hotel, airport, courts and back. I wish Paul was here but next month he becomes a dad and the junior tennis academy leader now, so his future is defined, wonder what mine will be, this tennis thing will only last so much.

I met Johan, with the two other players at noon, Johan was about 6'3", and had an accent I had a hard time understanding. I guess the South African version of English was something different. Anita and Isabel coming from Germany and Spain, had no problems understanding him, I often had to have him repeat what he was saying. Thirty-minute workout this afternoon so he could see my form, and he responded decent serve, nice slice, limited movement though, you need to work on lateral movement. Anita and I were given wild cards for the double's tournament. The singles qualifications would begin the next morning. The next three days nothing but practice, hotel stay and doing e-mails, weight training and then off to bed, a very boring existence. We did one thing as a group, we went to a place called "Hobbiton", and did a cave tour at the same location. It was good break in our routine and Johan said it was a good way for everyone to meet each other and have a little fun.

I did my running through the blocks around our hotel, I'm not a great person for the treadmill, or for the stationary bike, but with the nice warm weather, I did my running at 6 AM, and by 7 I was done ready for breakfast and then the day. I was able to call Larry it was like 9 at night, when I got back, he was getting ready to take a shower he had been at the gym, he said he was looking forward to waking up with Lilly.

"I said so am I but that is several months away."

"He laughed, I mean to see you play this morning, I think your match is scheduled at like 5 AM, so I will be waking up to Lilly. To watch your match, I had to buy an ap from the Tennis Channel, great for them but I only got it for you my future wife."

"I reminded him we still had 6 plus months before that was going to happen."

I got a text from Kiki that the designer for the bridesmaids' outfits were being told they had to be in pink, and with powder blue belt like material and pink shoes, she said those are your colors, so I guess we are stuck with them. I told her that they were paying for them as part of my endorsement deal for the year. She indicated they were gorgeous, from a French designer, but you need to get a third person, so they can start the final construction by March 1. Because I have already talked about the tournaments so much in my journal, I will just summarize the New Zealand results. I lost singles the second round, which still allowed me to make the 79th ranked player in the world, but Anita and I had fun in the doubles, getting to the finals before losing to 2 Russian players Svitolina and Anastasia Kuznetsov, we made a game of it before losing the match tiebreak 10-5. For the week with the combined results, I did manage to reap just under $10,000, in prize money, not a lot of money, but with expenses, discounted coaching, and John's fee I was still able to net about $4,000, for the week. I wondered what my friends with degrees earned at their desks in normal jobs.

It was time to check out of our hotel in New Zealand and go to the airport for 2 weeks or more in Australia. The other three were going straight to the Australian Open to start getting ready for the tournament, I was asked to do a photo shoot for Lacoste with the new line of "Athletic and Feminine", clothes, in Sydney. I would meet them on Tuesday afternoon in Melbourne. We had a hotel for this week outside of the city at a local club, one because there was more time available for practice and second with no prize money, we needed to keep the costs down. Anitia and I shared a room with 2 queen beds. It appears that Isabel and Johan, shared a room and from what Anita said to me doubted they needed to get 2 beds, that apparently had been lovers for a while.

Not much to do in Melbourne our room was equipped with a kitchen, Anita and I decided to save money and went shopping for food at a local farmers market and grocery store. We would do most of our meals in our room and explore the weekend for a couple of local restaurants before we left Saturday night for the closer location to the Australian Open.

If I hadn't said it earlier with all the wedding and holiday plans, I was notified that WTA had awarded me the "Most Improved Player Award". The plaque came to my parent's house right before I left for New Zealand. I'm sure it will go in the joint award cabinet along with James's All-American awards and top six awards. No money for this award.

At the Australian Open, I was going to be busy, I was playing singles, mixed doubles, and with Anita women's doubles, we were rated just high enough to get a main draw entry. Mike and I thought we would be awarded a seed after our run in New York, but with only 16 teams unlikely as a lot of good players were looking for the extra money.

It is the summer in Melbourne, Australia, they have great beaches and we had time on our hands. Anita apparently asked Johan for an afternoon off entirely and asked me to go with her to the beach. Anita is a gorgeous woman, 5'7" +, dark blond hair, long legs, and beautiful green eyes. She has done some modeling before, and she had a revealing bikini that she wanted to wear. I had no such swimming gear; I had a simple speedo bathing suit that I wore for swimming training when I needed to train and did not want to run. It was a print, mostly black with yellow prints on it, so I thought I could get away with it and Larry would not be upset. We decided on a trip to the Sandringham Beach, a little farther than another beach but we could get there by train and it was away far enough that we would not get bothered as tennis players. As I said, Anita is gorgeous, and it did not take long for the men to find her, fortunately they ignored the less attractive woman, well that was until someone pointed to me.

She came over to me and said, "you look like a tennis player who is also Eurasian, I said I bet there aren't that many of us that are blond and tall" She went away and Anita laughed at me you could have made her day. I told her it was ok, for me to be the ugly duckling, and she laughed, you really don't think you are very attractive. I told her about my life as a teenager, developing late, and not having a lot of curves. She said you want the name of my agent with your height and legs, you could do some modeling. Only Larry thinks I am attractive nowadays and that is all I care about. I will say that Anita was offered a few cell numbers and contacts for possible dates, I know she went on at least a couple of them coming home late each night. She was an extremely attractive woman, and the guys all wanted to take her out.

The last night before the qualifiers, Anita said to me, "I may have more of a shot at tennis, but your "Athletic and Feminine" brand will make you more money than you will ever make from tennis."

I had no idea what she meant but later you will see she may have known something that I did not.

Australian Open Experience:

I want to describe what it is like to go from 20's to 90's in Melbourne, but overall, the tennis was good enough to make a lot of money and get a little bit higher ranking. In doubles Anita and I won 2 matches before losing in straight sets to the number 12 seeds who ended up losing in the semifinals. My singles were not a bad result, making it to the third round, the seed in my section pulled out and we got the lucky loser, who I beat 6-2 and 6-3. I then won the second-round match in a tight second set 6-4, and 7-6, but fell to the eight seed from France, who was a fit player that got me running side to side and being desperate. I finally lost 6-4 and 6-1, but the 70 points would move me up to the top 60 of the worlds for the first time. Mike and I came close to getting a championship in the mixed doubles, we lost in the finals on Friday in straight sets 6-3, and 6-0. Mike was tired because he was still in the men's doubles with his partner and would eventually win his first major title. We received a nice plate for the mixed doubles finalist, that I sent home to Virginia, insured.

Larry here, I am inserting this because Lilly downplayed her Australian open. First, she pocketed nearly $250,000 in prize money, and her ranking after the week was 56 in the world, high enough to get into the main draw of Charleston. Her new friend Anita qualified into the main draw and won a first-round match which was her first in a major. The Lacoste ad came out for the new line of "Athletic and Feminine", and the photo shoot made me a little nervous that Lilly may have outgrown me. My fear was totally put away when Lilly arrived at Dulles airport and we made love and then bought a townhouse in Tysons Corner, VA, which would close right before Lilly would leave for Europe in April. Anita arrived three days after Lilly, and we met her at the airport, she said before she would agree to be in the wedding, she wanted to see the countryside of Virginia. Even after flying from Hawaii, the men could not stop looking at Anita, she is as attractive as Lilly described her, not sure I want my fiancé with that man magnet, but Anita and Lilly get along like they are sisters.

Anita landed at Dulles airport, and as soon as she got down, she was turning the heads of the passengers in the terminal. We spent the afternoon with Larry before we started down to Farmville to stay with Granny Miller, who was waiting for her granddaughter and friend. It did not take long the next day for Anita after seeing the church and then the venue to agree to be in the wedding. I let everyone know the third bridesmaid was confirmed in the wedding party. I was trying hard not to be Anita's "Duff", but she was a very attractive girl and like to tease the men getting their hopes up. They were rarely successful in getting more than a smile from her. Anita and I were back at Dulles airport three days later to fly to train in Florida, we had another tournament in Austin, TX to play. Anita had played in a 125, in Hawaii and now had enough points to get a direct entry in to Austin, I was the highest ranked player not to get a seed. Anita and I were signed up for doubles together, she would get men to the court to watch the matches.

The problem with having a coop coach is that while we were playing in Austin, Isabel was with Johan in Europe, they would next see us in Miami.

Two single women in Austin, TX could get into a lot of trouble a lot of bars to play and with Anita around a lot of Texas men wanting to buy her drinks. I had to remind Anita, we were here for tennis and not fooling around. She was disappointed, she was about the same age as the seniors at UT, and they found her model like body very attractive especially with her very thick German accent she used when she was with guys. We stayed together at the Hampton Inn, which was close to the tournament site, plus that way we got breakfast.

There are not a lot of tournaments in February and the top players skip these 250's awaiting the USA march swing. I needed points, so that was why we were here.

My tournament went as predicted; I made it to the quarters in singles moving me to 50th in the live rankings. Anita and I had to stay longer than expected even though she lost in the first round of singles, we made it to the finals in doubles, good for both of us in getting enough points for a direct entry in to another major. Since the finals were two weeks before California, for the first time in a while Anita went to Florida to train and I went home for a week. Larry would meet me in Radford, he had already vacated his New York apartment and was at his parents waiting for our new townhouse to be ready, they were installing the appliances this week. Anita was going to Orlando to train and to show off her bikini body at the pool, the poor men were going to go nuts. Another plate for the trophy case in Radford.

For a week, I was home and training with the coaches at the Country Club with the training program that Johan had sent me. I was doing a lot of lateral exercises to improve my ability to stay in points. They said this would help me in the clay court season, I had not played on European clay in 8 years, this was not going to be fun.

I really was not looking forward to three months of clay court season. I had no points to protect here but I also had like no experience on clay. I was enjoying my time with family and training locally, but March was coming and another 5 weeks on the road, before I would see my fiancé again.

Paul said his son Paul JR, had been born last week, he was a perfect boy about 7 pounds, Ann was doing well as was everyone else. I sent way too much in gifts for the baby, I probably should never have done it. I even got baby tennis clothes from Lacoste and baby shoes from Mizuno. I remitted to him, the first baby version of "Athletic and Feminine", Lacoste was just getting ready and I'm sure he would find someone that could use it. I was going to spoil my friend's child, Paul was like my big brother, and I wanted to spoil his child.

Time to heal, I missed my fiancé this travel was killing me, and my new little sister Anita, was away in Florida, again another lonely trip.

Chapter 21

The Journeyman

Time home from the tour and time to heal, I had to take three days off practice to let the calves heal. I took a drive to Winston Salem to order furniture for the townhouse, I think I spent my last tournaments proceeds and they were going to be delivered in April to the new townhouse. Afterwards, thought about I probably should have waited to show Larry before I bought them, but the bedroom set, and the dining room set, but they were a good sale and it happened. I will let him order the mattress for the queen size bed. I did not buy any furniture for the living room that was coming from Larry's apartment in New York, and well I was on my way to Europe and would get $100,000 at a minimum at the French Open so a little art may be purchased and sent home.

Finally, my calf was healed, and I resumed training in Virginia for a few more days with the family, and then flew to Florida to meet up with Johan and Anita for training. Isabel was already in Europe getting points in the clay courts, which left Johan in a lousy mood missing his girlfriend. I doubled up with Anita and while she was skipping Indian Wells, we were going to play Miami together in doubles. We were training near Orlando, and we would get up at about 9 each day play tennis until noon, and then the afternoon, we would go to the hotel pool. Anita would go to the pool for an hour each day and a different man would hit on her every afternoon, I did not have that problem, I guess a little too tall and thin as opposed to my mysterious German tennis friend who when she talked and batted her eyes, men ran all over to her to try to date her, funny thing she never went out with any of the male tennis players who were training at the same site. I will say she convinced me to buy a bikini, and realized my stomach was too white so tried to get tanned and ended up very burned, hurt like hell for two days to practice but I was not going to let Johan know what I had done he would have chewed me out. Anita later told me, that she sometimes wished she was homely, sometimes she wanted to just go to the pool without getting hit on by any single male in the place. I really did not have much sympathy for her, but I did not let on that I kind of envied her, athletic and one of the most beautiful women in the world.

Anita was going to play an ITF in Florida to get her singles points up while I was going to Indian Wells, I had never been to that part of the world. My first match was on a weird date, I was playing my first-round match on a Friday in the round of 128, half of the field played to get down to 64, players, the seeded players all 32 of them would not play until early the next week. I was not seeded and would play a qualifier in the first round. Unfortunately, if I won, I was going to play the number 2 seed, so sometimes your success is not dependent on your ability but also the draw, I did not get the best draw for this tournament. I beat a Mexican qualifier in the first round, Lorena Gonzales, 6-3 and 6-4, and then had Saturday off before playing again on Sunday. The tournament is a two-week tournament finishing on the second Saturday. I dropped the second match in 6-2 and 6-2, the coaches now knew I had a weakness was my lateral movement, and now I was known and tape on me, it was getting harder to surprise anyone. While there Larry informed me that he had a week off and would meet me in Miami, that was going to be a fun week, with him watching and Anita and me playing doubles together. Anita made it to the finals of the ITF and was now guaranteed a spot in the Miami draw allowing us to put in to play doubles together. Because I had no points to defend, just the one round moved me up to 49th, in the world. I flew to Florida to train for a week while the Indian Wells tournament was completing.

Between some Europeans deciding to leave early for the clay season, injuries, I was the highest rated player without a seed, and another injury came to a player in Indian Wells and for the first time in a 1000 tournament I was the 32nd seed, so I did not have to play until the second round, an additional three days of training in Orlando, but Johan was in Spain apparently getting engaged to Isabel. I called up Paul and he was not able to get out of the college tournament, so John had another coach be for Anita and me. The coach he had for us, was Thomas Johnston, I met him at Sea Colony last year. He had other tennis players but said he could take us on for the one tournament while we waited to go to Europe. I knew I would have Paul in Charleston, SC, and he has already told me that I was staying with the family that week. When you are not top 30 in the world it is hard to afford coaching, you can't get enough money to have your own. Anita was playing Friday in her first-round match. On Thursday we found out that we had been accepted into the doubles draw with 32 teams playing.

On Friday Maria Schindler won her match setting up a rematch from the US Open qualifications in the second round for me. Thomas is mostly a doubles coach but did have some things positive for me to work on, first he had me wrap my calf for the match and to baby it a little or use tape but keep it warm, second he said keep being aggressive, if it means getting passed at net do it, just don't let a clay court player get in to long rallies that is what they want and you aren't that type of player.

Anita won her match on Saturday and would play the three seed on Monday, doubles would start Monday, so they gave her an early match for Monday for singles and then us for doubles later. We drew the 2 seeds, so it was not going to be easy. Well, I say that now, but the night before, we received notice that the 2 seeds had pulled out of the tournament and the alternates were put in their place. What that meant was that the winner, had the inside track to get to the finals.

My match with Maria was a lot easier than I was expecting, I came out served and volleyed and took a lot of her strategy away and won the first set 6-2. She figured it out in the second and we went down to the wire, and I won the match 7-5, sending me to the third round of the tournament. My reward was to play Luna Marino, from France the 2 seed. I will tell you that the match did not go well on Wednesday, and I failed to make the fourth round losing 6-3, and 6-3, one break in each set was enough for her to move on. Anita had lost on Monday so neither went beyond the third round.

Our doubles were the story of the tournament, we routed the alternates 6-1 and 6-0. On Wednesday evening, we won again 6-3, and 6-4, so we had to play late into the tournament. On Thursday we again took down a seed, winning 10-6 in the match tiebreaker. Friday in the semi-finals, I thought we would be nervous, Thomas told a couple of stories and kept us loose. We took the four seeds down, 7-5 in the first set and 6-1, in the second, getting us to a major tournament final and a ton of money. The team share is $220,000, less coaching costs and we as a team made $100,000 in singles. We were both now fully funded for the remainder of the year.

In the finals we faced Caca Capo and Beatrice Berg, the three seeds who had upset the 1 seed in the semifinals. We were a very nervous team as we were first on Sunday. Anita and I had never been in a final like this and despite Thomas trying to get us focused, we were being outclassed and lost the first set 6-1. During the changeover, Thomas said go big to me, meaning biggest serves I had and blow them off a little and let Anita clean-up if they managed to get it back. We took the set 7-5 and forced a 10-point match tiebreak. We started off well, Anita double faulted, and the other team went up 6-4, and then Anita lost her serve, and we were down 7-4. Each team held our 2 points each and we then trailed 9-6, and we had a chance, but on the second match point I hit the return into the net for the other team to win 10-7. We may have lost but I found my doubles partner for the rest of the year. I will say Anita attracted a much larger male crowd than I would have expected for a doubles match, she was getting a following in Miami like Anna Kournikova, and Sports Illustrated was inking a contract for her for the next version of the swimsuit magazine. You noticed, they did not ask her doubles partner, the gangly looking Eurasian.

The points for this tournament put us both in the top 60 in doubles and for me I was now the 41st rated tennis player in the world, unfortunately the next 2 months were exclusively clay courts. In Europe

I would play red clay which I have not even viewed much less played on, not going to be an easy season but again I had almost no points to defend.

Larry was at the tournament the entire week, while we had some time together, this was my profession and the money I was winning this week was needed for the rest of the year. We did not even stay together in the hotel, that was left to Anita and me, someone had to keep the guys away from Anita, they tried always. I gave Larry my finalist dish for the double's tournament, he said he would take it to DC with him, and the townhouse would be ready by the time you get home from Charleston.

For me, the introduction of the girls sized shoes came out during the tournament, we heard there was an initial sale of 5,000, pairs before they were available, apparently moms wanted this for their little daughters.

Anita left the tournament and went to Europe, where I would meet up with her in four weeks, I had to quickly find a flight from Fort Lauderdale to Charleston, SC. I found Southwest had space on the flight leaving at 8 PM, it would get to Atlanta at 10, and then to Charleston at midnight. Waiting for me at the gate was Paul, he looked a little bit tanner than the last time I saw him. I yelled at him, "how is it going papa," and he gave me the biggest hug I had in a long time. I told him don't let Larry see you hugging me that way and I wanted to make sure he had opened his calendar for Farmville the third Saturday in July for the wedding.

Paul said, "not only had it on the calendar, but he was staying at a member of the country club's house they were going to be out of town, and we had the whole house for the weekend. I have been told by James to reserve Friday night for the guy's night out so we hope we will return your fiancé in time for the wedding."

The tournament in Charleston, is a 500-level tournament played on the green clay and not the red clay of Europe. The tournament this year had 28 players, the top 4 seeds getting a bye, so they won't play until Wednesday, I have a first day exception because of a travel rule from the WTA that I had never heard of before. The rule basically says they must give you a full day to travel between the former tournament and the current tournament, so I had Monday off.

"Paul said I will not want you to train today, I will send you to a physical therapist for your calf, it appears that the pain is getting worse, and you need to take some time off before this tournament. Fortunately, you are only playing singles, and after this week you have two weeks back in DC before going to Europe. I expect that you will take the 2 weeks to rest that calf and to do the physical therapy we will get you started today. You are suffering because this is your first year with this many matches and your calf is taking the abuse. You should skip going to Europe, but I know you won't because this is your vindication tour."

All I could say was "I need a day off anyway, I want to spoil your wife and son by giving her time to get her hair done, and me to play temporary auntie to the baby and maybe a little time with your stepdaughter after she gets home from school."

Paul was on leave from Hilton Head this week to coach, and he was going to just do the afternoons with College of Charleston, the girls this week were hostesses for the tournament to earn some money and some level of involvement in the community. Anita texted me that she was in Portugal for a tournament this week and would contact me later.

Larry was in DC all week and was not coming to see me play, unless I make the finals, then he will fly down on Saturday. The rest of the family also committed to other things, so I was pretty much on my own for the week and then to DC for almost three weeks. I realized that is how my life was going to be through July, nursing my calf, missing to see my family and fiancé, and trying to earn money. My graduate friends at Longwood had an easier life, not complaining because the money this year has been good, but it took 7 years.

It was so great staying with Paul and family, no hotel food and I felt a little spoiled. My opponent was Caca Capo, she had done the same thing as me. Leaving straight from Miami. She was leaving for Europe after this tournament and was already registered for the next week in Spain. When Paul saw it was Caca, he told me this won't be so hard, she is trying to be a singles player again and takes wild cards while she tries to win more doubles tournaments. Paul told me you are so lucky, you are first on Tuesday, 11:00, and after the work with the physio this afternoon you should be good to go. Ann made a great dinner for us and then left to feed Paul Jr; she was embarrassed to do it in front of company. I took some time to call Larry, and at the end he simply said I can't wait to see you next week when we close on the townhouse. (I love you by the way).

Tuesday morning and it was already 75 degrees and humid, welcome to Charleston SC, and this is April. The match was an interesting match, with me holding serve easily and Caca forcing me to run on her service games and usually winning. My calf while working was talking to me to do something and with that I returned and crashed the net forcing the action early and breaking to go up 5-3, I then served out the set easily. Using this much more aggressive method for the match I won the second set 6-2, and was now in the round of 16, playing the 2 seed Maria Bako of Hungary, who was a clay court specialist and had been practicing in Charleston for over a week. I went to the physical therapist for the tournament for stretching of my left calf, and it worked but she told me the only thing going to help that calf out was rest.

I texted Larry and told him my plan was to leave here Saturday morning and to meet me at Dulles airport in the afternoon. I had no pretense that I would make the finals here and wanted to be home with my fiancé for as long as possible. The match was scheduled for the third match on around 3:30 PM, on Wednesday. I did a takeout for the entire family at a barbeque place recommended and we spent the night talking stories about my time as an unpaid assistant coach, probably not the best way to spend the night before a match. Paul had beer while I got to drink flavored water.

The match on Wednesday just did not go well, I lost 6-2 and 6-3, just could not get into the slow movement of clay and the additional stress on my calf just did not want this much pressure on it. I received like $8500, for winning a round here and while not a great amount after paying Paul the minimum per week of $1000, it still paid for everything, and even the $425, to John for his cut. I could not wait until I went home on Saturday, meanwhile I spent 2 days with the physical therapist working on the strength and flexibility of my calf, it simply did not like all these matches and practice. I went to watch the College of Charleston win against Coastal Carolina on Friday and wore nothing that showed my colors. The points I won for this tournament did not move me up in position in the world staying at 41 in the live rankings with almost no points to defend through early July.

On Friday I called my mom and starting crying, "can I see you guys before I leave for Europe, I miss everyone and feel like I am all alone going to Europe, miss Larry and want to see everyone."

Mom and dad said they would be there the next weekend to see the new house. I asked them to bring the air mattresses, because not sure we would have much furniture yet, the North Carolina furniture was due earlier in the day.

My mother reminded me that for years I wanted to be a professional tennis player full-time, and now you see the other side of it. It is a lot of travel and a lot of time by yourself, not like you have Paul everyday like you did before. So maybe it is not as much as you had hoped the lifestyle you wanted. I did argue that I could make a lot of money this year, I had already made well over 1/3 of a million dollars.

With a hug and cries by all of us, I said goodbye to Paul and Ann and told them I will see you in three months in Farmville. I warned Ann, one of my bridesmaids is world class gorgeous so check your men at the door. I was only partially kidding.

I was so happy to be with Larry for the next few weeks, I trained every day at College Park under their coaches while waiting to leave for Europe. On Thursday we closed on our house and the furniture from New York was delivered on Friday. I bought a mattress for the furniture that came from North Carolina on Saturday. At 4 PM my parents showed up and things were better. I had my parents and my fiancé for a while, and the loneliness went away. My parents brought us some other items for the house including my trophies and dad built a brand-new trophy case for my tennis stuff, I added the Miami doubles finalist with the box of awards I had in Radford.

The townhouse was a nice 4-bedroom house that we used 2 bedrooms for offices, one for Larry as he went into the office 4 days a week and worked on Fridays from the house. I would use the very small bedroom as my office. There was almost no land and for the first year we did not have time to do any landscaping. Larry had them custom do my office with a powder blue paint job and pink corners. He had made 2 custom signs, "Athletic and Feminine Incorporated ". We were making a lot of money from it apparently this was taking over as a main line for Mizuno and Lacoste was having to increase production capacity. We had plank flooring in the office and a plastic protection under my office chair which was also powder blue.

My parents put the air mattresses in the last bedroom, and they brought furniture that Granny Miller said she wanted us to have that would make this room a nice guest bedroom.

I had 2 more weeks to buy things for the house, and train in College Park. I went to a few antique stores but not my style of furniture, did get a few paintings for the house at reasonable prices.

My training regimen was sent by Johan so the junior pro at College Park was limited in what he would do and was just a hitting partner. The calf treatments were daily and by the time I went to Europe it felt fine.

My parents left Tuesday morning. Larry and I did initiate the townhouse bedroom for several days afterwards and did not break the bed or the mattress. We met a few of the neighbors and I was very careful not to wear blue and pink while outside meeting them. When they asked me what I did for a living, I said promotions and a lot of travel, I was not willing to give up my privacy but I'm sure with the internet they knew very quickly that we had settled on the house and my last name was Jarman.

It was finally time for me to leave for the red clay season that would take me to various parts of Europe and meet up with Anita for doubles. We needed to make sure we qualified for the major as a team and we were getting closer. Larry was so good to me, and we spent our last night together in our bedroom and then to Dulles for a flight through Paris, for a tournament in northern Italy, then another in Bordeaux region of France before Roland Garros.

I discovered something that I had feared my game was 100% not a red clay court singles player by any means, way too much running and long points the courts were so slow. I lost in the first round of both tournaments basically just barely covering my costs, and Johan insisted that I do more running training to get used to the courts on my days off.

Doubles was my saving grace for the 2 tournaments with Anita. We made the semi-finals in Italy and the finals of the 125 in France. We then had a week off before the French Open. My calf was taking to the treatments well, but this was not my surface. The doubles money was as good as the singles money and we were invited to be in the French Open doubles, and Mike and I opted out of the mixed doubles too much time on the court. I have the small finalist plate with me, I ordered a case of wine to be at the wedding it was being sent through customs in June.

French Open:

Paris in the spring could get you in a lot of trouble, the air is finally warming up and so many sites to see. I knew that my run at Roland Garros was not going to go far, I had not won a match on the red clay leading up to the French Open, and this was not going to be an easy draw. I was lucky that I did not get a seed in the first round, but would face Beatrice Berg in the first round, again another doubles specialist that qualified for the tournament with a wild card. Anita and I would not find out who we would play doubles until Tuesday afternoon when they posted the tournament draw, we were possibly going to be a 16 seed based on our results and rankings. I missed getting a seed by a few spots which meant I would face a seed in the second round, my luck was going to face Marci Frankfort, this was her specialty, and it was not mine.

With a few days in Paris, Anita decided that we should go sightseeing, while I did not argue with that thought, when Anita went anywhere then men came shortly thereafter. Nothing like a 5' 7" + blond with green eyes, nice legs, and a great rack, to make the men go crazy. She told me she was a 34C but that just finished the package, and the men were attracted to her like bees to flowers. We did a lot of sites like the Eifel Tower, and the various castles and art museums, and walking along the parks. I made the mistake at the Eifel tower afternoon to wear "Athletic and Feminine", gear, when somebody asked me if I might be a tennis player. When I told her that I was, then she handed me a book and said, would you sign my book? I said who do you think I am, and she spoke. You are the founder of "Athletic and Feminine", Lilly Jarman, and I now started to realize that the saying was going global. I signed the book and then another few fans asked me to sign the same thing.

"Anita started to laugh, "see how it feels to have people chase you down and want to talk to you, that is my every day with men, always nervous because I don't know who wants to hurt me, so I always travel with a second person."

Before that I did not realize that she was always nervous about the men and someone possibly wanting to hurt her, so we were a pair, me for protection and Anita just the gorgeous friend, I was the Duff, but I loved Anita for her humor and genuine way of being. It was not her fault she also happened to be probably one of the most beautiful women in the world.

I lost the title of "Tall Girl" a long time ago, so many of the Russians and other Eastern Europeans women here were at the six-foot level at 5"10" I just felt normal. In Paris there were a lot of Eurasian women from the time that France occupied Vietnam, so I also felt very comfortable here, so different from Radford. When I saw these women, I only wanted Dea to be able to be with me, I had to satisfy myself with my mother Barbara. I received a text she was coming for the first few days of the tournament and would also meet me tomorrow at the dress fitting. My bridal dress was being designed by Donatelle Godart, a top designer who said that Lacoste had told her about me my measurements and how to incorporate my colors into the gown somehow. At first, she thought about doing a powder blue gown, and rejected the idea as this was going to be my first wedding and she said you deserve the bride treatment no matter what Lacoste said.

The day of the fitting, the first "Athletic and Feminine" bridal gown was unveiled. I know Larry and most men will not care about this, but it was absolutely gorgeous with beautiful lace all the way down the train was where she incorporated the blue and pink, the train was the same lace as the dress but sewn in to the center was a pale blue and pink stitching, and I told her it made it look like I had a skunk behind me, and we both laughed. She indicated I have a second train that I wasn't sure how you will like it, it is white lace down the middle and one side has pink and the other side is pale blue, and that is what I went with, if I was going to be stuck with it, I still wanted all my pictures with my white dress. Barbara saw the second design and indicated that will due, and then came the veil, and the pink and blue was on the border, so as the entire white veil portion would be what was viewed and photographed.

Anita looked at the dress and said, "I am taking this picture, if you think you are my "Duff", I want my agent to see you in this design, you sure you don't want to be a model?"

"I said not at 135 pounds they won't want me."

Anita responded, "maybe not for fashion, but for sports clothes the fashion models look horrible, you are not a twig like them. I really think this "Athletic and Feminine", is going crazy, I heard baby clothes went out this week and now I am told that Babolat is negotiating with your agent for the exclusive rights to a tennis racquet, using the: Athletic and Feminine", colors printed on it, and the check is supposedly going to north of $100,000, and a commission on the sales. I am also told that John is investigating a deal for "Athletic and Feminine" under garments and that a contract with Victoria's Secret is going to be worth another $100,000 upfront. I think by the end of the year, you will be a wealthy woman, and it won't be from your tennis winnings, and you still think you are my "Duff". If I were you, I would be starting to learn marketing from your agents because I think you can ride this brand to a life outside tennis. Venus Williams has done it why not Lilly Jarman."

I was stunned at what Anita said, the brand was taking off and by the end of the year Larry and I would share over a million dollars in royalties, agent got $50,000, but still going to be crazy, I realized for the first time, I was going to be wealthy, and with Larry making good money already this is going to be a different way of life. I am also going to get a royalty from the gown sales, I have been promised $200, per dress sold under this banner, Donatelle Godart was now a licensed provider and she had 10 orders she said as soon as I approve mine, and the others would not be available until September, we want your day as the first time this dress is released, I have a contract with Macy's and expect sales of up to 500 so nice little check for you. This was getting interesting.

Donatelle went to Anita and asked, "how would you like to be the model for me, I need a beautiful woman that is not a twig for my dresses." Anita then gave her the number of her agent and a deal was done by the end of the day.

With all the wedding-based events over I was again ready to concentrate on tennis. Donatelle said she would handle all of this for her beautiful new business partner.

Anita yells, "and she thinks she is my "Duff"."

"Donatelle started to laugh, she is attractive does she know it?"

"Anita responded no, and never will."

Tennis was going to be fun; I had a weird Sunday match, this was the only major that had three Sundays, I was playing second match on an outer court. Anita played later that afternoon. I will say that the dynamic duo somehow managed to win our matches Anita beat a poor qualifier 6-0, and 6-3, the poor girl looked lost. Anita was on the second court, and yes with her wiggling around the court, she had a lot of men watching her instead of their girlfriends. Marci proved to me that a big serve is still a big serve and I only needed to break once per set and ended up winning the match 6-4 and 6-4.

My mother on the other hand was going on a food consumption trip, she found out that Parisian food is something super fun. I went with her for dinner and ate only lightly and no wine. Larry called me during dinner and asked me how I was doing. I told him calf is fine, wedding plans are going great, wait until you see the bridesmaids' dresses. Anita looked stunning in them, and then again Anita looks stunning in anything she wears.

We both played on Tuesday, and I promptly lost 6-2, and 7-6, just not a lover of the red clay, even with 1 win only, my ranking went to number 39 in the world. Anita won both her singles match in the morning and our doubles match in the late afternoon, so we were still alive as a team. Johan told me to rest my calf and only do bicycling and walking in the hotel pool so I would be ready for the next doubles match. Anita lost on Thursday, and we won our second-round match in doubles, we were a pretty good team, and unfortunately for us as the 16 seed we were playing the 1 seed on Saturday. Caca and her new partner Genevieve Swanson, a great player from Norway, and I never thought of Norway as a tennis place, but again who would have thought Radford was either.

Mom left on Thursday morning she would fly to Dulles airport and stay a couple of days with Larry before my dad was coming for her on Saturday.

On Saturday, Anita and I lost in the round of 16, we stole the first set of 6-3, before they took over and won the second set and the third set 6-1, but Anita and I had done well against the double specialists. Even with our loss, we were now going to be seeded no worse than 14 at Wimbledon, and I was coming back to play Eastbourne on the grass an Anita and I would play together there.

Sunday came, and I packed for home. The tournament would play for another week, and I would miss the first grass courts and play the second week and rest the third week before Wimbledon. The wedding was now less than seven weeks away and I wanted to go see my fiancé. I had won over $125,000 in prize money for the time in France, I think I gave back $10000, to the local economy in art that was being sent to our new townhouse.

I had now played in three grand slams and was now top 40 in the world, I was getting money form "Athletic and Feminine", and it was outpacing my winnings it had taken off according to John.

I just wanted to get home now to see my fiancé, I love Anita and we had fun together, but I really wanted to be with Larry. Dad said that he and James would be up to Tysons to help put some things up for us this weekend.

I saw Larry at the airport waiting for me after customs, they looked at the metal plate from the doubles and started to laugh, so you are the famous Lilly Jarman, where is your blue and pink. With a hug and kiss I was in the arms of my fiancé for at least the next two weeks. Next stop England, and then our wedding in Farmville. Johns Memorial Episcopal Church was being fancied up getting ready for it.

Chapter 22

Wimbledon

Two weeks at home seemed like it went by way too fast, my time with Larry was great, and we were now just five weeks away from the wedding at Johns' Episcopal and I would become Mrs. Larry Wilson, well on paper, professionally I should be Lilly Jarman. John said we need it for the branding of "Athletic and Feminine", the world is going crazy with that product line, and now Lacoste is expanding to socks and then a warm-up set. The little girls Mizuno shoes he said had already sold over 10,000 pairs twice what they had expected and the factory in Vietnam was being asked to double production while it was still a hot market for them. He said that when it was all said and done Larry and I could expect a couple of million dollars within the next 2 years. So, we were going to be comfortable, and we should be considering how to do marketing and then possible charity work for women's sports. Dea's words were spreading faster than the flu.

Tennis was going to be the focus for the next three weeks, first to Eastbourne, then London and then I was going to play the ultimate event, Wimbledon. Anita had played a 125, to get her ranking up to the top 60 in singles and told me she was waiting for me in Eastbourne.

I will admit it, I have never played any tournament on grass in my life and had no idea how it will impact my game. I was told that a big serve is always a big serve, but Johan reminded me that my serve and volley game as an attack periodically worked better on grass, the ball moves faster than clay and does not jump up like hard courts so I will use Eastbourne to learn before I go to my first Wimbledon. Oh my god, I really said that I'm playing Wimbledon.

Wimbledon requires all white clothing for the court, so Lacoste had a warm-up jacket for me to use to show the colors, and the green alligator was on the white outfit. I was allowed my wrist bands as they were white with the flag of Korea on them, everything else was just for this tournament.

Who was going to be able to come to England and watch me play? Larry could not make it unless he said I made the final weekend, mom and dad were working with Granny Miller to get everything for the wedding done. Kiki said she would come to my first match, so I had one friend, and then James called and asked if he could sit in my box for the first-round match, he said Olivia was back at home starting the planning for their wedding the following June and by the way she loves the dress for the wedding. Paul was finishing the NCAA season and had his juniors, so he was not able to be there, so just a few people in my corner. Of course, Johan and Anita would be there but that was business. I think I need to see someone about the loneliness of tennis, it really sucks.

On Friday night I took the overnight flight to London on British Airways, and then a train to Eastbourne, to get ready for the tournament. The Posthouse Hotel was the tournament hotel, and while the rooms were decent, this was not a luxury hotel. It did have 2 things, a pool and gym facility, along with a nice pub where we could do dinners and meetings. Anita and I had adjoining rooms which made it a lot easier for us, Johan and Isabel were somewhere else sharing a room.

Eastbourne is a nice town on the Atlantic Ocean, but I was not going be doing anything but, tennis, and physical therapy to make sure that everything was ready for Wimbledon. I had special shoes that Mizuno provided, that had nubs all over it to give you better traction on the grass, apparently it can be very slippery especially trying to change direction. Because it was not Wimbledon, I was allowed to wear my normal colors, whites will wait.

The tournament is packed with a lot of high ranked players because there is such a short time between the French Open and Wimbledon and everyone wanted a tournament under their belt. With only 32 players and that many ranked players, it was going to be hard to make the finals. I managed to get 2 rounds but lost in the quarters in singles. Anita won her first-round match only to lose to the number 1 player in the world for her second round. Our doubles were the answer here, we got to the semi-finals beating a ranked team along the way. My parents said they saw me play using the Tennis Channel+ service they had acquired through the internet. We made some money for the tournament, and it helped me get to number 37 in the world, and with people out with injuries I was now the highest ranked player that would not get seeded at Wimbledon. Our doubles were going to get us the 12 seed in the doubles matches.

With our doubles match ending late Friday, we stayed in the city until Monday morning and took the train to London. We rented a townhouse for a month, that seemed the best thing to do, but at a cost of $15,000, this was going to be expensive. The master bedroom was shared by Johan and Isabel, Anita, and I both had the smaller bedrooms and shared a bathroom. We also signed up for a maid served to come in once per day to clean the place so when it was all over, we had to share $20,000, just for our lodging. Johan knew a chef in the area who worked at a great restaurant, and each day he cooked a meal at his restaurant for us and it was delivered for our dinners. I made breakfast most days for Anita and myself, I was always up first, and they were big breakfasts. We took a cab to our training center at a private club for conditioning and then 45 minutes on the court shared by all 4 of us. We would do this every day for the next 2 weeks, with one exception.

On the Sunday 1 week before the tournament started, we went sightseeing, to include the Piccadilly area, and walks around castles and the London Bridge, I got to be the photographer for pictures of Anita, that she was sending out for her publicity before Sports Illustrated. She really did not need any publicity, the men flocking to her were too many to count. Again, the one that counted for me was waiting in DC.

Qualification matches started on Monday for Wimbledon, none of the three of us had to qualify at the satellite location they used for qualifying. We trained at our alternate site each day, and I was invited to a Mizuno Party on Thursday night and a Lacoste party on Friday night as my sponsors and since Anita was now also on the Lacoste team, we were going to have some fun that night. The Mizuno party required business attire, so I was dressed for that, but the Lacoste party was basically formal, so on to Harrods for dresses for the 2 of us. I found a nice long dress for myself it was a light blue as requested by Lacoste. Anita chose a wine-colored dress which looked like it was custom made for her. She thought about a pink dress so when we came in together, we would be the proper colors.

I said, "please don't do this, Anita chose a new color thankfully."

The Mizuno party was about 2 hours with good food and drinks, mine was water and then orange juice, no drinking before a major. The Friday night was about being viewed at the event and shaking hands and doing autographs with sponsors and major patrons that had been invited for the event.

Saturday morning and the final draw for singles came out, I was the 32nd and last seed, which allowed me to be lucky and play a 17-year-old British wild card Betty Russell, supposedly the next British champion. The match will be on Monday late afternoon as we are number 4 on an out court. Anita plays on an out-court Tuesday second match on. We did our last practice before the tournament; we were taking off on Sunday for rest and to be ready for the matches. We submitted our doubles entry and would find out that we were the 11 seeds for the tournament. Mike said he was skipping mixed doubles as he was nursing an injury and did not want the added stress on his hamstring. I was ok as I was playing singles and doubles and that could be enough matches and off-day work in.

James told me he had cleared customs Sunday morning and was going to be with me on Monday. Kiki said her flight was getting her in late Sunday afternoon. Both were staying at a Hyatt about 5 miles from Wimbledon, a discount for families of players was arranged for that hotel. I was getting ready for the first time on the grass at Wimbledon, the shoes were odd as were the all-white clothes. Johan had a 15-minute meeting with me regarding what Betty does and does not do. He asked me to serve and volley about a quarter of the time whether receiving or serving. He said "I am not Paul but I'm pretty good at strategy here and this will drive the youngster crazy. We will warm-up you an Anita at noon on Monday and then we will chill at the players' lounge until it is time to go."

I was assigned court 17, third on with a women and men's match in front of me. The courts started play at 11:00, I was supposed to be ready by 2 PM, but with the men being best of 5 it could be as late as 4 PM.

I woke up at 7 AM British time, was going to send Larry a text then realized it would have been 2 in the morning, so I sent him an e-mail instead that would not wake him up. Breakfast was typical British with eggs, sausage and to that I added strawberries and bananas. Need to make it through the day, we would eat at Wimbledon after warm-up. I was very nervous about this match; it was going to be a very pro-British crowd and it was going to be hard to play against that.

Kiki here, I have the iPad from Lilly, and was designated to do the summary of the match. All of us Alumni were so thrilled to see Lilly play at Wimbledon, I took a picture of her right before she went out to the court. Then came the introductions, todays fourth match this afternoon, is a women's first round match. From Britain, in her first Wimbledon, is Betty Russell, she will be playing in both women's and juniors in this tournament. A good amount of clapping afterwards. Now introducing her opponent, who is also playing in her first Wimbledon, representing South Korea, the 32nd seed in the tournament, Lilly Jarman. A few clapping was heard and then "Athletic and Feminine", was heard. I would love to say this was a tremendous match and Lilly came out in historic style, but this was not the case, Betty was overmatched. Lilly won the first four games of the match before Betty won a game, and Lilly ended up winning the set 6-1, the second set, Lilly won the first 3 games and then Betty served and broke to get 3-2 and the British fans went crazy. Unfortunately for the crowd that is all that young Betty could muster against Lilly. Lilly won the match in just over an hour with a 6-1 and 6-2 victory, Betty was the number 4 seed in the juniors starting next week. After the match I gave Lilly, a big hug then saw her brother James who had been with the team in the player's box, I needed to be away from them so I could do the summary for Lilly.

In Lilly's box was her coach and a very attractive blonde who I later learned was her doubles partner Anita. She had a lot of male attention as she left the box. Lilly told me later; she would be in the next Sports Illustrated calendar and was going to be in Costa Rica in October for a photo shoot. I also realized she was also in the wedding, I was not going to be the most attractive women at this event, she might have to tone it down not to outshine Lilly that day. I introduced myself to Anita as the Maid of Honor, and asked how we can get Lilly away on Friday night.

"Anita said she can get it done, she will take her to Longwood to work out and then we can get her for the night when she has no other choice. Anita said she is searching for a male stripper for the night, it has not been easy, and she is on the phone with Barbara Jarman to help, she thinks some college students can be hired for it."

Lilly here, I can't imagine what they are planning together Anita and Kiki, but they better make sure I am at my wedding on time and in that beautiful dress waiting for me in like 4 weeks.

The doubles draw came out and as the number 11 seed, we were playing a non-seed on Wednesday, this was the fifth match on court 14, and would be late in the day, this also meant that I would be playing first or second on Wednesday for singles, while Anita would use this as her practice and competition, this also meant I had to have a hitting session on Tuesday.

I received texts from my parents, Larry and Paul about my victory and wishing me the best for the second round. Lacoste was apparently very pleased with my performance here and had sent four more outfits like the one I played with today, they were waiting for me at the townhouse.

It was getting late I connected with Anita, and we took a taxi back to our townhouse. Johan was with Isabel in her first-round match and would connect with us later tonight for a coaching session. I could go on about the day today, but we went out to a pub for dinner and Anita dressed down, so she was only attractive and not ultra-attractive. I was going to wear my sweats and remembered they would identify me, so I wore jeans and a white Lacoste shirt. This was just going to be a fish and chips dinner with iced tea instead of a good British ale like I wanted. We were good girls back in our townhouse by 9 PM, and Anita met with Johan for strategy for Tuesday. Johan told me we had a noon practice time, and I would be hitting with Isabel who had barely won her match today before it was dark. She was exhausted and had gone to bed after getting dinner at the lounge.

Tuesday was not a bad day, weather was like 70 degrees and the practice went well, I had no responsibilities so watched a couple of matches before going back to the townhouse. Anita had just come through her match in three sets, she had beaten the 24 seed who had made the quarters at the French Open. Johan laughed when he told me you are playing Caca Capo again in the second round. He said I could not have put a better match in for you for singles especially with you playing doubles late, we are number 1 on court 2, a show court.

Kiki was going to be here but that was going to be her last day, she had to go home to her job and husband. James was also staying for today only but would leave afterwards.

Second round day at Wimbledon, Isabel and I were playing first so Johan was going to be with her today, of course his fiancé and player versus just a player. James was going to be at the box and said he will coach today, then I registered Kiki for the day as my coach, she knew a lot more than James did. Both Isabel and I warmed up at 9:15, for thirty minutes and were done after that. Anita would warm-up later in the afternoon, while I was changing clothes and showering. I would then take a nap in the players' lounge and be ready for our match that would start around 5:30.

James here, with Kiki doing the coaching today, I am doing the summary for Lilly. Lilly was like 5'10" and her opponent was like 5' 3", so I know who the power would be. Lilly was told to get overly aggressive for this match and as the seed she was introduced last. Our first match this afternoon is a singles second round match. Introducing from Argentina, a winner of numerous doubles titles and grand slams, Caca Capo. Her opponent is at Wimbledon for the first time and is the thirty-two seed for the tournament, Lilly Jarman representing South Korea. This time the cheer came out the men yelling "Athletic and the women yelling "Feminine", it was great for Lilly. Caca won the toss and decided to receive, that decision may not have been a very smart decision, because after four points she was down 1-0. Lilly must have been running with way too much energy, as Kiki was telling her to pace herself, but Lilly broke immediately and then held for a 3-0 lead. By the time Caca won a serve she was down 5-0, and Lilly served out the first set 6-1. Lilly and Caca had a much more even second set and Lilly had to serve to force a second set tiebreaker. The tiebreaker went Lilly's way early and often winning it 7-2. The match was over before 1 PM giving Lilly time to shower, eat, and then do some light bicycle work to get her calf stretched. She went to the physio after the match for stretching her left calf. This was so different than the US Open, as a seed you get a lot more advantages.

Anita and Lilly warmed up against a pair of French wild cards in the late afternoon. Johan is back in the box after Isabel lost this afternoon. He told me that Lilly and Anita could go far in the double's tournament, Anita is pure speed and can serve and come in fast, where Lilly does not have as much speed, but she is 5"10" and is very aggressive at the net. They should never have let Lilly serve first; her slice serve was hard to manage on the grass it did not come up much and when it did Anita put it away. By the time Lilly served a second time they were already up 3-1 and would win the set 6-2. The French pair looked like they gave up at that point and Anita and Lilly won 6-1. Johan said this combination on grass was going to be remarkably interesting, your family may need to be back next week, don't be surprised if they upset their way to the semi-finals at least.

This is Lilly, I said goodbye to both Kiki and James after the match. Anita gave James a big hug, and I took a picture and told him if he did not behave, I would send the picture to Olivia. At the wedding, James and Olivia will walk together. Larry's brother will walk with Anita, I may need to tell Larry that his brother better behave with my adopted little sister.

My next matches would be Friday and again because I was playing doubles and singles, they would have me play early and then late. On Thursday Anita lost her second-round match in singles in a tough match where she lost 10-7, in a match tiebreak. I was there to console her and tell her know it is time for you to take the lead for our doubles and let us see how far we can go. I was starting to think of Anita as my little sister and I trusted her totally, even though she kept telling me that I need to look in the mirror, she said those debutantes really did a number on your confidence in your looks.

My practice with Isabel on Thursday was limited to thirty minutes, Johan wanted me to then go to the physio and have them work on my calf, he wanted me at full strength for a long run here.

I received a text from my dad, that Lacoste would cover his costs to come to Wimbledon if he had a passport, they thought I should have a family member in the box for the third round. He was taking the flight Thursday night with British Air out of Dulles Airport and would be off the plane at 6 AM. He would go to a nap room at the airport Hilton and then come for my noon match and the afternoon match with Anita. Mom was invited but said she is finishing wedding plans, so many people are saying yes, they are expanding the wedding to 175 people so they will be extra chairs added to the back of the church.

My opponent for the third round was Maria Romanoff, the two seed and number 2 in the world. Maria is the older sister; I had played her younger sister last year. Very few would have given me a chance in this match. Johan confirmed this in our coaching session Thursday night, but he told me to stay loose and to be able to serve and volley and cut off the points at any point. You never know what can happen and you will play no matter what as this stadium has a roof and a capacity of 12000, so be prepared for loud noise on court one. He said he will talk the strategy for doubles with Anita after the match.

Dad texted me he had landed and when I looked out of my room it was pouring rain so I knew my match would be indoors today. Warm-up would be on the indoor courts this morning and Isabel and I would be only on half a court and then I would be at the players' lounge until noon when it would be time to go to the stadium. The hitting session went well with Isabel and my serve was ridiculously hot. Dad is going to be outside and get the iPad before coming to the match. Anita and Johan will also be in the box so they can spread out a bit.

Ken here, Lilly was getting ready to enter the stadium, ESPN was interviewing her, she said nothing but easy statements nothing that could be used against her or made her look bad, what John had taught her regarding these interviews. Introducing the participants this afternoon for a third-round women's match. From South Korea, via Virginia USA, the 32nd seed Lilly Jarman, in her first Wimbledon. Her opponent this afternoon, the number 2 seed, and 2-time Wimbledon finalist, number 2 in the world currently, Maria Romanoff. The match was inside so every shot and grunt were going to be echoed. Did I mention in warm-up that Maria is a grunter, hard to hear the ball over her grunts. Maria won the right to serve and had no problem winning her serve, then Lilly in turn not even using her fast serves was able to hold. This pattern went through the complete set, big girl tennis serves in the 110 plus by Maria, but Lilly was using her slice serve only in the 90's. At 6-5, Maria finally had her first break point, only to have Lilly turn in her hard serve for the first time and win the game and force a tiebreak.

ESPN Studio, "we are doing split screen where Lilly Jarman has just earned a tiebreak with last year's finalist Maria Romanoff. This is big girl tennis, very few points going more than three exchanges. With the score 4-all and Lilly serving, Maria hits a great forehand down the line and Lilly could not get to. Maria is serving to win the set and proceeds to hit an ace and then a service winner. Maria wins the first set 7-6, and 7-4."

Ken here, Lilly instead of being dejected looked like she was up for a fight. She won her first serve of the second set with a big serve. Then Lilly went back to a slice serve up 15-0, and Maria hit the ball back to Lilly and as Maria was turning to get back to the court, she slipped and fell Lilly just hit the ball on the court.

ESPN Studios: Let us get over to court 1. Lindsey what is going on over there. Maria Romanoff, just fell ugly, let's show it to you. It looks like her foot went a different direction than her ankle. They are bringing the trainer to the court to see if she can continue the match she is sitting up and rubbing her ankle. Lilly is talking to her coach during this injury timeout, and she is hitting some serves. Maria is up with help from the trainer and sitting at her chair while they try to treat her. Maria is trying to walk, and she cannot put weight on her left ankle. She calls to Lilly to come over and shakes her hand and starts crying.

Ken here, with a handshake Maria was injured and cannot continue. The chair said that the match is over Maria Romanoff is unable to compete any further. Lilly did not cheer this time she gave Maria a hug and told her to get better soon. They brought in a wheelchair for Maria, and she exited the stadium.

ESPN Studio: Chris Evert speaking, "sometimes injuries end a match prematurely. We wish Maria a fast recovery, we have all been injured if we play this sport long enough. Lilly Jarman will get a pass to the round of sixteen, she will move to the top 30 in the live ranking with the points so far. A year ago, she was in the 600's and this show a run like hers can be magical just think what that wild card has managed to be for her."

Lilly here, this was not the victory I would have wanted but since I only played 45 minutes it saved stress on my calf, now on to the round of 16 on Monday, Wimbledon does not play on Sunday, a long tradition unless weird events like rain takes place. As I finished my match, they were starting to get the matches back on court about a 2-hour delay, meaning we would not play doubles until about 7 PM. I decided to invite dad to the players' lounge with me so we could eat a meal together and catch-up on events in Virginia. Anita called and said she would meet us at the lounge and start warming up afterwards with Isabel for the late doubles this evening.

Dad met Anita for the first time, and instantly you could tell that Anita liked him. She later explained that she had a strained relationship with her own father because he wanted to be her coach and she had refused, they had barely spoken a work to each other in the last year. My dad I guess made her comfortable, and she was asking him a ton of questions about Radford, and Farmville, and then I realized she was probing about places she could take me for my last night. God, I hope they do not do something stupid; ESPN is coming to record the wedding and I have sponsors coming so would hate to look horrible. I am already going to look like the country bumpkin compared to Anita.

Our Doubles was slated to start now at 7 PM, light in the area to about 8:45, so it is entirely possible, we would have to come back on Saturday to finish the match. Our opponent was Beatrice Berg and her new partner Janice Williamson, of the US. This was a very tall team; Beatrice is about six foot tall as was Janice. The two of them won the first-round match but had never played together before.

Ken here, I am covering the doubles match for Lilly. You could see that the combination against Lilly and Anita were strong hitters, but they looked somewhat stiff. Anita looked like a road runner with her ability to cover the court in warm-up and Lilly could match their opponent in power.

Beatrice and Janice won the toss and decided to serve first, the girls shifted from the first match and had Anita receive on the deuce side and Lilly receive on the advantage side. This must have surprised the two on the other side and immediately Lilly and Anita broke, everyone held serve until it was 5-3, and Lilly and Anita won the set 6-3 breaking as it was nearing a little after 8: PM. The next set went on all servers held and by the time the tiebreaker was getting ready to be done, it was too dark to play the tiebreak, so the umpire called the match for darkness, the fans were booing the decision. We then received a note that we would get to play the tiebreak and the third set indoors if required, on court one, in 30 minutes, a men's match had ended early, and they had a forty-five-minute break to fill.

The players were allowed ten minutes to warm-up and then the tiebreak and maybe a third set it was approaching 9 PM, when they got on.

ESPN Studios: Brad Gilbert and Patrick McEnroe reporting, we are going to show you the women's tennis match with Lilly and Anita up one set to none and 6-6 when it was dark outside. Brad commented can you imagine you are in an intense match, and they say, sorry you need to go to another court to finish the match tonight because we do not want to play on Sunday. Anita is the first to serve, and Beatrice drove it toward the center with Lilly poaching and hitting Janice on the foot for the first point. Beatrice then aced Lilly for a 1-1, but Anita hit a fierce return that Beatrice could not do anything with, and the team achieved the mini break. Up 2-1, Lilly hit an ace down the middle, time for Janice to serve. Again, she drove the first point wide and Lilly hits to the middle and Beatrice won the point. Anita hit a lob over Janice's head and Beatrice was able to get there and Lilly smashed a winner at the net to now lead 5-2. Anita served and was able to win the point to get the team to a match point. Beatrice won the next point so another match point. Beatrice won both of her serves to get within 6-5. Lilly then was up and served with a winner right down the middle at 109, she was possessed. The two women jumped up in the air and the fans chanted "Athletic and Feminine," the team deserved it.

Brad came down from the stands and congratulated the winning team. Anita spoke first and said she was proud of her older partner.

"Lilly said thanks I am not that old, yes but I will be a married women in three weeks' time." Lilly was asked about the wedding, and she thanked her mother and grandmother for doing all the planning while she was travelling and to Lacoste for connecting her with her wedding gown. The two girls then yelled on to another round.

Lilly here, we were tired and hungry, we found the pub down the corner and ordered a dinner from there and took it back to our room it was after 11 and we wanted some time on Saturday and Sunday to see the sites. We ate and then went to bed awaiting the next day.

Nothing to do over the weekend so we slept in and made breakfast just before noon. No practice today so we went out shopping, we had won a bit of money last night and Anita wanted some summer clothes for Virginia, we went to several trendy shops and spent a few hundred pounds each. Tennis would wait until Monday, and Larry said he was coming to be with me the second week, and I told him he could not stay with us, during the week or until I was done. I was hoping it would be a while before I could be with my fiancé although that sounds insane. I really wanted to do well here.

Anita and I went to see my dad on Sunday, we had brunch together at the Hilton, they had a discounted brunch for families of players, but since more than half of the players were done the room was not as filled as the previous Sunday. It was so great getting to see my dad and he was going to do some sightseeing this afternoon and take a double decker bus, he wanted to show pictures to mom, and he was worried that he had to leave after the Monday matches, he had an AM flight on Tuesday. I told him Larry was coming in on the flight tonight and would be there until I am ousted. Anita and dad seemed to get along, she was open to talk to him and had dressed down in sweats so that the men would leave her alone she just wanted to be with me and my dad to have fun.

We left dad to his wandering around town with another parent that had been there before and was also without his wife so I guess they could wander without worrying about getting mugged. Anita and I practiced together at 3 PM on the practice courts and when we got back to the townhouse, we decided we were going out to dinner. There was a nice restaurant near us, and when we called, they said they could only give us a table at 7:30 PM, and we had a little time to kill so I went through e-mails and was stunned when John sent me the financials for the year between prize money and endorsements and commissions I would make a million dollars, then when you took ten percent off for coaching and agent fees and then you put travel costs in, you could end up with only about half of that amount. It looked great but some of my friends were making nearly this every year and they did not have to travel and never really have a full day off.

Monday morning came and Johan was going to talk strategy about singles and would talk to Anita about our doubles. We were going to do a practice and then talk about Diana Lina my opponent for the day. She was from Mexico and although she was good on clay, she was also good on all other surfaces, she was the 15 seed and was probably not expecting to play me and she had to think she had a golden ticket to the quarters now. My match was on the number 2 court first on at 12:30, I guess with less matches on the show courts they gave us an extra half-hour. This court only has about 4000 fans and has a reputation of the death of seeds, I was hoping that would include the 15 seed. Larry had lied to me about getting here on Tuesday and before I got to the players' lounge, this fan came over to me and said he wanted to kiss the girl that was "Athletic and Feminine", I was going to get security but then he took off his sweatshirt and I just ran to him and kissed him. I wonder what other fans are going to try now.

The box was going to be 4 now for singles and doubles today. Anita in singles and Isabel in doubles would be our 4th. Now it was time to get focused on another singles match that was worth a lot of money. $100,000, for a win today, that is a lot of money and more for the doubles.

Ken here, Lilly handed me the iPad she said Larry was still suffering from jet lag, and she was afraid he would fall asleep. The introductions went as the last match and Diana was a dark-haired player about 5 "6" and was known to be an all-court player, never getting to a major final but she apparently was good at getting to the smaller tournaments and had won three this year alone mostly in South America. Lilly lost the coin flip but stated serving the match. Lilly was able to hold after getting to deuce and then hitting an ace and a service winner. Diana also went to two deuces on her serve until Lilly served and made it 6-5.

ESPN Lindsay Davenport – lets watch the match between Lilly Jarman and Diana Lina it is 5-6 and love thirty. Lilly just dumped the last point into the net for 15-30. Diana hit long with her first serve, and then Lilly hit a screaming return that we need to show you down the line. At set point, Lilly was too aggressive on the return and hit it out by a good ten feet, so Diana is serving to get the game all square. Diana again missed the first serve and Lilly moved inside the baseline. Diana saw that Lilly was getting ready to be aggressive and then proceeded to double fault the set away.

Ken here, Lilly was not going to let this match get away and after both held at 3 all Lilly hit 2 aces on her way to holding to take a 4-3 lead. Diana was laboring on her serve and double faulted at deuce and then Lilly jumped to the middle guessing the placement of her serve and hit a tremendous cross court forehand winner.

ESPN Lindsay Davenport let's show you match point on court 2, Lilly Jarman serving and what a serve wide at 40-15, she comes running in and finishes the match making her first major quarterfinal appearance on Wednesday. The 4000 in the crowd are saying what you all have heard since last year "Athletic and Feminine". Lilly will now move up another place in live rankings to we believe number 28 in the world.

Lilly had an interview with the British MC for the court, and said let us congratulate Lilly Jarman, and the cheers erupted again. Lilly who does you have in your box this afternoon. "Lilly responded my doubles partner Anita Krantze, my coach, my father, and the man I will be marrying in less than three weeks Larry my fiancé."

"What is the story about you and Anita, some people say that you treat her like she is your baby sister?

"Lilly said Well I'm her "Duff", I keep the men away from her and she makes sure that I smile and have fun."

"Well, everyone, let's hear it for our first winner of the afternoon Lilly Jarman."

Lilly got her stuff together and went outside and signed some tennis balls. I gave her back her iPad, and then I went back to my hotel for a couple of hours of rest.

The next 4 hours went like a blur, I did not even know the name of our opponents. I found out right before we played, they were two sisters from Australia by Eastern Europe, Romina and Elena Sansovich. They were our first doubles specialists we would play this tournament. I would like to say we won the match in a historic match, but Anita could have played the match by herself. Their coach had told them whatever they did to not hit at me when I was near the net, so they played right into Anita's massive ground strokes. The match did not last an hour as we won 6-2 and 6-2, we were in the quarterfinals. Dad would leave early in the morning, and he hugged me and said you are well cared for now, I am walking you down the aisle and by the way I like Larry.

Two days before we would play the quarters and I would spend time with Larry in London, with Anita as my beautiful kid sister and my partner coming along. With her lovely German accent and looks that were much nicer than Angie Kerber she will be famous as a tennis player, but many men just looked at her as a conquest. She was always nervous about men getting in her face or hurting her, she never went out alone. We did go out to see the London Bridge and other areas Anita in a hooded sweatshirt a size bigger than she needed to hide her assets and wearing sunglasses. I wore sunglasses and nothing blue and pink, I just wanted to be Larry's fiancé for a day. I should tell you that Anita was crazy about training regiments and would do at least 45 minutes on the treadmill every day, she was as fit as she was gorgeous. She had me working out on the treadmill which was helping my singles game.

With a physio visit late in the afternoon Tuesday and a light hitting practice right before, we were away from tennis until 9 PM, and Larry took us to a pub for dinner. Johan texted both of us be ready for a coaching meeting at 9 PM, so we had to cut our night short and get a taxi. I kissed my fiancé good night, and Anita just yelled so cute you two.

Johan led the conversation, "Lilly and Anita how do it feel to be here so far, well now the work begins. We are now in the quarters of both singles and doubles. The final three doubles teams played today and one of those will play you late in the afternoon on Wednesday. Maria Schindler has been playing with a very tall Slovak player, Evinka Milanovich, she is raw like you Lilly in tour experience but Lilly she is 6'1" with a rocket serve."

"I asked what it is we can do with this combination?"

"Johan said this one is so simple; I cannot believe it will take long to win this match. She is a statue; she wants high balls to hit overheads and you will nail in her in the stomach right off and lose the first game, but you will aim at her and hit her at least once. Once she gets hit, she tends to shy away from the net and the lovely Lilly here takes over. Anita with your ground strokes simply keep them cross court until Lilly decides it is time to end the point, just be careful because Maria is going to adjust and start lobbing and be ready with those lovely legs to win the point down the line."

Johan continues, "ok star athlete, you have a singles match at 12:30 on center court, you ready for the publicity. You have the lovely honor of playing Yelena Asinova, the three seed who has been a finalist here and wants this as her first major. She is taller than you can run like a deer and the only thing she does not have is a trophy with her name on it."

Wednesday morning hit and with it, a light rain had been overnight so we would play the match indoors. I warmed up with Isabel at 09:00, and the physio at 10:00. I texted Larry about the match upcoming and he was going to be near the Royal box, he told me he had the schedule already so relax. I was so nervous but in the end I really should not have been. I was thinking I was near the top level, but Yelena was the top level, I held my own in the early part of each set, but Yelena's experience and drive today was better than mine and won 6-3 and 6-4, it had been only 1 break per set, but that was enough. I was mad that I had lost but then I thought back, this time last year I was in the 600's in the world, and then moved up with the win at Sea Colony.

(I am inserting this because Yelena won Wimbledon for her first major title)

I thought I would be more disappointed in the loss, but I more was just tired, and had doubles again this afternoon. I went to Larry's room and took a 90-minute nap before coming back to the stadium ready for doubles.

The doubles match was last on this afternoon, on court one, not quite as nice as earlier today but not bad anyway. The stadium was about half full as we were last of the regular matches on here, there would be a men's doubles after us that was moved from court two because it had started to lightly rain and they were suspended.

I gave Larry my iPad for the match, and Anita gave him a hug, so you are going to be my adopted brother-in-law. The press ate it up and I am sure that picture will be on the cover of somewhere in the morning. Anita must explain that she is in Lilly's wedding party in a little over 2 weeks and Larry is Lilly's fiancé.

Larry here, I am sure by now you don't want to hear the introductions this time, so I will write the action. That poor Evinka, both Anita and Lilly went after her with hard shots right off the start. Lilly hit her in the shoulder, but at close range Anita hit her square in the stomach after that she stayed off the net. Those are the shots that hit, three more missed the court entirely, so Lilly and Anita were broken, but they quickly broke back and then Lilly served and volleyed to go up 2-1, the first set went the way of our girls easily finishing 6-2. The second set was much closer until Lilly hit Evinka again in the leg and she backed off again, our team won the match 6-4, and they did a side bump and then a hug as Lilly and her little sister were on to the semi-finals.

Johan said to me, "I knew we could intimidate them with heavy ground strokes and Lilly sitting there waiting for any errors. I bet tomorrow Evinka will have welts on her stomach from Anita's shot that was nasty and intentional. You would never think a woman that looks as nice as she is has a nasty side when she wants to hit an opponent, especially one that said things about her in the past. The good-looking woman got her statement to Evinka she's no fashion model."

Lilly here, it was a good ending to a sad day, I would stay in the top 30 in singles after today, but our doubles team was in the semi-final of the biggest tournament of the year. Larry told me he was extending his hotel room, and the hotel told him he had to get moved to another room, they needed his larger room for the weekend but found him a room. Mom and dad called congratulating us on the win to make the doubles. James and Olivia texted us are you ever coming to Virginia, or do you need to have a trophy before you get home. I just laughed.

ESPN- Chris Evert here. We just heard that the 11 seeds of Lilly Jaman and her partner Anita have just beaten the 6 seeds to make the semi-finals of the women's doubles. I guess Lilly won't be able to leave for Virginia for her wedding just yet. We have been told that the two are so close that people thought they were lovers, but Anita says Lilly treats me like I am her long-lost kid sister and protects me from the wrong kind of guy.

Johan sent me to the physio before going back to the townhouse, Isabel was leaving in the morning for a tournament in Italy on the clay, but Johan said he was staying until the end.

Thursday, we did a light workout with Johan and a junior tennis player who was available to hit with us after his match this morning. Larry said he went sightseeing, but I swear he wanted to buy some stuff for the house now that he was making more money, he felt comfortable buying things and did not want me writing the check from my tennis earnings, his ego.

Since Friday was the day of the men's semi-finals and our semi-finals for doubles, the men played on Center Court, and we were scheduled to play on Court 1. We would be the second match of the day with our match no earlier than 2 PM according to the program. Johan stopped by after seeing off Isabel and said give me thirty minutes then come to the kitchen area so we can talk about doubles tomorrow.

Kitchen area, we were getting close to out of breakfast stuff, so we were going to have to order some more to cook, we had at least one more morning and a couple more to be prepared for.

Johan led the conversation, "well, you two, congratulations for making it this far how about we win a couple more matches, the draw is wide open, all the top three teams have lost left are the 5 seeds and an unseeded team, on your side the number 11 and number 9 seeds are left. You are playing a Chinese player and a Japanese player that have been together for only a few months. The Japanese player is Risa Sade, she is about 5'2" and very good at both baseline and net. The Chinese player of course has a last name of Wang, and her first name is Nabing. She is a very mechanical player with a nice serve and will come up early and often, we must lob over Risa and attack, we just might get to the finals. Wouldn't you like a nice Wimbledon plate at least to show off at your wedding. They think that the two of you are weak because you have only been playing together since early this year, and that is there mistake, you 2 are way to close and can read each other's mind. It is uncanny so just let the play come to you and communicate and let's get a Wimbledon Plate. We will think about anything else afterwards."

The day of the semi-finals came, and both Anita and I were so nervous that as soon as we ate, we threw up. Ok, that was done, then we ate some toast and had some tea, which seemed to do the trick. We have just had the worst thing happen let's recover and start winning. We warmed up at 11:00 and finished before noon and went to the players' lounge it was nearly empty, with only about ten players left to play. Then came the announcement that the first match was in to the third set and be prepared for a 2:15 finish and be on court by 2:30.

Anita started crying, "I wish my parents were here."

I had been holding this back from her, but my dad had somehow done a miracle. Anita, look at my phone and read the message from my dad. Anita's parents flying in Friday morning from Frankfurt, Germany, should be waiting for you in box Lacoste has pulled a miracle.

Anita started crying again and hugged me, "I love my American family so now let's go out there with my parents in the box, and your future husband. Nothing is going to stop us from winning today."

We hugged one more time, and then Johan came over and said" it is time."

Larry here, I get the honor of summarizing this match for Lilly this afternoon. I was sitting next to Anita's parents, her dad spoke no English and her mom said so you are the famous fiancé, I heard about. There are times when it is said an athlete is in a zone and nothing can happen bad to them, that was the pair today, Anita had crazy good ground strokes, and Lilly poached and hit everything possible at the net. The pair won the first set easily 6-1 and I have never viewed Lilly this pumped. The second set was tighter until Lilly hit a backhand overhead at the net that went between the two players for a 5-4 lead.

ESPN Studio:

The sound from court 1 can be heard all the way over here. Brad what is going on over there. You can hear the crowd during the break yelling, "Athletic and Feminine." The team out there with less experience is serving for a spot in the women's doubles finals.

Larry here: Anita was serving and hit her first serve into the net and Lilly told her to just give us a chance and the slow second serve was out wide and as Nanbing hit it to the center where Lilly was waiting and hit a volley that Risa could not get to. Then Anita lost her second serve when Risa hit a winner down the line. That would be the last point the opposition would get today. At 40-15, Anita hit a serve at 104 down the service line where Nanbing popped it up, Lilly hit a smash overhead nobody was getting to this shot. The chair umpire said our team won two sets to none.

ESPN Studios:

We just heard the eruption that had to be Lilly Jarman. The unknown team has just pulled another upset and they just booked a shot at the doubles title, and I would love to know the odds that this team would make the finals. Let's talk to Brad, who is getting the team for an interview.

Brad led the conversation, "well ladies how does it feel to make your very first final of a grand slam?"

Anita spoke first, "thanked her unofficial big sister for playing with her, and in German thanked her parents for being at the match today. Then it was Lilly's turn.

With tears running down her face Lilly took a minute and then hugged Anita one more time. The fans loved it, she said "you know we have a bigger crowd than normal because I have an extremely attractive partner here and she gets a few extra fans to watch women's tennis. I would like to thank my fiancé for coming here I am sure he had to work a lot of meetings around to be here. I would also like to thank our coach Johan; we cannot wait until Sunday afternoon."

Brad stated, "well ladies' congratulations and welcome to the finals, do you know who your opponents are, and they said nope we will figure that out on Saturday, tonight we want to celebrate."

"Anita spoke in German one more time and her parents blew her a kiss."

Lilly here, oh my God did this just happen, we are either a plate or a trophy now and possible like $350,000 per person if we win. Anita invited Larry and me to join her parents at the pub tonight. I had other plans with Larry, but he said nothing until your tournament is over, so we held hands kissed and joined them. Anita's mom may be in her forty's, but it was obvious where the looks started, she was also extremely attractive.

Anita said something in German to her mom, and then Ingrid said to me, "so Lilly you are tall and unbelievably attractive, what is this "Duff" thing I hear about?"

"I almost choked, well next to your extremely attractive daughter who is going to be a swimsuit model, I am just a gawky girl."

"Ingrid came over to me and said, you are an incredibly attractive women in your own right, stop putting yourself down, your Eurasian looks are extremely sensual, and your fiancé agrees. I never want you putting yourself down for your looks again and if she does let you get away with it, I will yell at my daughter and yes, I know about the SI swimsuit contract. She kissed me on the cheek and said please thank your family for reuniting ours. She had tears in her eyes, I love my daughter and want to be in her life."

We left the pub, and Larry and Anita's parents shared a cab back to the hotel and Anita and I shared one back to the townhouse. Johan was waiting for us, he said he bought a couple more days of the breakfast stuff, and he said no talk of tennis tonight ladies. I have you scheduled to workout at noon on Saturday and for Lilly to see the physio at 1:30, she is opening her office just for you as she said the tournament is pretty much finished. I want you both to watch a movie together tonight and know you only have two things to decide, who serves first and do you want a plate or a trophy for Lilly's wedding. Now get out of here and enjoy a movie and get some rest.

Anita here, my adopted big sister fell asleep within 15 minutes of the movie in my room, I did not have the heart to wake her up and let her sleep the whole night on the sofa. She was very tired after singles and doubles this week, and we both needed rest.

Saturday morning and I made breakfast for everyone, scrambled eggs, sausage, toast, and bananas. We then had energy drinks and took our vitamins that have been certified for being clean to take. I got a knock on the door, and they made me go pea in front of the woman tester. The lovely life of a professional tennis player. When she left, Anita and I got dressed for our practice at noon. Johan was getting there early to look at tape of our opponents. We were working out when Mike and his partner came over to us and said they would like to be our hitting partners, but they were in their final in doubles today. They congratulated us on getting there, and we in turn said get the trophy. They did bring with them 2 junior players that had been hitting with them and they came over to do it with us. I received their names and made sure Lacoste treated them well this afternoon, I bet they got over $1000 each in gifts. They made us a sign a ball and sign it Wimbledon Champions, I started to tear-up again this was getting terrible.

Nothing else to do but meet Larry for a soda and my little sister went with me to the hotel where she had an early dinner with her parents. Larry said we should do the same, but I decided I wanted to sit next to him and put on my ring and hold hands with my future husband. By 6:30, Anita came over to me and said, on our way back to the townhouse, we need our sleep. Our match is first on at 12:30, and the men will be waiting for us. Mike texted me, that his partner and he had won, and he wanted a dance with me as a fellow champion on Sunday night. I did remind him that my fiancé was here, he said he has you forever I just get one dance. I showed the text to Anita, and she told me "Now we will win."

We were back in the townhouse for our last evening as a competitor.

Johan said, "see you in the kitchen in 30 minutes, you 2 are going to be glad you have 2 clay court specialists in the finals. Do not get overconfident, but Lucy Securro, and Jasmine deChambeau got through in a tight three sets. They are both top 50 singles players and had only played one doubles together so ladies you are a team, and they are individuals they can blast but so can you. As you can figure an Italian and a French woman cut their teeth as clay court specialists obviously, they are good enough to get here."

I had trouble sleeping and only fell asleep when I went on Anita's couch, I was just not wanting to be by myself. Anita fell asleep at 10:00, for me it was midnight before I could relax enough to sleep.

Finals Morning:

With a scream by Anita when she was going to sit on her couch and sat on my hips, we were both awake. Anita screamed, "when did you come in here?"

"I told her I wanted to talk to you, but you were asleep I just sat on the couch and fell asleep."

Anita and I shared breakfast duties and woke up Johan for breakfast.

We left for Wimbledon to warm-up and nobody else was there, we would be on Center Court at 12:30, maybe half full. We went to the players' lounge to hang out and other than the other doubles team and 1 junior player nobody else was there. It was so weird and then they let us know that the Royal Box would be empty so less pressure on us. The call for ten minutes came, and I hugged Anita, she gave me a kiss and whispered I want this one for you and me. I got my iPad to Larry for writing the summary and noticed that ESPN was already waiting for us. They asked us to take pictures before the match in the tunnel and it became real for us.

ESPN Coverage:

We are about to see the final of the Women's Doubles with none of the women ever being close to a final like this. One pair will win today their first and will always be able to tell everyone they were Wimbledon Champions.

Predictions please: Brad Gilbert predicts Lilly and Anita; Lindsay predicted the same as Brad.

Chris Evert then said, "I don't think they have a chance seriously; Anita is just in her second year on the tour and Lilly we all know about has not even completed her first year on the tour. The others have been on the tour for ten years each and this is going to be a blood bath, I predict 6-1 and 6-3, at worst."

Larry here, Introducing our competitors for the final of the women's doubles. Our first team was not seeded this week introducing from Italy, Lucy Securro and her partner from France Jasmine deChambeau. The two have beaten four seeded teams in this tournament. Now introducing their opponents, the 11 seed in this tournament, representing South Korea, and through the State of Virginia, Lilly Jaman, and her partner for this tournament from Germany, a former junior doubles finalist, Anita Krantze.

Lilly and Anita were decked out in identical clothing with, "Athletic and Feminine", Mizuno shoes and the Lacoste gear. The other team did not match with different manufacturers.

The crowd which was at least 7500 people started yelling our now getting annoying tag line and Lilly smiled when they did this. Anita patted her on the back and her parents said they are going to win today. Johan was so nervous he had never had a major champion either and this would be great for his business going forward.

The first set was upsetting for Lilly and Anita as the singles players simply outhit them and took the first set 6-4. Then the tide turned in the second set when Lilly started moving her feet and poached on the first shot of the second set and won the point. That got both ladies in a different frame of mind, and they won the second set as a team 6-2.

The third set was close at 4-4 and they tried to hit a lob over Lilly, which was a mistake and Lilly hit a backhand overhead between the two stunned players, our team was now up 5-4 in the third set with the title on the line. Lilly was serving and she was the better server on the team, but Anita was a cat at the net, and banged two points at the net for winners and the team was 2 points away from the win. The next point was a double fault by Lilly and Anita calmed her down and won another point at the net:

ESPN Coverage:

Lilly Jarman to serve for the title she is taking a little extra time, and just brushed her face with her wrist bands. A great toss and Lilly hit straight down the line and Lucy just touched the ball and a service winner. Listen to that scream by Lilly Jarman that is utter joy, and now she and her partner Anita just did a side bump. They came to the net and shook hands with their opponents. The two winners kept hugging each other and then listen to the crowd" Athletic and Feminine" they are singing this to Lilly and Anita and look at the two of them, both are in absolute tears.

Pam Shriver here, I did not get into the predictions, but I will interview the winners in a minute, Lilly is sitting at her chair with a towel over her head, she is sobbing deeply, and I look at her coach and partner and they are all in tears. For those that think doubles is just an afterthought for the players look at these three, not a dry eye here. Lilly's fiancé is here and so is Anita's parents, Lilly and Anita are running up to the players box and the entire box is jumping up and down. I think we will have to wait a few minutes of the awards ceremony.

Larry here, I will not go into the speeches by the finalists, but they did say congratulations to Anita and Lilly. Then the Wimbledon chairperson introduced the winning team. I would like to introduce our champions today, Anita Krantze and Lilly Jarman, congratulations today on winning your first championship.

Anita was first to speak after being handed her trophy. "I would like to thank the people that support this tournament from the ball kids to the officials to the people that make sure we are comforted in every way. I want to specifically thank my parents for being here and our coach Johan up there. In German she repeated her thanks to her parents so her dad would understand. I also want to thank the Jarman family for supporting us every day with Lilly's dad, brother, and her lover here every day."

Anita then went back to her chair and the chairperson asked Lilly the same question.

"I agree with Anita thanking everyone here, I want to specifically thank one person who is not here today, Dea Jarman, my grandmother who told me to pursue my dreams. I would like to thank the team in our box, including my fiancé, 2 weeks to go, coach and Anita's parents. I would like to thank my partner, Anita Krantze, yes, I have adopted you as my little sister. I want to thank the Jarman and Miller clan, who have been back in Virginia allowing me to play here only 2 weeks away from the wedding and doing everything for me today. I told you we had a reason to wait until 2 weeks after Wimbledon."

Pictures were taken and the pair walked together around the court. The cheer we all had gotten used to was being said. Right before they left, Lilly hugged Anita and the two faced each other and started to tear-up.

ESPN Studio: We are going to get the doubles winners up here in a few minutes, they want to clean-up a bit. Pam Shriver and Chris Evert at the desk.

Chris stated, "welcome to the desk, Lilly, did you know that you are the first person playing for South Korea, to win a championship, and for you Anita you are in a lengthy line of German women who have been champions at Wimbledon?"

"Anita spoke for the team and said thank you for having us here and yes, I acknowledge these talented players. I love my partner here; she is like my big sister I would have always wanted. When I was down, she reminded me of her journey here, can you imagine eight years playing in the lowest level for 7 years, and she finally got her chance, and she is here today. I want everyone to know Lilly is a beautiful and smart woman that is about to get married."

"Chris Evert then asked Anita, is it true you are going to be in Sports Illustrated next year?"

"It is, I have a photo shoot at the end of the year in Costa Rico, and I am proud to represent tennis in the magazine."

"Pam chimed in on a question of Lilly, you have been so quiet here letting Anita speak, so how is it that you and Anita clicked for this tournament?"

"Lilly waited a few seconds and simply said, my little sister by another mother tells me that I make her a better player doing the hard things on the court and blocking the men who want to date her. Just kidding, but she is in all sense a much more outgoing person than me and she pulled my best for playing with her."

Chris asked, "Lilly, we saw you had a towel over your head, can you tell people what was going on at that time?"

"All I could think of is how much I would have loved for my grandmother to be here today. Lilly started to tear-up again and said Dea, thanks for always being in my corner."

Chris Evert then said "well folks your Wimbledon champions, Anita Krantze and Lilly Jarman".

I handed back the iPad to Lilly, I needed to get back to the hotel, I was leaving tonight, and Lilly would leave Monday. Lilly and I spent some time together, before I left for my hotel, and she went walking around the site finishing her interviews. Ten minutes later the men's match was getting ready to be introduced and the ladies were done.

Lilly here, I will not change anything Larry has said about today. I have a dance tonight and I have a nice dress for the occasion, but Anita and I are going to go shoe shopping, neither of us brought formal shoes with us. We went to the townhouse and Johan, had finished packing, I will see you both in the states next month, I need to see my own fiancé. Lilly, I want you to keep having that calf of yours be treated and take some time for your brain to heal. I wish I could make it to your wedding, but Isabel needs to be in Europe getting more points, she never wants to do qualifications again.

We went out quickly and bought our shoes and then we decked ourselves out to be ready to go to the formal dance. Anita in her green dress was gorgeous, and her shoes were like 6-inch heels so finally she was taller than me. I was in pink which makes sense, and I had pink shoes I wanted to get blue shoes, but Anita said no.

The dance was great, and I danced with Mike as promised and he said, am I good enough to go out on a date with your partner. I heard later that they went out a few times, but Anita said she wanted nothing to do with another tennis player.

On Monday, Anita and I went to the airport with a lot of hardware, neither of us wanted to let ours out of our sight. We hugged each other and departed for our different airlines with the knowledge that ten days from now she would be in the states for my wedding.

My next chapter was only a few days away.

Chapter 23

Time for Mrs. Wilson

I was on United Airlines, and they were not full for this flight from Heathrow to Dulles Airport, so instead of me checking in the Wimbledon Trophy, they let me give it a seat. The captain met with me before we flew and asked can he have a picture with me he wanted to give to his daughter who is a junior tennis player. I said sure, and the co-captain took the picture.

"The captain announced we have an additional passenger here this morning, we are travelling with a Wimbledon Doubles trophy, because we have the pleasure of taking home "Athletic and Feminine" as a passenger today. Lilly Jarman and her trophy will be in the front of the plane for you to take pictures, we the crew ask you after that to let her be like any other passenger. She is on her way home after a few weeks in Europe and will sign autographs now and then we want her to have a great flight home."

"I thanked the captain because I was travelling in my gear sweats to go home."

Then it hit me, people wanted my autograph for their little girls, a year ago, they only wanted my signature to pay my credit card. The first little girl came in and we took a picture with the double's trophy, and I gave her a pair of my wrist bands. After ten minutes it was over as the captain had asked and I crashed until they woke me up for my lunch about 2 hours later.

I landed and went through customs; the trophy was an interesting conversation piece with the custom agents. One of them asked me to take a selfie with it and them and me. Waiting for me was the man of my heart, Larry, and a few people wondering why I was carrying a trophy with me. That thing was not ever going to be out of my sight. As soon as I activated my cell phone, Anita texted, "do I need to bring my trophy to Virginia or is one enough?" I laughed thinking one would be enough; it was going to Longwood for 6 months to be at the Athletic Hall to be on display after the wedding. Kiki's text said the light pink bridesmaid dresses were gorgeous the light blue belt she could do without, but she realized it had to be that way.

I had to admit I went home, put things in the washer, ate a little bit and did not wake-up until 6:30 the next morning, I had just slept for 10 hours. I had a request by the local Fox channel" WTTG". for an interview this afternoon and I said they had to go through my agent, and I provided them with the number. John was really worried about interviews and hurting the brand. The interview was conducted, and it was a light piece so only took a few minutes and I kept everything as John said very limited and nothing controversial.

I had to ask Larry what day it was it was so confusing with the travel and time zone changes; I was told it is Tuesday and you have a wedding in 11 days in some odd town of Farmville, Virgnia. This was a day to start getting up to date with wedding plans, so I called mom and asked what was going on.

Mom told me that the wedding is scheduled now 1 PM, on Saturday and that the wedding will take about an hour and then a procession and pictures, the reception will start at 4:30 with dinner starting at 5:30, and the room is reserved until 9:00 PM, You have the best room in the Hotel Weyanoke for the evening after the wedding. On Sunday, you will begin a seven-day honeymoon in a small island in the Bahamas, I hear you are flying to Miami, and then to Eleuthera which is a remote island. You and Larry come home and then you have a week back in Tysons Corner, play the DC tournament and have a week off and then

Cincinnati. Another week back here and then on to the US Open for the second time.

Johan had texted me not to play any tennis until Saturday to let my body rest. I was to go to the Physical Therapist each day, do stationary bicycling and then see a make-up artist for the wedding. He said that piece was what Isabel told him, that I needed to wear make-up for the wedding, and she had someone in Georgetown, for me to see. I could see this was getting out of hand already.

I thought that was the height of it, but then Anita called and asked my measurements, she was bringing with her special lingerie for the honeymoon, and a bathing suit from her friends at Sports Illustrated that they swear would be tasteful. She also said, "nothing in pink and blue during the honeymoon, so she is buying all the clothing."

I was afraid she had already mentioned everything that was to be included. She told me that Kiki and she were meeting in London, and then flying to Dulles together and would be there next Wednesday, they had plans for us on Thursday night. I made reservations for both at the Hilton in Tysons Corner until Friday, they then had 3 nights in Farmville.

Mom told me that my wedding dress and everything else is now in her old bedroom in Farmville. I was staying at her old bedroom she and dad were staying in one of the other bedrooms. Larry was going to stay Friday night in a hotel with his brother Chris next to his room. I hope Chris and Larry's boss don't do something stupid on Thursday night. James was going with them, but I know he was going to push the envelope with his future brother-in-law.

On Wednesday I worked out and went to a physical therapist to strengthen my calves, and to stretch them to avoid possible injuries.

"Anita called me again and stated she had a great long dress for dinners that she had for me in the clothing for the honeymoon, and some shorts and other tops for me, you may want to leave your bedroom a few times."

Olivia called me and said that the four of us are going out on Thursday night, she had a couple of places and a limousine that was reserved for us, Kiki and Anita are coming too. Kiki called and told me she was psyched to come and thanked Olivia for the party organization, we decided to do it 2 days ahead because DC had more possibilities, and it gave me all day Friday to get to Farmville.

The next week with Larry was great and I was worried that the amount of time I took travelling was going to be hard on us. I met Kiki and Anita at the airport the three of us hugged and screamed for at least 5 minutes. A few men looked oddly at us.

Kiki said, "I am excited to go out with you, but I may need to skip drinking, I need to go to a pharmacy and get a pregnancy test. (4 hours later we heard the call back to Denmark, she came back no alcohol for me)."

We hugged her and asked if she was feeling ok, and Kiki said, "nothing yet, hopefully nothing for this week."

I bought ginger ale for her anyway. I gave her a big hug and told her I was so happy for her.

"Kiki told me you may not be far behind, getting married this week."

"I told her I can't get pregnant, women tennis players never do well after having a child."

Mom called me and let me know everyone from the family was coming including Albert her younger brother who she has not been with for nearly 20 years. He is coming with his adopted daughter, "Elizabeth" who is 6 years-old, and is from Venezuela, she came to this country without a parent, and the couple adopted her. She will be the flower girl for the wedding we added her with Paul's daughter. Her brother Thomas was coming with his wife but not any of the kids, the three K brothers would be there with the spouses, as will be the Wilson contingent of 70 people. Granny Miller was coming with a male friend, and about 15 to 20 businesspeople including, Jacques and Allison, and somehow Paul is coming with Ann and the baby. 175 people in total. On Thursday morning I picked-up the marriage license and Larry finished work at 1 PM and would not return to work until after our honeymoon.

At 5 PM, the guys went out on the town, I reminded them to make sure my fiancé was able to make it to Farmville in time for our wedding.

I hope I never know what went on that night, Larry was more hung over than I was. He did though at least get home, something I was really worried they would dump him somewhere on GW parkway.

Olivia showed up at 7 PM with the limousine, we picked up the other girls at the Hilton, and we were out for the night. The first place we went to was a bar at Tysons 2, near the house, I had to wear a blue and pink balloon hat that Olivia had made. Next stop a restaurant in DC, a couple of appetizers and more drinks, I kept away from champagne, I know that makes me sick. Olivia had apparently found another club, this club had male strippers and apparently the people running it used to run the "Hangar Club", but this was not that bad the guys never got out of the "G String". I know I had way too many drinks and not enough to eat, but I was getting hungry, so we stopped at a pizza place near College Park, Md. (Ledo's), we were told they had square pizza. Between the greasy food and the extra amount of alcohol, I threw up in the bathroom, and truthfully then I felt better. I then went back and drank a beer and ate some garlic knots, I felt better. By the time we were done eating it was midnight, and then we went back to a club in DC, for a little dancing and more drinks. The room was spinning badly when I got home at 2 AM. I did survive my special night out. The three tennis players left for Farmville at noon after stops for a lot of aspirin and more ginger ale to settle my stomach. Along the way Anita had called her mom and her mom wanted to talk to me.

Jean wanted me to know how thankful for your stewardship of Anita over the last year, and that while she will be in Germany, she is thinking of you and don't let anyone ever tell you again that you are not a lovely and caring person. Anita is so much better for being your adopted little sister. In addition, tell your family thank you for reuniting ours, we are getting along better with her father just as a father. The Trophy in our house probably does not hurt either, he is building a case for Anita."

Larry was hurting a lot worse than I was apparently, and he and his brother did not leave for Farmville, until 3 PM, and caught the Friday night traffic, they were barely able to make the wedding party dinner at Longwood being catered by a restaurant in the area that Granny

Miller knew. I thought it was a dive, but apparently, they do cater better. Normally the night before is paid by the groom's family, but Granny Miller wanted this on her, and half the cost was being picked-up by Lacoste, so nobody argued.

Jean came to me and said, "we could not do a lot for you two because the way the wedding is being paid for by Lacoste, so we are going to do 2 things, first we are donating $5000, to the DC charity that promotes tennis in the intercity. Second, we saw your furniture in the townhouse, and noticed you did not have a patio or outdoor furniture, that will be constructed next month."

The dinner party consisted of the eight in the wedding, parents and grandmother and friend for 14 total. Toasts were made by Chris and then by Kiki.

Unscripted Anita decided to make a speech. "To my adopted big sister and her fiancé. I am so thrilled for the two of you, I don't know you well Larry other than the few times I have met you at tennis tournaments, but I will let you know that your fiancé is special to me, and without her I'm not sure I would ever get my ranking up, trust people, or allowed to grow up and have my father back. I love you Lilly Jarman, and you are not my "Duff", you are a gorgeous woman in your own way, and I want your long legs. By the way, I love the trophy that you and I were a part of this month and no matter what we do in tennis, we will always have Wimbledon Doubles Champions in our resume, nobody can take that away."

Victor stood up and talked about Larry and said, I have known men to chase their girlfriends, but this man has had to take days off to go all over the place to see his fiancé, including a strange place so she could get a trophy with the adopted little sister over there. And she told him he could not even stay with her. We know who will have wear the pants in this relationship. Larry is an athlete or used to be he played division 1 soccer, I know he chose not to pursue anything after that, but can you imagine the next generation that they will sire. An all-conference in soccer and an All-American and Wimbledon trophy winner as parents. I hope the kids choose swimming.

James jumped-up, sure say that Uncle James was an All-American swimmer. Olivia, hit him in the ribs you never told me you were that good.

"I jumped in, yes, he got his about 3 weeks ahead of mine, and does not tell everyone that dad was a football player at James Madison."

Victor resumed, so for everyone, Larry is smart, he did graduate Magna Cum Laude, and is doing quite well as an analyst for our firm.

ESPN, then came in and took some video as part of the documentary they were doing it was going to be about a 3-minute piece on "Sports Center" on Saturday night.

The dinner was done and most of the party left for hotels or Grandma Miller's house. Larry came over to me, gave me a very passionate kiss, and said you ready to be Mrs. Wilson? I told him yes, but he may know me as Lilly Jarman for business purposes, if he didn't mind. Lilly Jarman, I love you and don't care what name you go by as long as we are man and woman in the same roof, except when you are travelling for matches.

Wedding Day:

I had a hard time sleeping last night and finally stopped trying at 7:30 AM, I went to make myself breakfast when Grandma Miller came in and refused, she then proceeded to pamper me and made fried eggs and sausage, a couple of pieces of toast, and then gave me some coffee. I wish you would have let me get you hair cut at my place, but your ladies are coming over they said they are going to tame your long hair, and even give you some curls in that dark blond hair of yours.

I was told that every woman at the wedding was to have a Lacoste beach bag with a "Athletic and Feminine", T-shirt, and the new beach towel that was being released this week. The men would be getting a sweat jacket, green alligator with an embroidered my wife is "Athletic and Feminine", being released at the US Open. John had told me the saying was going all over the place and the next year Larry and you may each get over a million dollars from your share of the profits for this.

You could retire from tennis and live on what this will bring you for the next five years. So much for business this is my wedding day.

By nine, I had completed my shower and the tennis girls showed up shortly after they were in a rented car and ready to see me. Anita came prepared. She had the make-up kit the lady in Georgetown had made for me, she had a curling iron, and she was going to use something to help my hair look like it had more volume and untangled. Somewhere around 10:00, she had finished my hair and started to work on my make-up, when I said I could do it myself.

"Kiki laughed not today you won't, we want you to look good not like you do for the tennis court."

By the time, Anita and Kiki were finished I really had to admit I no longer looked like the "Duff" tennis player but a very different look for the Eurasian. I had lost 5 pounds since last year and now at 5'10" I was only 135 pounds; it was good because the dress I was wearing needed me to be as thin as possible. It had a very narrow waist. Larry had been working out and lifting so he could look buff as he said it, I think he will always be buff no matter what, but I am in love with him. It was after 11 AM by the time we were ready to go to the church. The dress was in the capable hands of my mother and was waiting for me at the church, along with my vail, shoes, and everything else.

I could not think of what to get my three girls as gifts for being in the wedding, I went out and bought them very nice watches, not Rolex but they cost nearly $1500, for the three of them. Larry apparently went on QVC and got nice watches for all three of his men. They were huge. I had engraved the ladies' watches, Larry, and Lillian Wilson wedding.

The preacher at Johns Episcopal Church is a woman, and she met with me and Larry separately before the wedding. Pastor Angela Smith, a very nice lady in her late forties had met me several times with Granny Miller, but Larry was a Methodist before but had wanted to be married here and will be a part of the church when we are here, we will find an Episcopal church in Fairfax County.

She was happy to see me, and simply asked one question. "So, MS Athletic and Feminine, are you ready to get married today".

I looked at her and started shaking, and finally said "yes."

She said "this is great for the church and the community of Farmville, ESPN has stated they will film no differently than any other wedding photographer, no commentators or anything else. She thanked me for choosing her church for the wedding and told me she was proud of me for overcoming the childhood bullying because you are beautiful, and the three women with you look gorgeous, and looking at Kiki, so you must be the pregnant one, you have that glow."

"Kiki started to smile and then started to leak, yes, I am but did someone tell you. Pastor Smith said you simply have the glow."

It was now noon, and the girls and I were now starting to get dressed in our room. I was told to hand the iPad over to Barbara and stop writing this down.

The rest of the writing was going to be done by my mother after the fact today.

This is Barbara, the mother of the bride:

At 1 PM, Larry and his best man, entered the church through the side and were at the altar awaiting the remainder of the party. Kiki went down the aisle and took up the position, then came the pair of Anita and Chris, followed 2 minutes later by James and Olivia. Such a diverse group. What seemed like an eternity, Lilly appeared at the rear of the church with Ken at her side. She looked radiant and tall as with her heels she was over 6 feet tall. The entire church turned and the gasped at how beautiful she looked in this gown. After saying he was offering his daughter for the wedding, Ken sat next to me.

The actual wedding ceremony took almost an hour to perform between the service and the vows that the two made. I really can't remember what Larry promised, but what Lilly said had me in tears. The flower girl and seeing my long-lost brother also had me in tears. I do remember that Larry said that when he first met Lilly and that old malibu, he thought it would be hard to convince her to go out with me. It took a while, but it was worth the effort, Lilly is everything I need and want in a partner. I just know something, I will never play her in tennis, I may be a pretty good athlete, not going to ruin my reputation and the trophy back there tells me not to challenge Lilly.

I will be stating how I remember it so I'm sure that the ESPN tape may say something different. Lilly stated that Larry saw her when she was poor, struggling in tennis and trying to overcome childhood bullying. Larry saw me for who I could be as a person, the tennis just seemed to come along with it and the childhood stuff did not matter anymore. Larry saw me as an athletic and beautiful woman, that had his heart from the moment we met. Then I had the famous proposal that was recorded. Larry has been so supportive as I traveled with my girls all over the globe and was there with my new little sister, when I had the moment in tennis people dream about. Today, I really get my dream because you are the dream person, I will share the rest of my life with. I am proud to be Lillian Jarman Wilson.

The two were declared husband and wife and had a very passionate first kiss shortly thereafter. They exchanged the rings, which were traditional and Lilly's fit next to that unique engagement ring. Then the recession of the wedding party began, and we had a photo and film session outside with the Magnolia's in bloom. By the time we finished at the photo shoot it was nearly 4 PM and time to go to the reception.

The ESPN crew left, and we were free of the press for the party that was to begin. We were ready to go to the Rotunda Building at Longwood University, which was being outfitted especially for us and guests. The school said they preferred this as opposed to the cafeteria; it was much more beautiful. This was going to be a catered affair, we had saved up for the event and since Lacoste was paying for half of the event, the food was upgraded. Most of the people were having a T-bone steak, while others chose leg of lamb, and we did have a vegan choice that looked good but there is no way, I would want it. We did have five people that did a trout alternative. Because we did not want people crazy drunk, we had chosen to offer beer and wine and no hard liquor, well except the K brothers all seemed to have a flask of some special moonshine. Lilly had no idea of what the wedding cake was going to look like, but she had assumed and was not far off. The top layer was pink, the subsequent layers all five of them, went from pink to light blue showing the 2 worlds. It had taken us 4 weeks to design the cake, and each layer was a different cake. The top was white cake, the bottom was a spice cake with blueberries in it. In between were raspberry and strawberry cakes, we really wanted to make them look good. Anita had added a dessert that made me laugh, she had paid for strawberries and cream, to be delivered apparently it had cost over a thousand dollars, but she said she had to have her strawberry and cream moment with Lilly and Larry, somehow Chris decided he should be in the photo with Anita. The first pieces of cake were cut, and Larry made sure that Lilly wore her slice, she then proceeded to do the same.

We decided not to have a band but to have a DJ, because they appear to get more people moving. The first dance with the two of them were followed with Ken dancing with Lilly, and then Jean dancing with Larry. Anita and Chris danced most of the night together, I think Chris was infatuated with the beautiful German tennis player.

There were two toasts to the wedding party besides the parents' toasts. "The first was from Victor, he had known Larry for the last 6 years. He was a workaholic until the day he met a woman in College Park while home for vacation. He said this tennis player was exotically beautiful, smart, and was not full of herself like a lot of professional tennis players. No offense Anita. Because Lilly was away at tournaments like every other weekend, my friend here learned about small towns to go to, funny thing though during these times, he would see Lilly, but because she was playing tennis, they could not date until she was eliminated. Fortunately, she did not go very far that first year, so they got to go out, and fell deeply in love with each other. Who in this crowd, does not know about Dea's dream for Lilly and their engagement. So, to the couple, may your life of travel be together, maybe you can get to share a hotel room."

"Kiki talked of Lilly's time in college and that she did not date much and had her miracle NCAA, and we were all stunned at that shy Eurasian girl with that funny accent, had really bloomed under our coach. Lilly and I have stayed in touch since her college days now almost 8 years ago, and she was always a dedicated and shy girl. With you Larry, Lilly has come out of her shell, and she does not try to hide those long, gorgeous legs. To the two of you, you are each other's best friend, to you Larry, you must have been something to get past Dea, I understand she was very particular."

We thought the toasts were done, and then Anita rose and said, "I have to say something today. You see that trophy in the back of the room, its mate is in Germany at my parents' home. I lost in my last round of the qualies when I first met Lilly, she told me, you are 21, you have so many more chances and I guess we did, she helped me through my first year and with learning how to be a professional. I saw their relationship over the last year and knew I wanted a husband someday, to be like Larry. I love both of you and Lilly, if you tell anyone else you are my "Duff", my mother has instructed me to fly to wherever you are and punch you in the arm. To the beautiful and sexy Lilly Jarman, and her amazing husband you need to know wherever I am if you want or need me, I will be there no matter what continent I am on."

Lilly, then said something funny, "So Anita, if you are on the beaches of Costa Rica and I call you will leave your photo shoot?"

Instead of saying anything Lilly and Anita hugged each other.

The evening ended about 9 PM, and then the bride tossed her bridal bouquet, and a cousin caught it. Larry and Lilly left in limousine to the hotel. The rest of us left within a few minutes, and I had the remainder of the cake that we took to my mothers. Something nobody saw coming, Anita and Chris left together, something was up with those two, but nobody said anything. Larry threw the garter, and his brother Chris caught it, I think he winked at Anita.

Before leaving Anita handed a suitcase to Lilly, we found out later that it was Lilly's clothing for the honeymoon, it did not look like a big bag.

Lilly and Larry left for the Bahama's and the rest of us had breakfast. Anita and Chris seemed so cute together. I do see why Lilly said Anita was gorgeous, she is a beautiful blonde with a sexy German accent that apparently Chris is smitten with.

Lilly here, the marriage was consummated at least twice in our hotel room Saturday night. The clothes that Anita packed for me were better than I thought and the 1-piece bathing suit she packed was extremely attractive and had only 1 side connected at the shoulder. It was a light black suit with blue stripes. The other things she packed were not blue but extremely full of lace and somewhat hard to figure out. Larry had no time undoing them as we spent a lot of time indoors enjoying our relationship. We did go out to the beach enough so that we had some tan. We even went out in the beautiful long dress that Anita packed. I did text her a thanks for the clothes she packed, they were all designer originals.

We flew back to DC a week later because I had the first round of the DC tournament, which I lost and blamed on Larry. For some reason I was a little more tired than I should have been. At least Anita and I made it to the semi-finals in the doubles before losing. Instead of going to Canada with Anita I stayed home for another week to get physical therapy and start hard tennis training again.

I did find out that while Chris was getting his master's degree at George Mason, he and Anita apparently became friendly. She asked if it was ok that she go out with Larry's younger brother. I said sure, but he will be a professional sports trainer when he is done with his degree in physical therapy and sports medicine. She just smiled, and I knew they were already dating.

Kiki was doing well at home, and she was now telling people she was pregnant she was now in her 12th week of pregnancy. James and Olivia were now living in an apartment together, the wedding was going to be 2 weeks before Wimbledon next year, I am hoping I can find a way to be with them.

Time to earn some more money going on the road again. I will be introduced at the US Open as Lilly Jarman Wilson.

Chapter 24

US Open Again

I gave my adopted little sister a dinner before she went to Montreal, we went down to Georgetown and tagging along was Chris, I get a feeling that he was infatuated with my little sister by another mother, and for once Anita was relaxed around him. I'm not sure how much they were dating but it was obvious that they at least liked each other. That was confirmed when I saw them holding hands when we walked to the dinner table. At least I knew the family he came from, and since I was now part of that family, I had to take blame for her dating someone I knew and liked.

I was encouraged to wear my Lacoste gear at times like this, but I was dressed up for a formal dinner. I was then told to wear everything in a blue and pink theme, so for this occasion, pink dress and blue bag, and a pair of pink shoes. I was not going to be looking silly with blue shoes. Anita with her world class beauty could have worn anything, but she decided to wear a powder blue dress, shoes and then somehow a pink clutch purse. I looked at her and said, "we must stop doing this."

Anita said to me "you started it; I'm just helping the team." Chris and Larry just decided to wear blue blazers and appeared happy with just being with us.

I know that Anita stayed with us in the townhouse, so nothing went on other than a goodbye kiss that night. As beautiful as Anita is, she

340

is very conservative about the physicality of her relationships, thinking that some men would like to conquer her and then never see her again, she was not that type of person. Her parents would approve of her choices, and I felt as her adopted big sister so did I.

I conceded to Chris to take Anita to Dulles Airport and see her off. I had work to do this morning we were setting up the "Pink and Blue" 501C3, legal charity, to help young women to be able to compete, by helping to bring tennis equipment to low-income areas. John, Jacques, and Allison were thrilled that we were doing it, and press was going out today. The public announcement would be this afternoon which is one of the reasons I did not go to Montreal, the other is my calf was sore again and I needed to have a day or two off from any tennis. Johan said we need to baby this calf to get through the US Open, and then you are off tour until Asia. 4 weeks of nothing but rehab and yes being with my love in our new townhouse.

Larry was working and skipped the public announcement of the creation of the foundation. I was asked what prompted me to do this, and I basically said to the reporter, tennis is a very expensive sport, and those that don't have a lot of money for travel, are forced to lower rankings not due to ability but due to finances. We will work with tennis facilities to identify upcoming women tennis players that if they were able to get some support, would be able to compete and get more opportunities for college scholarships. I was asked by another reporter, so you want to develop more women professionals they loved my answer.

The point of the funding is to increase the possibility that these lower income players have a chance to get recruited to play college tennis. If one or two can go professional after that, then that is a great result, but the purpose is for low resource women to gain chances to go to college on tennis and academic scholarships. This will only fund travel for tournaments and will be with the assistance of tennis facilities identifying these women and to vet the family.

The rest of the press conference went well, I was wearing the tools of my trade and with the colors I represented. Jacques was there and spoke about the support that Lacoste will do in supporting this effort.

Allison stood up and said that the company will also contribute 500 pairs of shoes for those identified by the vetting process.

What I did not know at the time, but this was going to be a big deal, I was now president of the "Pink and Blue Foundation". Athletes do charity all the time, but for me this was personal, and the reporter asked, would you have had an easier time had this been available to you?

I simply responded, "while I was thinking about me personally, our success in the last year we need more children especially the poor a chance to compete. The test area is going to be in Charleston, SC, and Coach Paul Nelson was going to vet three girls to be initially receive travel vouchers."

The local press ate this up and we received a 3-minute piece on all the local channels. I heard that ESPN mentioned something about it. I had made so much money this year it was time that I gave back. I was also funding one scholarship at Longwood for the next five years the name of the scholarship was" Dea Jarman", memorial scholarship $100,000, funded. It was for a student over 30, going to college for the first time. I know that this was a tax deduction, but it was time I gave back now that I had the money.

Jean and her friends said that they were taking up the "Pink and Blue" foundation. They were going to have some fund raisers at the local country clubs, and I was going to be expected to speak at them. I realized this was going to take up a lot of my time and energy away from the courts. I was going to have to ask the debutantes for money.

Back to the real world, I had a week with Larry before flying to Cincinnati, and the 1000. Anita was playing with Isabel this week in Montreal and got to the quarters before they lost, my little sister was becoming a great tennis player, and she even made the quarters of the singles. My lovely husband made sure that I did all my rehab exercises, and we even went on the runs together in our neighborhood. My life was so different, and I was not sure I really wanted to go back to tennis, but that was the source of my funds.

In Cincinnati, I was scheduled only to play singles, Anita and Isabel played doubles together. I went to the quarters before losing to the 2 seed here, and again my calf was aching by the end of the tournament.

Anita made it to the quarters on the upper side of the draw and lost a day earlier. Isabel and Anita won 2 rounds in doubles another quarter, they were playing well together. Isabel only played the doubles; she lost in the last round of qualifications.

Since Anita had played a lot of matches this summer, she chose to skip Cleveland but trained there with Johan. I had made the quarters when Johan said something to me that I thought I would never hear. He had basically indicated if we are going to play next week at the US Open, don't turn on those competitive juices, it is ok to lose most of the other seeds have already bowed out to give them time for next week. I had heard that this happens, but the points we needed were next week and not this week. Isabel and I won 2 rounds in doubles losing on Thursday so we would have three days to get to New York and get ready for the US Open. For me I took a detour and flew to DC, and then on Sunday I chose to take the bullet train from DC to New York, I was tired of the flights. I also got to see my husband for a night before the big tournament, he was not going to be able to make it next week, he just got promoted to a director level and at 36, he was one of the youngest and the money he was going to make was nice living even if I made nothing.

Because of my ongoing calf issues, the team decided that I was not going to play doubles with Anita, that would be Isabel. I would try to do mixed doubles and singles for the two weeks. I was going to miss playing with Anita, but everyone thought I was going to have trouble with all three and skipping the ladies' doubles meant less matches. I would miss not playing with Anita but now that I was 30th in the world life was different. I had also turned 30 in the last week; Larry and I celebrated in a romantic way when I was home.

I was treated by a friend on Saturday to get my left calf ready, it was still sore but with a couple of days off and no training over the weekend, I was going to make a run in New York.

US Open:

Because I am a superstitious, I ate at Elijah's bagels before practice on Monday, my first-round match was Tuesday third on the bull ring. My practice was with other people because both Anita and Isabel were on the top side of the draw, and each won Isabel over the 29th seed. Anita beat a qualifier, 6-3 and 6-2, she was getting more confident every day. I was proud of her like she was my real little sister and not just someone that I will always be connected to through Wimbledon.

This time we were able to get accommodations at a timeshare for the next two weeks from Wyndham, while it was a little slower to get there, we had two units next to each other, Anita and I were in a 2-bedroom unit and then Isabel and Johan were in a one bedroom, and we did the meals and meetings in our dining room.

On Monday night, we had ordered from an Irish restaurant at the bottom of the Wyndham. Johan congratulated the two that had played and let them know that they were playing doubles on Wednesday after they both played singles so make sure you hydrate well. He then said and to our married lady, you are playing a qualifier that is just out of the NCAA's. Juanita Gearhardt, who was Puerto Rican with a father that had immigrated from Germany, she looked like her mom, tanned and only about 5' tall. This is one that we want short points if you are past ten shots simply go for it no matter what. I don't want a 4-hour match. If you could manage to win this in an hour, I would appreciate it. Your practice partner on Tuesday will be 15 minutes of both of your partners in crime here. Then we send you to physio to get that calf taped with physio tape. Isabel and Anita, after you finish with Lilly you have another 15 minutes with me, and you get to go to physio for your stretching afterwards.

"Well ladies' good day, let's have another one on Tuesday."

I was on the phone to Larry and my parents they were all wishing me good luck, nobody was coming up this year until next week if I made it. I asked Lucy to come up on Tuesday and she said she would make it, but she was not going to do my iPad notes.

Tuesday came and I felt very good for the start of a big tournament as the 28 seed, I had a red number for this tournament 32 were seeds. Anita took my iPad and said I want to enter notes into the iPad. At 3 PM, we got called to the tournament and I handed the iPad to Anita to enter the notes for the match. Lucy sat in the back of the box.

Anita here, what a difference a year makes, in the introductions, Lilly was introduced second this time. Representing South Korea, playing in her second US Open, Lilly Jarman Wilson, Lilly is currently the doubles champion from Wimbledon, and was a final 16 player last year. I heard the now famous slogan, and it had to be intimidating for the very young Juanita. I say that because the poor thing looked so out of it during warm-up, she was having trouble putting the ball into the court in her overheads and her serves looked weak. She won the coin toss and decided to challenge Lilly by hitting the corners and while they were placed well Lilly pounced on them. Thirty minutes later, Lilly had won the first set 6-1. We thought she would challenge Lilly in the second set, but she was nervous, she did not force the long points that Johan has been warning Lilly about and lost the second set 6-1. Lilly took a little over an hour and because of that, Johan said Lilly we are going to warm-down today, then to the physio for you to get that calf stretched and then sending you to a whirlpool.

Lilly here, I received a text from everyone congratulating me on the win, it really was funny, that poor Juanita, needed to be at the ITF levels now she was just as green as I was. I received a text from Mike that our first round of the mixed doubles was going to be Friday. I was happy because that meant no practice that day.

Anita and I took an Uber back to Midtown. I called Larry from my bedroom after we got back and before I took a shower. We had a good conversation, because just winning today was worth a lot of money but beyond money, I was getting closer to matching my points. He told me that his mother said that they will need me back after the tournament, she has a lot of personal appearances for you to attend for the foundation, it was taking off. I took a shower and started to wonder am I playing for tennis or am I playing for the foundation. The two were now switching.

I called John about this, and he said truthfully, "Lilly your endorsements will end at the end of the year, and the money from "Athletic and Feminine", will eclipse your winnings next year. With all the outlets using this and how it is taking off, your commissions next year are now expected to be well over 1.5 million for both you and Larry. Every meeting that you do seems to only expand the demand, and you may not know it Lilly, but you are no longer just a tennis player, you have become a spokesperson for all those women that want to be athletic and open to being feminine also. I would love to represent you in but truthfully you are now going to be way more than a tennis player."

The night went well, and Anita came over to me she was nervous about playing the 12 seed and requested that I sit in her box to help calm me down.

"I told her if Johan was good with it, I would be honored."

Anita smiled, "it was already approved; I want my adopted big sister with me taking on my first top 20 in a major."

I agreed to come for the noon match on the bull ring. Anita came over and hugged me.

"I thought it was weird, she said you have no idea how much I love you."

On Wednesday, I was able to get up early and do the whirlpool, and some light hitting before I was expected into the box. Behind Johan and me, we had nobody in the box. Anita asked me to text Larry the results so he could tell his brother. I thought it was strange that she wanted to make sure Chris heard her results but did not do it directly. I think Anita was very nervous about dating she was a sex symbol by many and those of us that knew her, knew she was very shy and beautiful at the same time.

Anita should not have been nervous at 3-3 she broke Amanda Garcia from France and won her first set ten minutes later. When she went down 3-0, in the second set, I yelled at her you belong here, kick her butt. Johan was surprised at what I said, but Anita smiled. Amanda never won another game when the great returner came out of Anita. Anita had defeated a high seed 6-4 and 6-3. She told me later, my yelling at her made her laugh and relax, the rest came easy.

"Johan looked at me, you do remember I am her coach right. Johan stated, you have no idea how much Anita wants your approval, she really loves you like a big sister, that is uncommon, and no it is not a lesbian way. Her results are getting notice now."

I laughed I think I just told her to kick butt again.

Two hours later Isabel lost a tight match 7-5 and 7-6, she was out of singles. She had to get over it to be with Anita for the first round of doubles and as the ten seeds Isabel simply let Anita take over and truthfully it was 75% Anita and after a little over an hour the team had won 6-2, and 6-0. I went out and picked up a big pasta meal for all four of us that night and the two of them appeared happy about the doubles. Anita told me you helped me turn around my match I laughed, and I never do that on the court.

Thursday was coming and a second-round match against one of the Romanoff's again. I was number three on Ashe. I am writing that this match went much easier than I thought it could win 6-4 and 6-1. I was back in the round of 32 and needed one more match to keep my points from last year. The match has taken like 75 minutes and Johan was happy it had not been long he then sent me to the whirlpool again, this time I had a bathing suit to wear. The win was not as satisfying as I expected, it was worth $40,000, and money no longer appeared to be what was driving me. I really wanted to be home with Larry and creating our life together. I was more interested in the foundation now. Anita and Isabel worked out as a team right after my match, Did I mention that Isabel is very seductive also, so they had a lot of attention at the practice court. I had to rescue the two of them, with Johan so they could get out early.

Friday morning came and I went out to Elijah's to pick up breakfast for all four of us, the bagels were good as were the fruit and they had some nice coffee for Johan, the players could not have any. Anita was playing second on Armstrong, and then she was playing last on court 17 with Isabel in doubles. I was playing first with Mike in Mixed doubles. He had told me that due to the amount of tennis he had played this season, he was only playing doubles this tournament, he was hoping to go far and was close to qualifying for doubles in the year-end championships. We were first out on court 6, a small court at 11:00, I should be done in time to get over to Anita's singles match. Johan and Isabel wanted me to be out there for the doubles tonight that was last on the day session all the way out on 17.

Mike and I won our mixed match 6-3 and 6-4, it went well, it was not that hard, and the good thing meant I did not have to practice. I quickly got to the players' lounge and showered so I could get to Anita's box just as she was getting on the court for the second set. Anita had lost the first set, and when I got to the box yelled at her, come on Krantze, get your act together. She laughed, and proceeded to win the second set 6-2, and won the last set 6-4, in a match that took just under three hours.

"She was gracious in her interview and said thanks to the loud person in the stands that told me to get my act together."

"The interviewer looked up and realized it was either Johan or me that had yelled at her. I think it was your friend over there and he pointed at me, I was trying to duck. Well Anita, I think "Athletic and Feminine", was yelling at you."

"I spoke up, yeah, I told you to get your act together." Anita started to laugh and was about to say oh yeah, my Duff, but instead she held back and oh my darling friend over there. I watched Anita and Isabel win their second-round doubles match, what a long day, ten hours at the facility, I called Larry and told him I had won, he told me he had watched it, but wait until you see Sports Center, you are on yelling at Anita. He also said that Chris is happy you are helping Anita, I thought I bet he is something going on with those two and I'm not sure I really want to know.

Saturday morning came and another match at the US Open, my third round, and I played another faceless player that had upset a seed lower than me in theory this would make my life easier to the quarters. Aileen O'Hare was from Northern Ireland and played for Britain. I had not much tape on her, but she had red hair and was about my height, she just wasn't that good this morning at the Grandstand, she was not happy with the noon start time. I had no such problem, and she did not wake up until the second set. By that time, I was still ready to go and held on for a 7-5 second set win the match went under 2 hours and Johan sent me right back to the training room, another whirlpool anti-inflammatory, and then a massage on the left calf. This was getting old. Anita and Isabel had a practice that I watched from outside the fence and then back to the timeshare in Manhattan. Since it was only 4 PM, I took Anita shopping, she was willing to go with me until the stores close at 9, and we were ready for dinner when Anita read a text from Johan, you two get you asses back you have matches tomorrow. So, our shopping day ended, and the tennis people were back on, when we got back Irish food was waiting for us with a note, you need to stop acting like schoolgirls see you at 10:30. I knew we were going to get yelled at, Anita started laughing hysterically. We put our bags down, ate dinner and then Isabel and Johan came in.

"Anita broke the ice, you are going to yell at us, we just wanted to give you love birds time to play."

That ended the yelling at us Johan laughed, he just simply said, "we have a busy day. Anita you are first on at Ashe Stadium."

"I laughed no late night for you."

"Johan said not so nice for you either, you are 1 PM, second on Grandstand for your second-round doubles match. Then we have late afternoon with the lovely Isabel and her partner playing on Court 17 doubles last on about 6:30 PM."

Mike called me it was almost 11 PM and wondered what was up. He said "he had twisted his ankle in his doubles match, they had won, but he was icing down all night and would be taped up on Sunday and was hoping to just stay at the net because he needed another day to get the swelling down.

I was not happy about the prospects of losing the next round, but Mike needed to work on his men's doubles, if he and his partner won the next round, they got into the year-end doubles' championships.

Sunday morning came and we all warmed-up together. I gave Anita a hug and said your match and mine are near the same time, can you handle it if I can't be in the stands.

Anita's response "Yes, I can, can you handle not protecting me?" We both started to hug each other."

I know someone got a picture, I wonder if they thought we were lovers or something else. Right after we finished practice it started getting gloomy, and started to rain, my match was going to be postponed until at least 3 PM, so I decided to be in Anita's box.

"I received a call, and it showed Germany, it was Anita's mom and she asked me to make sure Anita knew we were supporting her, you know she idolizes you and wants your approval like you are her real big sister. I think that is why I also wanted to let you know that Chris will be in her box today, she wanted your approval that they go on dates."

"I laughed I thought something was up, sure and does he know no dating during tournaments?"

Mom, "that is what you are going to tell him, you trained your husband and Anita is worried that he will not understand." I agreed to sit in the box with Chris.

Anita looked up at the box and saw both Chris and me behind Johan, so I had to say something. Hey Krantze, kick some butt this afternoon. She started to laugh and then went out and played well winning in two tight sets 6-4 and 7-6.

I then had to say something to Chris, "I know you like Anita and given she is probably the most gorgeous woman I have ever known I want you to know that she is my good friend, and you can't mess with her performance during the tournament. No dating during tournaments, maybe a quick meal together, she can't have distractions during the matches, your brother knows."

Chris looked at me, and said nothing, I think he knew I would knock him on his butt if her did something to hurt Anita's career. Chris finally spoke, "she loves you like you are her big sister, so I get it and Larry sends his best for you. He will be at your round of 16."

"Anita was asked who was in her box today, she said you all know Lilly and Johan is my coach. Chris is Lilly's brother-in-law; he is up here to watch her play, I guess she made him come to my match since hers is delayed.

"Welcome Anita to the US Open quarters."

At 3 PM, we finally got on in our mixed doubles match, Mike was hurting, and I could only cover so much so we eventually lost 6-3 and

6-4, I really did not care though this was just a way to escape practice the money was no longer a big deal and Mike needed to rest for his doubles partner.

The Women's team of Anita and Isabel won but this time they had to win the third set, 3-6, 6-3 and 6-3, one break of serve in each set, it was dark by the time they were finished. We grabbed some food at the Players' lounge and went to the timeshare. Chris was not around, which was good, and I had to talk to Anita about keeping her head screwed on, no time for your male friend.

She then proceeded to punch my arm, "you had no problem with it."

"I said you know nothing but dinner and a movie no fooling around. Maybe you can learn from me and not repeat it."

Anita choking, "I would love to repeat certain parts like Larry and your relationship. A second team all-American footballer, and his lovely wife who happens to own the Wimbledon doubles tournament. The power couple."

Anita knew what I meant, and I had to get ready for my husband coming to the match round of 16, on Armstrong third on Monday. I was playing Amanda Knox; she had upset the lower seed so if I get through this, I get the quarters and who knows. I really did not care who it was I wanted to make the quarters and knew that I needed to get some rest and make sure John had Larry's credentials for Monday.

Monday match, I had the only match this time and so Anita and Isabel used my warm-up as their practice time. Since it was afternoon, I went to the players' lounge but before I could get there, a man in a hoodie said he would like to talk to MS Athletic and Feminine, I knew the voice, and pulled down the hoodie and kissed my husband. Of course, Anita said I thought you can't date and laughed I just kissed a fan if that is ok with you.

"Chris came up to Anita, can I do that also, and Anita said my big sister over there says no."

"Chris said you two don't look a lot alike did you have a different mother or father, and with a punch Anita delivered Chris knew to keep his arms and lips off her in public."

Larry here, I have the iPad for today and it felt different. After he had introduced Amanda, then came the introduction for Lilly. Introducing her opponent for this round of 16 match, representing South Korea and from the State of Virginia, well known for the phrase "Athletic and Feminine", Lilly Jarman Wilson, in her second round of 16 at the US Open. I had to make sure that I kept Anita and Chris away from each other, they really were not doing well near each other, and I wanted the focus on Lilly. Lilly started the match serving and took almost no time in winning her serve, and a few minutes later so did Amanda. The first set went into a tiebreaker, and that is when Lilly seized the moment she broke early and often for a 7-1 tiebreak win. The crowd was going crazy. Amanda looked dismayed, Lilly started serving and volleying to shorten the points and the next thing we knew she had finished Amanda off. Our team including Johan started cheering and yelling. Johan sent Lilly to the physio as soon as she was done with the interview. I did not see her for another hour she was hurting but would never let anyone know. She finally came out and to my surprise, Anita and Chris were holding hands, I had no idea. I can't imagine what my mother was going to say about another tennis girlfriend.

Lilly here, since all four of us were in town, we went out to an Italian restaurant. I made Anita sit with me on one side of the booth, nothing was going to go on tonight, she was still in the tournament, and I was still not so sure about Chris, and yes, I am protective of Anita. After dinner, we left in 2 Ubers, one for the men and one for the women tennis players back to the timeshare. Larry told me later the guys went out to a couple of bars; they did not have the issues that Anita and I had. I had a conversation with Anita to make sure where her head was at, she had the quarters in the morning and doubles quarters in the afternoon.

Tuesday morning, and we received a large delivery from Elijah's Bagels in the morning, I asked for a group of four bagels with eggs and sausage in them, along with fruit and cereal, it was going to be a busy day for the others. Anita was playing in her quarters number 2 on Arthur Ashe, the number 1 seed was playing another unseeded player. Anita was playing the 4 seed, Melanie Kush, so I thought it was funny Kush and Krantze, it sounded like a Rhine Wine. The doubles were going to be last on again on the Stadium Court, so it may be under the lights.

I was requested to go see the physio at 10:00, and then did a light workout. I had lunch with Larry on the square.

Anita said she wanted me in the box and I better yell for me and at me if I need it."

Larry was not going to be in the box as to our surprise Anita's mother was here for the event. Chris decided it would not be smart to be in the box at that point. So just Johan, her mom and me in the box. Isabel was told to get rest and be ready for doubles this afternoon.

What nobody knew was that Lacoste had asked me and was granted Anita the use of my colors and shoes for this round of the tournament. Her opponent was also sponsored by Lacoste so the change was apparent. I had to approve of it and had no problem, this was just going to provide more exposure for the clothes, and she is gorgeous, it won't hurt sales.

Anita was introduced first because she was unseeded, while Melanie was the 4 seed of the tournament. This is a quarterfinal of the women's singles, from Germany Anita Krantze, Anita is currently the Wimbledon Doubles champion. Her opponent this afternoon is the 4 seed for this tournament and has previously won the Australian Open and been a finalist at this tournament 3 years ago. Welcome Melanie Kush.

I have to say my adopted little sister was ready for the fight and stole the first set 6-3, before Melanie could adjust her game for the strong game that Anita had for her. The sound of "Athletic and Feminine", could be heard throughout Ashe stadium. Melanie was not going to go away easily, and she took the second set 7-5, when Anita double faulted on break point. The third set went break and break, and then all holds until a match tiebreaker was required. When Anita came over and got coaching from Johan, I yelled at her buck up Krantze, time to kick butt. The smile on her face told me she would be great in the tiebreak, and when she received a mini break to go up 9-7, she was lining up for the match point and proceeded to hit what looked like one of my shots very wide and won the point as she came in for the winning volley. She immediately fell to the ground and held her hands over her face. I got in trouble for yelling a little too soundly for her. Anita came to the net to shake hands and then got ready for the ESPN studios interview.

ESPN Brad Gilbert – "Well Anita I see the new colors and the fans yelling what your friend Lilly Initiated."

"Anita pointed to me, I needed some good luck to get through this match and my friend said I could wear her colors for this match, it was great."

Brad, "I see in your box is your friend Lilly Jarman, what did she say to you before the tiebreaker that made you laugh?"

"She said buck up Krantze, time to kick butt. Thanks, Lilly, for making me smile, it helped me concentrate."

I just waved at her.

I have one question what happens if you and Lilly make it to the finals?

"I would love to see it, and I think I can win. I want to thank my mom for getting here today, she has not watched me that much in my professional career."

Lilly here, Anita picked up her things and waved to the crowd and the chant was apparent. When I caught up with her, I said I think you are stealing my line. Anita simply hugged me and said thank you for your mentoring, I love you Lilly Wilson, you really helped me today just by being there.

"When Anita's mom came over, she said you look pretty good in those colors to her daughter, and then a surprise, she hugged me and whispered Lilly, you will always be welcome in my house, you have been so good for my daughter now she is going to have to learn to live with her fame as a tennis player not just her looks."

I understand Chris bought everyone a round of beer at the bar near the ESPN booth outside the Ashe stadium. Larry confirmed this and it was going to cost Chris a week's salary.

We had another 2 hours before the doubles for Isabel and Anita, so Larry and I went away from the stadium and went to Manhattan to go shopping for the house. I told Johan to make sure that Chris stayed away from Anita this afternoon she needed to rest for the doubles tonight. I should not have feared, Isabel had Anita in the players' lounge, and she had taken a nap. She had a hell of a singles match in just under 3 hours.

We got back at almost 6 PM, and the women's doubles was just about to get called on the stadium court. The team was playing Beatrice and Caca tonight and they were hungry for a championship. Apparently more than my girls, Anita and Isabel came back to win the second set 6-4 but lost the final set 6-3. Isabel was now done for the tournament, and she would gain in doubles points, but Anita had enough points that if I was able to come back for the Asian swing, we could be in the year-end doubles' championships. Chris came to see Anita as she was leaving the stadium and smart man, just shook her hand and told her, tough evening, you played well. I saw Anita smile even after the loss and the potential of the night with her new friend.

"I ended that thought and told her you are playing in the first semi-final of your life much less a major, you need to focus on tennis."

"Anita then told me then I needed to make sure my husband was not with me tonight."

I agreed only if she would help me ice my calf for the third time today, and then the icy hot to make it feel better.

"Anita finally asked how bad it is, Lilly?"

"I told her it only hurts if I walk, run, or stand but I will rest it after this tournament, and we will win together in the Asian swing."

My little sister helped me pack the ice and then went out of the room and got me an extra blanket and got herself changed and brought a movie in for the night. She ordered from a local pasta place for delivery and said I am taking care of you because you won't otherwise. I wanted to argue with her, the look on my friend Anita told me that I better let her help me tonight.

Anita asked, "does Johan and Larry know how bad you are hurt, and you probably should not even be thinking about playing tomorrow?"

"I started crying, I can't stop playing otherwise the brand and the foundation will be hurt".

"Anita said both will live far beyond your tennis career, I love you and I don't want to see you hurting like this."

I fell asleep apparently after the pain killers, Anita stayed in my room on my bed while I fell asleep on the sofa with my leg up on a pillow. The ice melted and I simply rolled over and put it on the ground.

Wednesday morning and it was time for my quarters this afternoon, I was playing a really good player Beatrice Northam, she was a top 3 seed, from Belgium. I had not ever played her or viewed her matches except on tape Monday night for a while. She was just about six feet tall, and while she was mostly known for clay, she had made the semifinals at both Wimbledon and the Australian Open. She had a decent serve, but she could cover the court insanely well. My match was number 2 on Armstrong, so I would not be until at least 2 PM, the men were first on the court so best of 5 will take a while.

Johan had me go to the physio before we did anything else this morning. After icing and then heating and adding physio tape, we then worked out at 11 AM. I went back to the players' lounge took a shower, had lunch, and then went to see Larry and Chris. We went under the shade, and I was doing my fluids, they were doing beer. To make sure I was not bothered, I wore nothing pink or blue and watched the large screen and saw that they had just split sets on my court, so I had at least an hour, it was almost 2 PM, and Johan texted me, time to get back in the players' lounge, we will look at tape on my iPad, to see what we can do. That took us to 3:00, they had just finished the third set, and the match was taking forever. Finally, at 4 PM, they said, match is 5-5, in the fifth set, expect 10 minutes. I had to take another anti-inflammatory and some food to make sure I could get through this match. I handed my iPad to Johan who was going to give it to Larry for notes for this quarter-final match.

Larry here, as they were getting ready to go to Armstrong, I got the iPad from Johan, and all three of us went towards the stadium. They were just finishing the interviews for the quarters from the previous match. Anita was already at the box waiting for us, Chris was not with her, she explained he was at the bar again, he did not want to be a distraction.

Truthfully, I was thinking back to last year and a proposal and now a marriage to the very beautiful and athletic Lilly Jarman Wilson. I was also thinking back to her struggles for so long as a kid and then as an athlete, being here was the ultimate. The foundation was going to take a lot of time, people were clamoring for it to succeed. We were going to make so much money from the licensing money that really tennis for Lilly was not required, but she loved her sport, and I did not want any chance of messing up her next few years. We still have time to think about kids and what we will do with our lives but in ten minutes Lilly would try to match her adopted little sister and make the semi-finals of the US Open. A little over a year ago, she won a small tournament in Bethany Beach, and it opened so many doors. The ESPN engagement, the Wimbledon title, all because of one opportunity she received. The funny thing I would have loved Lilly no matter what had happened she took my breath away from the moment I met her, even though she always seemed a little reserved. I think Anita has been a good influence on her, and no Lilly is not her "Duff" like a very good big sister.

Introducing our third quarterfinal match, from Radford, Virginia, the 29 seed, in her second US Open, Lilly Jarman Wilson. Lilly is the current doubles champion from Wimbledon. He opponent this afternoon, Beatrice Northam, she was a quarterfinalist last year, and has made the semi-finals in both Australia and Wimbledon. Beatrice is our number 3 seed of this tournament.

Lilly won the coin toss and chose to serve. Just from the warm-up you could see that Lilly could not just sit on the baseline with this girl she would need to finish the points earlier. Lilly had no want this to be long point and served wide and came up for the first two points on her serve. She served an ace down the middle and after a point that Beatrice won, Lilly won the first game of the match. Beatrice looked a little less sure of herself and Lilly was able to win the serve to go up 2-0. The two held serve from there on, and Lilly was able to win the set 6-3. The chant we all had been getting used to was erupting from the stadium. Anita was wearing the colors in our box, and she was chanting herself for Lilly. Johan, on the changeover told Lilly to stay in the moment, this is your time and a few other cliché's.

ESPN Studios:

Brad I am assuming by the yelling that Lilly Jarman Wilson has just won the first set. "Brad responded she won the first set by breaking early and the two women could not get another opportunity for the entire set. Lilly looked like she is now accustomed to this pressure."

Larry here, the second set was delayed because Beatrice decided to take a bathroom break, and at the same time changed her clothes. After a five-minute break, the second set began. Beatrice looked much crisper and was getting to shots that she had been missing in the first set. She held easily in her first service game, as did Lilly, the set went eventually to a tiebreaker and was 5-all. Beatrice served wide for the first time and while Lilly was able to return the serve, it had caused her to wince when she ran back to the court and lost the point, and trailed 5-6, and was only able to serve in the upper 90's which Beatrice hit cross court for the set winner.

Lilly called for the trainer, and they retaped he ankle and left calf, during the timeout between sets. Lilly was able to get on her feet, served big but they were always down the middle. She won three points easily and on the fourth Lilly just let the point go where in the past I know she could have reached it. Lilly managed to do a wide serve on the last serve and came to the net to win the game.

ESPN Studios:

Beatrice and Lilly Jarman are playing a very tight match with only 1 service break and that was early in the first set. We pick this up with Beatrice leading her serve 30-15. The serve was out wide, and it looked like Lilly got to the point, and it looked like she just fell as she turned to get back to the court. Lilly is trying to get up and she is looking back at her left calf. She is finally getting up and is very slowly and gingerly, trying to get back on the court. She is putting her hand up and asking for the trainer for a second time.

Larry here, I love my wife and I can't stand to see her in pain, she is literally trying to get taped up all the way from her knee to her foot, to try to finish the match. Finally, Johan is yelling at her to sit down and retire from the match. Lilly sat back down, and again tried to get up to move, and you could see she was unable to do anything but a feeble attempt to walk.

Johan was allowed to come down to the stadium floor and he says" no more Lilly. The world wants you Lilly Jarman, you are loved, and nobody wants you to get up and finish this match."

Lilly again tried to get up to play the final games of the final set."

"Anita, yelled at Lilly it is time to heal."

When Lilly looked-up at the box she shook her head and appeared to agree with Anita. Lilly called over Beatrice, who hugged Lilly. Lilly said something to the referee.

"Ladies and Gentlemen, Lilly Jarman is unable to continue the match. Beatrice Northam is the winner 3-6, 7-6, 0-1."

The wheelchair was brought into the court to a stunned filled Armstrong tennis stadium. Anita and I were allowed to help her get her things together. As soon as we helped her get her clothes on and she went into the wheelchair the entire stadium stood up and started clapping and for what appeared five minutes kept yelling "Athletic and Feminine". Even the stoic in the stands were yelling for Lilly as she was wheeled from the stadium.

Lilly was immediately taken to the waiting ambulance now waiting outside of the stadium. People who had been watching on the screen outside Ashe, were clapping for Lilly as she was lifted into the ambulance.

Lilly was rushed to Flushing Hospital Medical Center; we were 5 minutes behind her in a car driven by one of the security team from the US Open. Because they knew who she was the hospital had the orthopedist on call ready as she got there. The Xray showed no break, and then they ordered and MRI. The MRI results are normally not given right away to the doctor, but this was a professional athlete, and while it was not good news, the statement by the doctor said, Lilly has a major tear in her left calf, it will not require surgery, but this will take between 3 and 6 months to heal properly. Lilly won't be able to play tennis at least until January of next year. The US Open had a large SUV waiting after Johan called. Lilly was wearing a boot and she looked very dejected she whispered something to Anita, and Anita started to laugh.

When we finally got Lilly on the couch at the timeshare, I pulled her aside and said to her what did you say to Anita that made her laugh. Lilly told her to go kick ass on Thursday. Anita helped Lilly go to the bathroom to shower and change clothes, it was 9 PM, and the Irish restaurant came through for all and delivered to the suite a meal for 5. Somehow my brother Chris appeared with them, I know I did not ask him to come this had to be on Anita to help her get ready for her semi-final match. Lilly took the pain killer that was prescribed for her and before she could finish dinner, she fell asleep. Chris and I left for our hotel after I saw Anita give my brother a kiss. Anita pulled her stuff from her bedroom to sleep on the couch next to the recliner Lilly was asleep on. Anita was not going to let her big sister be alone tonight and since Johan kicked us out, she chose to protect Lilly and then sleep for her next match on Thursday.

I woke up Thursday morning and was still groggy from the pain killer last night, and realized I was still on the recliner that I had fallen asleep. I looked over at the sofa and Anita was sound asleep on the couch. I got up and with my foot in the boot, I was able to walk slowly to the bathroom to do my morning duties. I then called Elijah's to see about getting a meal ordered and delivered, they said someone named Johan had already ordered for you all it would be there in about ten minutes according to Uber.

With a knock on the door, breakfast was ready and then Johan knocked on the door to come in. We woke up Anita it was almost 8:30, I bet she had stayed up and watched over me for a while last night. She rushed to the bathroom, put on her robe, and then came out for breakfast and strategy with Johan. Even without make-up she was still gorgeous. What I had not known until yesterday was the depth of how she felt for me in just one year of knowing each other we had become very close and the tough exterior she tried to put on I saw through it; she was the most caring and loving person I had ever known.

The first thing Anita said to me, "can you make it to be at the box this afternoon?"

"I'm not sure I can walk that far," then from behind me was a cane presented by Johan, it was a very fancy cane. Anita sent him out this morning to a place she knew sold German unique items, this is an authentic Bavarian cane most use for mountain climbing we have a rubber tip on it for you.

I tried to get up and before I could Anita hugged me and told me, "I am so sorry your match ended the way it did. She kept hugging me and started to cry, so sorry I did not stop you from getting on the court, I knew you could not make it through."

I stood up and started using the cane, and yelled at Anita, "time for you to stop thinking about me, and be ready to win this match and get to the finals." I sat back on my recliner as Johan and Anita talked strategy. I texted Larry that I was going to the match for Anita. He had been told already by Johan, that Anita wanted you in the box. Larry said he was going home, and he was taking Chris with him. He knows Anita needs to focus on her matches and not him so we will be waiting for both of you in DC.

The second semi-final on Ashe was scheduled at 3 PM, between my boot and the cane, I was able to slowly make it to the players box, as I hobbled to the players box someone recognized me and started our now famous chant. The entire Stadium started clapping for me and I raised my hand to recognize the crowd. Anita's mom came up to me and nearly broke my ribs with her hug, I am so sorry for your injury would have loved to see my daughter and her adopted big sister in the finals together.

Anita came out on the stadium in our now common colors and again the stands erupted.

ESPN Studios:

We seldom show you the box of the players before the match, for Anita Krantze the stadium was rocking with chanting for an injured tennis player sitting in her box. When Anita came out in those same colors, the place rocked. You would think the match was going to be played in Germany.

Lilly here, I could not believe how well Anita warmed-up and focused she was. I would love to talk about an historic match, but Anita was on fire from the beginning, her opponent never knew what happened and after 75 minutes Anita had won 6-3 and 6-1. She would play in her first major final.

ESPN Studios:

Anita Krantze congratulations on your win this afternoon.
"Anita was gracious and thanked the fans for supporting her. I want to thank my coach and my mother in the box. I also want to recognize one additional person in my box this afternoon. Lilly Jarman, I know you could have gone home with your husband thanks for being with me today."

The stands erupted in the famous chant once again. Anita asked for me to stand up and the chants were great, I just pointed to her and then clapped for her.

"Anita's mom said you know Anita would never be here without you, you have no idea how you are loved not only by my family but for so many women across the world."

All I could do is say, "thank you."

I agreed to stay for the finals, Isabel went home to Spain and Johan would be with her the next week. They would get married in a small private ceremony in Sevilla.

Anita like a few others had spent her energy to get to the finals and never rallied in the finals. She lost the match 6-2 and 6-2 and was gracious in the awards ceremony thanking her team and her mom for being here. I had already told her not to mention me during the ceremony, so I was stood up with the rest of her team.

I flew home to DC Saturday night, and waiting for me was Larry. When we got back to the townhouse, my family was waiting for me, James, mom and dad, and Olivia. Granny Miller called and said you are now loved Lilly, even if you never play tennis again your life will never be the same.

On Monday morning, I received a call from Anita, asking me if I could meet her at Dulles airport at noon today. I said of course I can, why here though. She then told me Larry had called her Sunday morning and asked if I could come to see us before she leaves for the rest of the year. The plate was on its way back to Germany with her mother, but Anita wanted to stay with us she was dressed in clothing 2 sizes bigger than she needed, was wearing glasses and had a dark hair wig on. She came to our house and slept until Tuesday; she was exhausted. Chris came over Tuesday night, and I know nothing went on very romantically other than hand holding and a few kisses. I think Chris knew that he better behave, or I might do something he would have to deal with me. Anita left on Saturday for Germany, and then on to China for the tour, I would have to miss the rest of the season, but I received a call from Asia almost daily. I suspect so did Chris.

In November Anita was in Costa Rico getting her SI shoot, I know this because I met her there. I was asked to come to see the shoot, Chris was not invited. When I got there, SI said we have your bathing suit for your picture, and I laughed you want a picture of the" Duff". They said you are being nominated for most influential sports woman of the year and Anita wanted you to look both "Athletic and Feminine", we have you in a lovely one piece so get in the make-up tent, your photo shoot is in thirty minutes.

Larry and I were hosting Thanksgiving dinner, I did not cook, it was catered when Anita came in holding hands with Chris, she had landed this morning and said I want to see Lilly out of her boot. Ten weeks later I was just starting to train lightly again, I had not hit a tennis ball in nearly 12 weeks. The Wilsons came for this dinner the Jarmans were back in the country. Well except, for James and Olivia, they came late after having had dinner with the family in Radford.

15 months I had gone from unknown to known, and now not just for tennis because Jean told me the Foundation was growing insanely, it was going to have a 25 million budget for giving all over the world. My 15 minutes of fame had lasted 15 months. I had a new family in DC and an adopted family in Germany, and friend in Spain. My last ranking that came out after the Open revealed had made it to 25th in

the world. My adopted little sister was now 20. If I had not been injured, we would have played in the championship but that never happened.

Anita would play in it as a singles player the next year. Isabel and Johan traveled together the rest of the year, Isabel and Anita won a doubles tournament in Hong Kong and dedicated to their adopted big sister recovering at home, both wore pink and blue for the final.

US Open 5:

It has been three years since my injury in the quarterfinals of the US Open. I will be attending the semi-finals in the box of Anita as she is trying to make it to the finals for a second time. Chris will be in the box and there may be a surprise for Anita if she wins tonight, Larry has told Chris how to script this, her ring will be a full carat yellow diamond, with 2 pink and 2 blue sapphires. I had expressed, that in no way does she deserve to have the same ring as me. It would not be fair to either one of us, it would cheapen the moment, since Anita also favors the rose gold, the ring will be based on that color gold.

Isabel became a doubles specialist and with Anita, they won the doubles tournament at the Australian Open, while I was still recovering from my torn calf. She has won numerous double titles and makes a pretty good living being a doubles specialist. Isabel will not be playing tournaments for a while; she is four months pregnant with the baby due in February. They just found out it is a boy. Johan is Anita's standalone coach now that she is ranked number 5 in the world, he will be taking off right after the Australian Open.

Kiki and her husband are the proud parents of an older girl now 2 ½, and she is the proud mom to a boy that was born 3 months ago. She sent a text to Anita wishing her the best the other day, I forgot that they had conspired to whisk me away before my wedding day, they have stayed connected. I still remember throwing up at the pizza place because of them.

James and Olivia were married in June the year after my last US Open. Larry was best man, I begged out of duties for Olivia for the wedding, she had a lot of close friends that I did not want to have her to make a choice. The wedding was fantastic, it was an outdoor wedding somehow, they did it at the outside of the National Gallery of Art. I don't know how they did it, but the reception was after hours at the Natural History Museum, I was so happy for them. They are looking forward to being parents, they live in a townhouse in Georgetown, she is not pregnant that I know of. Talk about an interesting child, ¼ African American, 1/8th Asian, and 5/8th European. The child could be anything that he or she wants with a rich heritage. Olivia's parents are very accomplished graduates of American and Howard University, he is a department head in the DC Government and her mother is a chairperson of the local NAACP chapter. I have been asked to talk about being multi-cultural child and how my family overcame prejudice in rural Virginia. James has passed the bar and practices in Alexandria, VA he works hard and should be a partner in the next three years.

Granny Miller is now 80 something, she never tells anyone her age. She is living in sin with her male friend Frank Zumwalt. They decided they did not want to get married too many children and grandchildren to deal with, so they are just in love. Mom's younger brother now comes home for the holidays, it has been great to see him.

Paul and Ann now have 2 children together, and he has adopted his stepdaughter. Her real dad refused to pay any child support and Ann terminated his parental rights. Paul is now head coach of College of Charleston men's and women's tennis. His teams are doing well, he uses my journey to tell people you don't have to be going to a major university to have a shot at the pro's. I have given him the trophy he helped me win in Korea as a recruiting tool, it appears to work well. We call at least once a month, and he is regional director for the south of the "Pink and Blue Foundation", he has the final say on the 4 girls from the south that receive assistance to travel for tennis. There are 32 girls per year that receive assistance, in 3 age groups so just under 100 girls per year with funding, of $10,000, each. We opened it up this year for 48 boys in ages 14, and 16, so this year 150 almost in total.

My uncles are doing well, nothing in their lives changed they are still the rocks of the family. I can't even count the cousins I have, one of the little girls Marianne, looks a little like me she has Asian features, but she has light brown hair.

My great Aunt Lilly passed away in Seoul last year, I did not grieve for her, but I have at least heard from my cousins that they would like to establish some type of relationship going forward. It turns out that it was the matriarch of the family that kept the hate going and not the next generation had simply gone along with her choice.

As far as my mom and dad things are very different, Dad had a stroke about a year ago, he has a pronounced limp from his left side and limited use of his left hand. He has retired from Radford, and they have moved to a small ranch style house in Blacksburg, he said he feels more comfortable in his hometown. Mom just retired 2 weeks ago, she was tired of commuting, and dad really missed her during his rehab. They are still devoted to each other, and dad is now doing woodworking projects for people, he is a little slow, but he loves the work, and he has promised us a beautiful cradle.

I hear from some of the girls from Longwood University from time to time, but we are all in our new lives. We will always have the NCAA tournament and conference championships that we won together. Coach Wilson is still doing very well at Florida State, and he tells everyone, he is the reason I made it to the professional ranks, he is probably right, at least I have my third place and all-American awards due to his faith in me. I am asking him, to help look at the local kids in Florida to see who may be in need and worthy of the annual scholarship. He has identified 4 kids for this year, none are academy kids, they are sponsored or debutantes, and I don't support debutantes. Lucy has been inducted into the Hall of Fame, and we will get together next month for the first time. She says be expecting an announcement for me next summer.

I sometimes wonder what would have happened if the debutantes had not ostracized me as a lesbian, and simply let me be Lilly. Did they create for me the opportunity to succeed because I did not fall into the trap of debutante lifestyle.

Anita's family are doing so well, her dad comes to a few tournaments per year, not as her coach but simply as her father. Anita's mom is now part of our international expansion of "Pink and Blue", she is such a gracious lady. Somehow, we will be connected if somebody says yes tonight. How does, sisters-in-law, mother create a family relationship, I'm not sure. The truth is we have been in communication for a long time now, and while not my mother, she gives motherly advice, and she says she always has time for Anita's adopted big sister. We have been invited to see them in Frankfurt between Christmas, and when Anita leaves for Australia right after the new year. I plan to learn enough German by then to speak in both languages. She wants me to talk to some families about how tennis changed my life.

Larry is my love and we run most evenings around the neighborhood in Virginia. He still can run faster than me, that must be the soccer star in him. He asked the other day how much I missed tennis. I told him I still miss seeing my girls every day, but I realize that I would have been done likely anyway, I'm nearly 35, very few women would have been still playing well anyway. I am not Serena Williams; nobody would ever confuse my skills with hers.

If I am not playing tennis, what am I doing. Well, the calf did not heal as fast as they thought it would, it took a full six months before I could fully train for tennis again which meant I would have been ready for the clay season, which frankly I had no interest in doing. Losing all the ranking points from the swing and Australia, meant I would get into tournaments using a protected ranking, but with no tournaments I would quickly lose all my rankings and be where we started. Tennis was going to be a tough time back if at all.

I began training in Charleston with Paul and the College of Charleston team in late March, I did not want people to see me trying to get my groove back, plus training outside was better than indoors in the DC area. Larry came down one weekend for a second honeymoon and I guess we were a little carefree in Hilton Head. I found out 4 weeks later that I was indeed pregnant, so the comeback would have to wait, I decided that being mom at 32 was not a bad choice. Right after the Australian Open finals, Dea Jarman Wilson was born at Georgetown hospital, 7 pounds even. She has blond hair, and the only Asian feature is her beautiful dark almond eyes, my grandmother will always be watching over me. Dea is now 20 months old, is walking and talking and she is so spoiled by an extended family including the mythical grandparents in Germany, who visited us when Dea was only six months old.

Other mothers have come back to play tennis so why did I not go back to play. Clisters, Azarenka, Williams and a few others have come back to play so why not me. I can blame Jean Wilson for that, she loved the idea of the foundation, and her influential friends took this cause as a personal effort. We have raised millions of dollars on behalf of the foundation and that requires me to travel almost every week somewhere to make a speech on the magical 15 months and how it could have never happened. I have become a motivational speaker, funny for the girl that could not even make a coherent speech in front of her tennis team. My speaking engagements are like $5000 to ten thousand dollars plus travel, I do about twenty per year and the money is split between my salary and the foundation. I make a nice living partially as a nominal $50,000, as president of the foundation and with the money from the talking engagements, I pay the mortgage on the townhouse.

I started training tennis again this spring, and realized I had no competitive juices left in my body, the focus I used to have for tennis is now as a leader of the foundation and the mother of Dea. Larry makes a good living, and we don't need the money from tennis, and nobody will ever be able to take away that Wimbledon Trophy I won with Anita. We also receive a minimum of $300,000, per year in our contracts for using "Athletic and Feminine", with the various companies, including a new line for women's soccer and next year, field hockey equipment under so many brands that I must call John to figure that out. I just returned to my playing weight of 135, I had gained fifty pounds while I was pregnant. That darn German chocolate was to blame, as soon as I would think it was done another couple of pounds would arrive.

My main sponsors have benefitted from our arrangements, Lacoste had record profits last year and Mizuno now boasts 3 of the top ten tennis players that use the brand. Allison is now a VP of marketing and Jacques is president of sports related events for the company. He decides what events meet the Lacoste brand.

As for John Littleman, his little agency went from 2 people to 10 today. Anita is represented by him, and he no longer takes on direct new clients he has 7 agents that do that work now. Occasionally he has me interview potential new people for his agency to take on, they are those that others that have overlooked and may be a possible for the firm, so far, I have approved of one tennis player and one soccer player. Since I am no longer playing tennis those endorsement deals dried up for John, but he gets annually about $50,000, from the endorsement deals for our clothing lines that are growing each year, the last year we made over $500,000, so that was his cut last year alone. Not great but his work is done for us, it has blossomed. He has asked me to start thinking about doing more speeches at sites like Tennis clubs and training facilities, he will make 10% of those.

I just concluded a series of interviews with Pam Shriver, it will be shown on the Tennis Channel. The thirty-minute piece will be called" The Country Bumpkin Tennis Story, Lilly Jarman". They take me through the times with Jake Willis, to the Wimbledon doubles title. I will not be allowed to edit it, but they say it will be tasteful, it will be shown between Thanksgiving and the New Year, no live tennis, so a filler for content. It was still fun to look back and remember what suffering it took to make it possible. Anita is being interviewed after the US Open, don't want to disrupt her planning or playing.

I want to explain how far my adopted little sister has gone in the three years, she made the final of the French Open last year, and she and Isabel made the finals of Wimbledon in doubles, Anita made the quarters. She also won the Australian doubles with Isabel, so she has had 2 grand slam doubles titles. She is the number 4 seed and the lowest seed left she is in position to win her first grand slam. She has won Montreal, and Miami, at the 1000 level and has won 5 other singles titles, so she is doing fantastic in tennis. Her love life has been mostly unknown to the public, but since many of the dates started or ended at my townhouse in Fairfax County, I know that she and Chris were dating the entire time, when she was in the US. Chris also visited her last year in Germany, I was called beforehand regarding. I would not say that the relationship was hidden, but Anita is such a beautiful woman and now well known, she is very self-conscious and protective of her relationships. Her SI magazine went extremely well and there were only a few pictures I would consider too revealing, mine was not bad either, but I looked like the "Duff", as opposed to Anita. I am not allowed to say that according to Anita's mother, I have already received a directed punch in my arm when I said something after the SI issue hit the streets, that I was the Duff, that was apparently initiated from her mother.

I did not win the award of most influential woman in sports, but it was fun trying to find a dress for a tall woman 4 months pregnant and very self-conscious about her looks. A dress came from France, Lacoste says you need this, your wedding dress is selling well. It was a lovely yellow dress, and it was designed so they could release it if I sprouted more than expected.

Today is Anita's day. The first match starts at 1 PM, and her match this Thursday is scheduled no earlier than 3:30 PM. Pam Shriver and I had a private meeting this morning regarding what may happen after the match, I thought it a bad idea if she makes the finals, but the studio and the men wanted to do it like my proposal, this time, I will be waiting at the other side for support. Anita thinks her mom is still in Germany, she arrived last night and will not sit in the box, that is her dad today. In the box today will be Chris, Anita's dad, Johan, and myself. Larry will be with Anita's mom and little Dea they will come to see her adopted Aunt after the match. I guess shortly Dea's adopted aunt will become her real aunt.

Anita has taken to my habit of having someone take notes for the match. I thought it would be her father, but he asked me to do it, he said he would be too nervous.

Ashe Stadium, I was about to get seated into Anita's box when someone recognized me from my travels. Within a minute we heard the chant from the tennis crowd that I had not heard in a stadium for three years. Since Anita plays in those colors, she had to smile that she knew I was waiting for her and that the fans would be on her side.

Introducing the players for our second match this afternoon. … and her opponent our number 4 seed, she has been a finalist here, and has won 2 doubles major titles in Australia and in Wimbledon, from Germany, Anita Krantze.

When the applause had stopped, Johan came over to me and whispered now you can tell her. I stood up and yelled, Kick Ass Krantze. Anita started to smile, and I knew she would be ok for the match.

I won't tell you what I entered to her iPad, but mine will say, I supported my adopted little sister for about 90 minutes, after she qualified for the final, 6-4 and 7-5, she was just on fire. At the end of the match Chris blew her a kiss and then left to be with Anita's mother, Larry and little Dea. Anita was gracious to the crowd in her post match interview at the court, she pointed to her box, and I yelled at her again Kick Ass Krantze. The on-court interviewer asked who that was yelling for you this afternoon, and Anita responded, the CEO of the "Pink and Blue" Foundation", Lilly Jarman Wilson. The stadium erupted, but it was the first time I realized I was known for the foundation and not as a tennis player, the transition had happened and it was ok, Anita was taking on the mantra.

ESPN Studios – 30 minutes after the match ended.

"I know athletes are superstitious, but do you think Lilly Jarman Wilson at the match made it easier for Anita Krantze this afternoon, asked Pam Shriver?"

Chris Evert replied, "if I had someone in my corner that turned the crowd for me, I would have had them in my box too."

"Brad Gilbert agreed, sometimes you need that mental edge and you saw the smile on Anita's face when Lilly yelled at her."

"Pam Shriver here, for those that have never met you, congratulations Anita on making the finals let's hear a little about who is with you today. Anita who is with you this evening?"

Anita was so beautiful even though she had not showered yet she had a fresh pink shirt on.

"I have my coach Johan, you all know Lilly Jarman Wilson, and my dad Hans Krantze. I thought Lilly's brother-in-law Chris Wilson was here earlier, but he said he someplace to go."

"Pam says then who are these people?"

Anita lit up, "well the little girl is Lilly's daughter, Larry Wilson, and behind them is my mother." Anita scooped up Dea and hugged her and held her in her hands for the next five minutes of the interview, Dea knew Anita and was thrilled to be held by her while she could see her mother.

A puff question by Pam Shriver, "so if these are your posse for the night, who is this guy from the other side of the studio."

Chris walked into the studio from the other side and approached Anita. "Anita, you have watched Lilly and Larry's engagement so many times on the video, I wanted something special for you. Anita Krantze, we have been dating since I met you at Larry's and Lilly's wedding. I know that you are an incredibly beautiful woman who also happens to be a world class athlete that you showed today. I also know you as the person that has captured my heart, I know that I am a lowly professional trainer for the Washington Nationals and that you are a world class athlete. Anita Krantze, I love you and this evening I want to ask you, would you do the honor of becoming my partner in marriage."

Anita ran around the stage and came over to Chris. "Get up and hug me or Lilly will yell at me. The answer is yes you know the answer is yes."

The kiss they had was very passionate and then Larry handed the ring to Chris, and he put it on Anita's finger.

"Pam Shriver took control of the situation, and told the viewers, you need to see this ring, and then see Lilly Jarman's. I think the Wilson brothers must know about their ladies because they both have that similar sapphire pattern. Lilly comes here and let us compare the two rings."

Lilly said," you know that just like the two of us Anita's is prettier and fancier than mine. You understand I am Anita's Duff, and our rings show she is the queen."

The next thing I know is Anita punched me in the arm. "Mom said if you ever said that I was to punch you. Anita jumped into my arms. Oh My God we are really going to be related now."

Anita grabbed little Dea and said you little girl better be at the wedding. I broke down crying hugged both, and little Dea said I love you Aunt Anita. Anita then started to break down the look was going to be horrible on Sports Center tonight.

Hans wanted to take everyone out for dinner tonight, he had been saving money for this night, he just thought it would be home in Munich, not here in New York. Larry's boss got the reservation for the five of them. I bowed out because I had Dea, plus I had a test to take tonight, well a home pregnancy test tonight, I was 3 weeks late.

Larry said that the five of them had a very nice German based dinner, he had some leftovers for me, but I had already had a turkey club sandwich from the deli downstairs. I had fed Dea dinner and between bath time and sleep it was time that I had taken the test.

Larry, it is time we consider a larger house. He looked at me and asked why, we both travel and share the office we have next to Dea's room. I simply replied because we have a need for a second baby room. I just got my pregnancy test, and it was positive, I am assuming I am like 6 weeks at this point. He laughed, we only were together for about two times in the last six weeks, wow, you, and I must be in a rhythm together. I will follow-up when we get home with my doctor. Larry kissed me and our family will be so blessed.

Friday came and I was making sure to take care of myself, Larry, Dea and I went to Central Park, and then came a text from Anita, can you come to the timeshare this afternoon. I got to her timeshare at 4 PM and asked what the matter is.

"Anita said something I need to talk out. I am scared to win tomorrow."

I looked at her and asked, "what you are talking about?"

Anita looked at me, "I will be in a new class of women, that have won a grand slam singles title, the public pressure will be insane."

"Well Auntie Anita, you have already done a Sport Illustrated shoot, and became the sexiest woman on the planet, you have already been in the public light, now you are simply going to be the best player on the planet to go with it. No different than you have been just a new title on your resume."

Anita came to me, "how is it you always have the right answer for me?"

I wanted to say because I'm your "Duff", not wanting to get punched, "because you are my little sister, and I know how to look out for you."

Anita came over to hug me and I winced, she said "what's wrong?"

I simply said, "I don't want the baby to be crushed. I found out I was pregnant last night, probably due in Spring."

Anita then reached up and said, "Lilly Wilson, I love you and I need you always in my life."

"I laughed, well since it is very possible you will be my sister by marriage, I think the world is aligned." Now Anita Krantze, please get some rest, practice your speech because the world is ready for the next US Open Champion, and she just happens to be someone that is truly deserved of all the good things that can come to you. Don't ever let anyone say you don't deserve it; I have watched you in practice."

Anita asked, "Lilly, please be in the box on Saturday, I need you with me in case I do win. I am calling you so be prepared to be at the front row, Chris already told all the sponsors there are only six seats in the box, Johan gets one, Chris has one, Jacques has one, Allison has one, and dad has one. I thought mother Krantze would want to also, but Chris insisted that Lilly be there, not sure Anita will play unless her big sister is waiting for her. The others have a box upstairs and little Dea will be taken care of by my mom and Larry who have tickets courteous of Lacoste."

I don't know if it was being pregnant, but I started crying and told Anita, "I will always be there."

Anita responded, "Lilly Jarman how did I deserve you in my life, you are my big sister, it just took 22 years for me to find you."

Saturday came and I watched Anita do her practice, she was now in a zone her serve was big and her forehand looked exceptional. I had little Dea with me and at the end of practice, Anita asked for her to come on the court, I released her, and she walked over to Anita. Anita lifted Dea and so many people took pictures of the two of them, Anita was starting to relax.

Chris had the responsibility of the iPad today, he had never done it, but we figured a professional sports trainer could figure it out. I was decked out totally in the Izod uniform that was designed for me the last time I played at the US Open. Hans hugged me, and I told him it's Anita's day and he said please make sure you stand-up and yell for her. After the introductions just as Anita was taking off her sweats I stood up and yelled Kick Ass Krantze the stadium erupted in laughter, and Anita started to smile.

Chris reached over to me and gave me a kiss; "Larry chose well with you, and you made me grow-up and you shared your adopted sister with me. Wait until I go to the Mets stadium tonight to work."

I heard they showed the engagement of the Nationals trainer and the tennis star on the jumbo screen. The team made sure he came out from under the stadium and took a wave the stadium apparently erupted. I was told he got a Gatorade bath at the end of the game from the players and coaches. I think you chose well in Anita; she is gorgeous, smart, and extremely loyal to her friends and family.

The match was about to start, Chris will do the introductions in his iPad, I was simply looking at the match between Anita and Beatrice Northam. Yes, the same Beatrice who made the semi-finals in my last match when I had to retire injured. Anita had been looking at her tapes, this year Beatrice was the number 8 seed, so you had the 4 seed and the 8 seed for the finals, sometimes happens at the US Open, a lot of injuries by this time of the year.

Anita won the coin toss and chose to serve; I think she wanted to pound something to start the match. She hit a big serve on her first point and that through the entire game and she won easily. Anita's strength has always been returns and speed, and she proved her attributes in breaking Beatrice to lead 2-0. Anita and Beatrice then went on to hold the rest of the set with Anita winning the set 6-3.

I stood-up and yelled, "keep it going Krantze."

Anita's dad smiled at me, I thought he did not understand English but apparently, I was wrong.

"Johan looked at me and said really, when are you going to let me be her coach?"

I laughed, "was that what you were going to say."

Johan just shook his head, "not exactly."

The stadium saw me stand up and began the chant of "Athletic and Feminine", Anita soaked it up and began to smile during the TV timeout.

The second set was about to start, and this was not going to be easy, Beatrice held easily as did Anita, the pattern went that way until the match was 5-5. Beatrice tried to hit Anita with a body serve but my cat like friend simply moved and hit a backhand winner down the line. That point set Anita up for a break point, and she pounced on the opportunity by catching the serve and hitting it cross court, Beatrice got to it and Anita was waiting for the shot the net and placed the winner. Anita was now up 6-5 and serving for the match and her first major title. Beatrice did not give up and was at a break point of her own and Anita stepped up and hit a 111 first serve down the middle for an ace. 2 points to go and Anita was not to be stopped on match point she hit a slider and was waiting to put the match away at the net. Once the ball hit twice in the court, Anita fell on the court and realized that she had won her first major. She shook hands with Beatrice and fell to her knees again and let out a shriek that made mine look tame.

I wanted to yell something and decided the better of it, this was all Anita's time.

Johan came over to me and hugged me, you know you started this confident Anita when you let her wear your colors." Johan then asked, can you please get to the railing, I think Anita wants you in a picture now at the railing."

I laughed, "nobody remembers me now, just the beautiful and athletic Anita."

I ran to the opening and Anita came running to Chris and me. She hugged her future husband first and then came over to me and screamed, "Hey Jarman I kicked ass today." She whispered to me, this would never have happened without you in my life, I love your future sister-in-law.

I simply kissed her on the cheek and said "congratulations and yes today I am your "Duff", and she punched my arm."

Anita erupted laughing, "mom told me to do it."

I bet I will have a bruise on my arm. The entire stadium erupted into laughter.

The stadium was prepared for the trophy presentation, Beatrice was very gracious in her speech and said I only wished I had the support you all showed for the "Athletic and Feminine" team.

It was Anita's turn to speak after being handed a check and then her trophy.

"I want to thank the tournament the city, and the fans here today. To the people that work here for the last few weeks thank you for running this tournament. Anita's mom, Larry and Dea were now near the railing. I want to thank my team, first to my parents' thanks for being there on so many weekends. She then said some words in German directed at Hans alone. I want to thank my coach Johan, wow, can you believe this. To my trainer and future husband, I love you and hope you can get off early tonight, I want to celebrate. I think I want to mention someone else well two of them, can you stop hiding." She pointed at me and Little Dea, to my dearest Lilly, when nobody wanted to play with me or wanted to be my friend you were and will always be there. My colors came from you, "Athletic and Feminine", so many people need to know how you supported me, and apparently introduced me to my future husband. For the women in the crowd, you too can always be athletic and feminine too. Lilly, can I share the moment with my soon to be niece." Anita came over to the rail and grabbed Dea from me. Little Dea, your great grandmother started this, I know you won't understand today, but for us women it is alright to be both athletic and feminine."

Pictures were taken and little Dea hugged her future aunt and then Anita came over to the rail and returned Dea. I heard her say, stay here I want people to see the picture of all three of us.

The entire stadium started rocking with our favorite saying. I looked up and saw all three of us on the stadium screen.

ESPN Studios:

What a great tribute by our champion to her friend and soon to be sister-in-law. Anita Krantze, congratulations on your first singles championship.

Pam Shriver said, "there are a lot of men that were disappointed that Anita is off the market, how did she keep her relationship quiet?"

"Brad Gilbert said, apparently, she had one powerful friend who made sure we now know why she played DC every year."

Final Match update:

Anita and Chris tied the knot in a castle in Munich Germany in a small wedding February after the Australian Open. I was not allowed to travel but they showed the wedding live for me on zoom. Larry was best man and mom stayed with me. The honeymoon was delayed until the end of the Miami tournament they went to Key West for a week. On April 29th Brian Jarman-Krantze Wilson was born. He has dark hair and no other features that look Asian. I have no idea how this happened, but I heard a German accent as soon as I gave birth at Georgetown Hospital. Anita had flown in from Europe overnight on the word I was going into labor.

Instead of a hug she punched my arm, and said "I told you were beautiful", in her lovely German accent.

We both started to cry with joy.